CHRONICLE

THE BEST IN SCIENCE FICTION AND FANTASY

"THIS IS DENT, I'M GOING IN."

Sprinting forward, I dropped the muzzle of my CAW2K on the lock mechanism of the door to SW105. My computer shifted over to tactical and gave me a crosshairs that showed I was on target. Two bursts from the gun punched the lock and the knob, and I hit the door at full speed.

I caught it with my left shoulder and used the impact to rebound myself to the right. I pushed off with my right foot and sidesaddled my way across a desk set just to the right of the doorway. My butt and legs knocked phone, blotter, and a canister of pens flying, while my right hand came across the room's far wall. It tore up plaster and blasted glass from picture frames all along the wall, except in two places. In those places stood two Imperial guards in full combat armor.

I took a load of buckshot from the first one's assault shotgun square in the chest. It slammed me back against the wall. Breathless and stunned, I could not move. . . .

MUTANT CHRONICLES

MUTANT CHRONICLES

THE APOSTLE OF INSANITY TRILOGY

VOLUME THREE

DEMENTIA

by

Michael A. Stackpole

A ROC BOOK

ROC
Published by the Penguin Group
Penguin Books USA Inc., 375 Hudson Street,
New York, New York 10014, U.S.A.
Penguin Books Ltd, 27 Wrights Lane,
London W8 5TZ, England
Penguin Books Australia Ltd, Ringwood,
Victoria, Australia
Penguin Books Canada Ltd, 10 Alcorn Avenue,
Toronto, Ontario, Canada M4V 3B2
Penguin Books (N.Z.) Ltd, 182–190 Wairau Road,
Auckland 10, New Zealand

Penguin Books Ltd, Registered Offices:
Harmondsworth, Middlesex, England

First published by Roc, an imprint of Dutton Signet,
a division of Penguin Books USA Inc.

First Printing, December, 1994
10 9 8 7 6 5 4 3 2 1

To
Ken St. Andre,
Bear Peters,
and
Stephen MacAllister
For being good friends and greater thinkers
who never let me rest unless I have truly earned it.

Acknowledgments

The author would like to thank the following people for their contributions to this book. All errors herein are mine and most of the good stuff belongs to them.

Fred Malmberg, Nils Gulliksson, Henrik Strandberg, Mike Stenmark, and the other folks at Target Games who created this universe.

William F. Wu and John-Allen Price, who laid the groundwork for my book in their books and provided me good characters to work with in mine.

Sam Lewis, who gave me the time to do this book.

Christopher Schelling, Amy Stout, and Rick Taft, who made the book possible.

Liz Danforth and Jennifer Roberson, who endured hearing about this monster before, during, and after its completion.

BOOK I

People ought to start dead and then they would be honest so much earlier.

—Mark Twain

ONE

I didn't attend my funeral, but I've seen the video a number of times. My corporate masters at Cybertronic had thoughtfully edited out any clues to my identity, but that wasn't hard because most folks at a funeral don't speak the name of the dead. Those who eulogized me just used impersonal pronouns to refer to me, which was fine because, to them, I was no longer a person.

Not so to Cybertronic. After someone had snapped my spine in two and had driven a chunk of my skull into my brain, they saw me as corporate material. Apparently blunt instrument trauma made one a very attractive candidate for employment because they spent a lot of money to get me ready to enter the field again. As career opportunities for dead men usually involve vivisection, being pieced out for parts or sating unnatural desires, I opted for service with Cybertronic.

The flat-matte black of my little lozenge-shaped ash coffin reminded me of a suppository, and down here, in dusty, dark, Torricelli Trey looked like where they might have shoved it. Capitol is usually a bit better at keeping areas under its corporate sway cleaner, but the multilevel development in what had once been the Torricelli crater in the southeast quadrant of the moon's visible face was old and had long since decayed. Down here the thick, moisture-laden air leeched heat from my body and promoted the growth of more molds than I had any desire to know about.

The computer mounted inside my skull—taking up the

room made available through the removal of damaged brain tissue, used my olfactory nerves to sample the air. The fiber-optic cable that ran along my optic nerve and into my eyeballs displayed information on a spot that appeared to be toward the lower portion of my visual window, as if I was wearing bifocal glasses to read fine print. In glowing green letters, it scrolled out the names of all the things it had detected. It also declared that only *cladosporia lunaria* was in a dangerous concentration and that it had already begun to inhibit my body's histamine production.

That was the least of what the computers and the million or so terabytes of information could do. As usual, I ignored it and concentrated on my mission. After all, had this been something that a computer alone could have handled, Cybertronic would have sent an Attila unit out to complete it. The operation, my brief had said, required discretion, and no Attila had ever been described as discreet.

Wearing clothes that had stains on them older than I, I ducked into an alley and walked along it until the computer told me I was exactly 22.341 meters in from the street. I scraped away the rubbish and debris, then slumped down. I pressed my back to the wall of a cinderblock building aged to look older than lunar bedrock. I felt a flush come over me as the computer ordered capillary dilation and picked my heart rate up a bit—its equivalent of keeping my engine revving in case I required quick action.

First I had to set the scene so I would go unnoticed. Dressed as I was, and as far from the dark street as I had come, chances were I'd not be seen at all by most folks. Those who did notice me would likely figure me a duster—someone who lived on the streets long enough that lunar dust covered him like a second skin. Most dusters have a substance abuse problem, or live in alternate realities, so they have nothing worth stealing and, therefore, are left alone.

Being left alone was what I wanted. My covert entry into the building behind me would not be particularly difficult, but would require time. During that time my attention would be focused elsewhere, which meant my body would be very vulnerable.

Having died once already, I really had no desire to do it again.

Capitol, like Bauhaus, Imperial, and Mishima, had become paranoid about certain aspects of technology when the Dark Legion began to muck around in the affairs of men. They had good reason for their concern because the Dark Legion had the ability to warp humanity and technology to their own purposes. As a result, those corporations sanitized and isolated as much of their high-tech equipment. In simple safe houses like the building I leaned back against, this meant yanking out and discarding anything more complicated than a hot plate or telephone.

In their frenzy to clean things up, they relied heavily on "experts" who, because of ignorance or hefty bribes from Cybertronic, considered the optic cables and wires that had once connected the machines utterly harmless. They plugged blocking plates into the old outlets and declared everything safe. But safe is a relative term.

The truth of that concept proved itself quickly to me as I heard the clop of booted feet in the alley. With my arms hugged around my knees, I let my head tip back. I opened my mouth and kept my eyes closed, presenting the very picture of someone who had fallen asleep. I even gurgled and snorted a bit as the computer—using Doppler echo algorithms—counted down the meters until the pair of individuals reached me.

Closing my eyes did severely limit my visual input concerning the two people coming in toward me. The infrared sensors that had been inserted subdermally in my eyelids did provide me with a wealth of information that the computer digested in nanoseconds and delivered to me in a palatable form. It expanded its datafeed, letting the images play across what normally would have been my field of vision, so the yellow, red, and blue outlines occupied the same space the actual bodies would have taken up had my eyes been open.

She was taller than he was, but more nervous, which meant I would take her second, if I had to. They still could pass me by, saving all of us a lot of trouble.

"Hey, Holt, it's just a kid. Leave him." I liked her voice because it didn't betray her nervousness and even had a bit of compassion in it. Might have been maternal instinct, and mothering is nice. Standing practically on top of me meant the computer drew her in a crisp rainbow that reminded me of old Warhol prints of Marilyn Monroe, and that meant I'd forgive this woman being taller than me.

Holt, on the other hand, leaned down and got his face right in mine. About the same time the slender man realized he wasn't smelling flopsweat or narcstink from me, he started to finger something at his right hip. Neither the computer nor I could figure out what he was doing, as his body blocked our line of sight, so I had to act.

When Cybertronic made me over in their own image, they changed quite a bit about me. The alterations went deeper than the cosmetic changes to my face. Cybertronic trimmed an inch off all of my long bones, then reinforced the shortened bones with carbon fibers. The slack that procedure created in my muscles allowed them to reattach the muscles closer to the middle of the bone. As the woman discovered when my left leg snapped out and crushed her ankle, the shift in muscles gave me far more leverage and made me hit much harder than anyone would have expected.

Remaining in IR mode with my eyes closed, my right hand pulled a thin knife from the sheath on my right calf, and I stabbed upward. I caught Holt right below the sternum, then slashed down and back. A reddish-orange line appeared on the lower half of his torso, then a flood of molten gold poured down over my knife and hand.

A quick shove sent Holt flying across the alley and bouncing off the far wall. I stood and backhanded the kneeling woman. Something cracked in her face, and she went down hard.

The IR images dissolved as I opened my eyes. The computer started to exert some control on my autonomic nerves to slow my heartbeat, but I countermanded those directions. I wanted the elevated heartbeat and hypersenses the adrenaline rush gave me. It might hamper the latter part of my mission, but I wanted to be able to react quickly if a new threat presented itself.

I grabbed her by her unbroken ankle and dragged her deeper into the alley. Hoisting her up, I heaved her body into a battered old dumpster. Returning to Holt, I cleaned my knife on the legs of his pants, then I stripped from him the pistol he had been going for when I killed him. I popped the clip from the Ironfist and cleared the chamber. I tucked the ammo into my pocket, then tossed his body and the pistol into the dumpster.

As I walked back to my chosen position, the computer opened a cellular link into the Commnet. After a couple of rings a deadpan voice answered, "Tranquillity Preowned Furnishings." Though I didn't recognize the voice, I did catch the flat delivery, marking the speaker as a Cybertronic "vacationer," which meant I had the right place.

"I have a pickup. Two pieces, in a dumpster, Torricelli Trey. Priority Pickup Requested. Credit account RKX 571127."

I listened long enough to get a confirmation, then cut the vac off when he started to describe the specials they had. I normally have more patience with vacs, but the adrenaline and the possibilities of other attacks here in Capitol territory had me short-fused. For all I knew, the attack had delayed me to the point that I'd not be able to get the information I had been sent to collect.

The computer disagreed, since I was only five minutes off the Capitol schedule. Everyone knew that the obligatory reading of rights and warrants before any Capitol interrogation took place would set every substantive thing back a quarter of an hour. It reminded me that even if I went slower than I had on my first attempt at a covert entry like this, I'd still be able to hear 2.35 minutes of legalspeak.

With that for an incentive, I took my time. Sitting back down at the wall, I reached into my mouth and pulled a wisdom tooth loose from the right side of my upper jaw. It didn't hurt, but the spooling out of the fiber-optic cable attached to it did kind of tickle. I freed the plug from the crown and snapped the jack into the outlet on the building wall. Linked up, I set the computer to give me an intruder alert if anyone entered the alley, then I closed my eyes and went in.

The fiber-optic network inside the building branched from that outlet into a maze. Because the safe house they were using was located on Level Three of the Torricelli sector, I knew the interrogation unit would not be on the bottom floor. The building had no basement, as the basement of this house would be the penthouse of the building on Torricelli Four. The safest place for the interrogation would be dead center in the house, so that's where I went.

Going subreal is usually different for everyone—which makes sense since the world inside computers is a subjective reality. Some subreal systems, like the Cybertronic system, is almost surreal because the entity that owns it is able to impose certain laws and graphic impressions that are too difficult to morph into your own images. A fiber-optic network in a stripped building is free of such controlling interests, so my trip through it became exactly what I wanted it to be.

In this particular case I pictured myself swimming otter-like through a golden cylinder. Twisting, I went up, then cut back right and left, and dove down. I flashed past intersections, then raced around a long, right-hand turn, and split myself into four parts to cover all four of the outlets in the appropriate room.

I left the hard work to the computer, and it did it very well. Using IR data from the blocking plates—three in the walls about two feet from the floor and one overhead near a light fixture—the computer pinpointed the heat sources in the room. Using two sub-aural sonic pulses from the plates, it mapped the walls, furnishings, and people. As it gathered this data, the computer resolved it into a 3D model of the room, and I perched myself on the edge of a desk. The lack of an optical data source meant the people looked as if they had been molded from clay.

With the sonic sweep complete, the computer used the blocking plates to pull in the sound in the room. The three Capitol people in the room—two men and one woman—paced around the individual seated in what the computer indicated was a hard metal chair. I dedicated one IR sensor to her and ordered up a fine gradient resolution. I even chanced another sonic pulse and had the computer pull her face together into a varicolored landscape.

The image it put together felt hauntingly familiar, but was alien enough that I could not place it. Without knowing the color of her shoulder-length hair, without being able to see the color of her skin or eyes, I could not tell if I knew her or had seen a similar picture on a billboard or in some television drama. The computer did indicate a ninety-seven percent chance, based on gross physical characteristics, that the woman was of Northern European descent, but that meant she could have been anything from a blond Scandinavian to a redheaded Irishwoman or an olive-skinned, dark-haired Spaniard. And *that* would have been if she were a citizen of Bauhaus—if she were from Capitol, she could be almost anything the melting pot put together.

The legalspeak faded, and the computer increased my aural pickup. "Do you understand everything I have said to you?" The voice belonged to the more corpulent of the trio in the room. "Was that a nod? Did you see her nod?"

The other two shook their heads. "Give it a rest, Campbell. She's catatonic." The woman touched the seated woman on the shoulder. "I've got enough psycho-active drugs in her that I think I can get her to talk, but no promises."

The third person nodded. "Very good, Doctor. Mr. Campbell, please leave this to me. Those rights are only important if Mrs. Kovan here was undergoing a criminal investigation. We suspect her of nothing." That man stood tall and slender, and the computer colored him a steely gray. "Mrs. Kovan, you are on Luna and are among friends. I understand you have undergone some traumatic experiences, but they are over now. You are safe."

Steel modulated his voice well, and the computer's digitalization of it brought his sincerity through cleanly. "It is important, so that this never happens to anyone else, that you tell us what happened to you in Fairview and after that. Can you do that?"

Campbell pointed at her. "I saw a nod."

The doctor looked at a box beside me on the table. "Her pulse is becoming elevated. I think she did nod."

"Very well." The steel man reached out and squeezed Kovan's shoulder. "You are Mrs. Lorraine Kovan, and you resided with your husband and two children on Venus in the Capitol village of Fairview. You have lived there all your life. Very recently something that happened there caused you to leave. Can you describe what happened to me?"

This time even I saw the nod in the reddish collar that showed up on IR. "They came."

The doctor reacted as if Campbell had goosed her with a stunstick. "This must be a very strong memory. Her pulse is at 130."

The IR scan also showed heat building in her long muscles, as if she was running, but the drugs and restraints prevented her from moving.

Steel injected calm into his voice. "Mrs. Kovan, what you are reliving is a memory. They cannot get you here. They do not know you are here. You are safe. Now, who were they?"

"Black ship. Misshapen. Bulbous, like the corn when the fungus got in it."

Steel's head came up. "Mr. Campbell, you will leave the room, now!"

"But, but this is important if we're going to go to the Cartel to protest this action."

"Now, Mr. Campbell."

"This will be on your head. I'm going to your supervisor."

"Now!"

Campbell nodded to the doctor, then left the room. I punched a piece of myself off to see if the building had a phone cross-link so I could eavesdrop on any call Campbell made, but I set the datagathering on it to background.

Steel turned toward the doctor. "Recall, Doctor, that this patient is full of psychoactive drugs. What she may reveal might only be an impression of facts colored by her perception and the drugs you have pumped into her. In other words, it is likely *subjective,* not objective. You would be wise to avoid reporting what you hear to your colleagues."

"As you wish."

"Thank you. In your discretion I trust. Not so that lawyer."

"Your trust is well-founded."

"Now, Mrs. Kovan, you said you saw a black ship. What happened?"

The woman shuddered enough that the computer reported her movement as a jump. "They came out of it. Dead things. Metal and flesh. With guns."

"Pulse is at 135. Is that Cybertronic?"

Steel's features blurred as he shook his head. "Unlikely, despite the metal reference. Fairview was closer to Mishima and Imperial than Cybertronic. Rantings, remember, Doctor."

"Ah, yes, I understand."

"Mrs. Kovan, please, continue."

"Guns. They shot. They shot and shot and shot. Everyone." Her hands turned palm up, and her fingers flexed. "The blood. Everywhere. They go past me. Shooting. Screaming. Biting. Tearing. Little Niki, no! Niki, Niki!"

"Pulse 210! That's too high for her. I have to sedate."

Steel nodded as he crossed his arms. As the doctor worked on Lorraine Kovan, Steel paced and approached the table where I sat. "Doctor, what would you suggest this patient is speaking about?"

"Horrible trauma, to be certain. I have treated posttraumatic stress patients before, and the hallucinogenic portion of her report is outside the standard sort of exaggeration we find in most massacre survivors. Often we find time dilation and other perception anomalies, but seldom is the image of the perpetrator distorted. If I were forced to guess, I would say that she was abused as a child. It is not unusual for such memories to have been suppressed and then return quite virulently and violently in later life—leading to problems that include catatonia. She has created these rending, metal, and dead-flesh things to take the place of the perpetrators. This would lead me to believe that they . . ."

Steel turned to look at her. "These necro-mutants?"

"Sure, necro-mutants, if you like, are meant to replace her father or uncles or trusted members of her immediate family who abused her. Is her father dead? Was he a metalworker?"

"Quite perceptive of you, Doctor."

The doctor's cheeks took on a cherry glow as she smiled. "I am glad to be of service."

"I will see to it that your invoice is paid promptly."

"You are most kind." The doctor freed Lorraine's arm from a small restraint. "She needs a great deal of help, you know. I could treat her."

"I will relay that suggestion to her people. She has family here on Luna, and they are arranging to take care of her needs. Thank you again, Doctor, for your concern."

As Steel guided the doctor to the door, I pulled back into my own body and unjacked from the building. I returned my dental work to its correct position and stood up. I saw the dumpster had been hauled away while I had worked on gathering my data. I checked the intrusion log, and the computer had noticed the presence of an Oscar automated trash-hauler, but had not alerted me to its presence. Because it worked for Cybertronic, it presented no threat to me, hence it did not fulfill the parameters set out in my intruder alert system.

I shrugged and headed out of the alley. Had the Oscar remained around, I could have downloaded what I learned into its onboard memory and saved myself a trip to the Ptolemaeus district to report. That would have been appropriate, as what I figured I got was garbage. But if my masters felt it was important enough to gather, who was I to think different?

I laughed. At Cybertronic, I was paid precisely because I *did* think differently.

TWO

Actually, at Cybertronic, I'm not the only one to be paid to think differently. The employees at Cybertronic break down into two classes: vacationers or vacs and tiffs. Vacs are generally focused on their job and, like the person I spoke with on the phone, have no emotional spark in them. They have no stress, no urgency, just efficiency like someone on a package tour of the Grand Canal on Mars.

Tiffs, on the other hand, are just trouble. I heard that tiff became the letters *t* and *f* which, in turn, stood for *tempus fugit*. Unlike vacs, we notice things like the passage of time. We tend to be anxious to be finished with jobs, and we actually have some emotional content to our lives. The fact that tiff also refers to fighting is appropriate, too, because most of the truly efficient termination agents in Cybertronic's service are tiffs.

The difference between vacs and tiffs, to hear the boys down in Advanced Research and Development tell it, comes from the difference between the Mark I and Mark II versions of the drug we call brain-grease. All Cybertronic employees are dosed with it to speed up the neural processes that allow us to interface with the cybernetic portions of ourselves. The vast majority of employees have nothing more complex than a connection that allows them to bypass a computer keyboard, though some, like me, have been fully tricked out with plenty of hardware.

Vacs all have the initial version of the drug. It dampens their emotional brain centers, which makes them difficult to recruit as spies by other corporations. It also makes them boring as sin and provides them with killer poker faces when or if you can ever talk them into playing cards. Vacs like to be on the job and were they not required to go home to sleep and eat, I think most would remain at work until they died from exhaustion.

Tiffs are dosed with a newer version of the drug that does not suppress the emotions. The corporation found out very quickly that shutting off emotions also killed creativity. ARD and other selected portions of the corporate population are allowed free rein on their emotions because invention and innovation is the cornerstone to their contributions to Cybertronic. If you can't get excited about a discovery, then you aren't going to discover it.

To get back to Cybertronic headquarters and make my report, I had a choice of a number of routes. Each had benefits as well as drawbacks. If I wanted to drop down below street level, I could cruise through the storm and sewer tunnels beneath the city. They tend to be relatively uncrowded and safe, though they stink to high heaven. I've also heard of the occasional rumor about floods when a wall of sewage washes through, sweeping everything along with it. But the folks who claim that's true are also the ones who say all wastage is just pumped around the moon on a continual cycle because no one has the desire to or way to treat it.

The TubeLink was also an option. It smells the same as the sewers and is flooded with elbows, knees, and other knobby bits of humanity. Ordinarily I might have opted for it, or have taken a minicab so I could be in a steel box amid an unmoving crowd, but neither option appealed. I had a need for speed.

I also had a need to be inside my body and moving. I have found myself in this mood fairly often after I slip into an extracorporeal sensory network. I might, in fact, be a ghost in the machine, but I want to make sure I'm firmly locked back into my machine after I've been away from it.

After I died and Cybertronic brought me back, I spent a great deal of time becoming accustomed to the new look and new kinesthetics of my body. Being shorter and quicker took getting used to. I couldn't remember what life had been like before, mind you, but I *felt* it was wrong. Even now I occasionally wonder why something seems farther away than it should, or why what might have once seemed quick, now seems very slow.

My mood demanded I walk, so I set out. Rusty sets of iron stairs took me up to prime level, and I fell in with the meandering crowd. Like a child slipping through a mix of adults, I managed to work my way to the front of the wave and broke into the open space between it and the wave preceding us. In the clear I was able to look up and study the skyline. That helped soothe my feelings of dislocation.

The architecture that made up Luna City must have scared me as a child. Baroque and Byzantine, loaded with symbolism and flecked with neon, it looked as if it had been designed by Gaudí after he discovered LSD and Day-Glo paint. Clean-lined corporate towers emerged from the midst of squatting, black brick hovels. The corporate towers, in turn, surrounded the arcane spire of the Brotherhood's Cathedral.

Come to think of it, it was probably the Cathedral that scared me as a child.

There are some things you never outgrow.

The Brotherhood is one of those organizations that sees as its mission minding everyone else's business. It arose during the darkest period in the history of humanity, when we were doing our best to rip ourselves apart. The smoke-shrouded, gray planet hanging in the starry sky above the Cathedral bespeaks how close mankind came to destroying itself and the world that had given it birth.

The Brotherhood set itself up to be referees in the battles between nations and now the megacorps. Unfortunately for everyone, they can't help but get involved in the game. They infiltrate corporations and interrogate people from all walks of life, trying to ferret out bits of evil—or cap-D *Darkness* as they put it—amid the human population. That might serve a useful purpose, but their definition of evil is mutable and often serves only to promote the political goals they want to achieve.

Like the other buildings on Luna, the Cathedral is monumental, but has always struck me as being more organic than the corporate towers surrounding it. It looks as if it is a spike being thrust up through the surface of the planet, as if Luna has been impaled on the tusk of some mighty beast. The gargoyles festooning the Cathedral could be lice and ticks scuttling over the surface, ready to snatch up those who enter the Cathedral's precincts and find themselves judged tainted by Darkness.

With fantasies like that, you can see why I don't go to the Cathedral that often. Aside from not liking the Brotherhood—I find myself fighting down sudden urges to try out my new strength on the legion of street preachers clogging the streets—I avoid them because the Brotherhood does not like Cybertronic at all. Their infiltration efforts fail regularly because vacs make lousy spies, and tiffs think too freely to be locked into Brotherhood doctrine. In addition, the fact that a bunch of me consists of after-factory add-ons means that I'm considered a carrier of the Acquired Incurable Darkness Syndrome in their eyes. Any of their agents who were similarly altered would become heretics and be subject to Redemption with Extreme Prejudice.

I pushed on through the next knot of people, then stopped at a news kiosk. Both the *Daily Chronicles* and the *Independent Citizen* had headlines about corporate skirmishes on Venus, but one story contradicted the other. The Brotherhood published the *Chronicles* and probably had the more accurate story, but the *Citizen* would have turned some poor slob foot soldier into this week's hero and would be better reading.

The news stories really didn't interest me that much—I buy the paper for the classified ads and the personals. You can tell a paper by its personals. The *Citizen* was chock-full of human-interest stuff: lost animals, lost loves, and secret little messages from one person to another. The *Chronicles* only published *serious* personals like advertisements for Book of Law study groups or requests for family and genealogical information. Reading other folks' personals probably made me something of a voyeur, but there was something about the pleas that resonated with the human side of me for some reason.

I paid for a copy of the *Citizen* and picked up a packet of NyxStyx™ for Andy. I don't know how she can stand the things—they're flavored sugar with just enough nicotine and caffeine to give you a rush. Aside from reanimating dead bodies, NyxStyx™ were her only vice, so I indulged her. When you're a machine, you do what you must to keep your mechanic happy.

I didn't enter the Cybertronic tower directly. Instead of walking up the steps to the front door and attracting the attention of every watcher the Brotherhood employed to spy on us, I cut into a small Afghan-Caribbean Diner three blocks away. I nodded at the hostess, then walked back to the bathroom. Once inside I stared at the mirror and felt around under the washbasin for a lump of old chewing gum. I pressed down on it, and the button hidden beneath it, then initiated the recognition sequence.

The computer splashed a dizzying array of symbols and numbers against the lenses of my eyes, and an ultraviolet laser mounted behind the mirror read them. The toilet flushed to cover the sound of the side wall sliding up into the ceiling, and I stepped through into the small, closet-like dumbwaiter on the other side. The wall descended again, and when it locked into place, the box started its descent.

It would have been simple for someone to have faked up the recognition sequences that got me into the box—if the corps trusted their technology enough and had the right codes—but the transit to the tunnels below would have stopped them. As I descended, a whole battery of scanners measured, weighed, and analyzed everything from my oxygen intake to the nature of the stains on my clothes. Had anything inappropriate been detected, I would have been detained or destroyed.

As it was, I passed with flying colors and was released into a dimly lit corridor approximately five levels below the street. The computer added ultraviolet into the range of light I could visualize, and that provided me with all sorts of signs that would have been otherwise invisible. The UV lettering and symbols appeared to me in shimmering shades of gold, and the arrows along the floor that pointed me toward my destination had long ago prompted me to think of the path as the "yellow brick road."

That was appropriate because Advanced Research and Development for Cybertronic was the Land of Oz. It was not that it was overrun with Munchkins, as much as anything and everything could be found in the vast complex of subterranean rooms. This came both from the inventions the staff created and the fact that the staff was not allowed out on the streets. Their whims and desires had to be accommodated there, in Oz, to avoid any chance of another corp kidnapping them to learn what Cybertronic was up to.

Luckily for the corporation, the vast majority of ARD rats found their greatest pleasure in doing advanced research and development. While they put in long hours on the assignments the corporation gave them, they spent their leisure time puttering with pet projects that occasionally made the transition to corporate projects. And the things that didn't make the jump flew, crawled, or gathered dust somewhere in Oz.

From the secure corridor, I entered a well-lit lobby that rivaled any of those on the upper, accessible levels of the tower. Prim and proper, Miss Wickersham sat behind her desk and looked up at me as I approached her. No recognition flashed through her eyes, nor did her nose wrinkle in disgust at the odoriferous part of my disguise. "Good morning, Mr. Dent."

"Just say the word and we can run away to Tahiti and frolic naked in the surf."

"I appreciate the offer, Mr. Dent, but the Pacific Ocean is unfit for bathing, and the sun-exposure levels on Tahiti for one day have a positive correlation with an incidence of a malignant melanoma in 6.7 years from incidence of exposure."

I sighed. Vacs have no sense of romance, which is made worse when they come packaged for it the way she was. Tall, blond, with blue eyes and a body that benefited quite well from the company-mandated six hours of aerobic exercise a week, Miss Wickersham was enough to seduce a Brotherhood Inquisitor into forgetting his vows. Still, she was lost to me—and I took refuge in the idea that the drug kept us apart instead of daring to imagine she would have rejected me herself.

"You're breaking my heart, Maddy."

"I can place a call to Dr. Carter, and she can have you scheduled for maintenance."

I shook my head. "It will pass. I am on my way to see Dr. Carter now. Don't call ahead, I want to surprise her."

"Have a pleasant day, Mr. Dent."

As I stepped through the door beyond her position and into ARD, something black and skeletally bat-like detached itself from the false ceiling and swooped in at my head. Without thinking, I leaned to the right and brought the stiffened fingers of my left hand up like a knife blade. My blow caught the creature between its round head and ovoid thorax, severing them amid a shower of sparks.

"What the hell was that?" I looked up over a labyrinth of room partitions and saw two tall men applauding while a third cursed. I caught the head before it hit the ground and held it up as if it were Yorick's skull and I was Robo-Hamlet. The plastic sphere had two button sensors where eyes should have been and a pair of tall, pointed ears made of a fine Mylar mesh. A mouth had been painted on featuring garish vampire teeth.

"It's a Bat-Guardian Security Drone, Rev. 1," Simmons announced when he finished swearing.

My computer failed to come up with a project match code and told me so. "This is new."

Boggs, one of the other two scientists smiled. "It was originally a Boris the Bat™ Halloween Kids' Kompanion."

The computer brought that project file up, and I saw that the little bat-drone had shown to be unable to distinguish between legitimate targets and kids in scary masks. I frowned. "Hasn't the Brotherhood canceled Halloween anyway?"

"They're trying, but the Cartel is holding the holiday ransom against the trimming back of certain Inquisition inquiries." Simmons walked over and picked up the body of his broken toy. "It was coming to perch on your shoulder, having identified you as a 'friendly.'"

The sound of his voice made me think I'd kicked a puppy. "I'm sorry, Dr. Simmons, I thought it was attacking. Still, if I could take it out with my hand . . ." I let my voice trail off sympathetically.

The man frowned from his eyebrows to where thin hair fought a rearguard action against an invading forehead. "But the BGSD-1 has already shown it can dodge bullets.

The sonar send/receive relays are omnidirectional and create a detection sphere around the BGSD-1. I have twin broadcasting centers with double-redundant backups, digital oversampling, and pattern-matching software that can even identify the weapons shooting at them so their threat level can be accurately assessed."

I flipped him the head, then wiggled my fingers. "You didn't include a fingertip profile as a threat, did you?"

"I, ah, I think I have fist and hand-edge and foot and knee and elbow and . . ."

". . . And Boris got sucker-punched by my fingertips." I patted him on the shoulder. "Go digitize up some old Bruce Lee and Jean-Claude Van Damme movies and enter those moves into your threat assessment system."

"Yes, yes, then Boris will think small, fast men are threats."

"Could be, Doc, could be." I winked at him and walked on by. "But then I think he might have learned *that* lesson a second before he lost his head."

THREE

I left the three scientists debating whether or not old Boris needed a veterinarian or an electrician. Pushing on through the partition labyrinth, I turned left at the back wall and headed straight for the corner office. Down here none of the offices had a view, but the corners were bigger and possessing one was definitely a sign of corporate favor.

Dr. Andrea Carter definitely deserved all the favor Cybertronic could show her. I say this without fear of appearing biased, even though she was the person who did for me what all the King's Horses and Men couldn't do for Humpty Dumpty. I'm certainly grateful for what she did—the skill with which she worked had made my recovery nothing short of miraculous. According to the normal timetable for "reactivation," I should have been little better than Boris The Bat™ at distinguishing between friend and foe at this point in my career. Because of her, I was out on the street only eighteen months after dying.

Of course, Dr. Carter had been an inspiration to me. She stood taller than me—but after my surgery, most adults did—and had thick red hair that would fall in waves of ringlets over her shoulders, if she let it down. Her pale flesh had freckles that washed up over her pert nose and accentuated the cool blue of her eyes. She had very kissable lips that I'd often worked to see moving from pursed puzzlement to a smile of amazement. Her hands were both delicate and strong, capable of probing softly like digital radar or wrenching frozen joints apart without causing undue pain.

She was the kind of woman I would have gladly died for, and she was sharp enough to desire nothing of the kind from me. She did her best in putting me back together, and I worked as hard as possible to make her work pay off. So far things had paid off well, and her recent transfer to a corner office, I felt proudly, was due in no small part to her work with me.

I popped into her office without knocking and arced the NyxStyx™ at the far corner of the L-shaped room. The area nearest me, one foot of the L, had originally been intended as a conference area, but enough electronics and plastic things had been strewn across a long table and heaped upon the chairs to come close to building me a little brother.

Beyond the parts department, in the corner of the room, Andy had set up a cluttered work station and flanked it with full banks of shelves. Three different terminals had information scrolling across them in a blur, and the shelves were filled with binders that, in turn, were filled with optical disks of technical data. I knew, somewhere, I had been reduced to performance reports and stored there, but it beat being dead and shoved into a hole in lunar rock, so I didn't mind.

The other end of the L featured more electronics, but all of this stuff was in working order. Muted lights flickered in accord with an internal rhythm. In front of the computer bank sat a LinkCouch with which I had long since become intimately acquainted.

Dr. Carter snagged the NyxStyx™ from the air, then glanced up at me. "Only one package?"

In less time than it took me to shrug, the computer ran a check for me. "It's not your birthday."

Andy rubbed her eyes and stood up. "No, but you increased my workload today."

"Debriefs are a normal part of your work."

"Your debriefs are never normal."

"Having a postmortem perspective on life means little is normal."

"I thought I disallowed the 'death defense.' "

I smiled. "Point. What did I do this time?"

Andy opened the door that split her messy office from the Link suite and waved me on into the tiled examination room beyond. The woman from the alley lay on the stainless-steel table in the center of the room. Even being naked, with her right foot hanging oddly at the end of her leg and with her left cheekbone sunken in, she didn't look nearly as beautiful as she had before. I tried to stop the computer from updating my memory of her with this new image, but it was too fast for me and in a *click-whirr* she was gone.

"You do good work, Rex, but picking up after you can be a bitch. You broke her ankle and even chipped the knobs off her fibula and tibia."

"I thought you liked working on puzzles."

"Very few puzzles have powdered pieces."

I winced. "How about her cheek?"

"*That* you only broke into a half dozen pieces."

I frowned. "I didn't think I'd killed her. She was still breathing when I put her in the dumpster."

"Not your fault, really." Using the same type of cellular link I employed to call the trash-haulers, she commanded her computers to display an image. It downloaded the information to my onboard computer, and the image was projected onto my eye in a manner that made it appear to be hovering in midair above the patient. Andy pointed to the image of the woman's head in our consensual hallucination. "She had a weakened blood vessel here in her brain. In another twenty years it would have burst, and she'd have died of an aneurysm. Your blow ruptured it early, killing her. Luckily for us the damage was limited, and we got her here in time to stabilize her."

Andy patted the woman's cadaverous thigh. "Say hello to your little sister."

Something flip-flopped in my guts and neither the computer or I could figure it out. I didn't know if I'd been surprised at the idea that I might have had and killed my own, flesh and blood sister, or if I was seeing in this woman what Andy must have seen in me a year and a half ago. I knew I didn't recognize the woman from the tape of my funeral, but I had a lingering sense of familiarity associated with it. Could she have been someone I had known? Or was I just hoping for her to be a connection with my life before Cybertronic to prevent me from dwelling on my death and resurrection?

Or was I simply afraid of Andy having no time for me once she had a new toy?

I turned away and walked to the washbasin over on the wall. I drew the knife from the sheath on my right calf and started the water running. "What about the other one?"

"He was extremely dead."

"So was I."

"You only had skull fragments in your brain, not a tumor."

I winced. The fact that he had cancer had denied him the sort of revivification awaiting his partner, but not because it had destroyed brain tissue. Brain tissue could be replaced with cybernetic circuitry, as it had been in my case. The cancer doomed him because treating it and preventing metastasis cost too much and would take too much time for him to be useful. At least useful as an agent.

"You gonna ice him?"

Andy nodded. "He'll be good for some parts." She frowned at me. "You're not going to get that thing truly clean, you know. A chemical catalyst and a black light will show that it was blooded. I could type and match the trace blood there to the man you killed inside an hour and a half."

I smiled and glanced back at her over my shoulder. "I'm not worried about physical traces on the knife. Without a body, no one is going to be looking at a conviction. I'm just cleaning up my tools after finishing a job."

Andy arched an eyebrow. "You listen to some Brotherhood soothspewer on the way here? Are you getting metaphysical on me?"

I resheathed the knife, then turned and smiled with as much charm as I could muster. "I would love to get physical on you, Doctor."

"You couldn't handle it, Rex."

"You'd be surprised, Andy."

"No I wouldn't. I put you back together, remember? I know all of your capabilities."

"Really? Then I must have somehow forgotten what would have been a very memorable series of tests."

"Hysterical amnesia, Rex." Andrea forced a yawn. "The inability to deal with failure has often been known to induce it." She leaned back, resting her butt on the table with the cadaver. "Seriously, is something bothering you?"

I shook my head, but not well enough to convince her or me that I meant it. "I don't think so—at least nothing but your continued resistance to my obvious charms."

"What you lack in subtlety you make up for in persistence."

"Then there is a chance?"

"No, I prefer subtle." Her glacial eyes scanned me up and down again. "You've not reacted to a termination this way before, Rex. You've done Jacks and Jills before without problems."

"It's not the killing or the fact that I killed a woman." I rubbed my left hand down over my face, then folded my arms across my chest. "There's something else rolling around inside my brain. I think it's less the killing than it is the fact that the run wasn't as simple as it should have been. They shouldn't have been there looking for trouble, and the fact that they were, tells me that the data I picked up was a lot more valuable than it seemed when I got it."

Andy held her hands up. "Tell me nothing more. I don't want to know what you learned about."

"It was nothing special, honestly."

"I don't care." A note of anxiety entered her voice. "In theory I shouldn't even be talking to you right now."

"Excuse me? You do a preliminary debrief after all my runs, then I link into Bitwomb and download all my technical data."

"This run was different. I got an Alpha-One directive to have you link in to the computer as soon as feasible. The boys in the penthouses don't want me to know what you learned, and I respect that. If what you learned has an effect on you, though, I have to deal with that."

"They want you to get the stains out even though you don't know what got spilled?"

"That's why I have a corner office."

"I'm sorry for being such trouble." I nodded toward the door. "Can I link in through your set up in the office?"

Andy nodded. "I'll be working in here. I figure I've got six hours of reconstructive and integrative surgery, then thirty-six hours of intensive care before she's ready to run." She smiled. "I doubt she'll need a tenth of the rehabilitation time you did, though. The work I'm doing on her isn't nearly as extensive as it was on you. Thanks for not breaking her back."

I shrugged again. "We'd not been introduced, so I didn't feel I could do that."

"Always the gentleman."

I flashed her a smile. "I know how to treat a lady, if you'd just give me the chance."

"Take a hint, Rex. When I'm standing next to the corpse of a woman you killed, even at your most subtle, you're pretty obvious."

"I can see that."

"Maybe *she'll* like obvious when I get her up and going."

"Cardinal's blood, I hope not."

"No?"

"No." I started toward the door. "I'm not sure I want to be attractive to women who let me kill them before our first date."

FOUR

I retreated from Andy's operating theater and dropped myself into the cracked vinyl surface of the LinkCouch. I scrunched around a bit until my lips and shoulder blades found the familiar depressions in the pads, then I leaned my head back. As I closed my eyes, the computer flashed an inquiry asking if I wanted to link in to the main computer, and I gave my consent.

The glowing green letters of the question exploded into a galaxy of burning white lights that stabbed through my brain. It hurt for a second, then I was through the wall. I floated in a dark sky above a tiny world defined by neon vector-graphics. The vision could have been much more sophisticated, but I had long ago chosen to keep the world of the Bitwomb remote, alien, and crisply mathematically precise. I knew it would be very easy to allow the computer to project before me scenes that I could not distinguish from reality—and for all I knew that was exactly what it did for everything I considered my independent life. Even if that *was* the case and I really was nothing more than a brain in a jar thinking, I was living a full life. In *my* version of subjective reality, *I* would be in control.

Pointing my nose down at the world below me, I transformed my body into a sleek, stealthy fighter jet and flashed a head's-up display in front of me. Flicking my gaze over the mode selector for my weapons, I settled on a M-1716 Infobomb. Indulging me in my fantasy, the main computer packaged the data I'd gathered on my run into a little, aerodynamic bomb, then painted a golden target on the surface of the world. I sent myself into a long, low, swooping dive. When the HUD matched my aim point to the target, I let the Infobomb go, then I pulled up and made myself break to the right.

The bomblet exploded against the world. Shards of information whirled off through the subreal sky like lethal shrapnel as the computer analyzed and sorted everything out. I saw images of the two people I killed tumble on past me, and I laughed as they failed in their one last chance to get back at me for what I had done to them.

Then I felt a jolt, and my HUD began to flash. I turned my head, spinning the world around me, and saw that one of my two tail fins had been sliced away. A razor-edged image of the woman in the chair, with the rainbow changing and running like watercolors in a downpour, gnawed up the spine of what I had become. Almost halfway through me, it did enough damage that one of my twin engines ripped free of my skeleton and pushed up through me. The world spun, then boiled and erupted in a technicolor volcano that broke me apart.

I tumbled and fell through eternity, then stopped abruptly. I felt the pressure of the LinkCouch against my back and buttocks, but I knew I was still linked into the main Cybertronic computer. I found myself on a Link-Couch in a room with transparent walls. Across from me I saw a chair and a filled polygon figure seated in it. The spherical head with triangular ears nodded toward me. "Good Afternoon, Cyril."

"I've told you before to call me Rex."

"So you have." The figure tapped a yellow cylinder pencil against little ivory teeth. While I had been rendered in perfect graphical form, his resolution made his artificiality more than obvious. In other sessions I had told him he could make himself look as good as I did, but he opted to remain in crude construct form. "I shall indulge you at this time, but another time I want to explore with you the implications of the homonym for your chosen appellation."

"Right, no problem. Now tell me why you shot me down."

"Shot you down?"

I frowned and hoped the computer conveyed my displeasure in full. "I've used that little routine for data dumps before, and you never felt you had to bring me out of it so abruptly. You shot me down, made me crash."

"Ah, the crash." The thing I had named Carl looked at the notebook that grew up in his left hand. "Your communications protocol program did crash, but the Central Unit had nothing to do with that. The diagnostic programs indicate the fault came from your end when you tried to purge the image data from Lorraine Kovan. Do you know why that would happen?"

"Not a clue."

"Technically speaking, of course, the reason was that as the data packet went out, it was listed as containing 11,542 megabytes of data, but you tried to send 21,294 megabytes of data. Moreover, your operational logs indicate that you only isolated 11.5 megabytes of data about her on your run."

I was about to dismiss the problem, but I hesitated. "I had more data connected with that image than I had collected?" I felt a tingling sensation blossom between my shoulder blades. "Maybe I saw her somewhere before."

"Is that possible?"

"I don't know, Carl. You have to remember that I'm only eighteen months old here. My memories don't extend that far back. I don't remember seeing her, but I seem to recall you explaining things about the brain's 'holographic memory.' I could have seen her and just not consciously remember it. The doodads you've got inside my skull could have made that little connection and tried to integrate that sighting with this one."

"Plausible." The figure glanced at the pad again. "Have you ever been to the village of Fairview on Venus?"

I shook my head. "Not that I know of."

Carl gestured at the wall to my left, and it suddenly became opaque. It took me a moment to resolve the images being projected there, then I realized I was looking at a chopper's gun-camera record as the craft skimmed over the jungle on Venus. Once the dark foliage ended, the craft dipped down and did a figure eight over the fire-blackened ruins of what had once been a very small agricultural outpost. I didn't see any bodies, but there were little green outlines where bodies had stopped short grasses from burning. I counted a dozen of them before the scene tilted radically, then dissolved into hissing static.

"That was Fairview?"

Carl nodded. "We used a drone to make a quick pass over it. Capitol shot our unit down. They are being very protective of the area and anyone who has any connection to it. They evacuated Mrs. Kovan from Venus and brought her here for debriefing."

I shook my head. "I hate to say this, but that wasn't much of a debriefing. It seems to me they just wanted to make certain they had the right person. Steel—the guy doing the interrogating—cut her off and told the doctor that she was hallucinating. And that makes me think you knew Capitol had someone special there, and you just wanted to have me witness their verification of that fact."

"That certainly could be a valid interpretation of the orders you were given."

Both of my hands tightened down into fists. "I know you're supposed to evaluate my mental stability in these little meetings, but you don't have to be patronizing about it."

"I didn't mean to be patronizing, Rex." Carl's head swiveled toward me. "Why did you think I was?"

"I twig on to your reasons for giving me that mission, and you refuse to confirm my correct guess."

"Perhaps I have been given orders to confirm correct guesses, but to refrain from correcting errors."

I chewed on that for a moment. If I was wrong in assuming they had sent me out to pick up that little bit of data, then Cybertronic knew more than they were telling me. That wasn't unusual at all, of course, since the people in the trenches seldom know the minds of their corporate masters. We are not meant to know such things, nor are we intended to think our masters might not know everything.

That's the good thing about vacs—they question nothing. They have no curiosity. They have no desire to know more than they should. They're great little drones, and do their jobs, but they can't react to threats that require them to move outside their training and previous experience.

Tiffs, on the other hand, must constantly question things. Carl's carefully worded reply to me brought with it a number of questions. It clearly told me that my assumption about my mission was wrong. The information I had gathered could have been harvested by any number of means that would not have put me in jeopardy. I had to assume, absent evidence that Cybertronic wanted me dead, that they had wanted *me* to get that information. Why?

It was true that information storage required digitization, and that some data could get lost in that process. Had my bosses thought I might remember something that the data did not reflect? Had they hoped I would get some impression of Lorraine or the other people in the room that would not show up in the datadump? It was possible, but wouldn't *that* have been the first target of Carl's inquiry?

Setting that question aside for a moment, I reviewed the whole incident again. The two Capitol agents I'd eliminated shouldn't have been posted outside for something as mundane as what I had witnessed. Clearly they were there to safeguard the building and the folks inside of it. That suggested to me, rightly or wrongly, that someone else had an interest in the Kovan woman.

I glanced up at Carl. "When was the imaging of Fairview made? And when did Mrs. Kovan arrive on Luna?"

"Our imaging was made two months ago. Mrs. Kovan arrived on Luna four hours before you saw her."

"So there was a lag between Fairview's destruction and her transport here?"

"Quite a considerable one."

"Was there interference by any of the other corps?"

"The answer to that question is unknown right now, but the likelihood of that is high."

I nodded. "Silly question, I know." The corps regularly wage war on each other, so messing up special operations becomes just another way of annoying the enemy. Capitol and Cybertronic were not particularly antagonistic, but Bauhaus or Mishima would love to take a round out of

Capitol if they could. And Imperial hated Cybertronic enough to screw around with Capitol and try to lay the blame on us.

Carl scribbled a note on his pad, then both the pencil and pad vanished. "So, you have reached a conclusion?"

"Maybe. It seems you wanted *me* to be the one to get the information on Kovan, maybe because I ran into her before, which you remember but I don't. And apparently she's had a difficult time, and you don't know all there is to know about that. So, I guess, you want me to find out what I can about her, and you're hoping my native curiosity will make me do a good job."

I smiled at Carl. "Am I right? Are you going to order me to dig into her past?"

"There are no such orders for you at this point."

I shrugged my shoulders. "Then I'm stumped."

"I doubt that." Carl shifted in his chair, and the computer even supplied an appropriate squeak. "How do you feel about your work for Cybertronic?"

The shift in his question caught me mentally flat-footed. "Fine."

"No nightmares, no bad dreams?"

"Not that I know of. As I've told you before, I don't remember dreams very well."

"Or you suppress them. They could be painful for you. They could make you remember your time before you became one of us."

I shook my head. "You're always trying to suggest I need to resolve the crisis in identity I feel because of who I am now and who I was before. I keep telling you, I have no crisis. I don't want to know who I was before. I am RKX 571127. My cover identity is Cyril Dent, but I go by the nickname Rex. That's all I need to know."

"Is it?"

"If it isn't, wouldn't you have told me who I was?" I leaned forward and pointed at Carl with an unwavering finger. "You've allowed me access to my own funeral video-feed, but you took out any clue to my identity. Clearly who I was is not important."

"Perhaps."

"Always perhaps."

"Or perhaps it is not important *who* you were, but who

you *thought* you were. The funeral and eulogy gives you insights into the perception of others concerning you. The conflict arises not from who you were and what you are, but what you thought of yourself then, and what you think of yourself now. Your trauma-induced amnesia did not erase your core personality."

"You mean I was always a suave, charming, sophisticated man who had his way with women?"

"Perhaps. And perhaps your lack of success with women now is a conflict for you."

That stung. "I don't get a chance to meet many women, Carl. Dr. Carter doesn't want to get too close to me, and Cybertronic manufactures toasters with more personality than the vacs running around here."

"Dr. Carter and Ms. Wickersham are not the only women you have met."

"True, there was the babe I killed today."

"And Pam Afton and Fay Fan."

"They are business contacts who have helped me establish my cover as a freelancer here on Luna."

"The fact that they are business associates has not stopped you from attempting to seduce them."

"Flirting with them is not a seduction attempt."

"Would you care to see the readings from your autonomic nervous system the first time you spoke with Ms. Fan?"

"No, thank you very much." I wanted to snarl, but I wasn't sure how that would come out in subreal. "Well, us shorter guys have more trouble finding women."

"And you resent the fact that you are not as tall as you were before? You find the difference unsettling and dislocating?"

"No, no I don't." I forced myself to calm down. "'I am who I am."

"And you have named yourself Rex."

"That's right, I'm the king!"

"Or you are a wreck."

I said nothing for a moment in a vain attempt to keep that remark from sinking in. I failed. "Are we done playing these little games, Carl?"

"Do you want to see this as a game?"

"Yes, because then I can call for a time-out."

The Carl figure sat back in its chair. "Very well, Rex, you can have your time-out. Just be aware that you're entering into a new stage in your development as a member of Cybertronic. For the last eighteen months, your body has been integrating itself with your circuitry, and the marriage of the two has been going quite well. This means you have worked up an important series of synaptic connections that allow you to function fully. But that means things are going to change."

I didn't like the sound of that. "How so?"

"Continued integration may reestablish connections between parts of your brain that were traumatized when you were killed. You may find yourself dreaming or remembering things from before your death."

"Is that normal?"

"Every Chasseur we create is unique. Some of you deal with the problems easily, while others don't. You are very promising, Rex, and I don't want the inevitable to surprise you and destroy you."

"I appreciate that."

"Good. Our session is finished."

"Fantastic. Am I cleared to head out?"

"Yes, Cyril Dent, freelance troubleshooter is clear to leave. Where will you go?"

"I'm going to the Midnight Sun," I told Carl as subreal began to dissolve. "I'm going to get a drink, kill some brain cells, and delay the inevitable for as long as possible."

FIVE

I left Andy's office and cut through a side door to the employee locker room. Oz had a huge complex of athletic facilities and exercise rooms attached to it, but the eggheads in ARD seldom did anything that required them to break a sweat. As nearly as I knew, the only folks who made regular use of the facilities were chasseurs like me.

I stripped the old, stained clothes from me and put them in a burn bin. Lights flared in the tiled shower room as I stepped into it, and motion detectors started streams of steaming water spraying out. Their needlelike droplets stung me, but I relished the irritating sensation. After spending a half hour subreal, submitting myself to basic and occasionally painful stimulus was the quickest way to bring myself back to obreal.

And if that sounds even the least bit odd, just think of it as asking someone to pinch you so you know you're not dreaming. It's the same thing, but subreality can seem even more genuine than a dream, so a bit more help is needed to refocus on the objectively real world.

I had no doubt my last exchange with Carl had him making all sorts of notes for our next little episode. Keeping him back and out of my head was getting more difficult. He was becoming more insistent, but I figured he'd try to burrow in on my reference to alcohol to check me for signs of substance abuse, and that little cul-de-sac would sidetrack him long enough for me to work up other defenses.

At the core of his quest was a desire to know why I

didn't want to know who I had been. He saw that as abnormal—even vacs maintained cordial ties with their families and took pride in their identity as an individual. The fact that I clung so fiercely to what I had become disturbed him, and Carl was waiting for an explosion when the person I had been collided with the person I had become.

Carl assumed that collision would come because he felt I had no idea why I wanted to cut myself off from my past. If I had to guess what he thought I'd say that Carl believed me to be suffering from a gross insecurity complex. He felt I didn't want to know who I had been before my death because—citing my new size as an example—I clearly felt diminished.

Carl was wrong. He was wrong for one very simple reason. A reason I would die to prevent revealing it to him.

I didn't want to know who I had been because that person had ended up dead.

I'd lived in Luna City for my entire life. I knew the score. The world was dangerous. Corporations had assumed the roles previously assigned to nation-states, and they employed the full range of diplomatic weapons at a nation's disposal. This included everything from open and fair bargaining to waging war. Assassination was not unheard of and, in my case, clearly had been successful.

Death, contrary to fact of my current condition, is not a survival trait. Whoever I had been had been careless. He had been caught unaware. He had been taken and rendered helpless. His spine had been broken at L-1, and his skull had been crushed. He died.

I wasn't going to die a second time. I wasn't that person anymore, and I didn't want to know who he had been. He was a loser. I was determined to succeed where he had failed.

In nostalgic moments, I had tried to convince myself that in learning about my past—by following up subtle clues in the funeral video—I would learn how I had died and then never make that same mistake again. I could benefit from my previous experience. I'd not place myself in a position to be slain again.

The argument was convincing, but began to crumble as

my realistic faculties kicked in. If I learned who I was, there was no guarantee that I wouldn't make the same mistake. In fact, in returning to the life that had gotten me killed, I would make myself a target again. And I might *misidentify* the mistake that had led to my death. I might repeat my actions and be slain again because I underestimated the person or persons who wanted me dead.

I had been given an opportunity to live again, and I had no intention of squandering it. The old me had his spine crushed at the first lumbar vertebra. The injury severed the spinal cord. It denied me the use of my legs. It left me without bowel and bladder control. It destroyed all function below my waist. The old me, if he had ever regained consciousness, would have been trapped in a wheelchair for the rest of his life.

Through the use of micro-fine, fiber-optic cables that Andy had painstakingly snaked through my spinal column, I was given the lower half of my body back. Those cables were attached to integrated neurobiological circuits in my skull. Not only did that material give me control of my lower body, but they also more than replaced the damaged tissue that had been removed for their implantation. I now could download and access more information than I had ever learned before. I could process and access neural inputs beyond normal human capabilities. I could communicate with Cybertronic through cellular links, and the speed of my thought processes was increased by two orders of magnitude.

Cybertronic had rebuilt me. They had salvaged me from the wreck I had been in my previous incarnation. I had no reason or need to return to my previous existence and embrace it. I figured I could fend Carl off long enough until my track record at Cybertronic made his line of inquiries moot and rendered his fears immaterial.

As anyone with a metal detector or radio-frequency modulation monitor could easily discern, I had enough hardware in me to identify me as someone with a connection with Cybertronic. While there was a small community of expatriate Cybes in Luna City, all of us were tied back to the corporation by our need for spare parts and updates when bugs in chips were discovered. In short, apples from the Cybertronic tree never fell very far away.

Because there was no concealing my links with Cybertronic, I went ahead and dressed in one of the standard tunics with the stubby little faux collar and a pair of black slacks. The only nice thing about the half-inch collar was that it made wearing a tie kind of futile, and I'd not found myself comfortable wearing them. Part of me wondered if my murderer had partially strangled me, perhaps with my own tie, but I generally thrust that sort of speculation away.

I tucked the pants into Martian Trooper™ boots and snapped them shut. Straightening up, I looked every inch a Cybertronic vac, which meant I had to do something to change my image. The boys in ARD would have added a plastic pocket protector to the white shirt. I opted for an iridescent blue jacket with padded shoulders and a midi-cape that flared down and joined the spine at the hem. The jacket came to mid-thigh on me, which combined with the color to make it decidedly different from the tough-guy long coats most freelancers wore.

Fastening the top two buttons, I nodded at my reflection in the mirror, then shut my locker and headed out. Miss Wickersham paid me no attention at all, which meant I hadn't accidentally set myself on fire. I chose a covert route out of the building that got me one block closer to the Midnight Sun and dumped me on the street through the doorway of a candied-calamari shop.

Keeping the Brotherhood Cathedral at my back, I cut down two levels through steamy tunnels and wandered nonchalantly through the clumpy ribbon of humanity. Most of the people were normal, workaday types heading into, coming back from, or on lunch break during their shifts. Aside from most of them being taller than me, they were unremarkable. The sort of folks described by the phrase "innocent bystanders."

The ones that bore watching broke down into three classes. The first were the street toughs. They lounged around on stoops, or leaned on level supports, doing their best to look bored and menacing at the same time. A constantly obscene commentary ran from their mouths and intensified only when someone took offense or, better yet, appeared to be scared. Most of them were armed, but few of them with anything more heavy than a handgun.

I figured them for a low threat level, but kept my eyes on them nonetheless. Even though I was alone, I didn't walk like prey, so that kept them at bay. I just had to hope that one of them wasn't having a bad day, or had gotten bad drugs. Absent some external irritant, I was probably pretty safe.

The second set of folks I watched were the corporate patrols. Security for the various levels and sectors of Luna City was either supplied by the corporations in terms of house troops, or through subcontractors. A lot of freelancers like I was supposed to be took subcontracts when they didn't have anything big going. It was decent money, but a bit hazardous. Corps don't seem to mind as much if hired outsiders get shot up defending a facility, so subcontracted security details tend to see a bit more action than regular corps troops.

Most of the security folks on level three here were regulars in their appropriate paramilitary uniforms. They outgunned the gang-bangers and could call up reinforcements in an instant if needed. When one corps troop crossed paths with another, they saluted respectfully even though their corps might be trying to annihilate each other on Mars or Venus.

The Brotherhood did not take kindly to running corporate gun battles here on Luna, and their Inquisitors were more than capable of keeping the peace.

The vast majority of the security troops were on the lookout for members of the third group: freelancers. Mostly made up of ex-corporate troops, the freelancers take all sorts of jobs that require brains, firepower, discretion, and plausible deniability. Freelancers are part mercenary, part spy, and a whole bunch of cannon fodder. Most are also excitement junkies, which explains why they endure a life of mind-numbing boredom punctuated by jobs that could easily get them killed.

I opened the door to the Midnight Sun and saw more freelancers crowding the place than I had expected. While freelancers do hang out at the Midnight Sun, the population tends to stay relatively low since there's always some job requiring strong backs, weak minds, and ballistic ar-

mor. A quick-glance census told me most of the excess
traffic came from the guys who tended to work for Capitol, Bauhaus, and Mishima, which meant each of those
firms was waiting for something to break before continuing normal operations.

Stepping in, I cut to the left and toward a table where
my friends usually congregate. The Midnight Sun's decor
is early Landfill, with corrugated tin walls above a
lunarblock base, exposed wiring, old holographs, buzzing
neon, and an eclectic collection of beverage selections. In
fact, the only thing the liquors had in common was the
lack of any sort of tax stamp. I secretly assumed that none
of the stuff *in* the bottles had any relation to the labels *on*
the bottles. I ordered a bottle of John Greene's Raspberry
Weitzer—brewed only two levels down, I figured I could
trust it—then squeezed in toward the fiberplast cable reel
back in the corner.

Pam Afton noticed me first and, despite the fact she
was holding Lane Chung's hand beneath the level of the
tabletop, smiled brightly at me. "Hello, Cyril, it's been a
while." I caught relief in her voice, and that surprised me.
It sounded less her having been concerned for my well-
being than my presence had returned some degree of nor-
malcy to her life.

"It has been a while, Pam, but you're always a welcome sight." I meant that sincerely. Tall and slender, Pam
wore her blond hair stylishly short. Her blue eyes were a
degree warmer than Andy's eyes, and Pam favored skin-
tight jumpsuits to the stylish but less-revealing sort of
things Andy wore. Pam also wore a pistol on her hip and
was one of the cooler people I'd met under fire.

Lane Chung sat next to her. Smaller, dark-haired but
wiry, Lane tended toward being quiet except when talking
to Pam. I'd always figured he'd had it bad for Pam, starting back when they both served together in Capitol's
Martian banshees, but in the past they had been strictly
comrades-in-arms. The joining of their infrared outlines
below the level of the table suggested a change in that situation, and part of me wondered what would have finally
brought them together.

A greater mystery was what had brought Fay Fan and
Klaus Dahlen together with Pam and Lane. Like Lane,

Fay was of Asian extraction, but her mechanical eye replacements distorted the almond shape of her eyes. Despite that, her oval face was pretty and her black hair had been cut boyishly short. As nearly as I knew, she'd never worked with either Pam or Lane, though they were acquainted with each other from the Midnight Sun. While freelancers tended to be friendly with each other, I wouldn't have expected them to be socializing together.

The main impediment to that socialization was Klaus. Short—though an inch or two taller than me—and slender enough to be considered chicken-breasted, Klaus still held his head up with that Bauhausian air of superiority. While I agreed that Bauhaus manufactured highly reliable weaponry of uncompromising quality, the egos they issued their people were just this side of toxic. Klaus tended to whine about substandard this or that, which got on my nerves. Were he not with Fay, I would have considered tipping him out of his chair and appropriating it for myself.

Lane glanced down at the table self-consciously, then smiled up at me. "How did your baby-sitting job go?"

"No bugs, no rust, and no wear and tear on the machinery." I took my bottle of weitzer from the waitress and left a crumpled five piastre circle in its place. The others stared at my generosity, and I shrugged. To cover a month of refitting and adjustments, I'd said I had a bodyguard job for a Cybertronic executive. "The job paid well. Daddy finished his training course over in Aristillus sector, and no one threatened his family while he was gone."

Pam nodded, her expression a bit tight around her eyes. "Next time you get an assignment like that and you need help, let me know."

"Will do." I twisted the cap off the weitzer bottle and pocketed it—even chasseurs have to produce receipts to get their expenses covered. "You look a bit tired, Pam. Rough month?"

She was about to answer, but heat pulsed down where she held Lane's hand. She shook her head instead. "Not particularly. No more so than normal."

"That's good." I took a swallow of the beer and smiled at its crisp, semisweet bite. "Anything big going down soon? Lots of talent in the stable here."

Fay started replying, but something was wrong. Her voice came out all slow and incredibly deep. And the syllables didn't match the way her lips and jaw moved. In fact, I doubted she could have made some of the sounds I was hearing.

Then she started to turn into a monster.

I reached for the table, but it seemed very far away. My hands stretched out toward it, getting longer and longer. Blackness tinged the edges of my sight, and distantly I felt the weitzer bottle slip from my grasp. My knees buckled, and for a second I was afraid I was going to faint.

Then, as the world dissolved, I knew I wasn't going to faint.

With that realization, my terror redoubled itself and blackness slammed me to the ground.

SIX

If the wall I fell through had not been black, and had not
the blackness torn at me like a thousand fiery thorns, I
might have thought I was being dragged into some
horror-based subreal simulation. As it was, I felt shredded
by the transition. The Midnight Sun faded from view, and
I felt numb all over except for my stomach. It made me
nauseous, and my saliva tasted bitter and sulfurous.

The world slowly pieced itself back together, but that
did nothing to banish my ill ease. In fact, it heightened it
because I found myself trapped in a body that felt titanic,
yet incredibly light. I could not see details of it—I knew
I was seated and dark robes of a gangrenous velvet covered me. I had no control over the body in which I sat,
and felt very much a cartoon character trapped behind the
eyes of a huge idol.

Across the rough-hewn stone chamber from me, another creature knelt obeisantly. By comparing the huddled
figure with the few signs of humanity in that poorly lit
room, I knew the creature had to be huge—at least twice
the size of a normal man and much bigger than me—yet
the body I wore dwarfed it. Bulging muscles rippled beneath livid red flesh. As it straightened up and raised its
spike-festooned head, I saw its lipless mouth bristled with
serrated peg-shaped teeth designed for rending and tearing.

The robes it wore had been shredded over its chest and
belly. The flesh revealed by the holes in the robe appeared pinkish in color and had puckered around little

craters. The creature had clearly taken some heavy weapon's fire, and likely from close range, too. It disturbed me that something that nasty had apparently recovered from such wounds, and sufficiently quickly that it had not yet changed from the clothing it had worn when being shot. The other possibility—that the creature felt a moral or emotional need to wear the clothing in which it had been wounded—was no less frightening.

"Have mercy upon your pitiful servant, Master," it intoned as it pressed its forehead to the floor again. In its voice I detected a very real current of fear.

In me its plea inspired compassion, but the body I wore seized upon the fear as a delicious weakness. I did not reply to it immediately and felt the terror radiating off the creature like heat from an arc welder. I basked in the fear as if it were pure sunlight, and savored it as if a fine brandy rescued from the desiccated corpse of Mother Earth.

"Your inferiority as a nepharite amazes us, Ragathol. It seems to flow in direct proportion to your audacity. The only vaguely compensatory factor we have found is that we can predict how miserable your defeat will be by measuring the hubris surrounding your operation."

"I am wretched, Master." The nepharite shuddered, and I felt his shame as sharply as I might have felt an ice pick being shoved through my eye. I tried to pull back, but could not. I was as trapped as Ragathol, but I sensed no knowledge of my presence by the creature I inhabited. Without knowing how I knew it, I realized that my life and sanity depended upon my remaining unnoticed.

"You should someday aspire to being wretched, Ragathol. Have we not said your arrogance is the yardstick against which we measure your failure? We have not forgotten how you told us you have a vessel filled with insane visions that you wanted to give us. Yet now it appears you lost that token of your devotion to us—*if* it ever existed. You lost the vessel *and* your foothold on Luna."

"But I sowed the seeds of Dark Symmetry on Luna, on the world the humans count as their home. The farmer may not still tread the field, but the seed germinates and grows."

"Yes, some of your heretics are in useful positions, but

without the nurturing of a wise mind, they will wither and die." I felt a vibration course up through my body as the nepharite bashed his head into the floor. As he straightened up, I saw dark green blood flowing from a wound in his forehead. It coursed down between thick brows, over his broad nose, and disappeared like sewer water through the gate described by his teeth.

"You will have to do better than that, Ragathol, if we are to forgive you the greatest of your trespasses. You fled from Luna to Venus. You attracted the attention of human forces there . . ."

"I was in pursuit of the woman, my gift to you . . ."

"And your actions caused one of our forward bases to be destroyed by a handful of humans."

Ragathol pressed his thick hands against the scars on his stomach. "They were more than a handful, and were competent and well armed."

"But *you* are a nepharite. You are the elite of the Dark Legion."

"Had it been up to me, Master, I would have slain them all. I was ambushed."

"Do not attempt to deceive us, Ragathol. You were injured when a man, a lone man, found you preparing the warprift that brought you here. You had him enmeshed in Dark Symmetry . . ."

"He broke from my control."

"Impossible. No one, nothing can resist the Dark Symmetry! Your terror weakened your weaving of the Dark Symmetry. Would that you felt physical pain!"

"I know pain, Master." Again it smashed its head into the stone chamber's floor and again. Blood pooled around torn bits of flesh between the nepharite and me, and flashes of a dark fantasy featuring the nepharites severed head bobbing in a cauldron of boiling blood pulsed through my mind's-eye.

"Ragathol, you have mightily displeased us. The reason we allow you to continue your pitiful existence is because, somehow, your efforts have not attracted sufficient notice to pose a threat to us. Know that our trust in you has been mightily diminished."

"This causes me unbearable agonies."

"Yet you bear up beneath them."

"Only my will to atone allows me the strength, my lord."

I felt an urge to swat Ragathol down for his impudence, but I stayed my hand because, in the past, he had amused us so. We deigned to listen to him. "What is the nature of this atonement?"

"The woman—the vessel—is again on Luna. My assets there can obtain her and return her to me."

Outrage washed over us and in its wake we felt an unholy thrill. "That is your idea of suitable atonement? You would place the last shards of your operation on Luna at risk to get her back? You are quite mad, quite insane."

"But she was meant as a gift to you, my lord."

"She is *nothing*, Ragathol. A toy. An afterthought. Worthless."

"But, Master, her condition and her history have made her more than she was before. The terror she knew when I first offered her to you has doubled and redoubled because of her continual rescue and recapture. Her insanity has matured, Master, in ways that only you could truly appreciate."

An electric trickle of lust puckered our flesh. Our enemies were indeed diabolically clever. Insignificant morsel though she was, the woman could be diverting—surely nothing more than that. The pleasure would be minor, but the risk to obtain her would be negligible. Especially now that Ragathol had intrigued us enough concerning her that we actually *did* want her.

Not having her would niggle and dig, gnaw and burrow into us. It would infect our mind. It would fester and sour. It would build pressure, gathering strength with each nanosecond, compounding and swelling, an alien presence expanding to fill every moment, waking and otherwise, with the bitter, acidic knowledge that we had been denied sampling her madness. And when this obsession to possess her had built and built, it would explode, brain-gray venom gushing from every pore and orifice of our body, leaking without end, pulsing with our heartbeat, geysering out with every involuntary twitch of our body's muscles. It would have consumed us, destroyed us, and *that* we would not allow.

We looked at the nepharite and slowly nodded our head. "Obtain her and bring her to us. Do not fail."

"That possibility had not entered my mind."

"Nor had it before, but you still managed to let success slip from your grasp."

"Never again, Master."

"You had best hope not." Our tongue flicked out tasting the miasma of terror rising from Ragathol. "You will bring her, and I shall consume her." Our smile hid our afterthought: *Then, Ragathol, we shall consume you as well.*

The sensation of teeth crushing bones and sweet marrow sliding oyster-like down my throat caused a dislocating wrench that impaled me again on burning thorns. The world closed in on me, crushing me down. Pain exploded in my knees and forehead, then stars burst in front of my eyes. I felt warmth on my brow, seeping out from the pain, then I was flipped over and felt a weight descend on my chest.

I opened my eyes and found Pam with a knee planted on my breastbone and her pistol hovering just off the end of my nose. "What did you say, Cy?"

Without my conscious control of my body, I answered her question. "Then, Ragathol, we shall consume you as well."

She snapped her Bolter's safety lever off. "Explain how you know about Ragathol."

"If I can't, you kill me?"

Lane hovered over her shoulder. "If you can, you already know you're better off dead."

SEVEN

Pam shook her head. "Lane, I don't like this at all."

I tried to smile. "I'm not too partial to it, either."

"Don't push it, Rex." Her gun didn't waver. "Tell me about . . ."

She had begun to raise her voice, but Lane rested his hand on her shoulder and looked about. She followed his line of vision, then nodded. "I think it's best we take this elsewhere."

As that looked as close to a reprieve as I was going to get, I nodded in agreement. "Let's go."

Klaus sneered down at me. "I don't trust him. What if he has Dark Gifts?"

Lane rolled his eyes. "Cardinal's blood, Klaus, can it."

Without much help on my part, Pam pulled me to my feet. She didn't pull her gun off me, so I was very careful and slow in settling my coat in position and smoothing out the wrinkles. "Where to, my dear?"

"You'll find out when we get there. Fay, settle our tab and meet us there."

"Roger."

"Nice and easy, Rex." Pam forced a smile for the other freelancers in the Midnight Sun. Very few of them had turned around when she drew her gun, but a bunch more had noticed the click of the Bolter's safety coming off. It's odd how such a little metallic sound can cut through the din of a bar and attract attention. Noticing that sort of thing is, for freelancers, a survival trait.

So is evasion, but as I preceded Pam into the street, I

decided that my best bet was to do what she wanted me to do. She was jumpy enough that any odd action on my part might spook her. Pam Afton shot straight enough that she'd cut me in half with slugs from the Bolter before I had a chance to get away.

In addition to having to worry about her reactions, I didn't know what Lane and Klaus were carrying for hardware concealed beneath their long coats. Klaus was a sure bet for an MP-105 machine pistol, and the big question with him was whether or not he'd have it fitted with a grenade launcher. I decided he would—whiners always find ways to compensate for shortcomings.

Lane probably had a Bolter, just like Pam, but he moved stiffly enough that I wondered if he hadn't opted for a CAR-24 submachine gun. It's a nice weapon and spits out enough ordnance to clear the street in front of us. The fact that he'd be firing through me to do so diminished my appreciation for weapon's efficiency, but kept me mindful of its lethality.

If Lane was packing a CAR-24, that choice and Pam's clear anxiety told me they'd tangled with something very nasty and very recently. I'd have had to be as dense as Klaus not to figure the problem revolved around Ragathol and whatever he did on Luna. The coincidence of a woman having gone from Luna to Venus and back suggested to me that Lorraine Kovan might be involved in all this. Intentionally or otherwise, Cybertronic had tossed me in the middle of something that involved the Dark Legion, and the prospect of that was enough to make me beg Pam to pull the trigger.

The Dark Legion is something about which little is really known by most humanity. It's spoken of in hushed whispers, much in the same way the Mafia or Yakuza or Triads are discussed. Everyone wants to know more and to share rumors, but almost nothing of substance circulates concerning them. For those people who do think about the Dark Legion at all, it sounds like a sixth corporation rising up to oppose the Brotherhood and the corporate Cartel.

Most of the best stories about the Dark Legion come from folks like Pam and Lane. Ex-soldiers occasionally talk about things they saw in the jungles of Venus or on the wasted red surface of Mars. Animated and altered corpses and huge citadels dominate these tales, imbuing them with a mystical element that makes them easy to disbelieve. In fact, many people accept the idea of the Brotherhood's deliberate dissemination of such improbable stories to vilify a new, up-and-coming corps. Their anti-Cybertronic rhetoric is famous, and that bit of crying "Wolf" makes it harder for them to get across the idea of how much of a threat the Dark Legion poses to mankind.

Corps, being more prudent or alarmist than the general populace, had taken the threat as real enough to detechnify their offices and facilities. Cybertronic saw that as about as wise as cutting a hangnail at the knee. Despite their decision to cripple themselves, the other corps still managed to remain competitive. That included keeping troops in the field fighting against whatever the Dark Legion was.

It struck me that if that nepharite thing was real, and mentioning his name was enough to get a reaction out of Pam and the others, it meant they'd seen enough to convince them the Dark Legion was more than war stories and rumors. At least it was a working hypothesis, and I decided to put it to the test. "Which one of you pumped ordnance into Ragathol?"

Klaus frowned at me. "None of us shot him. Only Lane and Pam saw him, and they didn't even know his name until . . . ouch!" He grabbed his left ear, which was burning red from where Pam had cuffed him. "What did you do that for?"

"Think about how much intel you just gave him if he's one of *them*."

"Oh."

I let Klaus's expression hit the depths, then begin to soar back to Bauhausian heights before I spoke again. "So then, you weren't part of the crew that tagged him on Venus?"

I got a reaction from all three of them, but Pam shook her head once she'd wiped the surprise off her face. "Nice try, Rex."

"Just making conversation."

"Sure. Look, we'll take all the intel you want to give us."

"*Ja*, we can use it to confirm what you tell us later."

I screwed my head around and gave Klaus a wall-eyed stare. "The only thing I'll tell you, my boy, is how to

build up those pecs so your chest can have more definition than your chin."

"At ease, Klaus." Fay joined our little group and
caught Klaus's wrist before he could backhand me.
"Bill's paid, and our backtrail is clear."

"Good. We go down here." Pam waved me toward a
rusty old wrought-iron set of steps. Corrosion bubbles
cracked beneath the soles of my boots, and the metallic
clumping of our footfalls echoed between levels. We were
heading down to Level Four, which in this district was
built on bedrock. There were some building complexes
that did extend down farther into the Moon's ancient
flesh, but they were not part of a common level and could
only be accessed from within corporate towers.

We cut through an alley and came out into the middle
of what looked to be a confrontation between two street
gangs. Lane produced his CAR-24, and Klaus showed me
that his gun did have a grenade launcher grafted to it. That
display of hardware convinced the toad warriors they
wanted to give us a wide berth. We passed on through
without incident, then went down more steps to a pair of
basement apartments in a building that looked a lot like
the Capitol safe house in terms of age and upkeep.

Pam knocked on the door, then identified herself. A
skinny kid with a lank of black hair hanging down in front
of his almond eyes opened the door, then stood back.
"Zowee, Pam, you didn't say you captured a heretic."

"Quiet, Whiz." Pam dragged me over the threshold and
presented me to an Asian man whose stiff formality had
Mishima written all over it. Slender, but not emaciated like
the kid at the door, he wore his black hair in the stiff brush
cut a lot of Mishima troopers favored. His hair had gone
white at the temples, and I was surprised he'd not colored
it in keeping with his otherwise youthful appearance.

He looked me over, then shifted his gaze to Pam. "I am
pleased to see you, my friends, but I believed our business was finished some weeks back. What is the meaning
of this?"

Lane closed the door and took up a position beside it,
while Klaus appropriated what was a chair hiding beneath
dirty-clothes camouflage. Fay stood by Klaus, and Pam
kept her gun on me while the kid retreated to a computer

station, ducked his head within a virtual reality helmet, and started humming. Releasing the handful of my jacket's shoulder, Pam frowned heavily. "Something weird is going on, and it involves Ragathol."

The Mishima man did not react, but the kid offered "Triple Zowee!" as a measure of his surprise. Pam continued. "Rex met us in the Midnight Sun. He took a swig of a Greene's Weitzer, then passed out. Coming to, he mentioned Ragathol."

The man looked at me again, but kept his face impassive. "What did he say exactly?"

Klaus shifted around in the chair to get comfortable. "It sounded to me like, 'Then, Ragathol, I will consume you, too.' "

I shook my head. "I said, 'Then, Ragathol, we *shall* consume you as well.' You have to remember that imperial 'we,' Klaus." I extended my hand toward the Asian man. "Rex Dent, freelancer, at your service."

"Do I want your service, Mr. Dent?"

I kept my hand out. "Probably not as much as I apparently need your help, Mr. . . . ?"

He took my hand and shook it. "I am Yojimbo. What makes you think I can help you?"

"Mentioning the nepharite's name put the fear of the Cardinals into my friends here, and they immediately brought me to you. If I'd fallen down sick, I expect they would have taken me to a doctor. They saw something else wrong with me and brought me to you. I may not be an accountant, but I can add two and two."

"Your deduction is warranted, but I do not know if I can be of assistance to you. How did you come to know the name Ragathol?"

My brain clicked through a dozen different stories before I decided to tell the truth. Because of the Mark II drug supplied by Cybertronic, I analyzed and rejected my alternatives so quickly that no one in the room had any idea I'd hesitated. I opted for the truth because it minimized the chances of anything I said conflicting with information they had. With Pam still pointing her gun at me and with Lane at the door behind me, my life depended upon not disappointing Yojimbo.

"It works the way Pam laid it out, except that from the

inside I fell into some sort of fugue. I felt trapped inside a foreign body. I couldn't move more than bowing my head, but I wasn't really in control of things anyway. Ragathol knelt at my feet, and he was afraid of me."

"What *do* they put into that weitzer anyway? LSD?" clucked Klaus.

Pam hissed at him, and that shut him up.

I continued. "Whatever I was, I was reaming Ragathol out for failing. Specifically I was angry at his having screwed up here on the Moon. He lost something that further conversation told me was a woman. She ended up on Venus, and he made another grab at her. He failed in holding on to her there, and it cost the Dark Legion one of their citadels. This did not please us. Now the woman is back in Luna City, and Ragathol is going to try for her again."

Yojimbo's hands slowly tightened into fists. "This is most distressing. Whiz kid, can you get any confirmation on the location of the woman?"

The kid pulled the VR helmet on and started to work. Unlike Cybertronic folks, unmarked people have to use normal sensory inputs to access subreal. What I see when communicating with the computers that run Luna City is built out of images taken from my own brain. In the kid's case, everything he saw came from a graphics software package.

I had my onboard computer open my subreal receptors. Under normal circumstances they were kept shielded because the background inputs from watches, toasters, digital radios, and the occasional underground computer rig like the kid's were enough to drive us crazy. All computer chips put out radio waves, and we can pick them up, but unless we're in close proximity to them, they make no more sense than having a million songs playing at the same time.

The kid's apartment had enough shielding in the walls to keep his machine undetected from the outside. That meant the insulation was sufficient to filter out the incoming interference from outside the room. I was able to identify and block input from everyone else, leaving me open to eavesdrop on the operations of his computer network. Once my onboard system managed to find the right translator, I rode through subreal on the kid's shoulder.

He was good. He surfed on through the datawaves as

well as anyone I'd seen when I'd ventured out into the public networks. While the megacorps had cut down on their computers and isolated themselves from outside influence, the everyday existence and functioning of the world required data exchanges. The kid punched right into the nexus for the most traffic-intensive exchanges and settled himself into the waves rolling between the real world and insurance companies.

The kid sifted through Luna Port Authority reports to the big insurance carriers, and was able to isolate a passenger manifest for a Capitol ship named *Gabriella* that landed on Luna and had come in on a priority course from Atlantis station on Venus. While there were other ships that had arrived from Venus before the *Gabriella,* each of them had been traveling at more economical speeds, putting their time of departure from the second planet at more than a month back. I assumed his selection satisfied some internal criteria, because he came back out of subreal the second he snagged the list.

"Got something. The *Gabriella* came in straight from the big V. Only twenty-seven passengers and a half dozen of them were flagged 'duty-free.' They were also carrying a ton of equipment between them."

Lane whistled respectfully. "Those are some elite troops. In the Banshees we sometimes did Temporary Duty to show off for the bigwigs. TDY with our rigs and ammo always got us a 'duty-free' pass through customs."

"The *Gabriella* also had one specmed case. Supposed to be an eighty-year-old woman come back to Luna to see her family before she dies. Name is Loretta Corran."

I nodded. "I think her real name is Lorraine Kovan. Not terribly inventive when assigning aliases, those Capitol Clerk-2s."

Pam laughed. "Mitch Hunter, our CO in the Banshees used to pitch a fit about that. They called him Winchell Yaeger, which was not far enough from his own name to suit him."

The kid looked over at Pam. "Did you say Winchell Yaeger?"

"Is he on the list?"

"Duty-free and everything."

"Yojimbo, if Capitol wanted to keep the woman safe,

they'd have put her in Mitch's care." Lane eased himself back against the wall. "Mitch is tough enough to bite a nepharite's spikes off and use them to crucify the monster."

"Someone did pump some fire into Ragathol's middle."

"Probably Mitch." Pam gently nodded me with her Bolter. "Anything else you forgot to tell us?"

"You got it as straight as I do." I concentrated for a moment, then nodded. "Oh, yeah, Ragathol indicated there are still some folks loyal to the Dark Legion on Luna. I guess those would be the heretics the kid referred to?"

"Very good, Mr. Dent." Yojimbo thoughtfully cupped his chin with his left hand. "Are you one of them?"

"I tend to leave weird things alone. I even cross the street to stay out of the Cathedral's shadow."

"Given that the Brotherhood fights the Dark Legion, this does your case no good, Mr. Dent."

"I see that, Yojimbo. Ask Lane and Pam. They know me."

"Pam and I met him about sixteen months ago. We've done some light jobs together."

Pam nodded. "Dent's a sweet-talker who is good at distracting folks. Not bad in a fight. Never weird, though. He's a 'lancer with corps tastes."

Their testimony on my behalf appeared to satisfy Yojimbo, but I noticed Pam still didn't holster her pistol. I smiled, hoping to thaw her reserve, but her gun never even quivered. "I said I *know* you, Rex, but I'm still not sure how much I can *trust* you."

"I don't understand."

Yojimbo smiled easily enough that I felt uncomfortable. "You evidence some hostility toward the Brotherhood, yet you came up with a name that was provided to us by a Brotherhood contact."

"And you think I might be a Brotherhood plant trying to smoke out a leak?"

"That is a far more simple explanation than believing you stepped into the mind of something powerful enough to make a nepharite kneel before it. That story makes no sense."

"Good point, but truth is always going to be stranger than fiction because fiction has to make sense."

Yojimbo looked surprised. "You quote the philosopher Mark Twain."

"Actually that was in a fortune cookie I got a week ago in the Aristillus sector at the Tengu Tavern. The point is that I'm not lying to you. If I were an Inquisitor, I'd just kidnap the lot of you and see what you knew."

"Speaking of what you know, Mr. Dent, how did you know the woman's name was Lorraine Kovan?"

I met Yojimbo's questioning stare evenly. "How did you come to be chasing a nepharite around in Luna City?"

The Asian man clapped his hands once and laughed. "I am afraid that will have to be a secret, for now."

"And the answer to your question will have to remain a secret, for now."

"I respect this."

Klaus sniffed. "I can beat the answer out of him."

"You could *try*."

Pam slid her Bolter into its holster. "You accept what Rex's said?"

Yojimbo nodded. "Remnants of the heretic community here have had the better part of six weeks to try to avenge themselves on us, and they have not. Either they do not know who we are—in which case they could not have sent Mr. Dent to you—or they do know who we are and could have slain us when we buried Vic. The Brotherhood sanitized the Dark Legion enclave and, had they decided we were a risk, could have slain us easily. Parts of his story have been confirmed. I think, before we trust him, we should do more digging and consult our associates concerning the return of Ragathol to Luna City."

He gestured toward the door. "I suspect you have people you wish to speak with as well?"

"I do." A shiver ran down my spine, and I fought to control it. "This nepharite, this is serious trouble, yes?"

"It gets no more serious, Mr. Dent." Yojimbo waited for Lane to open the door, then he followed me and paused in the threshold. "Be careful, Mr. Dent. You have been touched by evil. Do not let it consume you."

EIGHT

Yojimbo's final comment flooded my guts with ice water. I walked up the steps rather mechanically, lost in thought. The one advantage to having a computer in my brain that controlled my lower legs was that I could issue a "home" order and it would get me there. That had been useful on nights when I'd sampled far too much weitzer at the Midnight Sun, and it was useful now because my concentration was shot all to hell.

I started to sort out all I felt and had learned in that encounter, and I began to find it all becoming more and more threatening. Pam and Lane obviously respected Yojimbo, which meant I considered him reliable and at least as sharp as either of the other two. When I asked how he had come to be chasing a nepharite through Luna City, he didn't deny that he had been, he just declined to give me details. Even so, from some of the other things he said, the Brotherhood had joined him in at least part of the operation and that operation had cost at least one life. He mentioned the name Vic, which I took to be Vic Baer—a former Cartel special mission operative, aka DoomTrooper and freelancer, who had vanished about the time I went in for my refit.

Without confirming a word of what I'd told them, Yojimbo had provided me with enough information to be able to puzzle things out for myself. It meant that I'd definitely done more than suffer delirium from some bad beer. The Dark Legion had been here and, apparently, on

Venus, but the knowledge of their incursions had been kept very quiet.

Walking along through the fourth level of Luna City, I realized that before now I'd generally bought into the theory that said the Dark Legion was a wannabe-corp. I'd judged it by the quality of its enemies, and in my estimation the fact that the Brotherhood wanted the Dark Legion destroyed meant it had to have some merit. Pam, Lane, and Yojimbo gave me another point of reference. If they didn't like the Dark Legion, I assumed there was something quite wrong with it.

Of course, my little fugue made me more than eager to think of the Dark Legion as abominable. The nepharite had not been easy to look at. Its abject subservience and abasement would have been comical had I not seen evidence of the damage it had taken and survived. The fact that I had been locked inside something that it feared so incredibly should have terrified me or revolted me. I felt neither reaction; instead I recalled enjoying Ragathol's pathetic groveling.

Knowing Ragathol had a big brother somewhere to which he answered served as a foundation for what really had me worried. Ragathol—a creature that shrugged off a belly full of bullets—was going to retake Lorraine Kovan. I knew that, and now Pam and her friends knew it. Capitol suspected something like that might happen, so they'd brought Mitch Hunter and his crew to Luna City.

From a corporate point of view all of this was interesting, but of no real value to my employers. At best, a direct confrontation with the Dark Legion could create a moment of weakness in Capitol's structure that Cybertronic might exploit. The value of Lorraine Kovan herself appeared to be minimal. The idea that denying her to some Dark Legion bigwig might cause him to blow a gasket was hard to quantify for a profit-and-loss statement. I doubted *any* corps would see that as a sufficient reason to safeguard the woman.

An anomaly detection subroutine in my navigation software sent a signal to me asking for input. If I didn't deal with it, the program would retrace my steps to a point before the anomaly was noted and try to work out another route home. Usually construction or an accident set the ADS off, but the roadway on Four was clear. I requested details.

The navigation program is really a modified version of a missile guidance program. At the start of any journey I look around, and the computer matches the surroundings to the local map it has in memory or, if I am in an unfamiliar place, it downloads a local map from the nearest Cybertronic remote connection. The computer then maps out the quickest, safest route to my destination. It gets up dates from local news, police, and public security unit radio networks and alters my route depending upon traffic and trouble.

The anomaly detection subroutine was originally put in to prevent the computer from running me around in circles when it reached a place where several routes were equally desirable. The computer matched the current visual scan to others in memory and if enough points matched, it alerted me so I could make a decision.

In this case I was not going around in circles. The computer had detected two individuals who appeared in every frame stored in memory. This meant they had been following me for at least five minutes. Given the time of day and general thinning of the crowd down on Four, it was possible they were innocently walking in my wake. The computer flashed their images up for me to see, and I decided they looked suspicious enough to run a check on my own.

Twenty meters later I stopped at a public phone booth. The two men slowed to a halt in front from a store window, keeping their distance. I pumped a decicard coin into the slot and dialed up the unlisted number of the cellular phone link my computer used. The computer immediately answered and provided me direct audio of the call. I spoke for a couple of seconds, stopped before the internal echo confused me, then paused to listen. While doing that I took the weitzer cap from my pocket and jammed it up under the phone's hook so when I settled the handset back on the hook, the connection remained unbroken.

I set off again, then stopped when my two shadows drew near the phone. Adopting their dodge, I stopped in front of a Grunge 'n' Go clothing boutique and tried to imagine myself attired in shredded plaid flannel and blowtorched denim. The two men following me dove for the phone as if it were the last seat in a game of musical chairs.

"He has detected us. We should move now and take him."

"Calm yourself, Brother. He is a freelancer wandering through the city."

"But he is the Get of the Great Silicon Whore."

"You don't know that."

"I can tell, Inquisitor. It is a gift."

"Then perhaps you are wasted here in the Second Directorate. Shall I request a transfer for you?"

I almost laughed as the older and shorter man rebuked his youthful companion, but then the white-haired Brotherhood Inquisitor picked up the phone and started to punch numbers in. He held the handset up to his ear to feign a conversation as I had, but immediately noticed the lack of a dial tone. He hit the hook once, then again, harder, and my bottle cap popped free.

The both of them watched it bounce along on the filthy ferrocrete sidewalk, then their heads came up and they stared in my direction. I tossed them a quick salute, then broke into a run. I didn't know if they would follow me, but I wasn't going to wait around to find out. The conversation had identified them as Brotherhood Inquisitors, and I could imagine them being a tad angry about the little trick I'd just played on them.

I cut right, posted myself off the narrow alley's wall, and shot off down its dark length. I leaped over heaping trash cans and scattered a pride of stray cats on my landing. Their hissing screeches echoed through the alley as I sprinted toward the low, corrugated tin fence at the far end. I knew, given our relative heights, clearing the top would be tough, so I ordered the computer to open the sluicegates and pump me full of adrenaline.

The computer did as I ordered, and I burst forward. The obstacle avoidance routine in the flight program I had on-line painted a scale over the image of the fence. It measured my velocity, then drew a nice little square on the ground that indicated the point at which I should begin my leap. My right foot hit the mark, and I jumped. Soaring through the air, I grazed the top of the fence with the hem of my coat, then landed cleanly as my pursuers shouted at me to stop.

On the other side I cut to the right and slammed my back against the warm surface of a steel door set in a recessed doorway. A second later light flashed through the alley on the far side of the fence and a neat little figure eight of bullet holes thundered through the tin. Shrapnel pinged off the walls, but missed me entirely. That would not have been the case had I still been running down the alley or, worse yet, still hanging from the top of the fence before dropping to the other side.

I turned around and looked at the door. The computer identified it as a standard five-centimeter thick door with a centimeter of steel on either face over a fiberplast structure. It also identified the lock for me and the manufacturer of the anti-jimmy plate bolted on the front to protect it. The door, located this deep in Luna City, had been designed to discourage even the best equipped of thieves. Anyone with a mind toward larceny would find easier pickings elsewhere.

I, on the other hand, was concerned with my survival, and I had so much adrenaline in me that I almost felt invincible enough to leap back over the wall and face those two Inquisitors straight up. Luckily my inclination to fight gave way to the wisdom of flight. I forced my fingers in under the anti-jimmy plate at the door jamb, then set my legs against the building's cinder-block wall.

As I began to pull, I felt my jacket begin to tear up the spine. My shoulders ground and my fingers began to bleed from the cuticles. The computer released endorphins, killing the sharpest pain, but left me some of it so I'd remember the precariousness of my position.

Slowly I straightened my wrists, and the metal plate started to bend. I heard a loud snapping and thought it might have been tendons in my forearms, but fiberplast dust filled the air as the plate and steel sheath on the outside of the door began to peel back. I gave it one more good, solid wrench, curling it up like the cover of a lunch-meat tin, then released and hammered a bloody fist against the exposed blond fiberplast. I ripped the lock out of it, then kicked the door in.

I dove through it into the black interior of the basement

a second before gunfire tore great divots out of the building's wall. My dive took me into and over several piles of debris. The basement stank of mold and rot. As the door rebounded from the other wall and closed, I came up shrouded in heavy, damp cloth and wondered where in hell I was.

The computer was unable to provide me a direct answer. It ran a series of holding companies past me, then got into some sort of a data loop and only stopped when I interrupted it. I had it project an amplified light image of the room on my eyes, and I quickly swung out of line with the doorway. I looked for anything I might employ as a weapon and seriously began to reconsider my refusal to carry a gun.

The first pass revealed nothing, and I heard voices at the door. I had to do something quickly. Grabbing a fiberplast hanger from the floor, I shucked my jacket and put it on the hanger. I hooked the hanger over one of the loops of electrical cable running between the fiberplast joists, then leaped over toward the door. I landed on cat's feet and crouched low in the darkness, with my back pressed against the building's wall.

And I put my hands over my ears.

The first Inquisitor kicked the door open, then came in leading with his gun. The weak light from outside splashed a little blue back into my jacket as it hung there rocking back and forth. The Inquisitor tightened down on the trigger of his Punisher. The automatic pistol stabbed flame into the room. Smoking cartridge casings rebounded from the rafters and soundlessly danced across the floor amid the gun's explosive din. The bullet hail hit on target and reduced my coat into so much lint.

Before he had a chance to even notice that I wasn't in my coat, I struck. Rising from my crouch, my left hand settled on his left wrist and my right hand hit him in the elbow. I pushed, once, hard, driving his elbow beyond its locking point. Tugging on his wrist unbalanced him, twisting it grated broken bones together and tossed him onto a mildewed pile of odd sheets and mashed pillows.

My left hand caught the Punisher his nerveless fingers had dropped before he or it hit the ground. Bringing the gun up, I hit the trigger once and caught the older Inquisitor framed in the threshold. The bullet hit him high in the chest, but still on the midline, and when he bounced back against the doorway, he left blood on the wall.

Turning away from him, I pounced on the younger man. His flesh sizzled when I pressed the hot muzzle of his gun to his cheek. "Why were you after me."

"You are damned for all time, infidel."

"You're staring at eternity yourself, ace. Why?"

"I'll never tell you."

"Your arm will heal. I can fix it so it won't. Why?"

"The Cardinal is my Guardian; I shall not fear."

"I can make you hurt very badly."

"He provides me purity and truth; he leads me to safe haven."

A strange heat spread from the base of my skull and on down to the break in my spine. I could smell the fear on the man and taste his pain in the air. I knew I had once felt as he had, when someone had broken me, and I wanted to be sympathetic, but I could not. The image of Ragathol and the echoes of his terror rippled through me. I tasted again the fear I had known before I died, and I wanted to scream.

I shifted the gun around, pressed it to the praying man's temple, and pulled the trigger.

Even Andy couldn't have put him back together.

NINE

Lying back on Andy's LinkCouch, I scuttled into subreal in the guise of a cockroach. I deposited my information in a sleek, brown egg case that immediately broke open. Thousands of millions of little cockroach bytes scampered off as the mainframe sorted them out and stored them.

I flipped myself over onto my back and let my legs hang stiffly in the air as a couch formed beneath me. Carl appeared in the vector-graphic room. He looked a little better resolved, especially in the face, and he wore a very sympathetic expression on his face. "Feeling in a Kafka mood, Rex?"

Looking down at my body, I saw it go from chitin to bronze, with my legs becoming gear-driven pieces of cast metal. Golden highlights flashed as I twitched. "I'm feeling less than human. You should pay attention to the last bit of stuff first. I hid the bodies as best I could, but I couldn't pull up information on who owned the building where I killed them, so I didn't know how to order a response."

Carl's face slackened for a second. "Ah, yes, I can see how the ownership nested loop would have caused a problem."

I clicked my mandibles at him. "So who owns it?"

"As of a second ago, we own it. Got it for an acceptable price as well—a gunfight in the alley beside it trimmed a thousand crowns from the price. Our agents have just taken possession." Carl focused on me again.

"I'm surprised, given the nature of the business there, you reported back here so quickly."

I wished cockroaches had eyebrows so I could frown appropriately. I settled for waggling my antennae at him. "I was only in the basement. When no one responded to gunshots, I assumed the place was abandoned."

"Hardly. It was a bordello—one considered something of a treasure by Imperial executives slumming on Level Four."

"No wonder no one noticed the gunshots."

"Yes, the place is well insulated for sound." Carl nodded slowly. "We have a disposal team on site. Mr. Beach relays his compliments on your shooting skill."

Whatever I had for internal plumbing lurched with that news. Mr. Beach was a Chasseur, like me, but they took every last bit of humanity out of him when they replaced some of his parts. He's a specialist in wet-work, with nerves of steel and antifreeze running in his veins. For him to be impressed with my shooting was high praise, yet it sent a shiver through me nonetheless.

Carl watched me closely. "Your use of the phone trick was quite resourceful. And the loss of your receipt is regrettable. The input you got does not indicate why they decided to kill you."

"I think that decision was made by the younger Inquisitor in reaction to my use of the phone. At the worst he felt I had jeopardized some operation, though I imagine he wanted to erase the embarrassment he felt at being tricked. In all seriousness, the Brotherhood has never needed a reason to want to kill someone from Cybertronic."

"Your point appears valid and within two standard deviations from the mean."

"That's my life goal: to be Statistically Correct."

"It is good you have a goal, Rex." Carl's pencil and pad appeared, and he jotted down a note. "Why were they following you?"

"I don't know for certain. Fay Fan reported that we were not followed from the Midnight Sun, and if she said that, I buy it. Those two were not very good at tailing me, and Fay would have picked them out as easily as I had. I would guess, then, that they were watching the apartment house where Yojimbo and this Whiz kid live. Yojimbo indicated a Brotherhood connection or alliance in their adventure here on Luna.

"The Brotherhood watchers saw me go in with Yojimbo's known associates and then come out alone. They followed me, perhaps pursuing me while others checked to see if I had killed Yojimbo and his people—Mr. Beach gives us chasseurs a bad reputation. The rest happened because I found them out and they wanted to cover their tracks. They might have even been afraid I'd beach them."

"That suffices as a working hypothesis. Your conversation with Yojimbo does correlate with abnormal activities within the last six weeks here on Luna. Vic Baer has apparently ceased to exist. There have been a number of gun battles that have not been matched to know corporate or gang activity. Your linking Lorraine Kovan with Yojimbo and these odd occurrences is likely valid."

"So the rest of it is true, too?"

"Let me finish processing . . ." Carl's image flickered in and out between a solid and a creature described by vector-graphics. The head turned toward me, only an outline, with burning red eyes in it. "Have you indulged in any psychoactive pharmacological products in the last forty-eight hours?"

"Just that beer."

"Insignificant." The image flickered more and just left the eyes in place. They grew larger, and I could see little data-streams scrolling up in the pupils. The irises looked like bloody suns, with fiery coronas alive and bleeding out flaming plasma tentacles. "Before we proceed, you must understand some things."

"Okay."

"First, you have knowledge of material for which you do not have clearance. In other words, the fact of nepharites existence is classified so far above your level that you could be considered a security risk. Were you not a chasseur, you would be placed in isolation for further study. It is critical that you do not share knowledge of what you have seen with anyone outside Cybertronic, and only those inside the corporation who I tell you are cleared for that information."

"But I already spoke with Yojimbo and the others."

"By luck, they possess the same level of information you do, so no harm was done. As a chasseur you are allowed some leeway—and you have showed good judgment in the past—but you should remain extremely conservative in sharing this information."

I nodded my head and clicked my mandibles in agreement.

"Second, you will instantly report any recurrence of this fugue state and relay all details about it to me. This order includes dreams about the incident and even a repeat of the incident you have already witnessed. Pay particular attention to time references, location references, and anything else that can enable us to pinpoint where and when these conversations are taking place."

I folded my legs in closer to my thorax and abdomen. "What was that whole thing?"

"Insufficient data to draw a conclusive answer."

"Have you a working hypothesis?"

Carl smiled briefly, then nodded. "I do, but you are not cleared to hear it."

"C'mon, one chasseur to another."

"I'm not a chasseur, technically speaking."

"This stuff is going on in *my* head. Don't you think I could have some valuable input on your theory?"

"You have a valid point." Carl scribbled something on his pad. "Your clearance is now Code Word: Ragathol. My working hypothesis is that you are involved in something of a tangle of psychic wires."

"Run that by me at something less than Mach 3."

"Very well. In the same way you were able to pick up on the RF mods from the kid's computer and read the data he was sending and receiving, so you picked up on the conversation between Ragathol and the party with whom he was speaking. Your growing affinity for the second party to the conversation suggests the leak is coming from him."

"But to pick up RF mods from a computer I have to be very close to it."

"Or you have to be extremely receptive."

I gnashed my mandibles. "Oh, joy, I've got a mental link with something in the Dark Legion!"

"Likely it is one of the Dark Apostles."

That crushed me down like a giant boot. "I don't even know what Dark Apostles are, but I know that's not good."

"It is known there are a number of them. Nepharites are to Apostles as his marshals were to Napoleon. Apostles command them and the nepharites are given resources to complete their missions. In some places ..."

"Venus and Mars?"

"You are free to infer that. In some places the Dark Legions have created Citadels and have garrisoned them with all manner of hideous troops."

"They lost one on Venus."

"There does seem to be some indication of this, yes." Carl's face sank into impassivity. "We do not know much about the Apostles other than each appears to have his own area of expertise and that they do not always work well together."

"Even with all the corps belonging to the Cartel, I don't recall seeing them work all that well together, either."

"True, but the Dark Legion poses more of a threat to humanity than the corps do to one another. Hence the decision of the Cartel to work at fighting against the Dark Legion."

My antennae whipped back and forth like wind-lashed trees. "If Yojimbo's action against the Dark Legion here on Luna was a Cartel operation then you would already know about it. The fact that you don't means it was done outside the Cartel, which seems to run counter to what you just said about the Cartel's Dark Legion policy. Why circumvent the organization tasked with fighting the Dark Legion?"

Carl nodded in my direction. "Astute observation, Rex. The core reason probably stems from the fact that the Cartel originally was created to be a forum for diplomatic discussions between corporations. While many saw it as a civilized step toward eliminating the lives being wasted in combat between corporations, in reality all the corporations knew that warfare was not that cost effective, largely because of collateral damage to facilities, equipment, and other assets."

"And the time needed to train personnel to replace those who have died."

Carl shrugged. "Most important personnel are evacuated in the face of an attack. In any event, the diplomatic nature of the Cartel means it is currently looking at the Dark Legion in two ways. The first is to assess the true extent of the threat the Dark Legion poses to everyone."

"I would have thought the presence of hostile Citadels on worlds in our solar system would have done that."

"Sarcasm aside, you are correct. A number of corps agree on the threat level, but even they are tempted to hold the Dark Legion hostage to curb the Brotherhood's actions. The Brotherhood, for example, wishes more oversight on internal corporate matters—presumably to root out those who have succumbed to Dark Legion influence—but the corporations are obviously reluctant to allow that. The corps withhold full participation in anti-Legion activities until the Brotherhood comes around.

"The second problem with the Cartel is that there are those who wish to negotiate with the Dark Legion. They believe that no situation is so hopeless that something cannot be gained through it."

The recollection of how I felt while speaking with Ragathol shook me. "The Dark Legion is the ultimate evil. What can be gained from working with them?"

"Nothing, in my assessment, but I do not always think along the lines of the other corps. For example, you know that terraforming the other planets is very costly. This is the reason we find it cheaper to fight for territory on rehabilitated worlds than to undertake the change of others. The Dark Legion has evidenced the ability to create creatures that do not require the same life support a normal human does. A deal struck with the Dark Legion could allow some corporation to have a worker base suitable for exploiting Jovian moons or some of the larger asteroids. Profits would be staggering."

I pressed my fingers together—and realized for the first time that I had unconsciously transformed myself back into a human. "So some corps, unconvinced of the threat the Dark Legion poses—or convinced they can control it—are doing nothing while the Dark Legion becomes bolder and bolder."

"There are other considerations, of course. Were the majority of humanity to know of the Dark Legion, they might react in unpredictable ways."

"Which would destroy the reliability of future product sales and development projections, cutting profits and forcing costly factory retooling to meet new demands."

"Well put." Carl tapped his pad with his pencil. "I think much of what you have supplied me here today can serve to sway some of the board members. We need to step up operations against the Dark Legion and, if nothing else, Yojimbo and this Mitch Hunter show that the Dark Legion is not invincible."

I swung my legs around and planted them firmly on a floor I could not see. "I am glad to be of service. What do you want me to do now? I can coordinate with Yojimbo and see what else I can learn."

"No, for now you shall do nothing."

I frowned. "Nothing? I don't like doing nothing."

"There are things in your experiences this evening that disturb me. I want time to analyze them to determine a response to them."

"Such as?"

"Such as the fact that you destroyed one Inquisitor's brain, eliminating the chance for us to make him into a chasseur. Your failure to report in promptly also made the other one useless to us."

"I wasn't thinking."

"On the contrary, you were thinking. This goes back to what we discussed earlier—the conflict between who you are and what you were. Your shooting shows you to be quite skilled with firearms, yet we have never trained you in their use. In fact, you chose to avoid firearms training and instead substituted more martial arts and knife training. That is the sign of a conflict that needs resolution."

Carl held up a hand to forestall my counterargument. "That conflict is immaterial at the moment. Your experience during the first fugue state indicates a complete lack of conscious bodily control. I am working from the hypothesis that you could have had more of these states, but something prevented it. You have spent an incredible amount of time subreal—nearly thirty percent of your time since you came to us—and if other messages had been passed during the time you were subreal, you might not have noticed them. I surmise this is because when you are subreal, your sensory inputs come via the computer, making it difficult for other things to get through.

"Your orders are to go home and refuse to go subreal. You will remain at your home until I summon you, or you have another report to make."

"I might have to go out to get food."

Carl shook his head. "By the time you return to your place of residence, you will have enough food for two weeks. If this situation persists beyond that, resupply will be affected." A smile blossomed on his face. "And supplies did include weitzer."

"There *is* a God."

"I prefer to think of myself in more modest terms."

I snorted a laugh. "Hey, if this fugue stuff could hit me at any time, how do you know I'll get home? Perhaps you should have Dr. Carter see me home and remain to monitor my situation."

"Dr. Carter is otherwise engaged."

"Oh, yeah, she's working on my playmate. How about Miss Wickersham?"

"You would find her less than stimulating."

"She *is* a bit stiff."

"Hazards of Mark 1." Carl smiled. "Your caution about a fugue coming on suddenly is well taken. I have just modified your navigation program so that if you do fugue, it will take you home. There, I've even linked it to your evasion and counterattack programs so your escape will include the normal élan with which you operate."

"You're too kind."

"I probably am, but given what you will endure if you fugue again, even this kindness is insufficient compensation."

TEN

I engaged my modified navigation program—putting myself on cruise control—and headed for home. In some ways I wished I could become the cockroach I had been while subreal because that way I could have climbed walls and moved between levels without using the normal modes of transport. Despite being back in my body, I really didn't feel terribly human. I knew Carl would have put that down to a conflict between Rex and the man who died to give him life, but I put it down to lingering bits of my Dark Legion counterpart lurking in my brain.

Carl had surprised me toward the end of our interview. Once he reviewed the Dark Legion fugue, he took a more serious and commanding role in our relationship. He gave me orders instead of asking me probing questions. His change in attitude didn't make him any more correct in his thinking about me, but it did give me a window on his truth depth, and that was enlightening.

I'd not have expected him to notice my proficiency with a gun. I'd known it was there from my first waking moment as Rex. When I moved, I felt an absence of a weight on my body. I was compensating for it and I thought, at first, that it came because of the long-bone length reductions that had been done on my body. That and connections with the computers, I decided, were giving me phantom sensations.

Then I strapped a gun on for the first time. With the weight of a Bolter on my right hip, or beneath my left arm or at the small of my back, I felt a little bit more right. I felt more complete. I felt more *myself*.

The problem was that the *myself* I felt wasn't me. It was the dead guy, not Rex. The dead guy clearly had been a crack shot. He had been able to handle himself under fire, but what did that get him? Had he believed himself invulnerable because of the pistol he wore? Had that false sense of security doomed him? Had he focused on his gun too much to be able to react well in some final situation?

I had no specific answer for any of those questions, but I had a general one: the guy with the gun was history. I had decided, therefore, any dependence on a gun would be history, too. I chose more personal methods of defending myself. I wove aikido, karate, *keupso chirigi,* and a host of knife-fighting techniques together into my personal self-defense system. Along with the extra power and extra speed that Cybertronic's alterations of my body had provided, these skills made certain I'd not be vulnerable to whatever had slain me.

My stomach growled, and it wasn't from nerves. I stopped at a Casa Shogun kiosk and studied a menu that I already knew by heart. Deciding I would eat while I continued walking home, I purchased a cup of miso soup and a soy burrito. Once I had the food in hand, I found it less appetizing than it had appeared on the menu, but that was normal and I appreciated the injection of some normality into my life.

Walking along it seemed to me that Carl had missed one point that disturbed me in my encounter with the two Inquisitors. He'd noted that I'd slain them in ways that made rendering them useless, as raw materials for Andy. He may have been right in the case of the younger man, but not so in the other case. I'd hidden that body and delayed reporting not because I didn't want that man made into a chasseur. I didn't care what happened to him.

I wanted to figure out what was happening to me.

I never should have killed the younger man. Had I been asked to gauge my response to that sort of situation before, I'd have said that I'd have knocked him out and then gotten him some help—Cybertronic help or otherwise. But I hadn't done that. I just put the gun to his head and blew his brains out.

Granted the man had tried to kill me, so he had unilaterally escalated our relationship into the realm of lethal play, but that didn't mean he deserved to die or that I had to kill him. Something in me had been worn down. I would have said it had broken, but the revulsion I felt at the killing told me it had not. Whatever internal brake I had against murder had been circumvented in that case, and I could only point to one thing that caused it to cut out.

The fugue.

The creature I had been would have murdered the Inquisitor as easily as I did. To that kind of mind—to an Apostle's mind—the man would have been insignificant. He would have been less than that. Killing him would have been like the folks on old Earth who used to kill and mount butterflies—creating memento mori because of the pleasure of viewing what they had once been.

What struck me as horrible was that I could understand the devaluation of life from the collector's point of view. What did snuffing the spark of life in an insect mean? What was the significance of its death? Could it be that the butterfly's only purpose in existence was to leave a beautiful carcass? For many people the value of life was relative: their own life was priceless, but any other life was open to negotiation and sale to the highest bidder.

As a human, I protested that human life was somehow different. The fact that an Apostle might be as far above me as I was above a butterfly did not justify my death. Worse yet, oddly enough, was the idea that my life might be seen as nothing more than a waste of time before my death could give a Dark Apostle pleasure. It was perverted and evil.

The obvious argument is that a man is sapient and an insect is not. But is not the test for sapience relative? By the time man had decided that dolphins and whales were truly sapient, we had ruined the oceans in which they lived, had destroyed their food supplies, and had trapped the luckless survivors in small pens in insufficient numbers for them to maintain a viable colony.

For all I knew, butterflies—back when they and flowers still existed in our solar system—had some sort of communication with others of their number. Perhaps in choosing which types of plants to pollinate, butterflies were making some sort of political statement. Perhaps they fought their wars by encouraging the propagation of plants that would push out the plants fertilized by a rival butterfly corporation.

Perhaps their form of communication was one so sophisticated we could not understand it. Carl had suggested my fugue state came about when spare thoughts leaked from the brain of a Dark Apostle—clearly imbuing them with psychic powers like telepathy. Could it be that butterflies had the ability to communicate that way? Could it be that any time I started to daydream, I was picking up a stray thought from a butterfly or cockroach or some other creature on Luna that I would not have credited with sapience?

Or could my confusion have to do with nothing more sinister than picking up stray thoughts from my own ghost. In defending myself I had begun to act as Rex, but as soon as I picked up the Punisher, I was the old me. Could I have been someone who was so callous that I would have willfully and remorselessly killed a helpless man? And if I was, am I not better off being Rex?

I arrived home and slumped down in my chair in front of my entertainment monitor with those same thoughts running around in my brain. As the navigation program performed its last check on the surroundings, I finished my burrito and drained the last of the miso from the plastfoam cup. I tossed it into a wastebasket, then picked up my remote control, brought the entertainment monitor to life, and started the first disk in my viewer spinning. The navigator shut off as the first pictures came up, and I once again became a ghostly voyeur at my own funeral.

Everyone there appeared well heeled and quite mannerly. The turnout was good. I'd have preferred standing room only, with thousands of mourners outside, but filling forty-seven of an available fifty-five seats can't be taken as bad. Some people even seemed to be genuinely upset. Would they have been upset at the passing of a stone-cold killer?

I settled myself back down into my chair, and an un-

conscious grin spread across my face as a man in the
front row got up and headed forward to deliver my eulogy. He paused for a second in front of the small, black
lozenge-shaped chest holding my ashes and lowered his
head respectfully. He said something, but I couldn't make
it out. Even going subreal with the video—which I had
done many times before but didn't do now—I couldn't
decipher what the man said. I decided that emotion had
choked him, so the words had never been vocalized.

It might not have been true, and hatred could have
done it as easily as love, but I took comfort in that illu-
sion.

And, after all, isn't that what funerals are for: comforting the living?

It impressed me that the man drew notes from his
pocket, then set them aside before beginning to speak.
"Thank you all for coming here this evening. I see so
many of you that [DELETED] knew and loved. Knowing
that he meant as much to you as you did to him would
have been of great comfort to him. Having known him all
my life, I have as hard a time as you do trying to come
to grips with the fact that he is gone. He may not be alive
in body, but he must live on in our memories."

Something began to itch in my brain as I watched the
video. I'd heard the eulogy dozen times before, but it was
different this time. I couldn't figure out why exactly, but
I had an inkling that I recognized something more in his
voice. I commanded the computer to check the speaker's
voiceprint against the voices of everyone I'd come in
contact with in the past week.

He'd barely gotten into his first recollection about me
when the computer came up with a match: Mr. Steel from
the Capitol interrogation of Lorraine Kovan! I immediately froze the video, then backed it to a good face-front
shot of the man. Isolating him from his background, I
flipped the video over to the infrared track and ordered
the computer to compare that image with the one of Steel
from the interrogation.

Click! The faces matched on thirty-seven of forty
points, and the mismatches concerned the length of his
hair. The man delivering my eulogy worked for Capitol,
and must have been high enough up in the corporate

structure to be trusted with a lot of information. Recalling the interrogation, I remembered how he had ordered the lawyer, Campbell, out of the room, and how he had misled the doctor into believing Lorraine was hallucinating.

That meant he knew enough to be able to obscure what the truth was. In Lorraine's case I knew, from Yojimbo and Ragathol, that what Lorraine had described must have been what truly happened to Fairview. The fact that Steel painted everything she said as delirium meant he knew it was true and wanted to limit the spread of that information.

In an instant I stopped the video viewer from actually displaying the rest of the funeral. I had the viewer download the entire disk's IR track into my computer, then I had the computer run a check against the faces of everyone who had attended. I wanted to see if Lorraine Kovan had been there. Somehow it had become important to me that she had been.

By the time it took me to remember that Steel had said she'd lived her whole life on Venus, the computer had completed its search. I almost didn't ask for the results because I knew she could not have been there and that the computer would show me every face in the video and describe, in turn, how each one compared to Lorraine's face. Any face with two eyes, a nose, a mouth, and a forehead would match on five points, so the recital would take some time.

I decided to endure it anyway. It would give me something to do while waiting for hunger or Ragathol.

Click! The first face, that of a thirty-year-old woman, matched on twenty-eight of forty points. A twenty-point match would have made them cousins, and twenty-eight meant they were siblings. The next two, an older man and woman, hit on fifteen and seventeen points respectively, making them her parents or possibly one pair of grandparents.

I hadn't found Lorraine Kovan, but I had found her family.

I had the computer pull back and give me the real faces to go beside the IR images. Then I pulled up the image I had of Lorraine, and had the computer create for me a colorless face template. From her sister I took flesh tones and filled in the skin. I was going to take the sister's blond hair, but I noticed some darker roots. Their color matched Lorraine's father's brown hair, so I filled her shoulder-length hair's outline with dark mahogany. Oddly enough, her father had bright blue eyes and her mother had dark brown. They combined in the sister for a nice hazel, and I used that to color Lorraine's eyes in.

Something inside me clicked, and it wasn't the computer. Lorraine's face, now with color, but still devoid of life, looked familiar. Discarding the parents, I had the computer scan the sister's movements during the funeral and used that to animate Lorraine's face. The eyes still had no spark in them, and the mannerisms appeared a bit stiff for her, but they were close. I knew I knew her.

It was more than just seeing a face that is vaguely common and deciding you've seen people who look like that before. The impression I had was intangible, but nonetheless real to me. I had known her. I didn't think we had been lovers or even that close, but it was something more than what Miss Wickersham and I had. Closer to what Andy and I had, but not that intimate. I was comfortable around her and relaxed.

At that point I almost blew off Carl's injunction against going subreal because I wanted to tag Lorraine's family with names. I hesitated before doing that and instead had the computer pull back and show me the sister and parents in context. The computer went back to the first occurrence of the woman in the video and placed her sitting next to Steel. As the image tightened in on them and masked everything but the two of them out, I saw they were holding hands right up until Steel got up to eulogize me.

I sat in my chair and shivered. Carl had assigned me the mission of covering Lorraine's identity confirmation because he knew I had known her and Steel. Steel should have known Lorraine. Perhaps he had been covering his recognition, just to keep the doctor from wondering about any connection between them. The presence of both of them in one room meant that Carl had hoped seeing and hearing them again would help me break through and reconcile my two halves.

At least, that was one explanation, but it didn't have to

be the only one, or all of the explanation. Perhaps Carl wanted to motivate me to work against the Dark Legion by showing how they had hurt someone I had known. He might even have known about the fugues before I became aware of them.

Ultimately, it struck me, Carl's reasons for assigning me the mission were immaterial—and I felt I'd used up my coincidence supply suffering a fugue in the company of folks who understood something I mumbled because of it. As Carl had been describing the Cartel and its reluctance to take action against the Dark Legion, I'd felt impatient to do something. The Cartel be damned, I knew where they had Lorraine Kovan, and I knew Ragathol was going to try to take her. I could get Pam and Lane and their people to be there to forestall Ragathol's effort.

"Hang on, Lorraine," I growled, "Ragathol may think of you as a prize, but you're not one he's going to get."

Intent on heading out to gather troops to protect Lorraine, I got out of my chair. I made it as far as standing upright when the fugue hit me. I continued forward and was gone long before I kissed carpet.

ELEVEN

We achieved integration almost instantly. We were one, but we were two and more than that. Still trapped behind glassy eyes through which we could not pass, we sensed shadowy figures lurking behind, around, above, and below. We could not name them, and none of them could name us, but we knew one of them was the creature whose corpse had become Rex.

But we were integrated, all cells in the same body. Before us, again prostrating himself, was the nepharite. From him we sensed a haughtiness and egotism. Those were the very traits that had drawn us to him originally. His sense of self superseded his need to be subservient, and that made him corruptible. His loyalty was to himself, and his dreams allowed him to believe he could one day ascend to be one of our peers. This meant he would someday betray us as he now betrayed his master, but by then we would be done with him and destroy him.

If the others did not get him first.

Still, his pride burned with a malevolent heat, and we luxuriated in it. It tempted us to swat him down and crush him, but that would require a display of power that might spell ruin for our long-range plans. The difficulty with Ragathol was, of course, that a failure to rein in his ego would mean that his overconfidence would bring him down. As we intended him to fall, but did not want him to fall quite yet, we had to be careful in how we treated him.

"You dare initiate contact with us, nepharite?" We put

anger and scorn in our voice, knowing he would use it against us momentarily.

"Forgive my impudence, Master, but developments warranted a report."

"In your opinion, Ragathol?"

"Wretched though my sense of judgment is, yes, Master."

Sarcasm ran through his voice like blood through an artery, but we deigned to ignore it. "What is so important that you jeopardize our mode of communication?"

The nepharite sat up, then rose to one knee. Keeping his head bowed, he spread his massive arms and left his hands opened in a gesture of peaceful abnegation. "As was your wish, Master, I have recovered the Vessel. She is once more in our possession and she is unharmed."

This surprised us—all of us. Given Ragathol's track record in covert operations, we had expected trouble and the request for resources. That he had not asked for assistance could mean he had been hiding from us the real strength of his assets on Luna. Such deception was expected, but the fact that he could hide something from us was disturbing. If he could do that, what else could he be concealing from us?

"How did you accomplish this feat?"

"Fortuitously, one of the last recruits to my circle on Luna was both industrious and connected with Imperial corporate security. Instead of arranging this operation as something for only our people, he convinced his superiors that the Vessel was an important resource. Imperial financed the raid and even now has the woman in custody. My agent is working to have the Vessel shifted to Mars for safekeeping. That will bring her closer to us, and our assets on the planet of blood are sufficient to blunt any human rescue effort."

"We would have thought a Citadel on Venus would have been similarly impregnable."

"It was not yet fully operational, and I was not in command."

"You will not be in command on Mars, either."

"No, but because Saladin's holdings on Mars are sufficiently demanding and diverse, he will accept my offer to oversee but a small piece of his realm."

A prideful pulse from Ragathol alerted us to a potential problem. Saladin, who answered to our brother Algeroth, was a nepharite overlord strong in the ways of the Dark Symmetry. What we read so clearly from Ragathol, Saladin would catch in fits and snatches. Saladin's steadfast loyalty to Algeroth meant he would report to his master any suspicions he had about Ragathol, and that could jeopardize our operation.

"You may proceed with your plans, Ragathol, but you will minimalize your contact with Saladin."

"I had thought I should avoid direct confrontations with him at all costs."

"Perhaps that is best. When will you go to Mars?"

The nepharite bowed his head again. "I had intended to direct operations from here. Preparations for the vessel's transfer to my custody and her journey here are already underway."

"She will be leaving Mars in the custody of Imperial?"

"As covertly as she departed Venus in the care of Capitol, Master."

"Very well. This improvement in your performance has been noted."

"I live only to serve."

"And you will only live *if* you serve, Ragathol."

The world suddenly went utterly black, but not in the sense of a lightless void. I felt reality crush around me and found myself drowning in a thick, swirling pool of bitter, burning liquid. My lungs ached for air, but breathing would kill me, and I knew it. I tried not to breath, and to struggle to the surface, but I had no clue as to which way was up.

I coughed and sucked the fiery goop into my lungs. An explosive cough wracked my body, then my arms felt something solid. I pushed off and rolled myself over. Gathering my hands and knees beneath me, I pushed up, fighting to get to air. Dizziness assaulted me, and another cough convulsed my lungs.

I opened my eyes and found myself crouched over a puddle of vomit tinted with blood. I tried to breathe in through my nose, but all that did was spray coppery blood against the back of my throat. I started coughing again, then retched dryly. Pain shook me, and I almost collapsed back into the reeking pool in the middle of my carpet.

I wiped my mouth on the back of my sleeve and weakly looked up at the ruin of my living room. I saw from a small pool of blood where I had hit the floor face first, splitting my lip and started my nose bleeding. From there I had thrashed right and left, smearing the blood and spewing vomit. I'd ended up on my back and almost drowned in what little of my lunch remained in my stomach. Seeing the mess, I was doubly pleased I had opted away from chili con tofu and jalapeño sushi at Casa Shogun.

The splintering of my fiberplast doorjamb terminated my contemplation of what had previously been digested in my stomach. At the sound of the door being kicked in, I rolled to my left hip and started to go for my knife, but my stomach hitched again and thick saliva bubbled upon my lips. As much as it made me feel like I was going to die, it probably saved my life.

Coral Beach came into my apartment before the dented door had finished pulling free of the hinges. He held the P-1000 pistol in his right hand, as if it weighed no more than a handful of lint, and used it to sweep the room. The gun dipped toward me and lingered through target-acquisition before Beach continued his check. We locked eyes for a second, and his computer sent an inquiry out to mine, prompting a plethora of data to scroll up the inside of my eyes.

I shook my head as he came erect and waved someone in from the hallway. I wiped my mouth as Andy Carter came in and dropped to her knees beside me. "Hi, Doc. Didn't know you made house calls."

"Give it a rest, Rex." I heard more worry than annoyance in her voice, and that combined with fatigue made me shut up. "How are you feeling?"

"I've been better." I glanced up at Beach. "Carl's got you picking up after me all over the place."

Beach shrugged. "You're the one who is tromping on *my* operation. I picked up an interest in Mitch Hunter and his team on Venus. I followed them here."

"Hold still, Rex." Andy pulled a small device that looked like a hearing aid from her little black bag. She inserted it into my right ear. I heard some squeals before it and some diagnostic circuitry agreed on a communications protocol, and started sharing data. "In a couple of minutes I'll know how badly you're hurt."

"Gotcha, Doc." I shivered as Beach completed a recon of my apartment—that in spite of the fact that my on-board systems had told him there had been no intruders present during my fugue.

Beach relaxed slightly, which was to say he pointed his bull-pup pistol at the ceiling instead of keeping it leveled and ready to spray the room. "All clear."

"How can you tell? My bedroom's a mess."

He shrugged. "IR was negative. And it wasn't that bad. New chasseurs are generally messy."

I raised an eyebrow. "Your first place like that?"

"Nope."

Beach had always struck me as one of those "a place for everything, everything in its place or else" kind of people. "Why weren't you messy?"

"Most new chasseurs find they are more concerned with who they are than appearances."

"And you weren't?"

"No?"

Beach gave me a smile that twisted my guts up again. "Most chasseurs are recruited, as you were. I volunteered."

"You *asked* for them to do you?"

Beach nodded slowly. "I am a perfectionist, Dent. Dr. Chandrapuri made me perfect."

"So you never forgot who you were?"

"My name is different, some of my attitudes have changed, but I have built myself on the foundation of who I was. After all, who and what we are comprise the only concrete clues to the fact that we are alive."

Andy plucked the device from my ear and plugged it into a handheld diagnostic interpreter, and words filled the small LCD display. "Sorry to interrupt what I am certain will be a fascinating romp through existentialism, but the test results are in. Your nose is broken, and you have a hematoma coming up on the left side of your face. Your eyes are fine, but you're going to look like you lost a boxing match with Beach's big brother."

I grinned at Beach. "You have a big brother?"

"An Attila unit was assigned to me. It is accompanying the slower member of our party." Beach looked as if he enjoyed having one of the fully robotic war machines following him around as much as I did. Part of my training had involved working with an Attila partner in some exercises, but the automatons were really designed for mass carnage, while I preferred to take a more low-key approach to things.

"Rex, you're a bit dehydrated, which is to be expected, your electrolytes are off and you need to get some sleep." Andy reached out and gingerly touched the bridge of my nose. "Does that hurt?"

"Not really. Dull ache. Do you need to set it?"

"It looks okay."

I reached up and grabbed her hand, then stared seriously into her eyes. "Doc, I want it to look smashing, not smashed."

Andy laughed and withdrew her hand from mine. "No damage done to your psyche."

"Ego's a bit bruised. I don't like having friends come over and find me lying in a pool of vomit."

"Do that often, do you?" Andy stood and walked over to the sink to wash her hands off. "Sit in your own vomit that is."

"Well, Cardinal knows I don't have friends over."

Beach looked down at me. "You'd have to have friends first, wouldn't you?"

"Oh, you were a comedian before you had Cybertronic spackle and cable you?"

"I know jokes that would just slay you."

I was about to tell him to fire away and put me out of my misery when a hulking creature ducked its head and twisted its shoulders sideways to get into my apartment. The synthedermis covering it made the Attila a bit more pale than Beach—Beach's Venusian tan being the reason for his bronze color. The Attila's blond hair had been trimmed very short, and his blue eyes vibrated back and forth for a moment as the robot digitized the apartment.

Aside from the robot's size, and the stupid grin it wore, the most remarkable thing about it was that its hands were free of weapons. Instead of any death-dealing devices, the Attila bore two mesh bags bulging with every-thing from first-aid ointments, bandages, and medications to enough cleaning solutions to sterilize all of Orontius Trey, where my apartment was located. I had no doubt the Attila had analyzed each item as it was placed in the bag, and even now knew which ones to combine together to create hideous explosives—but the fact that he had not begun to do so surprised me.

Even more surprisingly, Miss Wickersham followed the Attila through the doorway. She wore a white, sleeveless blouse knotted tight above her navel and a pair of khaki shorts that displayed her long legs to great advantage. She smiled sweetly at me, as if I were a date coming to take her out, not a man wallowing in blood and partially di-gested food.

"What's *she* doing here?"

Andy shook her head. "I suppose she was sent to help clean up."

"Great." I held my arms out and felt my sodden shirt pull away from my chest. "She can start with me."

"One place is as good as another." Miss Wickersham folded her arms. "Take off your clothes."

What little blood hadn't flowed out of me through my nose rose to my cheeks in a blush. "Miss Wickersham!"

"I'd do it, Dent, or she'll just toss you *and* your clothes in a washing machine."

I sneered at him. "I'm 'hand wash only.' "

"And drip-dry." Beach shook his head. "Get going, or I'll have Ashurbanipol shuck you out of your clothes."

I pulled my shirt off and used the dry part to wipe my chest down. "Maddy, will you run a bath for me?"

"Certainly Mr. Dent."

As she marched off to my bedroom and the master bath beyond, I nodded toward the others. "Thanks for coming, but I think I can take care of myself now. Gotta get cleaned up."

Beach finally slipped his P-1000 into the holster be-neath his left arm. "I'm sure you'd love for Miss Wickersham to fulfill your fantasies, but we've got orders to get you back to headquarters as soon as you're able. I put that at a five-minute shower away."

"So they did get her?"

Beach's head came up warily, but he said nothing.

Andy noticed his silence and shrugged. "You have things to discuss." She headed for the door. "I can find my own way back, gentlemen."

I pointed at the Attila. "Ash, see that she gets to Cybertronic safely." It occurred to me that Cybertronic's having let Andy out of ARD marked their concern over my condition. Mr. Beach and Ash had been sent out to safeguard her more than worry about me. For that I was thankful because I didn't want anything to happen to Andy.

After the two of them left, I turned to Beach again. "Capitol lost Lorraine Kovan to an operation tonight, right? She's gone?"

"That's about the size of it. We don't know where she's gotten to, nor who has her."

I tapped my head. "I do, courtesy of a nepharite who thinks he's brilliant."

Beach's dark eyes narrowed. "The Dark Legion. Good. I haven't shot anything since my return to Luna, and those heretics make just the greatest of targets."

TWELVE

Given the way things had been going for me over the past dozen hours or so, when I stepped from the shower I clothed myself with older items to which I had no particular emotional attachments. This resulted in my wearing a pair of canvas slacks, a white, single-pocket T-shirt and a blue nylon windbreaker over it. I did keep my boots and even pulled on an old Orontius Orioles baseball cap.

Beach, who had showed up at my place dressed in clean, well-pressed corporate casuals, shook his head at my appearance. "Apathetic chasseurs can be rather boring."

"Hey, I've had the best part of my wardrobe shot up or bled on today." I shoved my hands into the pockets of my jacket as we propped the dented door to my apartment up. "Do you think Miss Wickersham will be safe in there?"

"Now that you've left, probably."

Not feeling inclined toward being a whetstone for Beach's wit—and being a bit concerned about his reaction if I didn't laugh at one of his jokes—I sank into a sullen mood and wandered in his wake toward the Cybertronic building. A lot of different things ran through my mind as we walked, but I couldn't summon enough concentration to sort them out.

As if he'd read my mind, Beach dropped back and matched his pace to mine. "Most of your operations have been soft penetrations and scouting missions, right?"

I nodded. " 'Cept when I was sent with an Attila named Nebuchandnezzar to deal with some gang pilfering from one of our warehouses. That got a bit nasty, but Nebu used his AR3K to pretty good effect."

Beach's eyes narrowed. "That was the action against the Moonlions?"

"Six months ago. They were creating a 'spoilage' problem with warehouse 1045 down in Helicon Deuce."

"I reviewed that operation. You got three with your knife."

I shook my head. "Two. I got the third with my bare hands."

Beach nodded appreciatively. "You shoot very well, but you don't use a gun. Why not?"

"Don't want to be dependent on it. Guns jam, ammo runs out."

"But not many throwing knives can turn a crowd back." Beach settled a heavy hand on the back of my neck. "Now, what's the real reason you don't carry a gun?"

"Having a gun on me didn't stop me from becoming a candidate for Cybertronic's fitness regimen."

"But it might have delayed it."

I looked over at him. "What do you mean?"

"How'd you die?"

"My back was broken, and my skull crushed."

"I know that, Dent."

"Then why did you ask?"

"What were the circumstances behind your death?"

I shook my head as we headed up to the second level of the Ptolemaeus district. "I don't know."

"You don't know?"

"No, I *don't* know. I don't feel like dwelling on a morbid subject like that."

Beach's hand tightened slightly. "Then you watch funeral video records just for the fun of it."

"I consider it performance art."

"Why don't you want to know how you died?" Beach shook his head. "Most chasseurs ask for that information immediately and figure they'll go out and avenge themselves. That's why those records aren't available for a year after you join us. By then you've been judged able to handle it, or you've been deactivated."

I growled, and a steam shunt valve on the street hissed

sympathetically. "I don't want to know how I died because, I *died*. I don't want to repeat that mistake."

"Oh, you just assume you were stupid, do you?"

"I died, didn't I?"

Beach spun me around and slammed me up against a wall. His right fist came up and in at my head, but I'd already begun to twist free of his grip on my shoulder. I ducked away from the blow and drove my right fist into his ribs. He grunted with pain and bounced back, but my quick leg sweep banged his ankles together, and he went down.

I danced in at him, but he slapped the ferrocrete sidewalk three times with his bare hand, and I backed off. "What's the big idea?"

He slowly stood and brushed himself off. "The idea was to show you that you have skills and reactions that we could not give you. We built upon what you were, we didn't start with a tabula rasa. And we don't recruit stupid people. For all you know, you were a Free Marine on Venus who died from wounds sustained when you fought off a Bauhaus raid."

"Or I could have walked into an ambush."

"Or you could have died of smoke inhalation and sustained your injuries falling down stairs while saving children from a burning building."

"Or I could have been surprised by a jealous husband and killed with my pants down around my ankles." I poked a finger at him. "The bottom line is that I died, and I'm not going to do that again."

"Nice sentiment, Dent, but the things you're involved with now make that a long-odds proposition."

"But you said heretics make good targets."

"*They* do, but the other things that you'll run into don't. I prefer dealing with them when I'm on the blunt end of an SR-3500 rifle, with them in my scope and my finger on the trigger." Beach watched me for a reaction so I didn't give him one. "I consider myself very efficient at what I do, and I don't mind close combat, but the Legion's foot soldiers are the sort of things that rightfully inhabit nightmares."

We walked on, and I waited until the crowd thinned

around us before asking him a question. "Have you ever seen a nepharite?"

"With my own eyes, no. I've seen video of what appeared to be nepharites on Venus and Mars, and then what you saw during your first fugue."

"How big are they?"

"Four meters."

"That would dwarf Ash or Nebu."

"Not everything they have is that big, but a lot of it is incredibly hideous. They appear to reanimate our dead, and turn renegades and deserters into necro-mutants and Centurions. Razides are huge things, barely sentient, and Ezoghouls are centauroid death beasts. None of them appear to feel pain in any sort of way we do. They take a lot of killing."

"But they *do* die, right?"

"Sure, but seldom alone." Beach shook his head. "Better to be killed by them than be a prize for which they are fighting like this Kovan woman."

"Agreed."

He led me into a musty bookstore and down rickety stairs to the basement. Back in the science-fiction ghetto, he tugged on a book wedged on a head-high shelf, and the wall retracted. Lasers scanned both of us, then let us pass. Behind us the wall closed again, and we wandered through UV-blazed corridors to the Cybertronic tower.

"Isn't it risky using a book like that to open one of these doorways?"

"It was written by a short science-fiction writer who styled himself a literary genius. The late twentieth century was chock-full of them—one even retreated to France because he figured the French could truly understand him. Few enough people read these days that chances were poor that anyone would pick obscure, self-indulgent, self-important books to read."

I nodded. "His books were in the minority on the shelf there."

"What is in demand is what gets supplied."

We walked into the ARD annex of the Cybertronic tower and past a blond male version of Miss Wickersham. Once inside ARD we split up, but when I went subreal on

the couch in Andy's office, I saw Beach waiting for me
in Carl's office. "Evening, Carl."

"Good, now that you are here, we can bring you up-to-
date on what has happened to Mrs. Kovan."

I nodded. "One thing I wanted to check first—when
you modified my navigation program, you put in a subroutine that sends out a distress call when I fugue, right?"

The sphere and cylinder man nodded. "It monitors your
vital signs and calls for aid if your life is in jeopardy. You
went into convulsions almost immediately upon entering
your fugue state. Since you were in a known, relatively
safe environment, the program kept you there, then sent
for assistance.

"It was not a breach of trust, Rex, but a matter of concern for your safety."

"Just thought I'd check."

Beach nodded at the humanoid construct. "Carl, what
about the Kovan woman being taken?"

"One moment."

I looked at Beach. "You call him Carl, too?"

"For von Clausewitz, sure. You?"

"Yeah, but for Jüng."

We both smiled in appreciation at each other, then returned our attention to Carl. With his right index finger he
drew a box in the air, and its outline glowed green neon.
Black-and-white static filled it, then dissolved into an un-
steady video-feed that moved as if the cameraperson were
running. The images appeared familiar to me because
they had been shot in the safe house where Lorraine had
been held.

"A dozen armed individuals hit this location approximately two hours ago. The safe house was caught at the
end of a shift. The invaders posed as the relief crew and
took the others unawares. This video was taken by one of
our people who works in concert with a Capitol rescue
squad."

The video started in the back of the building and took
us down a corridor with blood smeared on the floor and
low on the walls. The trail curved off into a side chamber
where a dead body lay. The videographer continued his
journey into the building, following a trail of spent shells
and bullet holes. At the bottom of some stairs, two more

guards lay in a pool of blood and entrails. The videographer crouched and in the half-light I saw bloody footprints glistening on the stairway, coming up in his direction.

One of the three sets was barefoot, and I assumed that belonged to Lorraine. The fact that her footprints were irregular and highly smeared, I decided she came along reluctantly and might have even fought her captors. Given that putting up resistance was more of a reaction than I'd seen from her in the initial interview, I took that as a good sign.

Carl froze the picture on another pair of dead bodies. "Capitol operatives did manage to get a call out before they were killed."

"Total casualties for the operation?" asked Beach.

"At *this* facility five died, two are in critical condition. One of those will die, and the other will be crippled for life. Casualties for the other side are unknown at this point."

I frowned. "The way you phrased that, there is another site where there was difficulty?"

Carl nodded, and the picture shifted to the scene of a traffic accident. Mangled metal and shattered plastic made it difficult to figure out what had hit what, but if forced to make a guess, I would have said a black Puma Coupé going flat out hit head-on with a Yosemite family wagon. Bodies lay scattered amid the debris, and a thin thread of white smoke drifted up from the foam-covered wreckage. Beyond the fire trucks, I saw an ambulance and a small body being loaded into it.

"The girl in the ambulance was the only survivor of a family of seven. She said her father screamed about being blind before he swerved into oncoming traffic. The men in the Puma were a Capitol response team in pursuit of what was taken to be the raiders' vehicle. They never had a chance."

I raised an eyebrow. "That wasn't an accident?"

Beach answered me. "Those who have given themselves over to the Dark Legion are rewarded for their devotion. They sometimes possess what they call Dark Gifts. One of those is an ability to inflict blindness on a victim."

"But my fugue led me to believe the snatch was arranged as an Imperial operation. There was no mention of heretics being involved."

Carl nodded slowly. "It could very well be that whoever coordinated the attack directed the escape route through this particular intersection so any chase cars could be taken care of. The Imperial operatives may not have known they had help from heretics. Amend that—the probability of their knowledge is less than five percent."

"How do you figure that?"

"We just picked up a Capitol alert that identifies some of the raiders. They were all in units that saw action against Dark Legion forces on Mars."

Beach leaned forward in his chair. "Are they corrupted?"

"Unlikely."

I confirmed Carl's speculation. "Ragathol did not mention controlling them." I looked at Carl. "Does Capitol know this was an Imperial operation yet?"

"Apparently not. The raiders who have been identified worked as freelancers."

I smiled. "Good, then that means we have a chance to get Lorraine before Capitol does."

Carl's head came up. "Why would we want to do that?"

"Now I'm confused, Carl." I stared hard at him. "I did some thinking before I fugued, and I've made a connection between Lorraine Kovan and my past. I knew her. She is the sister of the wife of the man who eulogized me."

"Ah, then you wish to start integrating your past with your present?"

"No." I shook my head. "I am as adamant to keep the two things separate as I was in the past. What I do want to do is start fighting against the Dark Legion. You know, from my information dumps, everything I have experienced in those fugue states, but you don't know how they *felt*. Toward the end of the first one, I had begun to identify with Ragathol's overlord. From the start of the second, I was one with him."

"Which is why we believe your body reacted so violently from the start of that fugue."

"Well, my physical reaction produced physical results that I could clean up. What I can't clean up is my mind. I still know what it felt like to be inside the mind of an Apostle of the Dark Legion. I am tainted in that I know how he would react. I know what he likes and what he hates. I know what gives him pleasure and causes him pain. And I know how it feels to be *used* by the Dark Legion."

I pointed at the image of the car wreck. "You notice that the heretics blinded some hapless boob who happened to be driving his family somewhere? They deliberately chose to use a tool that would do maximum damage—both to their target and to humanity as a whole. That tragedy—which will doubtless be painted as wreckless drivers in a hot Puma slamming into a family—will erode hope with despair. Not only did it stop the Capitol pursuit, but it damages everyone who hears about it."

My subreal hand tapped my subreal chest. "I don't need to know who I was to be hurt by that action. And I don't have to be who I was to want to react to it. I might be an agent of Cybertronic, but I still possess *some* humanity. The fact that I once knew Lorraine Kovan means her case attracts my attention. The fact that I am human means I want to snatch her away from the Dark Legion and visit a bit of pain back on them."

Beach wore a smug expression that I didn't like, and Carl made notes before looking up at me. "How would you suggest we go about this rescue? We don't even know where she is."

"Start by getting every nanosecond of video from the accident from any and all sources available. Analyze it and isolate everyone in it. Sort them out by length of time they are there, eliminating those who arrive late or leave before the ambulance takes the girl away. After that, study the individuals alone and then in whatever groups they appear to form. Check them for appearances of ecstasy or fascination with the accident. Pay special attention to those who seem to have knowledge of exactly how it happened."

I narrowed my eyes. "A heretic is going to be like a pyromaniac—he'll get a thrill from watching the aftermath of what he caused. Rank very highly anyone who seems anxious to talk to the security forces. Tap the security forces for names and addresses of the witnesses. Then compile dossiers on all of the likely folks and place them under surveillance. Research their known associates and, eventually, we'll get back to someone in the first or second level of Imperial security. Lorraine won't be far from him and is probably being held in some satellite facility near the spaceport for easy transport to Mars.

"And working backward from the Capitol identifications of freelancers will probably work, but I expect those freelancers to be dead before they're paid off, so they'll be useless."

Beach clapped his hands. "Bravo, Rex, that's an excellent start."

"I take it you see other things that need to be done at this point?"

He nodded. "Imperial's facilities—at least the sort you suspect will hold Kovan—are often built on one of three or four different floor plans. We can begin an assault analysis of those plans to determine the resources necessary to crack one open. Its actual location will affect the rescue operation in terms of ingress and egress, response times and perimeter isolation, but little more. We can be a jump ahead of ourselves if we start looking at what we need early. We can even begin to procure materials before finalizing our plan."

"You're using the term 'we' rather freely there. You want a piece of this operation?"

Beach nodded. "You'll need an assault coordinator. I'll take the job if it's open."

"It's filled now." I looked over at Carl. "You can handle the computer stuff, right?"

"I've taken the liberty of beginning the isolation and analysis of the videos already. We can manage that and the planning of a theoretical raid on an Imperial facility before we need corporate clearance. Anything much beyond that would be premature."

"Does premature include my rounding up some freelancers for this operation?" I started to tick points off on my fingers. "We want freelancers for plausible deniability. We want particular freelancers because they've seen Kovan before—if I get hit, they can still identify her and extract her. We want those same freelancers because they've had experience fighting Dark Legion heretics before, and if there are any involved in keeping Lorraine captive, their experience might prove very helpful."

Carl started to nod, but Beach cut him off. "If we consider them outside consultants for our planning of this theoretical raid, we hire them for their expertise, not action. That we can do."

The construct smiled. "Well-done, Coral. You outmaneuver the regulations very adroitly."

"Coming from you, that's high praise."

I smiled. "Okay, then, things have a weak green light. I'll go find Pam and Lane and get their crew together. Once we have a location and a plan to take it, we can get clearance to get Lorraine back."

Beach shook his head. "Ragathol will not be pleased."

"No he won't. Nor will his master." I smiled in spite of myself. "And even though I'll pay quite a price for it, that's not a show I want to miss."

THIRTEEN

I came out of subreal and found Ash hovering over me. Swinging my feet off the couch, I peered around him and saw Andy sitting at her desk, sucking on a NyxStik™. "How am I doing, Doc?"

She shrugged, letting the hissed sucking sound communicate her lack of concern. "That black eye looks really very combative. Other than that you're fine, though you will hit a wall if you don't get some sleep."

"Plenty of time to sleep when I'm dead."

"Found it that restful, did you?"

I winced. "Touché, Andy. I've got an errand to run, then I will get sleep, I promise."

"I believe you." She looked up at the Attila unit. "Ash, if he violates this promise, you will put him in a bed and sit on him until he goes to sleep."

"Acknowledged."

I glanced up at the death machine. "I'm not going out with him in tow."

"You're not going out without him."

"I don't need a baby-sitter."

The door to her office opened, and Beach came into the room. "You will take Ash with you in case the Brotherhood has any ideas of avenging their operatives."

Ash reached out and helped me to my feet. "Your safety is paramount."

I rolled my eyes. "Take a long walk off a short pier, okay, Ash?" I shifted my attention to Beach. "Having an Attila backing me up will ruin my freelance cover."

"When this operation goes down, your cover will be in tatters anyway. If these freelancers you're going to meet are acquainted with the enemy, they will welcome your corporate ties. If they don't, you can't use them."

As much as I wanted to deny what Beach was saying, I knew he was right. My cover as a freelancer had been of limited value and limited life anyway. With Fay Fan's experience as a Cybertronic expatriate for an example, Lane, Pam, and the others must have assumed I had some sort of a sweetheart deal with Cybertronic anyway. While I did complain about the availability and cost of spare parts the same way Fay did, I never seemed to have as much trouble coming up with them or the money to pay for them as she did.

"All right, Ash, c'mon." I started toward the door, but the Attila unit didn't move. "Ash? You coming?"

The blond behemoth blinked his eyes twice. "Pardon. Compliance with your initial instructions required the completing of the information download."

"Download?"

"A comprehensive survey of every known pier to facilitate running a statistical analysis that yielded the specifications for 'short' as it relates to piers. Subsequent to that will be a similar survey of 'walks' to their lengths. Do you wish this procedure aborted?"

"Yes, for the moment, yes." I nodded at Beach and Andy. "I'll see you later, I hope. And then it will be lights out."

I decided to let Ash follow me instead of using him like a cutter to split the crowds on the street. If he saw anything that tripped his surveillance-and-protection-program protocols he could reach out and touch me, or use our cellular phone links to covertly supply me with information. I did not expect trouble, but I didn't want to be taken unaware. In spite of myself, I felt good about having him there, but my sharing that with him would mean nothing to him, and my self-esteem didn't need the knock of realizing I needed a bodyguard.

I knew I'd have to catch up with Lane and Pam at the Midnight Sun because a visit to Yojimbo's apartment would put me under Brotherhood surveillance again. With their operatives having failed to report in after they started trailing me, I felt alerting the Brotherhood to my presence was not a survival trait. Lorraine's survival depended upon *my* survival, so I opted for the easier course and headed to the bar.

Surviving the Midnight Sun, on the other hand, was not always that easy. A lot of the patrons had left for the night, but my friends were formed up in their customary knot at the table where I'd found them before. A few patrons sat at the tables scattered through the center of the bar, but the next largest cluster came in the form of a half dozen men and women at a table at the opposite end of the bar from our table. From the collection of beer pitchers pyramided on their table, they had been drinking steadily for a while.

I smiled at them and nodded. In an instant I surveyed their personal firearms, and my computer decompressed the data about them. I knew what they looked like, how many bullets they carried, how fast they could shoot them, and even what the digitized soundprint of firing them would look like. In the Midnight Sun, their threat level was relatively low, though the copious amount of beer did raise it a notch. The obvious tension in the air between them and my friends raised it yet again, but it never got close to where I was concerned about trouble.

Pam smiled at me as I came walking over. "How are you doing, Rex?"

"I've been better." I pointed Ash to a position next to the wall. "Things have gotten a bit more complex since I saw you earlier this evening. I think I need you for an operation."

Lane and Klaus instantly became more interested, but Fay paid a lot of attention to Ash. "Odd friend you have here, Rex."

"He's my little brother. I put him together from a kit." I looked at the others. "Right now I can authorize your participation as consultants. We do the planning for a theoretical operation, and you get first crack if it goes live."

Pam leaned forward with her elbows on the cable drum's surface. "How much firepower are you going to need? We can get backup."

Lane frowned at her. "We don't know that. We left Mitch a message to find us here. He may not be interested in freelancing."

"Hey, look," shouted a voice from across the bar, "it's Abacus and Costello."

I glanced back over my shoulder at the people at the table and sneered at them.

"Ignore them. They rolled in an hour ago and started sopping up beer like sponges. They've been making remarks at Fay, so we figure they're Imperial nullbrains." Pam reached out and gave Fay's hand a squeeze. "Freelancers have to learn to let old corps ties die."

"Back to your original question, Pam, I don't know how much we'll need in the way of firepower. That's part of the planning. You four, Yojimbo, and anyone else you can think of who has experience in dealing with weird stuff will be welcome."

Pam nodded her head, a strand of blond hair slipping down to caress her cheek. "How much?"

"In the planning phase, twenty percent of your normal rate."

"That's not what a consultant for a corporate matter would be paid."

"Good point. Twenty-five crowns per hour?" I glanced at Fay. "And you can take yours in parts at cost, if you want."

Her dark eyes narrowed to slits a second before I heard a man burp behind me. I turned and stared at a big man weaving ever so slightly about a table away. "Can I help you?"

The guy gave me a drunken smile and what he clearly hoped was a hard-eyed smile. "Answer a question, 'kay?"

"What."

He sniffed and wiped his nose with his sleeve. "How come Cybertronic makes weenie folks like you and the little minx there?"

"They tried making larger models like you, but something in your size just can't help being stupid."

That hit him between the eyes, but comprehension just didn't take place. "You got special parts?"

"Ask your wife."

"What?"

"Well, they're not special," I turned fully in my chair and faced him. "Just *bigger*."

"You're a goddamn machine." He pulled himself up and smiled at a trio of newcomers entering the bar. "You run on batteries."

"And I keep going and going and going."

I saw him begin to move around the table to brace me more directly, then one of the newcomers gestured and the whole world went black.

"Who turned out the lights?" the man yelled. Then all hell broke loose.

One advantage of being a Cybertronic agent is that my brain functions so much faster than other peoples do that what seems to occur simultaneously to them becomes a clearly delineated chronology of events to me. For example, even as I began to tip my chair over to drop me to the floor, I felt a warm spray cover me. A gunshot and the sound of a bullet impacting its target followed, then I hit the floor and a body fell in front of me.

The blindness surprised me, but my chasseur training took over and forced away the panic rising in my throat. In an instant I opened a cellular link to Ash and requested visual data. I got a confirmation that it was coming, but when I saw nothing I realized that the blindness was not an absence of light, as my dead companion had thought, nor was it a dazzling of the eyes. It went straight to my visual cortex and prevented me from seeing anything or interpreting any input visually.

Instantly I switched to my default, and kicked special interpretive software in. It processed everything I heard, and fed it directly into the balance and position centers in my brain. The computer created for me a three-dimensional, kinesthetic array that pinpointed me and the sound sources within the confines of the echo-reflective surfaces surrounding me. A separate feed of the same data from Ash provided triangulation inputs that confirmed direction and range.

I reached out to the dead man's body and slid an Aggressor from the holster on his right hip. It was a pig of a weapon, complete with a stubby snout, but it beat the hell out of throwing a knife in a firefight. I snapped the safety off and charged the gun, then came up on one knee and pulled the trigger.

Relying on passive sonar to locate and eliminate targets in a firefight is a weird experience. The human body tends to absorb sound, so it can be detected by the absence of noise coming through it. However, in a firefight, there's more than enough sound to mask any void. A human with a gun only has two sound sources: the gun and the voice box/mouth combination. Luckily the latter is on the body midline and makes a dandy target in and of itself.

My first shot sent a bullet out that knocked a body tumbling back into tables and chairs. The explosion from my gun echoed back off the tipping and toppling surfaces, and the computer placed this new terrain in my kinesthetic landscape. As that sound source went from being crisp and explosive to wheezy, I shifted my aim point to the left and fired again.

This time I triggered two shots, and one of them hit. The target spun back to the right and spotted itself by screaming. That told me it was not dead, and I decided to finish it. Two more bullets silenced it and with its death, my sight returned.

Being able to see again almost killed me. Visual inputs immediately overrode the aural ones, but my brain was still feeding data to my kinesthetic faculties. As I brought my gun around to target the last heretic, I lost my balance and began to fall to the right. My trigger finger twitched prematurely, sending a shot wide of my target, and the recoil ripped the Aggressor half out of my grip.

A smile blossoming on his face, the last heretic brought his Ronin knockoff around to finish me.

A burst of automatic submachine gun from behind me caught the heretic in the middle and folded him double, as if he were a cardboard cutout. A second burst punched down through the crown of his head and drove him butt first into the bar's far wall. On impact his body straightened up again, and a third burst blew his heart out of his back and left it in a smear on the wall.

Ash scanned the bar, then tucked the CAW 2000 away again. "Threat Assessment Evaluation equals zero."

I nodded. The heretics had been interested in killing the drunk Imperials. Ash hadn't seen them as a threat to me until one of them turned his gun on me. At that point the Attila reacted instantly, eliminating the threat to my safety. Such literal-minded devotion to duty made Attila units wonderful as combat support, but their lack of flexibility meant they required mentally dexterous leadership.

I tossed the Aggressor on the body of the man from

whom I'd taken it. Most of the top of his head was missing and most of what had been in it had splattered over me and the others. The three heretics were down for good—I'd hit the first one in the throat and the second one in the torso. The other Imperials were also down, but cries for help indicated someone had survived.

I used my cell link to call for medical assistance. I wanted the Imperials treated by Cybertronic so we could get information from them. I ordered Ash to immediately dump his visual record of firefight to Carl in the hopes that these heretics might have been at the accident scene. That done, I turned back to the others. "You all okay?"

Lane shivered. "What was all that about? How did those heretics manage to miss us?"

Pam gave Lane's shoulder a squeeze. "They weren't after us, lover. We were blinded to eliminate witnesses."

I slapped my hand against my forehead. "Of course. I expected it, but not this soon."

Pam frowned at me. "What did you expect, Rex?"

"You in as my consultants? You'll sign a nondisclosure agreement?"

Everyone nodded.

"A freelance operation sponsored by a heretic inside Imperial took Lorraine Kovan away from Capitol earlier this evening. The freelancers who snatched her didn't know they were tied up with the Dark Legion. They got away because they had some heretical help on their escape. I told my people that I expected the Legion to kill them to tie up some loose ends. It should have occurred to me that this place, being a freelancers' watering hole and all was a likely place for the hit. After all, we've chosen it for the easy access that makes getaways quick, haven't we?"

Lane looked hard at me. "What 'we' white man? You're no freelancer."

"True, but right now I'm the guy who's got the backing to take on the Dark Legion and rescue Lorraine Kovan. That okay by you?"

"You pay the bills, you call the shots, boss." Lane clapped me on the shoulders, and all six of us headed back to Cybertronic to do some consulting.

FOURTEEN

Fay Fan shivered as we walked into Cybertronic headquarters. "They say you can never come home again."

"Whoever said that never needed spare parts." I ushered the others into an elevator, and we ascended to the fifth floor. A conference room on that level had been made available for us. When we walked in, we found an assortment of foods and beverages that had undoubtedly been selected by a program that tried to generalize concerning what freelancers would enjoy eating. This meant we were supplied with cheap alcoholic beverages, a cold-meat platter, and pastries. It wasn't a bad selection, but not the sort of spartan, high-caffeine fare conducive to planning a lightning assault on an enemy facility.

I sent Ash to find an urn of coffee. Pam used a phone to call Yojimbo and get him to join us. Klaus started picking through the food, and Lane fell in line behind him. Fay just stretched out on the black leather couch in the back and began leafing through the latest Cybertronic catalog. With everyone occupied, I went subreal, sucked up an information packet, and was back out before anyone noticed my departure.

The packet contained a number of things, all of them good news. While I'd been away, Carl had been hard at work with his analysis, and he'd even shown some initiative. Keying off my remark that a heretic at the crash would have been like a pyromaniac at a fire and would have stayed around to watch the aftermath of the accident, he pulled psychological evaluations for as many

people as he could and started looking for obsessive/
compulsive individuals. The data that Ash shot him from
the firefight helped narrow the search down, and Carl
matched one person at the scene with the second heretic
I'd shot.

His widow, it turned out, came from a family with a
long history with Imperial. Her brother worked for their
security division and, according to information taken
from an internal Imperial newsletter, had been promoted
to Acting Security Supervisor for a plant over in the
Furnerius sector. That put it almost on top of the Luna
City spaceport, so it fulfilled our criterion for the place
where they would hold Lorraine.

Once Yojimbo and the Whiz kid arrived, Mr. Beach
joined us and gave us a video presentation on the facility
in question. "Ford Wilson heads up security at an Imperial BXR5S3 building. The BX designation means the
building itself has an outer box with corridors and offices
connecting the four corners of the box. This leaves four
triangular courtyards north, south, east, and west of the
central cross. They extend all the way up for the two
floors that are above Furnerius Cinq. The courtyards are
used as gardens and cafeteria seating, so they are over-
grown with plants. They are small, but organic material
might interfere with fields of fire.

"Below the ground you have three floors. They were
carved out of lunar bedrock, so there is nothing but rock
where you have gardens above. Consider the crossed
square belowground a prison from which the only route
out is up."

Beach froze the presentation at a schematic of the
building. "The R in the facility designation indicates it is
a research lab. As such, the bottom floors have their own
life-support systems and are isolated from each other. The
lowest level was originally designated for medical research and has rooms suitable for human habitation, both
patients and staff. We suspect Kovan can be found down
there."

Beach started things again, and the video zoomed in on
the building. Interior details became clear, and I saw we
were dealing with a much larger amount of space than I
had originally imagined. Instead of each section of the

building being a corridor with rooms off to either side, the sections had three corridors each. All of them provided access to labs on either side, with rooms jammed back-to-back in the center. Firefights down there could go from a room in bedrock to a corridor, into two more rooms, another corridor, two rooms, a corridor and a dead end in bedrock on the other side of the building arm. The schematic didn't show the crossing corridors, but the interior rooms had clearly been constructed to allow for quick alteration, so corridors could be anywhere.

Yojimbo pointed toward the video monitor. "The size of this facility makes rather difficult the possibility of finding Mrs. Kovan and getting her out quickly, does it not?"

Beach nodded. "It would, but we have some advantages. This plant, which is called Furnerius Larkspur, was built right before Imperial decided to lease the Mercurial settlement of Fukido from Mishima. It had been a pet project of one of the MacGuires and was all but abandoned when that MacGuire was assassinated for his opposition to the leasing agreement. Without him to lobby in the Parliament's Chamber of Lords for funding, Larkspur languished. Only recently has it been given funding, and that's pretty much just enough to get its equipment up and running so they can decide what to do with it.

"In that capacity, only the lowest level has its life-support systems functioning fully. The other two subterranean floors are dead and while not vacuum or filled with poison gases, they are stagnant and unused. The above-ground sections of the building have long been leased out to private, freelance companies that Imperial has wanted to support and, eventually, buy out."

That was typical operating procedure for Imperial. Most of the other corporations organized and funded their own research and development projects. Imperial preferred to use its vast wealth as investment capital and buy up young but promising companies. They even funded efforts by people who had left other corporations—luring them away from their employers by promises of untold wealth. The reason that Imperial hated Cybertronic so much stemmed from the fact that Cybertronic employees seldom leave the fold, resulting in Imperial having no way to get its hands on Cybertronic developments.

I tapped into more of the infopacket I got when I went subreal. "As it turns out, Cybertronic managed to set up a small corporation that Imperial wants to buy. Imperial does not know of the Cybertronic connection and offered us space in Larkspur. The offices opened two months ago, and we can all gain access to the building through Hexargos Industrial." I searched the file that came out of the information packet for details about supplies. "Mr. Beach, are weapons on-site already?"

"A limited number of them are, yes. More are being brought in. We expect to have the supplies you need by Saturday, which is when we suggest the operation goes off."

Pam looked up from some notes she had taken. "How do we know Kovan won't be moved before that?"

"We don't, but Ford Wilson has reserved two berths on a Capitol ship—the *Red Corsair*—for a run to Mars. The ship will dock at Furnerius a week from now." Beach shrugged. "Wilson is under surveillance. If he moves early, we will be alerted."

Klaus quickly swallowed a bite of Danish. "Any special security modifications? I don't like surprises."

"The original design of the building did not call for anything unusual, and other BXR5S3 units have not yielded any surprises when explored. On the other hand, it is possible that Wilson, in bringing the facility up, has updated and improved the security measures and devices. He could even have used Dark Legion necrotechnology or funds to put things in there that Imperial does not know about. Our people in Hexargos have not been informed of any new procedures for security in the upper floors, but none of them have access to the lower levels, so they don't know what is down there."

Lane clearly didn't like the unknown. "Let's start running it down. Assuming we're in clear through Hexargos, how do we get to the lower levels?"

"Ingress comes through the elevators. Four shafts run through the building, though only one has access to the lower levels. It is key operated and the use of the key, which is magnetically coded, turns on a camera that the security staff, located down in level five, uses to inspect the passengers and clear the elevator for descent."

Klaus frowned at Beach. "Unless you have a man in Security down there, you can't bypass that clearance system. And if you have a man down there, you don't have to worry about it."

Beach remained impassive. "All the shafts go down, but the elevator circuitry in the other three does not recognize the presence of the lower floors."

Klaus smiled. "So we blow the floor of an elevator and rappel down to the bottom."

Pam shook her head. "No go, Klaus. Security would hear the explosion, and getting Lorraine out will be a bitch because the last time I saw her, she was comatose, not ambulatory. We need a way to get that elevator down there."

"No," Beach corrected her, "you need a way to get *one* elevator down there. Tonight, tomorrow, and Saturday morning, Hexargos employees are replacing the circuitry in the other three elevators with boards that will allow the elevators to descend all the way down. You'll have devices that can summon the elevators as you need them. Because Imperial only thought to rig one elevator to go all the way down, they have no way of even monitoring when or if the others head down."

"That's stupid," Klaus grumbled.

"But fiscally responsible." I smiled carefully. "Okay, we're down. What next?"

Beach outlined the rest of the job as a snatch and grab. Surveillance suggested that Imperial had only put three dozen security people on the staff there, split into three shifts. Going in late on a Saturday night meant we would have a minimal number of noncombatants on the site. He finished by going over the closest response garrisons for Imperial, and provided us with numerous escape routes as well as an overview of the methods he'd be using to discourage pursuit.

I looked at the others. "What do you think?"

Yojimbo furrowed his brow. "We know how many security people work at the site, but with facilities for staff down on level five, we do not know how many permanent individuals we could have down there. Given Wilson's involvement with heretics, it is possible he has a dozen or so stashed down there."

Beach nodded. "We have considered snatching guards coming off duty and subjecting them to narco-interrogation, but we think that would alert Wilson to our impending operation. I would point out to you that Rex will have Ash with him and that the heretic ability to blind does not affect Ash."

"But will he shoot heretics?"

"He will, Klaus." I opened my hands. "At the Midnight Sun he did not see the heretics as a threat to me as they were intent upon shooting the Imperials. On this operation he'll consider anything that is not Lorraine or one of us a threat. If it initiates hostile action, it dies."

Yojimbo nodded. "I believe the rest of the risks are within acceptable limits."

"Provided the money's right." Pam turned toward me like a tiger stalking prey. "How much?"

I shrugged easily. "Twenty thousand, four now, the rest after the operation, with only half being paid if you die in an unsuccessful effort."

"Twenty?" Pam sat back and opened her arms. "We're talking Cybertronic, Rex. Twenty? Try forty."

"Forty? For that much I could hire Snow White and six more dwarves like Ash to do the job. Twenty-five, seventy-five hundred down, same terms."

"Thirty-five, ten now, twenty after and five deferred for sixty days, same terms otherwise."

"If you go thirty, with ten now, fifteen after and five deferred, you have a deal."

Pam smiled and took my outstretched hand. "That's each, Rex, and a good deal."

"It's each of you, I know." I smiled openly. "Glad to have you aboard."

We spent the next two days refining our plans and watching surveillance video of the site. The team remained at Cybertronic in case Wilson decided to move Lorraine prematurely. Since Cybertronic was supplying equipment for the raid, the two-day vacation at our headquarters allowed the others to get used to the weapons Cybertronic manufactures.

The time they spent training, I spent sleeping. When I first lay down and tried to relax, too many thoughts stormed through my head. Even though we had everything figured out, we could have been planning based on the tip of the iceberg, and that meant we could have a rude surprise waiting for us when we went in. I knew Beach was trying to minimalize that possibility, and the things he didn't think to check, Yojimbo asked about anyway.

Leaving all the planning up to them allowed me to drift off to sleep, but anxiety haunted me in my dreams. I found myself alone in a room filled with gray mist. It swirled around me as I walked forward. The mist itself glowed, giving me what little light I had to work with. I tried to shift over to IR and UV light, but in my dream I could not. This frightened me because I knew that meant I was locked into the body I had been before Cybertronic had made me better.

The mist cleared off to my right, and I turned to face it. There, trapped in a mirrorlike glass panel, I saw Lorraine Kovan. A smile lit her face, and the laughter in her eyes made her positively radiant. "You are a caution. I see why Anna couldn't get away from Nicholas. When I asked her to see if there were any more at home like him, I didn't expect you'd be the answer."

"Lorraine? What are you talking about?"

"There you go again! It's me, Cassandra. You pledged your life in my defense if need be, and you were my rock. 'Be true to yourself,' you said." Her smile began to die, and her features began to slacken. "Because of you we went to Venus. And what did you do? You died."

"I don't understand."

"I never thought you'd take the easy way out."

The word "out" echoed through the mists as Lorraine exploded into a tinkling hail of a million glass shards. I felt them rip through me, but their sting came to me as if as distant as the echoes of her voice. The pain I felt was a twin of the pain I had felt at her departure for Venus. It hurt, but did not destroy me.

Silence never had a chance to again command the dream realm. Slow and insistent, beginning as something I felt more than I heard, a muted tapping sound entered my dream. As the sound grew, the pounding bass tones fluttered through my chest and set up a rhythm in the mist. Its translucency fluctuated with the sound, becoming nearly transparent as the noise hammered me, and shrouding me in solid gray in the valleys within the thunderous assault.

A final boom dropped me to my knees. Looking up I saw myself before an ornate wooden door—real wood, not fiberplast. A golden sheen marked highlights on the mahogany panels. It struck me as being of an odd shape, but the significance of that shape, of the narrowing at the top and bottom and the bulging a third of the way down, did not come to me immediately. Only as I reached for the doorknob, which I found to be cold, and twisted it did I realize the door was the lid to a coffin.

It opened on creaking hinges. Nestled within the pink satin quilting I saw a fire-blackened skeleton with inch-wide gaps in its long bones. The first of the large, lumbar vertebrae had been crushed to a powder. Looking up into its empty eye sockets I could see through its shattered crown to the lace pillow behind its head.

The skeleton wore a shoulder holster with a Bolter in it. It hadn't been there when I first opened the coffin, but with the logic that comes in dreams I knew it always had been there. Then, without motion on the skeleton's part, the gun was drawn and held pointing in my direction. The skeletal hand that held it did not waver, and the gun's weight posed no problem for an arm missing segments from its long bones.

The skeleton's mandible slowly opened. "Do you know why the dead hate the living?"

"You're a dream."

"I'm a nightmare. Do you know what death is?"

"The cessation of life."

"No. It is an eternity of frustration. All your hopes. All your dreams. All your whims are destroyed. All your pain and your fear and your private terrors will never know relief. They are all you have left. They are all you have left me."

The voice was my own. Its timbre and quality were slightly different, but the words and how they were strung together was me. "I've taken nothing from you."

"But you have. You have my body. You have my skills."

"You weren't using them."

"But you have not used them as I would have. You are our second chance."

"I'm my own *first* chance."

"You are not separate from me."

"I have nothing to do with you."

"You *are* me. We are each other. Death does not wipe the slate clean. Everything I had at the moment of my death, you inherited at the moment of your birth."

"I want nothing from you. You failed. You died."

"And without me, you will die again."

"We'll see about that."

"So we will." The skeleton lowered the gun, and the tableau began to dissolve. "Remember, not dying is not really living. Without me, survive though you may, you will never be alive."

FIFTEEN

Insertion into the Hexargos Industrial suite on Saturday went easily enough, and that was good because I found myself rather edgy. The skeleton and I replayed our little conversation every time I laid myself down to sleep. That had me second-guessing myself and wondering if I was doing certain things certain ways because that's how Rex does them, or how the skeleton used to do them.

The team was brought into Hexargos under the guise of being individuals who were looking to defect from their corporations and join Hexargos. Security for that sort of thing demanded they come in on Saturday, when most folks only worked half a day anyway. That minimized the chance of their being recognized and, for us, reduced the chance of innocent bystanders being caught in any firefights.

The Whiz kid and Mr. Beach took up positions in the tech center at Hexargos, and in jig time the kid had patched his equipment into the aboveground security network. He didn't push down into the lower-level security because we didn't want any slips to alert the people on Level Five that we were working an operation. While such caution might have seemed foolish in the face of possible support troops hidden down there, our primary concern was in establishing surprise.

We did this very simply. With the kid in place early on, he tapped the security video-feeds running down to the command center. While our personnel were in the building legitimately, he was able to isolate and animate images of them leaving the building by morphing together their images with other people's departures. As the majority of folks in the building started to leave, we sent a video record of our own people going out. The kid doctored the monitors within Hexargos, including the surveillance devices Imperial had secreted in the suite, and by seven in the evening the folks in the security center down on five had every indication that Hexargos was empty.

We prepared to go in at one in the morning. In addition to our own personal selection of a sidearm—I went with a Punisher just because I'd liked it more than the Aggressor I'd used in the bar—everyone carried a CAW 2000 submachine gun. The advantages of carrying a lighter weapon like that came in that we would be fighting in an enclosed area. The compact CAW2K wouldn't get hung up on door frames and still kicked out a lot of ordnance when needed.

The two exceptions to the above were Ash and Klaus. We gave Ash an AR3000 assault rifle. He was big enough that the AR3K was to him what a CAW2K was to the rest of us. In addition, the built-in grenade launcher provided us some seriously heavy firepower if things really started to go bad. The fact that Ash would take a lot of damage before going down meant we'd have heavy-weapons backup on demand, and that might well be the difference between life and death.

Klaus is contrary by nature, so I suggested he carry a SA-SG 7200i combat shotgun. He complained, as I expected, about the fact that it was only semiautomatic, but he did like the fact that the gun was all but jam-proof. He also liked the fact that I was willing to let him mix loads of slugs and buckshot in any configuration he saw fit to use. I figured the shotgun would be less useful on security folks and heretics than it would be on any Dark Legion creatures, and if we had to leave Klaus guarding our butts as we ran from some monster, well, it would give him something to complain about.

The most difficult choice we had made came concerning body armor. Yojimbo had agitated early on to be able to return to his apartment to get his heavy battle armor. The Mishima heavy armor is impressive. It turns their soldiers into these giant samurai warriors, and it protects them rather well from gunfire. If it has a drawback—and this is true of all corporate heavy armor—it is that the same massive size that makes it so visually intimidating also makes it cumbersome and dangerous in the sort of close-quarters combat we would be facing.

While all of us would have loved that level of protection, we opted for something more reasonable. Head to toe we dressed in ballistic nylon. It would stop most small-arms fire, though it would leave a nasty bruise behind. Over that we put on light composite backplates and breastplates that were articulated enough to allow flexibility while they covered us from groin to throat on both sides. Side panels snugged uncomfortably up into our armpits, but a bullet in there would be given free access to lungs and heart, so the discomfort could be managed. Our combat boots were likewise armored and included knee pads for protecting kneecaps. Armored gloves, composite helmets, and faceplates completed our protective gear and would stop the vast majority of what we were likely to meet down there.

Ash, of course, wore no armor at all. He dressed in a black T-shirt and black fatigues. He looked more suited to a night in a club than he did to any attack. With him, the lack of armor did not really matter because of the armor he already wore beneath his plastic flesh. While there was armor made for Attila units, smuggling it into Hexargos would have been difficult and would only have made him that much bigger.

Radios linked us all with each other and Beach. He was to remain in Hexargos with the Whiz kid, directing things from there and providing the kid protection. He also had an external link with some chasseur and cuirassier teams on the outside who were protecting our escape routes. I knew he'd have preferred to be in the thick of things, but I welcomed having a cooler head directing our assault and in position to offer immediate help.

Lane and Fay carried some simple explosives in case we needed to open the cell in which they were keeping Lorraine. Pam had a medical kit and had been designated as the primary caregiver to Lorraine, while Klaus had been given a rucksack that contained a ballistic armor jumpsuit for Lorraine. The rest of us were just along to get to Lorraine and to help Pam get out with her.

Loaded up and ready to roll, we stole from the Hexargos offices, and Beach contacted me by radio. «Video-feeds to elevators are negative and null, Ace.»

«Roger, base.» I waved the rest of the team forward. "We're clear to the elevators. The kid has them blanked."

Cautiously we worked our way down the corridor to the elevators. We kept our backs to the walls and covered doors as we went past them. Yojimbo, Pam, and Lane— radio call signs Deuce, Trey, and Cat respectively— covered the north wall while Klaus, Fay, and Ash followed me. Klaus and Fay answered to Sink and Cease on the radio and the kid became Keys, while Ash was just Ash. After all, he didn't have an identity to protect in the real world, while the rest of us did.

Yojimbo reached the elevator first and summoned it. Lane and I checked it for passengers, then ushered the rest of the team into it. We let Ash stand in front of the doors so he'd soak up any fire from an ambush. I hit the "door close" button, then held down the "Down" button. With it depressed, I hit 2 and then 1, for a total of three, and that sent the elevator down three levels.

Our elevator opened on the side of the central column facing away from the security center. As we came around with guns drawn, three of the four technicians in the brightly lit center raised their hands. The fourth raised only one hand and extended a single finger in an ancient sign of defiance, then turned and hit an alarm button on the wall behind him.

"Cover, everyone. Ash, blow the center."

The Attila brought his gun up, and the grenade launcher married to the underside of the barrel vomited out a rifle grenade. It hit the bulletproof glass between us and the security center, and punched through. Even so, the resistance it met going in triggered the grenade's charge. In an instant the center became a roiling ball of fire, most of which blew the glass back out into the corridor.

One whole sheet of it came out of its fittings and flew at Ash. As if it were a sheet of water, it wrapped him in a elastic cocoon. Then it shattered, instantly becoming a lethal silicon mist that would have reduced a man to raw, bloody meat as it swirled around him. The Attila weathered it without complaint even though it left his synthetic flesh and clothing hanging in tatters from his ferrotitanium body.

Hunkered down behind the elevator column, the glass typhoon missed our humans, but enough smoke filled the core to cut visibility. Staying low, our team moved out, and I keyed the radio. «Base, four were in the center. They're gone. Alarm went out.»

«Roger, Ace. Alarm in process of being squelched.»

«We need a loc on two guards.»

«Keys confirms your target is in SW105. Guards, searching.»

«Roger. Moving to SW105.»

As I looked around the core, the computer flashed up the corridor designations. I pointed off down the southwest passage. Yojimbo and Klaus headed off down it, with Fay and Lane following closely behind. Pam and I brought up the rear, with Ash stalking down the center of the corridor between us. I almost ordered him to one side or another, but stopped when I realized that he'd attract the most attention for any enemies, and that would mean those of us who can bleed would not be the initial target.

«Ace.»

«Go, Base.»

«Negative scan on your guards. Keys is in security net five and has no visual in southwest, west, or south corridors.»

«Roger, base. Team, eyes open because we're alone right now.»

SW105 was a suite of rooms at the juncture of the south, west, and southwest corridors. We headed for it with all due dispatch. I assumed any resistance would crop up at the suite, but we all played it very carefully. Our pace slowed as we entered the last third of the southwest corridor. With hand signals, I designated myself and Yojimbo as the first two attackers, with Klaus and Fay to follow.

«Ace.»

«Go, base.»

«Keys says something odd is happening down there. What's in your six?»

I turned and looked back down the corridor. Behind us the walls were shifting and twisting to cut off our retreat.

«Base, I have wall movement. Someone's building a maze. Can Keys stop it?»

«He's on it. Looks like it is a security program. Working on it.»

«Roger, we're going in.»

Sprinting forward slightly ahead of Yojimbo, I dropped the muzzle of my CAW2K on the lock mechanism of the door to SW105. My computer shifted over to tactical and gave me a crosshair that showed I was on target. Two bursts from the gun punched the lock and the knob, and I hit the door at full speed.

I caught it with my left shoulder and used the impact to rebound myself to the right. I pushed off with my right foot and sidesaddled my way across a desk set just to the right of the doorway. My butt and legs knocked phone, blotter, and a canister of pens flying, while my right hand came across in a sweeping motion and traced a line of fire across the room's far wall. It tore up plaster and blasted glass from picture frames all along the wall, except in two places.

In those places stood Imperial guards in full heavy combat armor.

I took a load of buckshot from the first one's assault shotgun square in the chest. It slammed me back up against the wall, then unceremoniously dumped me down into the secretary's chair behind the desk. I overbalanced the chair so it flipped over and toppled down across my legs. Breathless and stunned, I could do nothing, physically.

Yojimbo had earned the attention of the second guard, but the Mishima expatriate had executed an elegant assault maneuver that made mine look like the clumsy stumbling of a drunken idiot. As he came in, he executed a shoulder roll to the left that took him out of line with the door and below my line of fire. Coming up, he stitched fire across the belly of his guard while that man's first shot missed wide and high.

Yojimbo's burst of fire had driven his man more toward the center of the room, but the CAW2K's bullets were too small to core through the heavy composite armor. Klaus appeared in the doorway, crouching low, and thrust his shotgun at the guard. Light flashed through the room as he pulled the trigger. The slug caught the guard right above the navel and smashed an oblong hole through his armor.

The guard who had shot me swung his Mandible shotgun toward Klaus, but before he could pull the trigger, the wall above my head burst in toward him. Three slugs from Ash's assault rifle, being aimed in accordance with the visual data I fed the Attila, ripped through the wall and hit the man in the head and shoulders. One shattered his helmet and left the head beneath it in not much better shape.

I kicked myself free of the chair and pulled myself upright with the desk's help. I waved Yojimbo and Klaus toward the room's other door. Pam, Lane, and Fay entered the office and followed those two through to the back room while Ash took up a position in the back room.

I heard Pam's voice over the radio. «Ace, we have the prize.»

«Good,» I managed to cough out. «Base, what's with the maze?»

«We have the process stopped. All paths out are blocked west, south, and southwest.»

Gunfire sounded from outside, and some slugs ricocheted off Ash's chest. He returned fire down the west corridor. Leaving him there, I ran to the back room and felt a jolt run through me as Pam and Fay zipped Sandy into her body armor.

She was exactly what I thought she'd be, except conscious and laughing as in the start of the dream. Slender and slightly on the small side, with her hair cut shorter than I remembered it. Her face had lines at the corners of her eyes and mouth, yet sleeping they were barely noticeable. Those lines, and the few wisps of white in her hair, marked the harshness of her life since I'd known her, but the Sandy I knew would have toughed it out through anything.

Sandy? Where the hell did I come up with Sandy?

Yojimbo looked at me. "What is it?"

"Nothing significant. We're taking fire from the west corridor. You guys will go out the south corridor, then work your way back to the elevators along the southeast corridor. Ash and I will play rearguard so you can get Sandy out of here."

Pam's head came up. "Sandy?"

Lane looked at me as if I'd suddenly sprouted nepharite spikes. "This is Lorraine, isn't it? I mean, she's the one we rescued before."

"Yes, she is." I frowned at him. "Look, just get her ready to go. Ash and I will buy you some time."

Yojimbo shook his head. "We're not leaving without you."

"Don't worry, we're not suicidal." I winked at him and headed back out into the antechamber. "It's just that you're all a heretic or two ahead of me from the last time you rescued San ... her. I just want to even the score. See you topside."

SIXTEEN

While it was true that I didn't feel suicidal, I *did* feel like killing something. Rolling back into the antechamber, I looked over at Ash. "Grenade 'em. We're taking the west corridor."

My choice of the west corridor had been made based on the original plan for Larkspur. The west corridor contained the staff housing, so we assumed that whoever opposed us came from there. Some of them doubtlessly would head toward the elevators to cut them off—at least I would have sent some of my people there—but it was possible that if there were Wilson's Dark Legion compatriots, they might not think about cutting off our escape.

A muffled explosion sprayed bits of partitions into the start of the west corridor. Ash moved out first, and I followed in his wake, going low and taking to whatever cover there was. The wall partitions were not dense enough to stop bullets, but they did obstruct vision, so they offered some protection against fire. In addition to having them for cover, the movements of the walls did nothing to clear out the furnishings of the rooms the walls had once contained. Desks, chairs, and some permanent plumbing fixtures offered other chances to hide behind something.

The first line of walls—the ones Ash's grenade had chopped into fiberplast splinters—hid what was left of two bodies. Neither one wore body armor, and the clothes were of civilian cut. Being as how both had been near ground zero for a rifle-grenade blast, it was difficult to tell if their clothes had been dirty before or just soiled during the blast, but I was willing to bet these guys had been down here for as long as Sandy had been a captive.

«Base, concentrate on clearing the south corridor. Double-A is rolling up west. The others have the prize. Get them clear.»

«As planned. Opposition?»

«Strictly amateur west, so far.»

«Roger. Will inform of progress.»

«Thanks.»

The maze in the west corridor had me feeling a bit claustrophobic. The ceilings were just over three meters high, and the walls packed things in close. Ash caught fire down a long, narrow corridor that was clogged with desk chairs. The video-feed I got from him showed a hand firing down along the wall. Despite the fact that his limbs had independent chip assemblies that functioned like dinosaur auxiliary brains, without visual sensors, they were no better at shooting than the sniper down the hall.

He kept shooting high to avoid the desks, so with a running start I slid myself across the corridor's narrow mouth and took up a position opposite Ash. I don't think the sniper saw me go. The shooter ripped off a clip of ammo at Ash—allowing his Interceptor SMG to recoil up and chip the concrete ceiling—then withdrew his arm to reload.

As he did that, I popped up and brought the CAW2K to bear. Without waiting for him to show himself again, I triggered a long burst at the corner behind which he hid. I tooled the muzzle around to give myself a nice little figure-eight pattern, but by the time I'd gotten to four, the heretic twisted and danced out into the corridor. His limp body cartwheeled back into the wall, then collapsed in the middle of the intersection.

Ash and I immediately moved forward. He got a bit in front of me as I slowed. Something didn't feel right to me. Two guards in heavy armor had been placed in the front room of the suite where they had housed Sandy, but only three lightly armed and unarmored folks had opposed us so far. That made sense if the light opposition were the first people to respond and their goal was to buy time for others to come up.

I switched vision over to infrared and saw heat signatures moving down both corridors that ran parallel to the one we advanced along. Had we been more cautious in our approach to eliminating the man holding the corridor, these other troops would have come around behind us.

«Deuce, Ace here. You could have some imps in your six o'clock. We'll try to waylay them.»

«Thanks, Ace. Keys is moving things. I'll have him cut pursuit off.»

"Ash, move it. We've got heretics east and west of us." I pointed him off toward the west. About ten meters down a corridor headed north, and five more beyond that one headed south. That southern corridor was our goal, since the larger of the two parties I'd heat-sensed moving past us went down that way. "Speed is of the essence."

Ash started to run, but as he entered the intersection with the northern corridor, he flew up into the air. A piercing whine filled the whole level as the Attila unit did a mechanical imitation of the sniper who lay behind me in a pool of blood. Bits and pieces of Ash clouded the air with metal. One second he was tattered, but whole and functional. In the next, as I hit the floor, his body had evaporated.

His skull bounced back and landed in my hands. One half of his face was gone, and his braincase showed serious denting. His computing core shot me a visual image of two cylinders hanging down from the ceiling about twenty-five meters on into the corridor. Each sprouted the muzzle of a Gatling cannon. His data packet included their designation—HMG MK. XIXB Chargers—which made them capable of filling the air with almost one hundred of their 16.7mm projectiles per second. The little sensor balls mounted in front of the foregrip provided the guns with the ability to target radio-frequency modulations. Radio calls and noncomputer equipment operated on frequencies that didn't trigger the Chargers, but Ash had been one big target when he stepped into death alley.

«Base, Ace here. Any security stuff available on the west corridor?»

«Keys is trying now. He says he's picking up overripe men through the smoke detectors. No telling the number.»

«Going away or coming toward me?»

«Waiting. South corridor is sealed, so everyone will have to come back in your direction.»

«Ask Keys about cracking codes on cannon canisters in this wing.»

«Say again?»

«Ceiling mounted Charger canisters. RF mod reactions. Cease will trip them.»

«So will you and Ash.»

«He has. I don't plan to if I can avoid it.»

«Given Imperial's attitude, we should have anticipated these things. Keys has canister codes. Says the place is covered with them. They're new and codes will be tough.»

«Roger. Clear south and southeast first.»

«Keys has people coming in your direction.»

«East or west of me?»

«Both.»

«Shit. I need time.»

«He'll shift walls.»

«Roger. Get him clearing the way for the prize. That is paramount.»

«Base out.»

The heretics coming after me knew from the whine where at least parts of someone or something were. They thought they would have a limited area to sweep to find any intruders because no one or nothing would get past the Gatling cannons. As long as they swept the area south of the cannons, they'd have their prey.

In thinking that, they missed one important fact about the cannons themselves. The heretics hadn't been shot by them when they passed down the corridor. The reason for that was because the cannons had been specifically designed for use against agents of Imperial's mortal corporate enemy: Cybertronic. The RF targeting system, while sophisticated and deadly, was useless against anyone who didn't have a computer on them.

Depressing a button in the inside of Ash's eye socket, I popped the top of his head open and withdrew the plum-sized core that was everything Ash was, except for being big and strong. It was virtually indestructible and probably a good deal more immortal than the soul the Brotherhood like to prattle on about. I brought the core's single little IR sensor up to my right eyeball, and it read a shutdown code from my computer and turned itself off. Until

I manipulated some buttons on the back of the egg-shaped core, Ash would sleep like a dead man.

Which is exactly how I would sleep if I couldn't get past the cannons. I tucked Ash's core away in my left gauntlet and let the CAW2K hang across my back on its sling. Lying flat on my belly, with my head pointing toward Ash's smoking wreckage, I took a deep breath. Then I ordered my computer to turn itself off.

It refused. It told me that deactivating it during a combat situation was suicidal.

I overrode its refusal.

Again it refused, noting my mobility would be cut to almost nothing if I shut it off.

I noted I'd be cut to nothing if I didn't shut it off.

This time the override took. The computer shut itself down. The light in my eyes went out. My legs went numb and then dead. The last function the computer performed was to reset three buttons that clicked up beneath the flesh behind my right ear. I could feel them pressing against my flesh, and they began to itch.

Even half-asleep I would have swiped at them with my hand and, quite likely, depressed them. That was the computer's fail-safe. If it ever went down, the buttons would pop up, and what little was left of my brain would make me bat them down again. It was a foolproof system, but one that would get me killed if I gave in to it.

Of course, had my brain still contained a lot of the left brain tissue that allows me cold and logical thinking, I would have been able to restrain myself. It did not. The computer served that function for me, so what little thinking tissue I had left had long since forgotten how to work on its own. While the drugs Cybertronic had given me allowed me to think fast, the rational part of my brain could do very little thinking at all.

I gave it one job. That was to focus on getting me to the far end of the corridor and past the cannons.

The part of my brain that did work started to work overtime. Freed from the overwatch of my silicon brain, the emotional side of me rejoiced. It flooded all sorts of wonderful emotions through me. I wanted to laugh. I wanted to cry. I mourned the loss of my legs yet celebrated the return of my humanity. I was whole again, even though I was broken, and that was good because dying as part machine was no way to die at all.

My few thinking brain cells seized on that and used it. They funneled my fear of death down into a beautiful neon fiber that glowed with the vitality of life. Twisting it into a knot, they then split the line and stretched it out until they could plug it back into two other parts of my brain.

For one connection point they shot past the upper brain and got straight down into my medulla oblongata. They shot past what my brain had been as a man and went straight for things that had been hardwired into my neural network before I was born. They went back to a time before computers. They went back before machines and before the invention of the species that created machines. They stabbed that neon lightning bolt into cells that knew the fear of pursuit and knew how to react to it. They triggered the flight response at the core of every living thing, and that sent me scrambling on my belly down the corridor toward the dormant cannons.

The other sizzling neon thread whipped back into my right brain. It wove itself around the original fear fireball that gave it life, than searched out the emotions that fear had driven into the shadows. The neon point narrowed to a needle, then threaded together courage and hope. Turning back on itself, it sliced a small piece of urgency from the emotional blanket enfolding fear and sewed that into the mix.

Five meters and then ten. I clawed at the ground with my hands and pulled myself along. My shoulders began to ache, and every second I knew someone or something was going to appear behind me and unload every weapon in the world into me. They would start with my feet, with my toes, and little by slowly grind every bit of me into protoplasmic paste. And I would never it know it until they got above my waist. The pain would overwhelm me, and I would die screaming in untold agonies.

Snarling as the neon found defiance and stitched it into my emotional engine, I slid myself over toward the juncture of wall and floor. My right hand found purchase on the wall easier, and I started making greater progress. The voices I heard behind me—I could not make sense of their words because my thinking brain was otherwise engaged—pulsed new urgency through me. The fingers of my right hand actually stabbed into the plasterboard partitions and gave me a better grip.

Fifteen meters in and I picked up my pace. I could taste freedom from fear as I neared the things that had destroyed Ash. They were to be feared, but not at the moment. They were quiet, though smoke drifted up from their muzzles, and the scent of cordite slicked the back of my throat.

The cordite almost doomed me. There in that corridor it was so overpowering that it made fear swell up to gargantuan proportions. All the fear I had ever felt in any firefight ever poured into my fear bucket and geysered on out. Fear started to erode me and everything I was. Fear became my reality. Anything I would do would be wrong—that I knew. Each attempt at a decision ran into a wall of fear, and I stopped.

I lay there on my stomach in the corridor beached and motionless like a dying fish. With cannons ahead of me and voices growing in volume behind me, my fear paralyzed me. I could not go forward, nor could I go back. All I could do was fear. I would lay there in fear until I died.

And then, as the skeleton told me, all I would have was my fear.

Fear of having nothing but fear jolted life back into my arms. A decision might move me into greater fear, but it would also move me away from other things I feared. I had a purpose, and that was to know something other than fear. If I moved in one direction, even if I were hurtling into some terrible and terrifying fear-nova, at least part of me would exist in the safe haven of my shadow. One part of me would know less fear, and that was enough to push me on farther.

Tile by tile on the floor, the distance between me and the cannons, dropped away. Gnashing my teeth, I pulled myself past the twenty-meter mark and onward and onward. Three meters, then two, then mere centimeters separated me from the oasis in the middle of the corridor of death. At my goal I laughed aloud and flipped myself over onto my back. Staring up at the bases of the canisters, I knew I had reached the halfway point and I was safe.

Then I saw movement at the end of the corridor I had quitted. My right hand slapped the side of my helmet, and my computer immediately came back up. Above me the Charger barrels began to spin, but because they could not locate a target in their firing arcs, they did not begin shooting. Their motion did attract the attention of the three individuals in heavy armor at the far end of the corridor, and one of them beckoned unseen companions into combat.

Heavily armored though they might have been, they were not combat trained. I burned a clip from the CAW2K and scattered them. The submachine gun didn't have enough power to burn through their armor, but they ran for cover as if I were using the Chargers on them.

«Base, this is Ace. Status.»

«Where have you been, Ace? Prize is at the elevators. You can run.»

«Not at the moment.»

«You better. Keys has people south of you and more working around to the north. Won't be able to help you much longer.»

«Get out. As we planned.»

«Wilco, Ace.»

«Base?»

«Yes?»

«Get Andy some NyxStyx™ from me and say goodbye to Carl.»

«If you don't first. Gotta go.»

Another burst from the CAW2K kept the heretics back until one of them stepped out into the corridor and trained an assault rifle on me. I fired at him, but he didn't shoot at me. He turned back toward his fellows and said something to them, then turned back at me and gestured at me to get my hands up.

I dropped the CAW2K as more of the heretics filled the corridor. They started forward, then stopped, and hung back as something else entered the corridor behind them. Even the leader hugged a piece of wall as the huge creature shouldered his way past. Floor tiles popped beneath its steely claws. It carried a Dragonfire Gatling cannon with the ease Ash had managed the AR3000. In fact, with its bulging muscles and burning red eyes, the creature looked as if it might have been the Dark Legion's answer to Attila units like Ash.

Or Attila units might have been created to deal with things like this.

The leader of the heretics called out to me from behind the thing slowly stalking down the corridor. "You are wise, infidel, to surrender, for you could never stand against the might of a Razide." To the creature in front of him, he added, "Take him alive. We may trade him for the woman, if we cannot find her."

The neckless Razide turned back to nod at the human, and that gave me a chance to act. I poured Ash's memory core into the palm of my right hand, hit his reset buttons, and sidearmed his consciousness down the corridor. It hit once, slid a bit, then rebounded off the wall and smacked the Razide right where his head met his shoulders.

Supplied with a computer-active target, albeit a small one, the Chargers blazed into action. The cannons' heavy shells beat the Razide's bullet-shaped head into a gray-green mist. That might have instantly killed the creature, but it did not stop it. The Razide turned back toward the cannons and stumbled forward. Its long arms kept it upright, and some of the shells actually ricocheted off parts of the creature that were not organic in origin.

Fortunately for me, the same shots that decapitated the Razide punched Ash's core farther down the corridor. Its irregular shape, and the fact that it kept bouncing off various heretics, forced the Charger cannons to spray their streams of fire back and forth along the corridor. The storm of 16.7mm cannon shells dismembered the Razide. Only because of his size were any recognizable pieces left behind. The same could not be said of the heretics who took fire once he stopped shielding them.

I scooped my CAW2K up and fired at both Chargers. The whirling barrels were made of metal and had grown quite hot with the friction and fire from their shooting. My submachine gun's bullets, while tiny, were able to dent hot barrels enough to warp them. That, in turn, caused the gun's projectiles to explode in the barrels, and in short order the guns tore themselves apart.

I did a quick radio check for Beach or the others, but all I got was static. Running back down the corridor I had so recently traversed on my stomach, I found Ash's core, wiped the blood off, and tucked it into the pocket of my trousers. I patted it gently, then slapped a fresh clip into my gun.

"It's just you and me, Ash. The others did the hard part." I moved off toward the east, and hoped I'd see the enemy before they saw me.

SEVENTEEN

As it turned out, I *did* see them before they saw me, but that didn't materially help my situation. There were a lot *more* of them than there were of me. Being small and relatively quiet, I was able to work my way on through the maze before they began searching for me in any sort of logical pattern. When they did start a formal search, they had people positioned to cut off all escape, so I retreated to a custodial closet and waited.

In many ways my situation was academic. My CAW2K, for which I had two full clips left, really was too light to pop through their heavy armor. Apparently Yojimbo and his crew had done enough damage to Dark Legion forces here on Luna that they got very serious about arming and armoring themselves. While they had little training, even an idiot could hold his finger down on a trigger and with a dozen or so of them out there, the law of averages said that I'd lose to a bullet or two before the night was out.

If I'd had Fay's explosives, I might have been able to do something that would deal with more of the enemy all at once. A nice little ball of Semtek studded with the nails and screws on the shelf beside the door would have worked nicely against the heretics. Unfortunately for me I had no Semtek, and even using the powder from all the shells I had for my guns would only produce a minor bang.

I looked around and shook my head. Having a two-meter-deep, meter-and-a-half-wide, and three-meter-tall

janitor's closet for my mausoleum just didn't sit well.
While it was true that I had an eternity's worth of polish
for my casket, and enough wax and other things to keep
the whole vault spic and span, I'd never been much for
housework, and I doubted that after being dead I'd take to
it much. I knew that to have been true from the first time
around—after all I left Miss Wickersham to clean up my
apartment after the second fugue.

Something clicked in the back of my head, and I dug
for Ash's core. Holding the IR sensor up to my eye, I in-
terrogated the unit about the chemistry involved in turning common household cleaning agents into lethal
weapons. Ash cheerfully started downloading material
into my computer, and under his able tutelage I managed
to construct all sorts of fun stuff from Mishima's Finest
Hogosha Furniture Polish, Capitol's Drainex, and Capitol's Mr. Keen™ Cleaning and Solvent Solution.

I knew I was working with limited time because someone among the heretics would figure out that the Chargers
had been shooting at something giving off RF mods.
Since the cannons had shot up some heretics, someone
was bound to conclude that whatever the guns had been
shooting at had gotten *behind* the heretics. The presence
of my bloody footprints heading away from the scene
would let them know the target was still ambulatory. That
meant someone would find an RF mod scanner and track
me.

I put together the most explosive mixtures possible and
sealed them tightly in aluminum floor wax canisters. I
had enough to fill three of them, and all three stood upright in a galvanized tin bucket. Around them I packed a
number of mop heads, and I sprinkled nails and screws
liberally through their threads. I soaked the mop tops
down with more flammable liquids, tied the bucket's handle to a regular mop, and got everything in position for
my wait.

My attack definitely had to be a counterpunch.

Of course, the only problem with a counterpunch is
that you have to be hit first before you can throw it.

The fact that my opposition was not made up of professionals saved me. From what they said in the corridor
outside my little stronghold, they did have an RF mod

scanner. "We know you're in there. Come out now with your hands up, or else."

"This is your *last chance!*"

It was my *only* chance. I remained silent.

They opened fire. Every single one of them put as much fire through the door to the closet as his gun would kick out. The fiberplast door exploded into dust thick enough to walk on. The bullets that had torn it apart continued unabated and gnawed their way through the closet's back plasterboard wall and ricocheted through the conference room behind it.

The firing became more sporadic as heretics paused and reloaded, then burned second and third clips. Finally someone shouted at them to stop firing. With only two clips to my name, I found their profligate expenditure of bullets rather offensive, but I was also pleased that they thought me deadly enough to warrant such overwhelming firepower.

"Reload, reload."

"I don't see nothing."

"After all that shooting, there isn't going to be anything to see."

"Serve him right for what he did to Epsilon Team."

"Let's check it out."

"Careful."

"Of what? He'd have to be invulnerable to have survived that."

Invulnerable, or aware of a little flaw in the way people tend to think. Seldom do people look up above eye level. I don't know why, I just know it must be true because when being trained as an agent for Cybertronic I was taught to break that habit. Without training, I felt certain the heretics would still have it. Actually I had to hope they still had it, which is why I climbed up and wedged myself in the upper corner of the closet, above the door.

The heretics, imagining me cowering in the back corner of the room, had filled the closet with bullets from the two meter height of the door down. Only one or two had let their guns get away from them, but those shots missed me by at least three centimeters, so I knew I'd chosen right.

They'd given it their best shot.

Now I got to counterpunch.

I brought my right hand forward, and it pulled the mop and bucket from the top closet shelf. It swung down perfectly, despite being an awkward and unusual-looking pendulum. When I felt the mop handle hit the top of the door, I let it go and spin out in the corridor. Without waiting to hear their reactions to the bucket and stick flying through their midst, I dropped from the ceiling and filled my right hand with the Punisher.

My gun came up as all of them turned to watch the flying bomb. One of two had begun to swing their guns in line with the bucket, but they didn't get a shot off before my finger twitched on the trigger. In fact, the closest one of them got to shooting it was getting a burst off into a man across the way from him as my slug hit the bucket and exploded the wax canisters.

The makeshift bomb's detonation was crude, and its blast radius was small, but the fiery explosion served its purpose well. Heretics reeled away with pieces of burning mop strung over them like incendiary spaghetti. The nails and screws that didn't pierce armor got under foot and acted like ball bearings to trip up the scattering heretics. Their screams and blind flailing about filled the corridor with chaos.

Moving in and among them, I stuffed my Punisher into armpits or other chinks in their heavy armor and dispatched the heretics who could still do me harm. A shot up under a chin here or into the hip joint there, and I'd disabled the last of the ambulatory heretics. From one of them I appropriated an ammo belt with reloads for my CAW2K and found nestled among the shells a grenade. Running up the horridor to the north, I tossed the grenade back behind me and trusted in it to discourage pursuit.

Farther along the corridor I came to the area we had identified as the staff quarters and likely housing for the heretics. Deciding they'd not expect me to trap myself in their den, I cut into it. Even though it got me no closer to the elevators, I had to hope I might be able to crack whatever they had for an armory and possibly appropriate better armor. In fact, if I were able to disguise myself as one of them, I might be able to get clear much more easily.

A cursory search of their quarters confirmed that the

heretics had been stationed here. The suite's large common room had been ringed with double bunks. Two of the rooms off the common area had their doors open and appeared at a glance to have been housing for one of their commanders and the Razide. I kicked a third door open and found the armory. It had only bits and pieces of armor, but I did find an Imperial Assailant Sniper rifle. With the stock closed it wasn't that much longer than my CAW2K, so I took it and some clips because it would punch through even the heaviest armor.

Moving past the kitchenette, I approached the last door off the common room. It had two locks, both of which were new, so I knew something special had to reside behind it. Given the size of the complex and the fact that we hadn't seen enough folks going in and out to even guess at a garrison force of two dozen, I wondered if it didn't lead to some secret passage up to ground level of Furnerius Cinq.

Using my Punisher lock pick, I had the door open in short order. A musky, cold breeze blew out of the dark room beyond the doorway. Shifting over to IR and UV vision didn't get me anything—the flat-matte black of the interior seemed to greedily suck up all electromagnetic radiation. The only light I got came through the doorway, and despite the fact that leaving it open would leave an obvious clue to where I had gone, I didn't want to close it.

This room had been shaped out of the lunar bedrock. I normally would have said *carved* from the Moon's cold flesh, but I saw no evidence of tool scars or drill marks on the tenebrous stone surfaces. Part of me wanted to think acid had been used to etch the odd shapes and imposing forms from the stone, but another part of me was afraid that this place had been here since the time it was formed out of molten lunar rock.

The surface architecture of Luna itself is industrial gothic. It towers over the people, with its sheer mass giving it legitimacy. The clean lines mark mechanical precision, and the shapes celebrate the incredible array of tools man has created in conquering his universe. The towers even rise to heights that trap the dirty brown ball that is Earth as it courses through the sky, making it a jewel in the crown that marks the apex of man's achievement—the reshaping of his home world into something he can no longer inhabit.

This room's architecture was different. It struck me as funeral gothic because the shapes loomed and were oppressive, but the symbolism had been taken from death and horrors worse than death. Mind-twisting creatures and tortured beings knitted their limbs and bodies together in double-helix arches. Stalactite corpses hung down from overhead, their feet visible in the light but their bloated faces nothing more than swollen shadows in the vaults. The obsidian floor glistened like black ice, and if I looked at it very long, I saw faces of people frozen beneath it. Their eyes bugged out and cheeks bulged as they fought for air in the stone void beneath my feet.

I didn't know what the place was, but I found it evil and, perversely, comforting. I tried to tell myself I took comfort in it because I knew none of the heretics would willingly tread into this unholy desecratorium, but I knew that was not it. Part of me was familiar with this place.

Part of me had come home again.

I caught movement in the corner of my eye, and I turned toward it as I brought the Assailant up. I stared at my own image in a black mirror. A snarl stole the humanity of my expression, but even as my face softened into a smile, I saw the fierce mask on my reflection stay the same.

I approached the mirror and saw new images of me, with my face becoming more puzzled and then horrified. Each new image dwarfed and engulfed the old ones, and yet the old images remained there faintly. They hovered like a legion of revenants, waiting to rend the new image.

The mirror did not report the new image accurately. Though I stood with my nose so close to the glass that my breath left fog on it, the image it showed was two inches taller than me. I saw a man who looked like me, though he stood taller and wore his hair in one of the shaved-side cuts popular among Capitol's elite. His face resembled mine, yet showed an innocence I had never even dreamed of possessing. In his eyes I saw myself and felt curiosity running in tandem with anger.

"Why anger?" I asked him.

"Because now you have destroyed us both."

Suddenly his pink flesh swelled up and burst like a flesh balloon. In its place, with bits of gore splattered over it, a creature grew up to tower over me. His robes were a riot of color and images, all clashing and shifting with the only discernible pattern being that which would do maximum violence to the eyes. Skinny arms extended beyond the sleeves and ended in sensuously slender hands and fingers. The claws on each finger curved inward, delicately, and glistened with a venom that I knew to be distilled delirium.

Looking up, I saw his head as he looked down at me. Fat white corpse worms moved in and out through his skull. A worm displaced an eye and crawled across his pale brow to burrow in through the creature's ear, yet the creature seemed to take no notice. Instead of striking at the offending worm, the creature's hands played with the barbed chain that girded its waist and plucked at imagined imperfections in its garment.

The creature opened its mouth, and a worm functioned as its tongue. "We are Muawijhe, He who is known as the Lord of Visions. We have a bond."

I tried to move back, to move away, but I could not. "No, I have no bond with you."

"Oh, you do Quentin Kell, a very strong bond." Muawijhe's eyes half closed, as if he regretted something. "It was a useful bond, but no more."

The worm that was his tongue lunged forward and passed through the mirror as if passing through the flesh of a soap bubble. The glass clung to it, wreathing it in a writhing corona of light reflected from Muawijhe's robe. "A useful bond, but one we shall now sever."

I felt the worm's cold kiss on my brow, then the universe imploded and left me alone with all the fear I had ever known in both of my lifetimes.

EIGHTEEN

```
RUNLOG ON

  SYSTEM CHECK IS OK
    INIT EVASION.NAV
    INIT EVALUATION.NAV
      CURRLOC_VAL= 60E,36S,5-.3Z
      TARGLOC_VAL= 04W,40S,3.2Z
    INIT UP
      INTERRUPT UP
        EXIT_VAL = 0
    INIT SURVEY.EXT
      EXIT_VAL = .1
      INIT EVALUATION.TGT
        THREAT_ASSESS LEVEL = 0
        STRUCT_INTEGRITY LEVEL = 3
      INIT EVALUATION.WPN
      INIT CAW2K.ONE
      CONT EVALUATION.TGT
        THREAT_ASSESS LEVEL = 0
        STRUCT_INTEGRITY LEVEL = 0
        EXIT_VAL = 1
      CONT UP
        CURRLOC_VAL= 60E,36S,5-.2Z
      CONT UP
        CURRLOC_VAL= 60E,36S,5-.1Z
      CONT UP
        CURRLOC_VAL= 60E,36S,5Z
      CONT EVALUATION.NAV
```

```
INTERRUPT EVALUATION.NAV
  INIT EVALUATION.TGT
    THREAT_ASSESS LEVEL TGT.1 = 4
    THREAT_ASSESS LEVEL TGT.2 = 2
    THREAT_ASSESS LEVEL TGT.3 = 3
    THREAT_ASSESS LEVEL TGT.4 = 2
      PRIME_TGT=1
      INIT CAW2K.MLT
      CONT EVALUATION.TGT
        THREAT_ASSESS LEVEL TGT.1 = 0
        THREAT_ASSESS LEVEL TGT.2 = 3
        THREAT_ASSESS LEVEL TGT.3 = 4
        THREAT_ASSESS LEVEL TGT.4 = 2
          PRIME_TGT=3
          CONT CAW2K.MLT
            INIT CAW2K.RLD
            INIT EVASION.CBT
            CONT EVALUATION.TGT
              THREAT_ASSESS LEVEL TGT.2 = 4
              THREAT_ASSESS LEVEL TGT.3 = 0
              THREAT_ASSESS LEVEL TGT.4 = 1
                PRIME_TGT=2
                CONT CAW2K.MLT
                CONT EVALUATION.CBT
                  THREAT_ASSESS LEVEL = 0
CONT EVALUATION.NAV
  CURRLOC_VAL= 60E,36S,5Z
  CONT UP
  INIT SOUTH
  CONT SOUTH
    CURRLOC_VAL=60E,40S,4Z
  INIT WEST
  CONT UP
INTERRUPT EVALUATION.NAV
  INIT EVALUATION.TGT
    THREAT_ASSESS LEVEL TGT.1 = 1
    THREAT_ASSESS LEVEL TGT.2 = 1
    THREAT_ASSESS LEVEL TGT.3 = 1
    THREAT_ASSESS LEVEL TGT.4 = 2
    THREAT_ASSESS LEVEL TGT.5 = 1
    THREAT_ASSESS LEVEL TGT.6 = 1
    THREAT_ASSESS LEVEL TGT.7 = 1
```

```
      THREAT_ASSESS LEVEL TGT.8 = 1
   INIT DISPLAY.WPN
   CONT EVALUATION.TGT
      THREAT_ASSESS LEVEL TGT.1 = 0
      THREAT_ASSESS LEVEL TGT.2 = 0
      THREAT_ASSESS LEVEL TGT.3 = 0
      THREAT_ASSESS LEVEL TGT.4 = 0
      THREAT_ASSESS LEVEL TGT.5 = 0
      THREAT_ASSESS LEVEL TGT.6 = 0
      THREAT_ASSESS LEVEL TGT.7 = 0
      THREAT_ASSESS LEVEL TGT.8 = 0
CONT EVALUATION. NAV
   CURRLOC_VAL=45E,40S,3Z
   CONT WEST
   CONT WEST
      INIT HAIL_TAXI.NAV
      INIT DIRECTIONS.TLK
      INIT COURTESY.TLK
      INIT SMALL.TLK
      CONT SMALL.TLK
         SUB ORONTIUS_OREOLES.TLK
      CONT SMALL.TLK
         SUB PROFANITY.TLK
      INIT GRATUITY.CLC
         CONT SMALL.TLK
            SUB PROFANITY.TLK
CONT EVALUATION.NAV
   CURRLOC_VAL=04W,40S,3Z
   CONT UP
   CONT UP
      INIT ENTRE.ACT
CONT EVALUATION.NAV
   SUB EVAL_HOME.NAV
      HOME_MATCH_VAL=32
END EVALUATION.NAV
END EVASION.NAV
INIT DISTRESS.MSG
RUNLOG OFF
```

BOOK II

The reports of my death are greatly exaggerated.
—MARK TWAIN

NINETEEN

I awoke in a bed I did not recognize. I awoke with my left arm draped around the shoulders of a naked woman I did not recognize. I even awoke in a body I didn't recognize.

I decided it had to be a Monday.

Of the three immediate problems, the body bothered me the most. The bed, while a little like a prison with the brass bars at head and foot, was comfortable. Rex had used enough of my esthetic sense to avoid black sheets and silk sheets or combinations thereof, so I avoided the momentary shock of thinking I'd awakened in some corporate joy house.

The woman was the least of my problems, though her left arm did lay somewhat possessively across my bare chest. Her blond hair smelled faintly of some synthetic flower fragrance, and she murmured out a kittenish purr as I tried to ease her head from my shoulder and onto the other pillow. Her long legs had ensnared my left leg, so extricating myself was not going to be simple. Despite her slender physique, generating the leverage needed to move her gently was not going to be easy.

Ms. Wickersham—Madeline I seemed to recall from Rex's fantasy life—snuggled back closer to me, shutting the door on my escape. She trapped me within her arms and within the body Cybertronic had given Rex. Despite her loveliness and the eroticism inherent in our situation, I wanted to crawl out of my skin and run screaming through the night.

That image struck me as funny, but only because I had waited eighteen months to get back *into* my body. I'd actually always been in it, but it had taken that long for me to figure out how to get back in control of it. By the time I had worked my way through the maze of synapses and neural-interface circuits, Rex's personality had grown strong enough to oppose me and fight me for control. It was a battle he would lose, eventually, but a hard-fought battle nonetheless. I would have enjoyed winning, but I accepted taking over after he retired from the field of combat.

I knew I shouldn't be upset with my body. Getting it back after a year and a half wasn't like picking up a suit from the cleaners. I held my right hand out and stretched, noticing that my hand was just that much closer to my face than it had been before. *Perhaps it* is *like getting a suit back from the cleaners—things do shrink.*

Even though I was aware that my hand *looked* wrong to me, it did not *feel* wrong, and that miracle I owed to Rex's hard work during rehabilitation. He had been determined to take command of the shell in which he found himself. Of course, I'd not left it in such poor shape that his job was impossible, but the speed at which he recovered was remarkable.

I suddenly realized that I had to stop thinking of Rex as a separate individual because everything he had done had been built upon a foundation I had supplied him. What I was now was a synthesis of what I had been and what Rex had done in creating himself. Even the computer had a share of what we were—without it, we would have died.

It was not a question of which one of us had taken over the body, but really more one of a merger between rival firms. As the current chairperson of the board—elected to that position because of my long association with the firm—I directed operations. It was a post I had held before and, aside from one unfortunate circumstance, I had been quite successful in it.

I decided, lying there in bed in Ms. Wickersham's embrace, that my first order of business was not to realize the explicit fantasies of the old CEO. Instead I chose to face the thing he would not. I chose to try and pierce the

veil surrounding the circumstances of my death. I recalled
Beach saying this was not something Cybertronic encour-
aged in new chasseurs, but I was hardly new, and I already had access to the information they would have
given Rex had he but asked.

Before death I had been Quentin Kell—of the Capitol
Kells. Second son of Archibald Kell, a minor but
powerful-in-his-own-way executive within the Capitol
corporate structure. My father had seen very early on that
the taste in consumer items changes and *had* to change
for a corporation to profit. Managers who championed
new products that succeeded could rocket to the top of
the corporate structure, but if the fickle public turned on
them, or their new ideas did not match their old ideas,
those managers tumbled from their lofty seats. The corporate world was controlled chaos, and when you lost your
grip on it, you were consumed, digested, and eliminated.

My father realized that in that paradigm he had isolated
a bit of firmament in the corporate universe. No matter
what products the corporations put out for a profit, they
always put another product out and never profited from it.
Corporate waste—rubbish, garbage, refuse—was an open
wound that bled Cardinal's crowns for every company.
He resolved to staunch the wound as much as possible.
While moving into waste resource management was not a
glamorous route to power, everyone needed my father, so
they accepted him and respected him.

My older brother's first coup in corporate life came in
the form of an idea that he suggested to my father. Nicholas asked him if information leaks were not really just a
subset of waste management. Bad information, like useless garbage, could be eliminated, and good information,
like wastes that formed the raw material for other enter-
prises, had to be retained. It struck my brother that corporate security—dirty work, after all—should fall into my
father's corporate fiefdom.

With Nicholas's help, my father organized a power
play that gave him control of Capitol's internal security.
My father offered Nicholas control of Security, but the
offer was refused. Instead my brother convinced my father to create a special Internal Security Investigation

Unit that was supposed to initiate counterespionage and disinformation efforts against the other corporations.

Other corporations and the Brotherhood.

The corporate gods in their Olympian penthouse suites decided this plan was good, and it was implemented. Nicholas hired specialists to train his agents in anything and everything they would need to complete their missions. His goal was to create agents who were to covert operations what the Cartel's DoomTroopers were to military actions. His trainers were uncompromising and demanding, but those who graduated from their program were an amalgam of all their skills, making them lethal chameleons who could slip into any setting, establish themselves, and begin their missions immediately.

I know because I was the first graduate.

My first couple of missions involved getting close to Imperial and Bauhaus agents in Capitol satellite facilities. I learned what they knew and passed on to them enough information that their controllers decided they were very reliable. Once that had been done, I gave them a story that made their corporate masters buy heavily in the stock of worthless subsidiaries. Capitol sold what the others were buying and made enough in profits to fund my brother's operations through his next two Five-Year Plans.

Those operations were just warm-ups because Nicholas and I both wanted to crack the Brotherhood. That order, we agreed, had exerted influence well beyond its worth. Unfortunately the Brotherhood had enough supporters in key positions that defying it was impossible. If one of the Brotherhood's corporate toadies saw another executive as a threat, the Brotherhood would find a way to discredit the threat, and their man would gain in prestige and power.

The problem with this purge-and-promote system was that no one was certain that what the Brotherhood sought to eradicate even existed. We had all heard of the Dark Legion, but only in the way that people speak of organized crime. We accepted it existed, but no one could point a finger at it and say "There it is." Having shared a mind with an Apostle and having watched a Razide in action, I now had a new yardstick against which to measure rumors of the Dark Legion, but back before my death I did not.

Nicholas and I staged some very visible and violent arguments. I started drinking, and eventually people from the Brotherhood approached me. They offered me their strength and solace. Though I never found myself enmeshed with any of them as I was with Miss Wickersham, I had no doubt that the Brotherhood's acolytes would have been willing to go that far and farther to bring me into the fold.

I played hard to get, and they persisted. I let them wear me down and settle me down. I returned to my status as a model employee at Capitol. People sympathetic to the Brotherhood within Capitol brought me into their social circles. Once they decided I passed muster, the Brotherhood even approached me about joining the order on a permanent basis. I demurred, but they insisted, and I let them put me through a battery of tests.

The results must have been positive because my Brotherhood contacts insisted I would be of greater service to humanity if I joined the Brotherhood. Again I hesitated and put them off. My joining the Brotherhood as more than a lay member went further than my brother or I had intended, and I was not going to take that step without consulting him.

We met and decided I would refuse. I remember feeling relief as we both agreed that things had been too successful. We would settle for the partial picture of Brotherhood influence in Capitol and make sure I didn't get sucked in too far. We shook hands, and I left him in the apartment suite he shared with his wife Anastasia and their children Garrett and Laura.

I got nothing more.

I backed up and dealt with each discrete memory as if they were individual beads in a rosary. The offer. The tests. The insistence on my joining. My brother. The handshake.

Nothing.

I smashed my balled fist down on the bed and was surprised by the tearing sound of the sheets and mattress cover. *That shift in leverage really did do the job. I wonder . . .*

I twisted onto my left hip and placed my left hand on Ms. Wickersham's spine. I left her head resting on my left forearm, then snaked my right hand beneath her ribs at her right breast and gently lifted her torso. It worked better than I had imagined it would. Slipping my left leg from between her thighs, I pulled the coverlet up to her neck, stroked her cheek, and stepped out of bed.

I got a good look at myself in the full-length mirror on the closet door. I appeared smaller than I remembered and, because of it, my torso looked stockier. My hair was longer than I liked, especially on the sides, and the hollows around my eyes gave me a haunted look—one I deserved after what I had gone through. Recalling the last time I'd looked in a mirror sent a shiver through me. I gave the looking glass a wide berth as I headed for the bathroom.

The tiles felt cold beneath my bare feet, but not as cold as the marble that had paved my bathroom at home. It struck me that the bathroom in my home would have been large enough to contain the back half of this apartment, and the furnishings were far more elegant than anything this apartment would ever house. That realization did not spark in me the horror it might have in my peers at Capitol. While I would have preferred marble to tile, this apartment had everything I needed to live contently. Had I a choice, I could have lived nicely in a place as small as this.

Being Archibald Kell's son did not give me such a choice. As offspring of a corporate officer and significant stockholder, modest accommodations could not be mine. If I lived below my family's means, on a level in a tower below our due, people would start talking about how my father's grip on power was slipping. Were I to date outside my proper social circle, people would reason that other corporate officers saw no value in linking my family with their own.

Corporate status, though it was the source of all benefits, did demand a price. Enduring creature comforts for the sake of keeping up appearances is hardly penance. The very real restrictions on who one could see socially, on the other hand, chafed and even threatened to smother people. Those who could live with it, like me, did so. Those who could not revolted.

Like Lucifer in his heavenly rebellion, those who did not want to be part of Capitol were cast out, and never was their name to be spoken again.

A shiver shook me, so I stepped into the shower and desperately tried to remember the proper handle position so the water wouldn't scald me. I got it pretty close and let the water run hot to warm me up. I took the dry soap from the little alcove built beneath the nozzle and worked it up into a lather. I took refuge in the simple act of washing myself and wished, for a moment, that the totality of my life could be that simple.

Then I felt other hands on my back. "Making the soap available to me will facilitate the cleansing of the dorsal region of your anatomy."

I remained facing the shower head. "Ms. Wickersham, while I appreciate the help, I wonder if you're supposed to be doing this."

"My instructions were to monitor your recovery and assist in any way I could."

I swallowed hard because I found the sensation of her hands soaping my back quite soothing. It was also helping me recover other functions. While she might have been willing to aid me in discovering the full extent of my recovery in that area, I had no desire to take advantage of a living automaton who was just following orders.

"You know how you could really help me, Ms. Wickersham?"

"Please tell me, Mr. Dent."

"Prepare for me a big, steaming cup of coffee."

"As you wish, Mr. Dent." Her hands left my body, and I sighed.

"One more thing, Ms. Wickersham."

"Yes, Mr. Dent?"

"Put some clothes on."

"If that is what you desire, Mr. Dent."

"It is, Ms. Wickersham," I mumbled as I switched the shower to cold water. "It is."

TWENTY

I managed to convince Ms. Wickersham that she didn't need to physically help me dress by allowing her to select what I would be wearing that day. While she sorted through the clothes hanging in my closet, I pulled on ballistic nylon torso armor and tightened the straps to hold it in place. Over that I donned the white shirt and olive three-piece suit she picked out for me. I put a narrow knot on the tie, then buttoned down the shirt's collar.

The only footgear I had were boots, and they were equipped with lifts. The right one also had a knife sheath built in, and I transferred the thin blade from a heavier pair of boots to the one I was wearing. Though Ms. Wickersham and I both searched the apartment for it, I found no shoulder holster for the Punisher, so I put the pistol in a briefcase and we headed out.

After crowding into the LunarTrak train in Orontius, we got off again at Thebit so Ms. Wickersham could go to her apartment and change into more suitable office attire. Her apartment was not much bigger than mine, but it had more by way of decorations. Small-framed display cases were filled with metal and porcelain thimbles. The collection boasted a few thimbles made before Earth was abandoned, but many more that were issued on momentous occasions here on Luna—like the installation of Cardinal Ian Durand as the head of the Brotherhood or Charles Colding's election as President of Capitol half a dozen years back.

Her collection appeared to be an outgrowth of her passion for embroidery. I know it seems impossible to imagine the term *passion* having anything to do with a vac, but it seemed appropriate in this case. Exquisitely detailed embroidery decorated the wall hangings, table runners, and pillows throughout the apartment. While it did strike me that a vac's ability to pay specific attention to tasks that others would see as mindlessly boring would make doing a repetitive task like embroidery possible, the decision to actually *do* it, and the choices involving patterns and color schemes hinted at some creativity.

It might be that the Mark I drug did not rob vacs of their creativity and emotion, just suppressed it and forced it to come out in other ways. I found myself hoping that my observation reflected the truth, because in it I found reason to dispute what the Brotherhood found so pernicious about Cybertronic. How could the dehumanizing·of employees not seem evil to the Brotherhood? If vacs could display creativity, it meant their humanity was not stolen but just deferred, and somehow that difference was very important to me at the moment.

Ms. Wickersham returned dressed in a khaki jacket and skirt combination over a white blouse. "I apologize for any delay, Mr. Dent."

"I did not notice any delay, Ms. Wickersham." I pointed to one of the pillows that had Capitol's Striking Eagle crest stitched into it. "Your handiwork is very good."

She watched me for a moment, a vacuity behind her flawless blue eyes, then she nodded. "Thank you. I set a quota for myself each month. I give them to friends."

"Your friends are quite lucky."

"Friends are important."

I smiled politely at her. "They *are* important. I am glad to have you as a friend."

A stiffness entered her posture as she looked at me. "Do you consider me a friend?"

"Yes."

"Then why do you denigrate my intelligence, Mr. Dent?"

I blinked my eyes. "I am not sure I understand what you mean?"

"You engage in verbal communication that reveals an

underestimation of my value as an individual. Friends do not treat friends with such a lack of respect."

Flashes of Rex's nearly constant flirtation with Ms. Wickersham vibrated through my brain like the sound of fingernails being raked across slate. "I apologize for my conduct. I know it was inappropriate but, at the time, I was incapable of operating correctly. That's not an excuse, just an explanation."

"Accepted." She preceded me to the door, and I fought to refrain from watching her walk. "We should be going."

We returned to the train station and took the North line to the center of Luna City. The walk from the central station to the Cybertronic headquarters was not too far, and we entered the building through the main entrance. A knot of Brotherhood novices at the base of the steps did make me uneasy, but I got past them by affecting Ms. Wickersham's indifference to them.

I left her at her desk which, I noticed consciously for the first time, had embroidered covers for her computer console and chair. She buzzed me into the ARD land of Oz and a small winged construct swooped down and flew a circle around me. It looped me again, darting in at my face before flapping its way back out to a more elliptical orbit.

Two men in white frocks cheered. "It works, Rex. It knows you have a gun and wants to disarm you."

"Really?" I set my briefcase on the edge of a partition and popped it open. The little bat creature sped up and made a fast circuit, then dove in at the Punisher in my briefcase. Like a vampire falling on the neck of a victim, it dropped onto the pistol's heavy barrel and clamped its teeth down on the metal. Its wings unfurled, and it began to drag the gun away.

I closed the briefcase.

Boris the Bat™ beat his wings frantically against the inside of the case. I snapped the locks shut, then handed the closed case to Simmons. "Be careful. The gun is loaded."

The slender scientist looked crushed. I shook my head and walked back to Dr. Carter's office. I knocked once, then waited to be invited in.

Dr. Carter looked up from her desk. "Oh, it's you,

Rex." She held her right hand up, then looked strangely at me. "No NyxStyx™?"

"They're bad for you, Doctor."

Her hand came down as she slowly stood and stared hard at me. "Is that you, Rex?"

I nodded. "It's me, more or less."

She frowned. "Can you explain that?"

"I don't know, given what I have to explain. Perhaps we can come to an understanding if you can answer some questions for me."

"I'll try."

"I take it, by your reaction just now, you were unaware of anything unusual happening to me recently?" I smiled. "And, yes, I realize that is an odd question to ask of the person who brought me back to life."

"Did something else happen? Aside from the seizure the day Beach took me to your apartment?"

"Probably. So you've had no contact with me since telling me I needed sleep?"

Dr. Carter shook her head. "I reviewed diagnostics on your cybernetic components early yesterday. Nothing odd there."

"You didn't examine me yourself?"

"No, the data was sent to me through the mainframe. I was told they had sent Ms. Wickersham over to take the readings. You were resting after an operation on Saturday."

My eyes narrowed as I looked at her desk. "Do you still have the data? Does it include an electroencephalogram?"

Dr. Carter returned to her chair and swiveled around to her terminal. "I think it's still here." She hit some keys, then nodded. "It's here. You can go subreal and find the specific information you want more quickly."

I held my hands up. "Not just yet. Can you check that EEG against old EEG records and see if you get an exact match."

"Rex, no two EEGs are going to match exactly."

"Humor me."

Andrea Carter was nothing if not good. She looked at the pattern displayed on the screen and hit keys in rapid succession. "Looks like a sleeping EEG. That cuts down the search. Let me see here."

It took her five minutes, then her terminal beeped, and she smiled up at me. "Not a perfect match, but close enough. Someone has been doctoring my data. The EEG on the diagnostic I saw from the day before yesterday was about two months old."

She set her keyboard down on her desk. "So what happened to you?"

"I don't exactly know." I walked over to the Link-Couch and sat down. "I imagine, though, Carl has a good idea. After I speak with him, I'm going to talk to you again and explain as much as I can." Smiling at her, I lay back and went subreal.

Before my death I had never gone subreal. Capitol shared all the other corporations paranoia about computers and the things the Dark Legion could do to them. Though I knew of people who interfaced through networks like those the Whiz kid used so effectively, exploring computer networks wasn't something Archie's sons would do. Computers were unreliable and risky, and my father's skill at avoiding unnecessary risk passed full on to his sons.

I materialized in the room that Carl and I used for our conversations, but I did not lie down on the couch. When Carl appeared, I made my onboard computer resolve him into a clear image of another human being, then I offered him my hand. "Thank you for seeing me, Carl, without notice."

"My pleasure." He shook my hand, then stepped back. "You *are* RKX 571127."

"I am, but not quite the same one you knew before last weekend."

Carl nodded solemnly. "I gathered that from your willingness to see me as something more than a cartoon construct."

"The old Rex knew, deep down, that he was not a fully rounded individual. He feared that integration with me would result in his death, and he was determined that he would not die again. To reassure himself that he was complete, he viewed you as less so within this forum.

Only by making his judge less real than he was could he continue to believe he was whole."

Carl arched an eyebrow at me. "Fascinating." He gestured at the couch, and it metamorphosed into a chair similar to his with a table set between us. The room surrounding us dissolved into a mountaintop patio looking out over the arid red vista of Mars. "I hope you don't mind a change of scenery."

"Not at all." I looked around, then smiled. "Mare Cimmerium, isn't it?"

"I didn't know you had been to Mars."

I shook my head. "Never been there, but once I had to make someone believe I had."

"I see. Yes, this is Mars. I have an old image running here—recent constructions have marred the vista."

"The Brotherhood's Chapel of Eternal Vigilance?"

"You *did* do your homework."

"Better safe than sorry."

"I never heard Rex say that before." Carl sat, and I joined him. "What shall I call *you*?"

"Rex still works, though I prefer the original connotation of the name over the homophonous one."

"And I applaud that change in attitude." Carl thought for a moment, then frowned. "You are suggesting, are you not, that before integration Rex was, in essence, insane."

"Possibly, but I was certainly functional. I think the closest explanation comes from the realm of multiple-personality disorders in which a traumatic event causes the birth of a personality to accept the stresses of that situation."

Carl smiled. "Dying would certainly qualify as a traumatic event."

"It was. Rex cobbled together a lot of my aggression and anger and molded it into a personality. One of the reasons I had trouble asserting myself to force integration was because I was no longer aggressive. Rex's lack of depth is obvious when one looks at his inability to deal with women as anything more than sexual objects."

"An interesting analysis, Rex."

"An understanding of human psychology is important in preparing for deep cover work. I am interested, though, why you are trying to analyze Rex and determine if he was sane or not?"

Carl opened his hands and in the left one appeared a cut crystal goblet filled with a burgundy whose flowery bouquet I could easily pick out of the dry, Martian air. "He—you—has or had an affinity for a Dark Legion Apostle named Muawijhe. He is also known as the Demon of Screaming Insanity. My operating thesis has been that Rex's connection in the fugue states has come through his insanity."

I smiled and found a glass of the same vintage sitting on the table in front of me. "You have been unable to reconcile the fact that *all* insane people are not undergoing the same fugue states with your theory, correct?"

"Even our attempts to provide the insane with the same mechanical aids you have, while alleviating their symptoms, have not resulted in successful duplication of the fugue links."

"That's because there is no significant correlation between Rex's insanity and the fugue states. It's something much more simple, yet far more strange." I lifted my glass and drank some of the wine. It cut the dust in my throat, and its stout flavor made me smile. "Had I known the pleasures of subjective reality, I might have come over to Cybertronic on my own."

"The simulation is close, but the real thing is better." Carl set his goblet down and folded his arms together. "What was the link?"

"When I died, Dr. Carter took bone fragments and brain tissue from me, as well as removing bone from my long bones and the remains of L-1. You combined those bits of bone with the ashes of another body and returned them to my family."

"We did that in case there was ever a time Capitol decided to check your remains for DNA to confirm your death."

"So I understand. What you did not know, and what Capitol does not know, is that my ashes were stolen before they were sealed in the ash casket. One of Ragathol's minions took them on the orders of his master." I held my hands up. "From trace impressions that Rex missed during the fugues, I know they were not looking for *my* ashes, but the remains of someone—anyone."

I sat back and watched the inverted Martian sunset through the stem of my goblet. "The ashes and bones were combined with mortar to create a life-size statue of Muawijhe in Ragathol's Holy of Holies. The statue itself serves as a communications device between Ragathol and the Lord of Visions, yet because my bones are part of it, the energy expended is muted and changed to avoid detection by other Apostles."

"You form a cutout, facilitating communication without revealing the fact that it is taking place."

"I believe I did, yes. Since I was supposed to be dead, the conversations could not be overheard. As Ragathol is in service to Algeroth, his dealings with Muawijhe would doom him. And, seen from Muawijhe's point of view, Ragathol's failure can embarrass Algeroth as easily as his successes can empower Muawijhe."

"Muawijhe is in a no-lose situation as regards Ragathol."

"I don't know that is entirely true. I believe Lorraine Kovan's very existence could compromise Ragathol and, through him, hurt Muawijhe."

Carl nodded, then sipped some of his wine. "I feel sorry for the woman, caught in the middle as she is."

My mind flashed back to something Carl had said earlier. "Do you think Cybertronic implants could unlock Lorraine's mind? Could Dr. Carter help her?"

"Treatment showed great promise with catatonic patients."

"Good, then you will take care of her? I know she'll be a wonderful asset for Cybertronic."

"I believe you. You have shown excellent judgment in the past, incomplete though you were." Carl shrugged. "If it were in my power, I would help her."

I frowned. "But?"

"I can't help her."

"Why not?"

"Because as of eight hours ago, we turned her over to Capitol and right now I have no idea where they've put her."

TWENTY-ONE

"You did *what* with her?"

Carl shrugged. but I got the distinct impression he was less alarmed about Sandra's situation than I was. "In the thirty hours you remained unconscious after the extraction, things moved quickly. Imperial used Ash's remains to show we had taken Lorraine Kovan, and Capitol asked for her to be returned to them. A number of deals were on the line."

"Deals? We're talking about a woman's life here."

Carl frowned at me. "You expect Capitol to kill her?"

"No, but if she is someone you would give up so easily, why did we go to the trouble of taking her from Imperial?"

Carl got up and opened his arms. "We took her because that action was an excellent investment of minimal resources to get a big profit. That sort of dealing is exactly why I can afford this mountaintop retreat on Mars, or I can enjoy a villa in the rain forests of Venus. We took her because it was a good business decision to do so."

I swirled wine around in my goblet but did not drink. "You lost an Attila unit and paid for mercenaries to invade an Imperial facility, then you give away the prize. How do you figure a profit from that?"

He folded his arms across his chest. "I think you can answer your own question, Mr. Dent. I'll fill in anything you miss."

I groaned and immediately saw a lot more credits than debits on the operation's balance sheet. Imperial lost personnel and suffered damage to a facility—probably enough to shut it down forever. One of their security force was shown to have Dark Legion ties, which meant a purge of their internal security force and increased training costs as they rebuilt their organization. They'd also have to hire freelancers to fill in for the holes left in their security outfit, and that would mean a material drain.

I looked up at Carl. "You told Capitol that you had held on to Lorraine Kovan only long enough to stabilize her, then you turned her over to them?"

Carl nodded. "In fact, we had her evaluated by a specialist that Capitol uses for their stockholders. She was able to explain she saw no evidence of alterations. Kovan's rescue and return bought us an incalculable amount of goodwill from Capitol."

"And the exposure of heretics in Imperial has likely sent shock waves through both it and the Brotherhood."

"It is as if, to use an old Earth expression, 'someone kicked over an anthill.' "

"With that, and the material damage done to Imperial, I can definitely see how you think we profited."

A smile slowly spread across Carl's face. "You miss one more very important thing we got out of this raid."

"Yes?"

He pointed at me. "You are whole again. Eighteen months ago we found you shortly after your body had been dumped on the streets. We identified you and put Dr. Carter on your case immediately. We knew who you were because of our interest in the security networks of the other corporations, their leaders and their families. Had we not been able to harvest you, we likely would have recruited you."

"I'm not certain I understand."

"I think you do, Rex." Carl began to pace, and the table evaporated, though our goblets still hovered in the air in defiance of subreal gravity. "When Cybertronic was born, I realized that we would require three types of individuals to make it successful. The first—those you refer to as vacs—were easy to recruit. We could take a bored worker, and by using Mark I on him, we could turn him into a productive, content, law-abiding individual. The suppression of emotion would limit creativity, but it also limited the influence of evil. Face it, to break the rules of society one must have enough imagination to figure out how to do that, and enough ego to think you can get away with it.

."The second type—creative tiffs—were also simple to bring into the corporation. All of the denizens of Oz leaped at the chance to have their brains enhanced and turbocharged. The distrust of technology rampant in other corporations frustrated them, and their decision to pursue projects on their own made them the objects of Brotherhood scrutiny. We gave them a chance to come into a safe harbor where they would be appreciated for their work, rewarded for it, and, best of all, be given creative freedom to push mankind to the next level of evolutionary development."

As Carl paced he passed between our goblets, and the wine trembled with his steps. "The third type of individual we needed was more difficult to procure. Tiffs and vacs are content with lives of isolation. While they do not reject social human contact, they prefer a smaller circle of friends because it limits confusion and potential hurt. Some, like many of the scientists in Oz, have such poor socialization skills that letting them remain technohermits is a service to their fellow humans. Others, like Ms. Wickersham, just want a quiet life."

"That leaves people like Beach and me."

"Yes, the third constituency in the Cybertronic trinity. I needed people who already had interpersonal skills and diplomatic abilities, yet people who were not unthinking toadies or worthless middle-management types. I needed people to be hard-nosed negotiators and sharp marketing strategists. I needed the sort of agent your brother made you into: someone capable of functioning anywhere, any time; loyal, yet capable of taking independent action that would benefit the company in the long run.

"Beach came to Cybertronic and offered his services to us. He saw us entering into a symbiotic relationship with him, and I have never regretted the decision in accepting his offer. Most of the rest of our Diamonds—you are called that for your value and multiple-faceted abilities—are recruited from the ranks of people the Brotherhood drives from other corporations. A few, like you, are salvaged at great risk and expense."

What should have been clear from the beginning exploded in my brain. "So the original mission of seeing my brother was a deliberate step in forcing the integration of my personalities."

"The process was occurring at a slow rate anyway. As you worked on the problem of Lorraine Kovan, Rex began to rely upon more and more of your skills. In the beginning he was a carefree individual who had little problems with wetwork. As you were able to assert yourself, he resisted but succumbed eventually."

"But was there an urgency in forcing integration, or were you just making use of a convenient situation?"

Carl paused and clasped his hands behind is back. "Originally I wanted you to see your brother and start working on him. When you kept after Lorraine, I decided that was a viable course to pursue, assuming it would bring you in contact with your brother again. I did not realize until now that you knew Kovan, and I am unclear about your connection with her."

I felt a warm, Martian breeze caress my face and saw it ruffle Carl's hair. "Her real name is Cassandra Raleigh. She is the sister of Anastasia Kell, my brother's wife. Cassandra and I dated once or twice, and we served as maid of honor and best man respectively at my brother's wedding. She and I were thrown together socially because of our family ties, but we both knew early on that we'd only be friends.

"She met Munnsinger Ellsworth, a funny little man who she shouldn't have given a second glance. He was twice her age, chubby enough that he didn't really seem to have a neck and was as bald as an abbot. Her weekly clothing allowance was more than he made in a month in his job as a dispatcher of garbage trucks for my father."

I smiled in spite of myself. "I thought she was crazy for liking him until I met him. Munn had a great sense of humor and a way with folks that made you think he really cared about you. He had a great memory and would do little things for you without asking anything in return. One time he called me and asked if I thought it would be presumptuous of him to buy Anna a birthday present. I'd forgotten Anna's birthday was coming up, and I think he knew that. His question reminded me of it, and he even got me out of the office long enough so I could help *him* pick out something appropriate for her. Of course, I bought my gift for her at the same time and avoided gross embarrassment."

I shook my head. "Talk about your Diamonds, Munn certainly was one."

Carl's face echoed my smile. "But he was a pauper, and she was a princess."

"That's it in a nutshell. Her father, Winchester Raleigh, demanded that Sandra stop seeing Munn. She refused. He threatened to cut her off completely. She told him to go ahead and do it. He threatened to destroy Munn, and that's when Sandra told her father that they had gotten married in a civil ceremony, and she was already pregnant."

Carl concentrated for a moment. "This was five years ago?"

"Yes, about that time."

"Winchester Raleigh was passed over for promotion, and Capitol Consumer Products started its own new transportation company instead of continuing to do business with his division." Carl tapped his chin with a finger. "Raleigh had a daughter who died at that time, which combined with the corporate defeat to give him a breakdown. At least that's what we interpreted his Martian vacation to have been."

"Winchester did run a bit amok. He thought he'd lost the contract because of the social stigma attached to Sandra's situation. What he'd missed was that his executive assistant was in bed with Comprodiv's comptroller, so business bids were rigged, and he lost out. His EA and the comptroller moved over to the new Compro Shipping division, but Win saw that as the man trying to distance himself from the disaster Win's career had become.

"Win placed all the blame on Munn's 'defilement' of his family. Win decided that Munn was wastage and needed to be dealt with. He came to my brother and asked Nick to have Munnsinger and his family killed. Nick protested, saying that would result in Sandra's death, too. Win was adamant—he said he had no daughter named Cassandra, and that those who hurt his family must pay the ultimate price."

Carl smiled slowly. "So you and your brother arranged for a fatal accident and shipped Lorraine Kovan and her husband off to Venus."

"Who better than Internal Security for fixing up false identification? We did it all the time for our agents. We told them we'd bring them back after Win calmed down or died." I fought a lump rising in my throat. "The only contact we had with them came in the form of a personal ad placed in the *Independent Citizen* once a year. It admonished me to wish Anna a Happy Birthday."

I sipped my wine and choked it past the thickness in my throat. "So there is a very real chance that Lorraine Kovan's life might be in jeopardy in Capitol hands. In addition, Winchester could make things very difficult for my father and brother if he finds out about the deception. Over and above that, of course, I'd like to see if we can help her. Sandra would be a Diamond, trust me. If we can get her back from Capitol, you'll have gotten me and a brand-new Diamond out of the deal—doubling your profit."

"Interesting observation." Carl nodded slowly. "I think it would be a good idea if we asked for her return. I just wish it would be more simple."

"I doubt my brother would like communication from beyond the grave, but I could go through him."

"Only if things could be that simple."   .

"I'm missing something here."

Carl frowned. "An hour ago the Brotherhood representative to the Cartel's High Council called a meeting to discuss the presence of the Dark Legion on Luna. They have asked the corporations to be ready to turn over all personnel who have had contact with the Dark Legion."

"That means Sandra is becoming an artifact over which the corporations will fight."

"And if we cannot find a way to win her, I believe the Brotherhood will demand, at the very least, proof that she has been cleansed of any Darkness. They will even offer to take care of her."

"The cleansing procedure will be a success, but the patient will die."

"The Brotherhood is nothing if not efficient." Carl quaffed the last of his wine, then crushed the glass in his hand and scattered its glittering diamond shards up into the starfield arching over our heads. "We must do what we can to make sure she does not fall into their hands."

TWENTY-TWO

I came out of subreal, and Dr. Carter looked at me expectantly. "Well?"

"I'm not the Rex you knew, but I am the Rex you were supposed to put together a year and a half ago." I stood from the LinkCouch and bowed my head toward her. "Thank you for the work you did."

"My pleasure." A smile blossomed on Andy's face. "So does this mean I won't have to put up with your clumsy attempts at seduction anymore?"

I blinked in surprise at her. "Excuse me?"

"You heard me. Your hearing is fine—I know."

"Is the change in me that obvious?"

"Not entirely." She tossed me a flat, laminated card with my picture and the name Cyril Dent on it. "Ms. Wickersham came in with this ID card to get you into the Cartel building. She said it was fitting that someone like you would represent us at the Cartel, and she was happy to have washed your back on this, the morning of your glory."

Andy watched me closely. "I'm your doctor, Rex. You can tell me what happened."

"Nothing happened, Doctor."

"*That* I gathered from Maddy's remarks. What I want to know is why *not*?"

"Medically I was perfectly functional, Doctor." I tucked the identification card in my jacket pocket. "Ethically I couldn't abide the idea of taking advantage of her. She'd been ordered to see to my needs, and would have done so. I don't think she would have done so willingly, and I had no desire to celebrate my return to life with rape. I guess I'm just funny that way."

Andy looked surprised, then smiled. "Even before this transformation, you weren't the type to insist when you had been rebuffed."

"But I was persistent."

"And your idea of impressing me was to get my NyxStyx™."

I rolled my eyes. "I assure you, Doctor, if I decide to pursue you, my conduct, taste, and style will be greatly improved."

"You're not the man of my dreams, Rex, but perhaps the man of some wishful thinking. We'll see."

"So we shall. Adieu, Doctor."

Only three blocks away from the Cybertronic tower, the Cartel building rose from the center of Luna City like a monolithic memorial to some hero of antiquity. Its clean lines and the lack of ghoulish decoration marked it as quite different from the other buildings surrounding it. The only project all the corporations and the Brotherhood have worked on together, it remained plain because its owners could not decide among themselves how it should be decorated.

That inability to make a decision marked many Cartel proceedings. The Imperial and Bauhaus representatives were figureheads only and could not agree to any plan without corporate oversight. Cybertronic's representatives had more leeway, but the Brotherhood did all it could to ignore them. Capitol and Mishima had some influence, but internecine battling within the Mishima delegation made it quirky and hard to negotiate with. Capitol had more direction and power within the Cartel, but they would be opposing the Brotherhood in the matter of Lorraine's custody, so that crushed almost any chance of reaching a consensus in the High Council.

Coral Beach met me in the lobby and took me up to the High Council chamber annex in Cybertronic's elevator. "First time here, correct?"

I nodded. "Even in my previous life I never got this far."

"Consider this the reward in your afterlife."

"That could be taken as a threat."

"And I thought you said you'd not been to one of these

sessions before." The door opened, and Beach waved me through it. "This is our home away from home. Make yourself comfortable."

Though I had not expected it, making myself comfortable would not be difficult to do. Our annex was more like a luxury apartment than it was any sort of working area. Four doors led to small suites complete with bedrooms, bathrooms, and windows looking out over Luna City. In the main room a full kitchenette and wet bar took up one wall, with comfortable chairs, couches, and low tables gathered into conversation nooks in front of it. A thick pile carpet with the Cybertronic logo woven into it covered the floor.

The working area of the annex lay toward the front of the suite. Three tiers of seats with long tables in front of them looked out through a glass wall toward the High Council chamber itself. Phones, terminals, a scattering of optical disks, and some dirty plates covered most of the farthest forward table. A man sat hunched over in the middle of the mess, and if he noticed our entry he gave no sign of it.

The chamber itself was a work of art. Glass made up the entirety of the north wall and provided an exquisite view of the city stretching out before it. As darkness began to fall, the various buildings glowed with a rainbow of neon shades. Many of the decorations gave the impression of the darkening city being transformed into a stone jungle for the night, but this high up it only looked intriguing and not menacing the way it did down on street level.

The other corporations' annex suites surrounded the chamber on three sides, but were set higher than floor level so observers in annexes had the impression of looking down on a grand sporting event. The chamber's bowl had been decorated with wood laid out in a beautiful parquet design. The wood was genuine and had been obtained by sacrificing thousands upon thousands of antiques that had been brought from Earth to Luna during the exodus.

The furnishings consisted of six tables with two chairs at each. The tables did not touch each other, but were arranged to form a large hexagon. The Brotherhood's table faced away from the window, placing their delegates' backs to the panorama. I understood that had been their choice and had been made so their annex appeared to be the whole of Luna. Bauhaus and Imperial sat on their right and left respectively. Cybertronic took the desk directly opposite the Brotherhood, with Capitol to its right and Mishima on its left.

A debate already raged down below. Beach hit a switch that flooded our annex with the sound of the Brotherhood's representative speaking. "So you are saying, Ambassador Robertson, that while Capitol believes the reports of Dark Legion presence and influence on Luna, you hold yourselves above the rest of us by refusing to turn over the woman who has been at the center of so much activity?"

Thom Robertson tugged at his vest before he answered the question. "Capitol, which I shall remind you was the corporation that instigated the formation of this very body, does not hold itself apart from our esteemed peers. We have ever been cooperative and, I would say, even *aggressive* in pressing for measures to be taken against the Dark Legion. Moreover, and this is a crucial point, no one has advanced an identification of this woman in question. In addition, no one has even hinted at her being willingly involved in any Dark Legion activity. Finally, all reports on this matter, sketchy though they may be, say the woman is utterly uncommunicative and may even be in an advanced vegetative state, so suggesting she might have intelligence value is absurd."

I grinned over at Beach. "Nice parry."

"Robertson is good." Beach nodded as the man seated next to Robertson got up and headed back toward a small doorway set beneath the edge of the Capitol annex. "He's about to get better because he's bringing in a new deputy."

The rules of conduct inside the High Council specified that each corporation could only have two people at their tables during a debate. The telephones on the desks did allow for conversation between an ambassador and his annex staff, but reliance on the phone was seen as a sign of weakness. Imperial and Bauhaus ambassadors did nothing without direct communications from their superiors, but the others tended only to use the phones to call for aide substitution.

The man sitting in front of our annex half turned back toward me and spoke with bored indifference. "The new

Capitol guy coming in is Nicholas Kell, part of their Waste Management staff."

Beach smiled. "Thanks, McNelly. Kell is really Internal Security at Capitol."

"So I understand." I leaned forward on one of the observation tables to study my brother more carefully. He looked a lot older than I remembered—even older than he appeared in the video of my funeral. His brown hair was shot with gray at the temples, and he was beginning to get the bags under his eyes that had made my father look as if he seldom slept. Nick had kept in better shape than our father, so he appeared trim, but his suit's vest strained a bit against the buttons when he sat down.

Seeing him again shocked me. Though he had changed, he hadn't changed enough for me to fail to recognize him. Though I knew he couldn't see me behind the smoked-glass fronting of our annex, I could easily imagine the smile he'd have on his face when he saw me again. Despite the changes I had undergone, I *was* still his brother.

The tall, slender Brotherhood representative waited for Nick to take his place before he answered Robertson's questions. "The lack of identification of this woman is not because such does not exist, Ambassador. She came to Venus on one of your ships as Loretta Corran. We understand her real name is Lorraine Kovan, and she was a citizen of yours who lived in a Venusian settlement called Fairview. Need I go on?"

Robertson leaned down toward my brother, nodded once at whatever Nick whispered to him. As he straightened up again, he gave the Brotherhood diplomat a cold smile. "I am afraid, Bishop Fulgencio, you will have to be more specific in your identification. My aide informs me we have no records of a Lorraine Kovan or a settlement on Venus called Fairview."

Fulgencio calmly smoothed the red tabard he wore over his black robe before he replied. "I am aware of Mr. Kell and his efforts for your corporation. He is misinformed."

"Perhaps, Bishop, you could provide us with some of your sources so we could have a better grasp upon our own corporate structures."

"I am certain Mr. Kell would love a list of those in Capitol who oppose the Dark Legion."

"Surely, Bishop, that would comprise the entire staff of our corporation."

"I believe, Mr. Robertson, many would be surprised at the omissions on that list."

"That could be so, Bishop, but I doubt it sincerely. However, in view of your reluctance to provide us with material proof of this woman's existence, I see no reason we should continue any inquiry about her."

I frowned. "Wait a minute. If they kill the discussion right here, we've got no chance at getting her back."

Beach nodded. "I believe Ambassador Grayson knows that, but she did not expect Capitol to stonewall the woman's existence."

"But she has proof Lorraine Kovan exists. She can use the video from the operation that rescued Lorraine." I avoided calling her Sandra because of the threat to her that the discovery of her true identity could produce. "Why doesn't she say anything?"

McNelly looked back over his shoulder at me with irritation clearly evident on his face. "The data you gathered was pulled together in a manner that we don't want to reveal. The Brotherhood is already very wary of anything we say or do. If we gave them even a hint of what we knew and were capable of discovering, they would step up efforts to destroy us."

"But if we don't intervene and get Capitol to admit she exists, they'll bury her, and we'll never be able to help her recover."

McNelly shrugged. "There's plenty more where she came from."

"No there isn't, that's part of the problem." I slammed my fist down on the table and Formica shattered. "She was a friend of mine, and I'm not going to let her get stuffed into a hole somewhere. What happened to her was not her fault, and she shouldn't have to pay for it."

"You can't . . ." McNelly started, but stopped when Beach held his hand up.

"What can you do, Dent?" Beach pointed at Robertson and my brother. "They say she doesn't exist, and that adamant a stonewalling effort is a tough defense to break down."

"Unless you've got a big enough battering ram." I

came around and sat down in the first row of the annex's viewing porch. "Can I call the Capitol table from here?"

"It better be very important . . ." McNelly shook his head. "I forgot, this is life and death."

He gave me a number, and I punched it in. I saw a small red light glowing on the Capitol desk, then my brother answered the phone in a hushed voice. "Kell."

"Nicky, admit Lorraine Kovan exists."

"Who is this?" Confusion ran through his voice. "This is no time to be playing a trick."

"No tricks, Nicky, just time for the truth. She can get help, but you have to admit she exists."

"What are you talking about? Who are you?"

"Nick, admit she exists, or the truth about Cassandra Ellsworth will come out."

I saw him stiffen, then lean forward and rest his forehead on the heel of his left hand. "Who are you?"

I almost told him, but I held back for a moment in case I needed more leverage. "Munnsinger Ellsworth had too many friends who cared for him to leave all of them thinking he was dead. Admit to Lorraine Kovan, or the truth could get out and hurt a lot of people."

"This is a horrible joke." He tried to sound convincing, but surprise had taken its toll. "Lorraine Kovan does not exist."

"Nick, you don't want to see her like that for the rest of her life. She can be helped." I choked back a lump in my throat. "Admit she exists, and Anna will have her sister back."

My brother returned the phone to its cradle and beckoned Robertson close. They discussed things quickly, then Robertson patted my brother on the shoulder and turned to address the chamber. "Mr. Kell's staff has just reported that they discovered records involving a Lorraine Kovan, and she was one of our people. She came to Luna for treatment of a nervous disorder and has been discharged from care."

That admission brought murmurings from the other representatives, but Bishop Fulgencio accepted it gracefully. "My compliments to Mr. Kell's staff and their diligence. You will turn the woman over to us, will you not?"

Robertson smiled painfully. "There is a problem with

that, Excellency. Mrs. Kovan is no longer on Luna. She departed twelve hours ago—nearly ten hours before you called for this meeting—on the *Black Queen*. She is bound for Mars."

Harry Murdoch, dressed in a suit made from his family's green and black hunting tartan, rose from behind the Imperial table. "Now that you've admitted you have the woman, Robertson, you'll be bringing her back."

Robertson stalled as my brother retreated to the Capitol annex and another aide came to take this place. "Bring her back? What do you mean, Ambassador Murdoch?"

"Being so obvious that you can understand me, Robertson, I mean that you'll be bringing the *Black Queen* back here so you can turn the woman over to the ministrations of the Brotherhood, of course."

"Ah, I see." Robertson got coaching from his aide, then shook his head. "I regret to say, ladies and gentlemen, that we will not be recalling the *Black Queen.*"

Erika Richthausen glared at Robertson from the Bauhaus table. "You risk a charge of Contempt of Council, *mein herr.*" Appearing every bit a Valkyrie, she pointed at him and dared him to contradict her. "First she does not exist, then she does, and now you will not return her to us?"

"I meant to suggest nothing of the sort, Madam Ambassador. We will not be recalling the ship, this is true. My colleague, Mr. Newmar of our Transit Division, informs me that recalling the *Black Queen* would result in an expenditure of a half-million Cardinal's crowns."

Erika transformed her frown into a predatory grin. "Then you will have to pay it, will you not, Ambassador Robertson?"

"Not all of it, Ambassador. Bauhaus has cargo comprising twenty-five percent of the ship's manifest. You will absorb that cost, in accord with your contract." Robertson shrugged easily. "That is just the flat cost of fuel, of course. The delays caused by those supplies not reaching their destinations on Mars could be economically disastrous. Imagine, for example, if some of those things *you* are shipping—or that Mishima has going out there on that ship—are spare parts for your security forces. The delay might prove to be very problematic, and

I doubt you wish to force a decision upon me and my company that will cause you harm."

Both Richthausen and Murdoch read the threat in Robertson's words and blanched. If others learned they had cost their companies that much money and trouble, they would themselves be consigned to methane recovery on Pluto. Robertson looked from one ambassador to the other, and finally stopped at Olivia Grayson. "Has Cybertronic an interest in this matter?"

Though a petite woman, Grayson moved with a fluid grace that made her seem more powerful than one would have expected. Being seated behind her I could not see her facial expression, but Robertson's reaction to it indicated he did not like it. "Thank you, Ambassador. We are merely concerned with this woman's well-being. We would suggest sending a party out to get Mrs. Kovan and return her here to Luna. We are prepared to offer personnel and equipment in this effort."

Mishima's Ambassador Kentoro concurred. "Mishima is likewise willing to aid in this matter. The Overlord himself directs all efforts be taken to assure this woman is returned to Luna."

The Brotherhood ambassador smiled. "You see, Mr. Robertson, admit the truth and many helping hands will be held out to you. You will permit this multi-partisan mission to bring Mrs. Kovan back to Luna?"

"Your kind offers are most appreciated." Robertson bowed his head to his peers. "I cannot render this decision myself. I need to consult with my superiors."

Fulgencio returned the bow. "That is understood. Shall we adjourn?"

As the High Council broke, Beach poured himself a glass of water from a pitcher on the bar. "Tomorrow Capitol will agree, and Mrs. Kovan will be as good as back in our hands."

"I hope you're right, Beach."

He frowned at me. "What is it, Dent?"

"Probably nothing." I sighed and tried to banish the knot congealing in my stomach. "It's just that Ragathol intended his people to bring Lorraine to Mars. I can't help but think that even if we were to set out after her right now, we'd still be too late."

TWENTY-THREE

I returned to the Cartel building the next morning after having spent most of the evening just wandering around through parts of Luna City. I consciously avoided known Capitol hangouts, mixed freely with people elsewhere. I reveled in my friendly anonymity and got used to my body. Aside from the loss of height, it seemed to function as well as or better than the one I had been born with, and in accepting it I made peace with all but the very last smidgen of Parabellum Rex.

Beach greeted me with a smile as the elevator opened to admit me to the Cybertronic Annex. "Have you seen the morning's *Chronicle*?"

I shook my head. "Something important?"

"The Cardinal himself has a letter on the editorial page."

Ambassador Grayson fastened on a diamond earring as she came out of one of the annex apartments. "That letter means today should go much more easily." She extended her hand to me, and I shook it firmly. "I understand you are responsible for Capitol's reversal yesterday, Mr. Dent?"

I shrugged. "McNelly led me to believe that Capitol's tactics were a problem. I had some leverage, and I used it. It seems to me—and I would like your opinion on this—that Capitol's admitting Lorraine Kovan exists is far from their agreeing to letting the Cartel send people to take her back from Mars."

The fox-faced woman gave me a smile that, had it been

inviting, would have melted Parabellum Rex's brain. "Your assessment would be accurate, were all this taking place in a vacuum. The Cardinal's letter is designed to bring pressure to bear on Capitol and to reward Mishima for its support."

"That must be *some* letter."

Beach nodded and held a finger up. "It's got a lot of the normal Brotherhood nonsense in it about eternal vigilance, but the cogent piece comes in one simple paragraph. Quote, 'As you know, brethren, the world is a complex place in which evil is able to cloak itself in a number of guises. There are ways to separate evil from good, and some of them yield pleasure in the discovery of the work of other good people like ourselves. I was recently acquainted with a Mishima product, the *Dainuibari* sewing machine. In its solid construction and simple yet elegant functionality, it is a pure and rewarding tool. It will free your creativity so you may produce raiments that will celebrate the sanctity of life itself.' "

My jaw dropped. "That sort of advertising Mishima couldn't buy."

Grayson nodded solemnly. "But they did, with Kentoro's statement. Sales on the *Dainuibari* are skyrocketing and the sales of our NDS3000 and the Capitol Betsy Ross Seamstress machines have died. The implication is quite clear—the Brotherhood will not be ignored concerning Lorraine Kovan, and Capitol will pay dearly if they refuse to comply with the Brotherhood's wishes in this matter."

I nodded. "I imagine their wishes will be for an Inquisitorial team to travel to Mars to bring Lorraine back."

"That's what they would like, but that's not what they will get, and they know it." Grayson ticked points off on her fingers. "Mishima will lose face if they are not allowed to send even a token force along. Capitol will claim the right to escort her because she is one of their citizens—and they'll probably have the unit that brought her to Luna from Venus be the one to fetch her back." She looked up at me, and her brown eyes flashed mischievously. "And you'll be leading our team on the expedition."

"Me?" I looked over at Beach. "He's got a lot more experience than I do."

"I have other duties. Carl advanced you himself."

"Who else goes?"

"Ash and a new chasseur, Jan Terant. It will be her first mission."

I frowned. "Who is she?"

"I believe you first made her acquaintance in an alley about a week ago, when you recruited her for us."

"There's no way she's ready." I shook my head. "Dr. Carter just put her back together a week ago. I took months before I was operational."

"I don't make the assignments, Dent, I just report them." Beach shrugged. "She didn't need as much work as you did, and we've not invested that much into her training so far."

"So she's expendable?"

"You disagree?"

"No, but I don't like the implication that Ash and I are as well."

The ambassador laughed lightly. "I don't think things will go so badly that any of you will be expended. The fact is that Jan Terant, until a week ago, worked for Capitol. She's bright, knows how they work, and can relate to many of their people. She might learn things you could not. The trip from Luna to Mars will take over a week and will be on a Capitol ship, so this could be an intelligence bonanza for us."

"That's fine, but I don't want to lose sight of the real goal here: getting Lorraine Kovan back here so we can help her."

Grayson smiled at Beach. "I think Carl should recruit more idealists."

I growled at the both of them. "Is that not our goal?"

"Returning Lorraine Kovan is the *mission* goal. Cybertronic's goal is to earn, through this joint effort, some respect from the Brotherhood. Normally they see us as the antithesis of Imperial, and view us as a great evil. Imperial's embarrassment in this whole contretemps has caused a slight rift between them and the Brotherhood. We may not gain much ground at this time, but even an inch gives us a toehold in our fight to reach some sort of an understanding with the Brotherhood."

I nodded slowly. "I see that. I don't think the mission and our goal contradict each other."

Grayson watched me closely. "What will you do if a conflict arises? Which way will you jump?"

I gave her back my version of her earlier smile. "I don't know, but the fun's in the not knowing. And *that* is why Carl only recruits idealists on a very limited basis."

The Cartel session went very much the way Grayson predicted. That was not because she was precognitive, but because she and her staff had worked throughout the night to put together the compromise she had outlined. Bauhaus made a preemptive bid to upset the deal by offering to send a ship out from Mars to take custody of Lorraine in mid-flight, but Capitol balked, and the Brotherhood—who would have been cut out by that plan—killed it.

Everyone broke for lunch, and during that time the Cartel staff made arrangements for all the team members to get together for a basic orientation meeting that afternoon. Somewhere Cybertronic found a dark blue suit in a size to fit Ash. With a new body, there was no way to tell him apart from the old Ash—or, for that matter, any other Attila unit. He escorted Jan up to the annex and, like him, she looked normal except for wearing a better class of clothing than usual. In her case she'd been given a cream-colored skirt cut to knee-length and a white silken blouse to wear beneath the jacket.

We exchanged greetings, and I saw no recognition flash in her eyes. As with all of us, our moment of death is lost. Normal brain function takes about ten minutes to transfer information from short-term memory to medium-term and on into permanent storage. With head injuries and concussion, short-term amnesia is not unexpected. I would have been surprised if she even remembered the day she died.

Of course, since Cybertronic did have a record of her death, it would be available to her whenever she wanted to fill in that last gap in her life story. I didn't have that luxury since, to the best of my knowledge, no one at

Cybertronic had been present to make a record of my death. At this point had such a thing been available, I think Carl would have given it to me to view. As he had not, I had to content myself with the realization that I'd never know how I died.

And, as I told Ambassador Grayson, the fun is in not knowing.

Whatever the staff had expected in bringing the various corporate contingents together, I think they were disappointed. Given the contentious nature of the Cartel itself, they probably expected an instant battle between all of us. It could have happened, of course, because the sort of folks chosen for special missions invariably have egos.

Of course, a run to Mars to bring a catatonic woman back to Luna was hardly the sort of heroic mission that suited itself to a grand investment of ego. It might be something that would get put on a résumé, but only under "Miscellaneous Projects." We were all present because of the need for our employers to maintain face and parity with each other, not because Lorraine needed so big an escort.

The nature of the mission was not the reason we didn't fight. Nor was our respect for each other or our standing as professionals. Avoiding conflict for those reasons would have made us noble enough to warrant *two* whole paragraphs in a letter from the Cardinal, but the reality of the situation was a lot more basic.

We didn't fight because we found many of us already knew each other.

Mishima had chosen Yojimbo as its representative. Grayson mentioned that Overlord Mishima had hand-picked Yojimbo, and Mishima's son, Lord Moya, had not opposed his father in this because Moya would have preferred to stay out of it entirely. In granting his father's request, Moya had hoped the mission would distract the old man enough that Moya could consolidate his position within the Mishima Corporation.

Yojimbo, as the Overlord's agent, could not travel without retainers. He hired Pam Afton and Lane Chung to attend him. Seeing the three of them in the room heartened me because they had risked their lives more than once to help Lorraine. If there ever did come a point when Lorraine's safety had to be put ahead of corporate ambitions, I knew I could count on them to help me out.

Lane and Pam knew Captain Mitch Hunter, the leader of the Capitol squad. Hunter had eight other people with him, which matched Capitol's people one for one with counterparts from each other's corporation while leaving Mitch free to run the operation. Clad in special forces dress uniforms, Mitch and his squad looked uneasy until they welcomed their friends from the Mishima contingent.

Yojimbo also knew one of the two Brotherhood representatives. Titus Gallicus's balding head with its fringe of white hair made him look to be the eldest member of the team. Tall and slender, he smiled sincerely enough to make me postpone my instinctive dislike for Brotherhood Inquisitors. The fact that he appeared to get along quite well with Yojimbo further eroded my reservations, but that still left me well shy of warming up to the man.

In Titus's shadow walked the other Brotherhood agent. Though not as tall as Titus, she was even more skeletally slender than he was. While her black clothes and the big black cloak draped over her shoulders revealed little about her body, the sharp angles of her face and the bony nature of her jaw and shoulders heightened an impression of androgyny. Her blond-white hair had been raggedly cut away from her face and, had she smiled at all, might have seemed a very chic sort of styling. Her expressionlessness, which ran from her dark eyes through her whole being, made me think of a snow-capped volcano—dormant on the outside, while seething on the inside.

Her pale flesh was cold when I shook her hand. Titus introduced her as "Inquisitor Scythia Scipio," but I suspected she was a Mortificator. The Brotherhood's fanatical assassins were known to be ruthless and efficient. If the Brotherhood decided Lorraine was a trap or of use to the Dark Legion in some way, I had no doubt Scythia would kill her to save the rest of humanity.

Despite the damper Scythia put on my mood, the team meeting almost immediately degenerated into the sort of story-swapping informality needed to allay suspicions and bind the group together. Aside from Ash, who did not have the programming necessary to tell a story or to listen to one either, and the brooding Brotherhood witch, the team members mixed quite quickly and started to get along famously.

This dismayed the staff. They made some attempts to usher us toward the far side of the room where they had set up chairs and video viewscreens for a briefing, but we wanted none of it. Almost without exception, all of us had participated in an earlier effort to rescue Lorraine Kovan, so our stories were our bona fides and also a sharing of experience from which other team members could benefit.

The staff decided to appeal to a higher authority to get us organized. Since the mission was to be run under the Cartel with a Capitol leader, they decided to get someone who could move the Caps to their chairs and get the meeting started. Because I was standing toward the rear of the circle of friends, keeping an eye on Scythia, and because I headed up the Cybertronic delegation, I became the logical first target for the staff's attempts at coercion.

A staffer gently tapped me the shoulder. "Mr. Dent. I'd like to introduce the man who will be briefing you once things get underway."

I turned and offered my hand before I'd seen to whom she referred. The other man took my hand and smiled down at me. "I'm Nicholas Kell."

A jolt shook me, and Nick felt it through our grip. "I know. We've met."

"Have we?"

"In a previous life." I pumped his arm stoutly. "In a previous life, when I was your brother."

TWENTY-FOUR

Nick's reaction to my statement showed me he'd not slowed down any since my death. His face registered shock for a moment followed almost instantly by disbelief. Then his hazel eyes narrowed, and he studied me for a moment. He even bent his knees slightly, lowering his eye level to bring me back up to my proper height. "I knew there was something familiar about the voice on the phone yesterday."

"Sorry about that, but it had to be done."

The woman who had introduced us gently touched Nick's elbow. "The briefing, sir?"

Nick dismissed her curtly. "There will be plenty of time for briefings on the way to Mars."

She looked puzzled. "But you're not going to . . ."

"I am now, Agnes. Clear my schedule for the next three weeks. I'll call my wife and explain it to her myself. Right now Mr. Dent and I have a lot to discuss."

As she retreated, Nick steered me to a corner of the room. "What happened? We had a funeral and everything. There wasn't an empty seat."

"Actually there were eight open places."

"What?"

"I've seen the video. It was a beautiful eulogy—even with the brother references edited out." I kept a pleasant grin on my face despite the conflicting emotions crashing around inside of me. "I never intended to betray you, nor have I. I only learned of our connection yesterday."

I saw from the sharpening of his features that he didn't

fully accept my explanation, so I went into more detail. "A year and a half ago Cybertronic found my body dumped into the street. I was dead from massive head and spinal trauma. They identified me and put me back together, physically, but my brain was a bit messed up. I wasn't quite myself. While Cybertronic *did* see my regaining knowledge of who I had been as important to my full recovery, they concentrated on my rehabilitation for the first year. By then I didn't want to know who I was because I thought that would destroy me somehow."

That struck a chord with Nick. "When you went deep cover on ops, you never wanted to resurface until things were over. You were good at submerging your real self so you'd not be exposed by a slip."

"That explains how I managed to resist Cybertronic's efforts to bring me to the fore again." My hands curled into fists. "The last thing I remember is leaving your apartment. What happened after that?"

Nick sighed and tipped his face toward the tiled ceiling as he forced his mind back. "You were out of touch for a couple of days, which wasn't unusual, then we had a call from the Luna City Morgue. They said you had been in an accident and then had been mixed up with another body, so you were cremated before we had a chance to identify you. The coroner told me you'd been pretty messed up, so it was just as well. They gave us your ashes, and we had a funeral."

"Okay, that's the cosmetic stuff. What did you find out?"

Nick hesitated. "Nothing useful."

I reached out and firmly grabbed his shoulders. "Nick, this is me, Quentin. I look a little different, and you're not expecting me to be here, but it is me."

"How do I truly know that?"

"Nick, I know you have a small black dot on your back from where you asked me to give you a tattoo during your fascination with stories about Yakuza on old Earth. You were seventeen and wanted to impress Suzy Coulson."

"That's a story that my brother used to tell from time to time." His face sharpened with concentration. "When did you lose your virginity?"

"You're going to say it was when I was sixteen, after my first Future Executives of Capitol Cotillion. With Patty Lyons."

"That's when it was."

I shook my head. "Actually, it wasn't."

"What?"

I swallowed hard. "Remember when you were sick and asked me to talk Suzy Coulson into visiting you by asking her to bring you review notes for your physiology exam."

"Vaguely."

"Well, she decided to use me as study aid to review the chapters on human sexuality."

"You lie."

"You could ask her, I guess." I let my hands fall back to my sides. "I never told you because you had this thing for her, and I realized, after the fact, that I would have hurt you."

Nick remained stone-faced. "Then why did you do it?"

"Well, at the time I was angry with you for ordering me around to do your dirty work. I thought it was fitting revenge. And it was fun to be able to do something you'd not been able to do." I blushed. "And she was cute as all hell, and I was fifteen and full or hormones."

He reached out and gently cuffed me, as had been his wont in our youth. "Okay, you're Quentin. If you'd stuck with the Patty Lyons story, I would have known you were lying."

My mouth opened in surprise. "You *knew* about Suzy and me? How and for how long? I never told that story to anyone."

"I know, and I appreciate your sparing my feelings." Nick folded his arms across his chest. "Sandra threw a party for Anna before we got married—a bachelorette party—and Suzy was invited. After some drinking—heavy drinking—they started swapping stories about horrible things they had done to boyfriends or guys who had been interested in them. Suzy confessed to having seduced you. Anna told me about it after you died. We laughed and cried a bit."

He glanced down for a second, then his eyes met mine. "And it's just as well you were dead at the time, because

I would have killed you for doing that to me." We both burst out laughing at the mock anger in his voice. Nick balled a fist and raised it theatrically as if he was going to hit me, but before he could even feign a punch, Ash had grabbed his wrist.

"Ow!"

"Ash, stop."

The Attila unit looked at me. "Maintenance of your structural integrity is a prime operational directive."

"That's fine, Ash, I appreciate your attention to detail, but this man won't hurt me."

"Identification and analysis indicates Nicholas Sebastian Kell is rated at .347 on the Norris Lethality Index in unarmed combat."

"Ignore this NLI, Ash. He wouldn't hurt me."

Nick threw his arm around my shoulder. "That's right, we're brothers. If we fight among ourselves, it's only so we sharpen each other up to deal with outsiders who would hurt us."

Nick did get up and address the team briefly. He told us that we'd be heading to Mars on the *Red Corsair* and would arrive there roughly a week after Lorraine Kovan. Because of her condition, she was being sent to a private hospital in San Dorado. Once on the planet we would make arrangements to bring her back to Luna, and the *Red Corsair* would remain on the red planet until we were ready to return.

San Dorado, Capitol's capital on Mars, sat between the Mariner Valley and the dry reach of plains known as the Erythraeum Sea. Though small in comparison with Luna City, San Dorado is still the second largest city in the solar system. Like Luna City, it is a bustling metropolis that has plenty of facilities from each of the corporations, so we'd all have local contact people to help us once we got there.

Even though none of us expected trouble in bringing Lorraine Kovan back, we would all be traveling with a full complement of personal combat equipment. Since we were officially a Cartel operation, we could elect to use weapons that had been developed exclusively for the use of Cartel DoomTroopers. While I elected to stay with

Cybertronic weapons, I was not surprised when I learned Jan had decided to add a plasma carbine to her personal weapons manifest.

Within three days the whole lot of us embarked on the *Red Corsair* for Mars. Aside from daily briefings on the Martian situation, including data on the presence of a Dark Legion Citadel—I should have been able to see from the simulated heights of Carl's Martian Hide-away—we were largely left to ourselves. Most of us spent our time socializing in the ship's lounge, though an information packet my brother gave me after liftoff occupied a fair amount of my time.

It contained copies of everything he had been able to learn in his investigation of my death. He had been more than diligent in trying to learn what happened to me. He located some people who reported seeing me to get into a black Vinciano-Traffaux sedan with darkened windows. That wasn't unusual—all of the Bauhaus luxury vehicles had darkened windows and half the senior executives in Luna City owned one. The other half just lusted after the cars, and I knew plenty of people who had them. The witnesses didn't remember license tags, and the description of the driver as being an older man meant it could have been just about anyone from Capitol to any other corp.

Nick had concentrated on the possibility that someone from one of the deep cover jobs I had done had recognized me and had me killed. The accident story didn't seem right to him, and the witnesses said I'd been in no distress when I entered the vehicle, so he assumed I knew the driver. He had been able to determine that I'd not visited home since I left his place, so he knew I had been taken shortly after he last saw me.

Nick's subsequent investigations left him with nothing. Everyone who would have had a revenge motive checked out with alibis. Because there had been a finding of "accidental death" in my case, Capitol was reluctant to spend much money on a continuing investigation. As his leads petered out to nothing, Nick stopped digging.

It felt strange to be reading about my death and feeling very detached from it. I should have been outraged because when Cybertronic found my body, it was fresh. Given the time of my disappearance, it meant I could have been held for upward of twenty-four to thirty-six hours before being killed. That suggested interrogation, and even though I had been trained in ways to resist, I knew there was a limit to human endurance. I must have suffered unbelievably, but without being able to recall the pain and torture, the anger my brutal death should have spawned wasn't there.

Before, I didn't want to know about my death. Now, in knowing all there was to know, I was faced with a gap that I probably could never fill in. While my death was a traumatic event, I had no way to touch the trauma, and that meant my death became nothing more than a transformative event. And, given the way I went through the transformation, it was as if I had gone to sleep one day and woken up eighteen months later, better than I had been before.

I could recall times when relationships had soured and crumbled apart. The pain crushed me down into depression. I'd not want to eat or do anything. All I was capable of doing was hurting, and even though I knew I had to get on with my life, there seemed no reason to put any effort into it. What I fervently wished during those times was that I could wake up a month or two down the line and be fully recovered.

Gain without the pain.

Of course, the saying older than the corps themselves still applies: there's no such thing as a free lunch. While I'd not suffered the pain of my death, Parabellum Rex had suffered being incomplete because of it. I realized he sought to protect me from the pain by absorbing it all himself as fear of dying again. He sheltered me and filtered enough of the pain out that I was able to recover. Once I was strong enough to challenge him for control, he knew his job had been done and he surrendered to me.

My death shifted from being an object of fear or a source of anger into being a mystery that I might never be able to solve. I accepted that fact, and knew I'd poke around in the mystery when I returned to Luna, but I'd not push too hard. Dying again trying to figure out how I died the first time would be stupid. If I was going to die again, I wanted it to count for something—like protecting and helping Sandra lead a normal life.

On final approach into San Dorado's Rutan Space Center, I joined my brother in his suite. Once we came within range of the city's communications network, he placed a call to the Morency Clinic and channeled it through the video monitor in his cabin. A youngish switchboard operator put us through to Dr. Rajiv Singh's office. "Hello, Dr. Singh, this is Nicholas Kell with Capitol. We spoke two weeks ago when I told you we were sending you a patient."

The dark-haired doctor nodded. "I remember. I see you are calling from the *Red Corsair*. You decided to accompany the patient yourself, then?"

"No." Nick leaned as far forward as the landing belts would allow. "Elizabeth Walters was sent to you on the *Black Queen*."

"Oh, no, Mr. Kell, she was not. We got a message from you saying there had been a delay and she had not embarked on the *Black Queen* as planned."

"But she did, Doctor." My brother stared at the man in the monitor. "I put her on the ship myself."

Dr. Singh held his hands up helplessly. "This message came through Capitol's Rutan office. We assumed you would inform us once alternate transportation had been arranged. I am sorry."

"Thank you, Doctor."

"Her case sounded very interesting. If you find her, Mr. Kell, do bring her by."

"I will, Doctor." Nick closed the connection and killed the static-filled monitor. "She got here, Quentin. I had reports all the way and confirmation of her arrival."

"Okay, you know she made it to Mars."

"Right, she's on Mars. But where?"

I shook my head. "I don't know, but I hope we find a good answer fast. If Ragathol and the Dark Legion figure out she's here, her location is likely to change fast, and even if this little crew we have with us can find her again, we aren't likely to be able to get her back."

TWENTY-FIVE

Finding Lorraine Kovan was easy. The second the shuttle-crawler from the *Red Corsair* got us to the Rutan Terminal, my brother raced to the Capitol Operations Center. Flashing his identification he got both of us in. Within a minute we were in the manager's office, and the sweating man was pounding furiously on his computer's keyboard. "I was just following orders, Mr. Kell."

"I'm certain you thought you were, Mr. Cusder, but there was an error in what you did." Nick, standing beside the seated manager, laid his left hand heavily on the man's right shoulder. "You say you remember a comatose woman coming off the *Black Queen*."

"Yes, sir, I do. I remember it because orders came through regarding how we were to treat her. I was to send a message to Dr. Singh with your regrets, then turn her over to two people who gave me a password." Cusder tapped the screen, then raked stubby fingers back through thinning hair. "See, she was turned over to Mr. and Mrs. Jones of San Dorado."

I swore. "That's useless as far as identification goes. They could be anywhere in San Dorado."

Cusder shook his head. "No, sir, I doubt it."

I saw my brother's grip on Cusder's shoulder tighten. "Explain."

"Well, they took her to a chopper out on the commuter side of the terminal."

"And?" Nick brought his face down so he could stare

into Cusder's beady little eyes. "Where did the chopper take her?"

"They didn't tell me."

The computer in my head flashed a chart of Cusder's rising pulse inside of my eyes, right above the graph of the stress analysis of his voice. "Mr. Cusder, my brother is a patient man, but I am not and you are deceiving us."

"I'm not a liar."

"No, just deceptive. He asked where the chopper took her. You replied that you were not told the destination. That does not mean you do not know where they went."

"It's important, Cusder." My brother's voice implied a favor given for the one he was asking.

That prompted Cusder to smile. "Well, it does just so happen that I noticed that particular helicopter did happen to refuel twice going out and twice coming back. And the pilot said he hated the crosswinds coming down off the Cimmerian Mountains. That means he put down at the Chapel of Eternal Vigilance."

My brother and I groaned at the same time, which would have been funny, except for the circumstances that prompted it. On our briefings on the way into Mars, we had been brought up to speed on the current situation on the planet, and the Chapel had figured in a few discussions. On the opposite side of the planet from San Dorado, the Dark Legion has established a huge Citadel run by a nepharite known as Saladin. Constructed in territory that Imperial had taken away from Cybertronic a long time ago, the Citadel remained intact because Imperial resisted any attempts to destroy the Legion by other corporations. Imperial wanted the glory of eradicating the Dark Legion for themselves, and refused to let anyone else take direct action against the Citadel.

Imperial did, however, allow the Brotherhood to build a proto-cathedral only one hundred kilometers away from one of the Citadel's outposts. I'd known it existed because Brotherhood folks had mentioned it to me during my infiltration of the order. Despite my knowledge of its existence and location, until Titus briefed us on it, I had no idea what the Brotherhood did there.

Eternal Vigilance was an important place for the Brotherhood. They sent people out there for training in ways to become sensitive to the Dark Legion and the things it did with Dark Symmetry. From the way Titus Gallicus had spoken of it, Eternal Vigilance was as close to a spa as the Brotherhood maintained, and being chosen to visit there was an honor just this side of having a private audience with Cardinal Durand.

I looked up at Nick. "We're going to have to get out there. Can you get us transport?"

Nick patted Cusder on the shoulder. "I'm sure my friend can find us transport."

"I don't think so, Mr. Kell."

"What?"

"That whole area is being quarantined, by order of the Brotherhood." Cusder's pale skin took on a grayish hue. "No one is supposed to know, but there's fighting out there. Imperial is making a push, and there has been a counterattack. When they start going hard, you can feel the vibrations from the bombs here in San Dorado."

Nick looked up at me. "A Brotherhood blackout must mean someone is getting beaten out there."

"More Inquisitors to keep peace in heaven."

"Blasphemy." Anger flushed some color back into Cusder's cheeks. "No one would dare attack a Chapel!"

If only you knew what we know about the Dark Legion . . . "Blackout or no, we have to get out there and get Elizabeth Walters back out. She's not supposed to be there. Does Eternal Vigilance have an airstrip?"

"It does, but I'm not going to give you any of my aircraft to take out there."

My brother produced his identification card. "Reconsider."

"I don't work for you or the Waste Management Division."

"You could. I could have you surfing effluent waves in the tunnels below Luna City inside two weeks." Nick shook his head. "If *I* ask for you, *my father* will ask for you, and when he does, do you think Transport will deny the requested transfer?"

Cusder's head came up, and he smiled. "I have friends in high places."

"Unless you're Winchester Raleigh's golf partner when he comes to Mars, you'll be mine inside six hours."

"You don't scare me."

I smiled at him. "Be careful, Cusder, Mr. Kell is Winchester Raleigh's son-in-law."

That made Cusder hesitate, but his canary-eating cat grin returned quickly. "I'm happy for him. Perhaps I'll see him in a social setting when I next visit Luna."

Both of Archie Kell's sons instantly read the handwriting on the wall. I got up and double-checked the door to make certain it was closed. I saw that it was and made a show of locking the door. "I think you have to bring him into confidence concerning the *investigation*."

Nick didn't miss a beat. "We've been investigating some improprieties concerning Winchester Raleigh. There is some evidence that he is looking at jumping ship from Capitol to one of our competitors. Elizabeth Walters is a courier who is carrying on negotiations on behalf of Raleigh."

Cusder shook his head. "But Raleigh is on Luna. Why send a courier to Mars?"

I shook my head. "What's wrong with you, Cusder? Haven't you ever heard of a cutout or a dead drop? She brings things to Mars and leaves them here. The other side picks them up and ships them back to Luna. It's all very difficult to trace, which is the point."

"What kind of stuff?"

"We're not at liberty to discuss that, but it is very important stuff."

My brother nodded solemnly. "*Very* important stuff. We'd not have gotten this far except my father-in-law originally authorized the Walters trip here in my name— just in the same way he told you to send regrets in my name to Dr. Singh. Yes?"

Cusder nodded. "I did think it was odd that he would send an order in your name."

"He thought it was clever for the mouse to be using the cat's tools. Thought he could implicate me and get me tossed off the case." My brother took out a pen and wrote a number down for him. "In six hours—six hours after your plane takes us to Eternal Vigilance—call this number. They'll have a new duty assignment for you at a ten percent raise, and you'll get boosted to the next transfer back to Luna. You'll get a new identity so Raleigh

can't get to you. You're going to be important in wrap-
ping this up and saving Capitol trillions of crowns. And
we don't forget our friends."

Cusder's eyes brightened. "With this new identity,
you're going to put a female agent on me to watch
me, right, like a bodyguard?"

"Splendid idea. The plane we'll need requires VTOL,
should be armed, and capable of carrying twenty passengers with full combat equipment." Nick slapped the man
on the back, upsetting Cusder's spectacles. "Thank you."

"The agent, she'll be blonde?"

"Hair like spun gold."

"I'm clearing a SkyRay 838 for you at the Executive
terminal."

Nick gave the man a thumb's-up as I opened the office
door. "Six hours and we'll have him."

Heading back to the holding lounge, I looked over at
Nick. "Cusder's attitude told us that the orders to send
Sandra to Eternal Vigilance came from Win. How did he
find out about Sandra being on the *Black Queen*?"

"I'm guessing, but he must have been notified when
the Council suggested turning the ship around and bringing it back to Luna. The figures Robertson were given to
argue against that idea sounded like the kinds of things
Win would have put together. If Win looked at the passenger and cargo manifests to try to figure out why the
ship was coming back, he could have spotted Sandra's
picture in the manifest. I didn't have time to dummy
something up, and didn't think it was needed since all old
records of her are gone. Only the fact that Win knew her
allowed him to identify her."

"So why send her to Eternal Vigilance?"

Nick remained silent for a while because he knew what
my question really was: did Win send her there to be
helped by the Brotherhood or to put her in a place that,
at some point, had to be the subject of a Dark Legion assault? Either one of us would have defended Win against
a charge of wanting his daughter dead, but we *had* been
approached by him to kill her. However, that had been
right in the midst of his breakdown, and he'd been a lot
better since coming back from his vacation.

"Dammit, Nick, Winchester came here, to Mars, to recover from his breakdown."

"But he didn't do so at Eternal Vigilance."

"It doesn't mean he didn't make contacts here. Possibly Brotherhood contacts."

Nick shook his head. "Win was never named by anyone in your investigation as being part of the Brotherhood, and he seemed as hostile to your becoming involved in it as anyone else."

"The Brotherhood plays the long game, Nick. Try this scenario: Winchester was down and needed support. They recruit him and help him rebuild his mind around the fact that he's their sleeper agent inside Capitol. He's supposed to be there and play innocent until he moves up. If the Brotherhood managed to convert other stockholders over to their way of thinking, Winchester could have even been voted in as President of Capitol."

"That scenario is not very improbable at all." Nick nodded slowly. "Win's laying low, then he sees Sandra's image on the ship's manifest and begins to crack. He contacts someone within the Brotherhood to deal with Sandra, and she's diverted to Eternal Vigilance."

"And Eternal Vigilance is in the middle of a war zone." I finished my sentence as we walked into the lounge area.

Mitch Hunter looked up from the seat in which he had stretched out. "War zone?"

"Yeah, war zone." Others started to gather as I answered Hunter. "Turns out our lady isn't in a sanitarium here, but out at the Chapel of Eternal Vigilance. And it, in turn, is in the middle of a battle between Imperial and our shadowy friends. Sorry to disappoint any of you who packed your golf clubs, but we've got real work to do."

"Roger that, Mr. Dent." Hunter stood and stretched like a jungle cat. "But, you know, putting things into holes isn't that much different than putting holes into things. Shoot straight and make your shots count, it's all basics."

"I hope so, Mitch," I smiled, "because if we hit into the rough on this one, we'll be up to our armpits in bogeys, and there's worse things out there than sand traps and water hazards."

TWENTY-SIX

Lieutenant Julia Alverez kept the SkyRay screaming along barely a hundred meters off the red planet's tortured landscape. In our approach, which had taken us down over the southern pole and then brought us in using the Cimmerian Mountains as cover, she kept the flying wing at five hundred knots. Even at that speed, the trip from San Dorado took seven hours and twice required refueling in the air. We'd gotten no warnings from the Hostile Threat Assessment Systems, which meant we might have surprise on our side, but the biggest surprise lay beyond the mountains at the northern edge of the Cimmerian Desert.

As we came up and over the plateau where Carl and I had sipped wine and discussed my mental health, I saw enough to confirm why he had chosen to put his private hideaway here. The plateau provided him an unobstructed view of Martian landscape. Twisted, pitted, and scourged as it had been by nature, it possessed a majesty that Luna City's gray landscape and even the Venusian jungles could not match.

At the far edge of the plateau, I saw why Carl had never updated his simulation. Fifty kilometers ahead a fetid black wound stained the planet's red flesh. Citadel towers, all full of barbs and spikes, pierced the landscape like a toxic weed. Even at this great a distance, the general shapes reminded me of the shadowed chamber in Larkspur, and I shivered.

Closer to us, literally at the base of the plateau five

kilometers downslope, Eternal Vigilance defiantly thrust its towers into the air. Fires burned around the Chapel as if it were an idol to which the offer of sacrifices was appropriate. The compound, which was marked by remnants of barbed-wire fences entangled around bestial corpses, had been seeded with bodies. Some buildings burned, other just sagged in on themselves. Circles of destruction showed where the defenders had put up resistance, then had fallen back as the Dark Legion pressed them harder and harder.

"Mitch, I think they're in the Chapel already. No visuals of defenders on the ground."

"Roger, Julia." Mitch looked at the rest of us from within his heavy armor. "Stay with your team, spread out, but support each other. White and Green teams will watch our backs, Red and Blue go straight for the Chapel, Purple get ready to direct traffic inside."

The transfer to vertical traverse mode started the SkyRay vibrating, but the Capitol soldiers appeared not to notice. Hunter had divided his people among three teams: Green and Red had three each, and Wendy Levin had been added to Purple team with the two Brotherhood representatives. Ash, Jan, and I made up Blue team while Yojimbo, Pam, and Lane were White team.

Jeff Taylor, Alverez's navigator and gunner, counted off the seconds to touchdown. "Three, two, one—rear hatch descending. Go!"

We hit with a bit of a bump, then poured out the back end of the aircraft. Running as fast as I could, I broke left and joined Jan and Ash hunting up cover. My heavy armor slowed me down a bit, and the helmet's faceplate restricted my field of vision ever so slightly, but dropping into a war zone without it would have been suicidal.

Behind us Julia took the plane vertical as the hatch closed, then shot off back toward the south. She was going to orbit the base and come back when we called—if we called. She and Jeff would also use the rockets mounted beneath the SkyRay's wings to keep Dark Legion aircraft off us. Strafing runs might drive back Dark Legion ground troops, but if we found ourselves in a position where we required that sort of ground support, we knew we were in serious trouble.

Clouds of smoke drifted across my field of vision, but the computer flashed infrared data images into my eyes to show me what was beyond the clouds. Bodies and puddles of viscous liquids predominated. The company of Brotherhood troopers stationed at Eternal Vigilance had sold their lives dearly. Everywhere, at their machine-gun nests and at the edges of the moat surrounding the Chapel itself, Dark Legion bodies lay heaped in leaking piles.

Moving forward, we followed the Dark Legion's line of advance. As we grew closer to the Chapel the numbers of bodies increased, both among defenders and attackers. At one point the still smoking ruin of a vehicle lay surrounded by body parts and ruined buildings.

Mitch shook his head. "Suicide bombing by a defender. Legion must have been massing."

Scythia's voice purred coolly through the radio. "The faithful will do anything to prevent the defilement of the Chapel."

The fact that more Dark Legion bodies sprawled over the wide steps leading to the hollow doorway in the Gaudían tower meant the defenders had not succeeded in stopping the Legion. Sprinting closer, I began to hear sounds of gunfire from within the Chapel itself. At the base of the steps I waved Ash forward, and Hunter likewise brought Ted Halston up. We followed in their wake and entered the world of some nightmare godling's vision of hell.

The entryway extended for two dozen meters and brought us to the head of steep stairs that led twenty meters down into the common worship area. A thousand meters square, the nave writhed with hundreds of Dark Legion warriors. Razides dotted the roiling ocean like islands in a stormy sea. Centauroid Ezoghouls leaped above the undead Legionnaires and stamped their steelshod hooves down on sacred statuary or the occasional defender who had not already been ripped to pieces.

As much as this had once been a sacred place, the Dark Legion had desecrated it and anointed it with the blood of its defenders. What once had been pews were now splintered pikes with human heads impaled on them. Pages from The Book of Law fluttered through the air like snowflakes while growls and snarls and screams echoed from walls that previously had only heard the vows and prayers of believers. Corruption ran thicker than blood, and cheers arose when necro-mutants pushing onward and upward through the high corridors tossed maimed and dying defenders down to the ravening horde below.

The obscene tableau so brutally assaulted our humanity that it stunned us.

Thus it was Ash who opened fire first. The whirling triple-barrels of his SSW4200P Gatling cannon vomited fire and armor-piercing projectiles. The backlight from the muzzle flashes burnished red and yellow highlights over Ash's stainless-still armor. Discarded shells streamed from the gun's ejection port, cascading down the stairs toward the Dark Legion horde below us. In the fire, with whining thunder of his weapon echoing through the Chapel, he appeared every centimeter an avenging force hammered from inanimate metal by Vulcan, the blacksmith god of human antiquity.

Ash scythed fire back and forth across the milling, screaming mass of undead at the base of the stairs. Moving at hypersonic speeds, 12.5mm projectiles designed to tear apart light vehicles barely slowed as they blew through Legionnaires. Warriors who had once been human before reanimation by the Dark Legion exploded into gobbets of gangrenous flesh and rotting bones. The lucky ones were cut in half—the others disintegrated and contributed to the wet, stinking, sodden mass of protoplasm lapping at the feet of the stairs.

Even with the unforgiving nature of his assault, Ash barely decimated the horde before the barrels of his gun glowed red, forcing him to pull back. In his place Mitch Hunter, Ted Halston, and I stepped up. Using the 37mm grenade launcher mated to the underside of my AR3000, I sent a round sizzling out at an Ezoghoul galloping toward us. My shell hit the massive creature in the left hip and glanced off. The grenade exploded in a huddle of necro-mutants, scattering their constituent parts and spraying gore over the Ezoghoul's flank.

Mitch Hunter's M50 launched a grenade that flew more accurately than mine had. It hit the Ezoghoul in the head and exploded on impact. That set the creature back on its heels, crushing more necro-mutants beneath its bunched haunches. As the monster shook its head, bits and pieces of the device it had worn over its nose and mouth flew out over the horde. Looking stricken, and getting a bit blue in color, the Ezoghoul clutched at its own throat and went mad.

Its stomping and prancing panicked the necro-mutants so badly they rushed the stairs. Fighting up and over the grim harvest Ash's fire had created, they came at us and there was no doubt we would quickly be overwhelmed. Hunter and I both unloaded our assault rifles, but even slaying the front rank barely slowed the onslaught.

Then Halston cut loose with his Gehenna Puker. The Cartel's heavy flame thrower spat out a fiery dragon's tongue that vaporized the lead element of the onrushing necro-mutants. Their high-pitched howls of agony lost in a battle with the Puker's throaty roar, and Halston lifted the fire-stream and arced it out into the center of the nave. In a volcanic flood it washed down and incinerated necro-mutants in an ever-growing circle.

The Dark Legion forces returned fire at us, but their small arms—rifles and submachine guns mostly—had difficulty penetrating our heavy armor. Bullets ricocheting off my armor's broad shoulder pads and squat helmet sounded like popcorn exploding in a battered tin pot. The sheer force of the return fire did drive me back, and I felt pain as bullet fragments found chinks in my armor, but the computer quickly damped my pain sensations.

Razides shouldered their way through the milling Legionnaires and necro-mutants. The heavy machine guns they bore could do to us what Ash's SSW4200P had done to their forces, but the panicked throng made aiming difficult. More importantly, Green team's two snipers, Venneti and Harris, used their Mephisto Sniper Rifles with devastating accuracy. Spread out to my right in the narthex of the Chapel, they calmly picked out the most dangerous targets and put a bullet through them or, in some cases, through their weapon.

Titus's voice came through our helmet radios. "We have the Cardinal's path open."

"Pull back, Green and Red. Blue, you're rear. White first." Mitch retreated slowly to the entryway and waved

Purple team through the darkened alcove after White had raced through. Green and Red teams went after them, leaving my team to bring up the rear. I was the last one in and closed the alcove entrance.

Scythia, who had spent time here at Eternal Vigilance, had mentioned two things on the flight that figured prominently in our plans if we had to enter the Chapel itself to find Sandra. The first was that an individual with Sandra's symptoms—cognitive dysfunction and catatonia—would be cared for in the special psychiatric infirmary high up in the Chapel. Up there the Brotherhood maintained a special staff who had been trained in dealing with severe mental illnesses and traumas, as those things often prompted family and friends to send people off on retreat.

The second thing she told us about—and very reluctantly at that—was of the existence of a special, secret passageway built into the walls and accessible from several points in the Chapel itself. While the Brotherhood made a big show of all celebrities being treated the same as anyone else in their eyes, the fact that a celebrity could disturb the concentration of another pilgrim on retreat just by his very presence meant that a covert way of moving folks around was required. She had described the passageway as narrow and twisted, but thanks to the Brotherhood's taste for armor and clothing as ostentatious and broad as our was functional, we were all able to fit in the passage—though if Ash squared his shoulders, he did strike sparks from the rough stones on either side of the passage.

Though the tunnel had been meant to be a secret, the Brotherhood's architects had not been stupid when they created it. Every twenty meters or so it leveled off and broadened out into a circle roughly three meters in diameter. The passages leading out of that point would twist at ninety degrees and or pitch up or down sharply. Because of the zigzag pattern, it became impossible to direct a stream of fire any farther than twenty meters, and that made the passage very easy to defend.

Yet even before we reached the first circle, I heard a sharp crack from down below, and light flooded the passage. I triggered the grenade launcher, and the explosion blew stone and shrapnel back out into the entryway. Moving through the smoke I saw more figures, so I tightened my finger down on the assault rifle's trigger. The weapon sprayed bullets back down the passage, but stopped abruptly when a shell jammed.

The necro-mutants poured into the passage. I fought to clear the jammed round, but my grip slipped on the AR3000's charging lever. I started to backpedaled up the stairs, but a burst of gunfire caught me in the chest. Though the bullets bounced from my armor, the force of the impact threw me onto my back. I hit hard on the steep stairs and lost my footing.

My armor, unyielding and rigid to protect me, angled to deflect projectiles and shrapnel, offered me no purchase on the stairs. As helpless as a turtle flipped onto his back at the top of an icy slope, I started to slide. Picking up speed, I bumped my way down to the horde of necro-mutants eagerly awaiting me below.

TWENTY-SEVEN

Two necro-mutants locked their hands on my ankles and would have pulled me apart had the narrow confines not prevented it. Shrieking maniacally they beat my legs against the steps and their lumpy fists against my legs. My armor made a horrible clacking as they assaulted it, and somewhere in their spoonful of brains that sound told them they were breaking me into little bits.

This made them laugh even more forcefully, unhinging their jaws like boa constrictors who intended to swallow me whole.

While the necro-mutant on the left tried to twist my foot off, I stuffed the barrel of the AR3000 in the mouth of the one on my right. His laughter died a second before I hit the grenade launcher switch. The 37mm grenade blasted out through the back of its head, then bounced off the tunnel's ceiling and careened down to explode in the mass of necro-mutants at the doorway.

I pulled my left leg back and threw the necro-mutant hanging on to it off balance. He released my foot and finally regained his balance a couple of steps down. Bracing his hands on either side of the passage, the necro-mutant rose above my spread-eagle body and roared at me. Homicidal fire lighting its eyes, it lunged at me.

I scissored my legs. My right foot caught the side of his head, and my left foot swept through his neck. Pain shot up my left leg, but the gurgled scream filling the tunnel came from the necro-mutant. Black blood geysered up to coat the tunnel's ceiling as the head caromed back down the stairs. The headless corpse stood upright in the passage, its limbs spasming as if it stood on a live wire. For a second it blocked the tunnel, then exploded as gunfire from below ripped it to pieces.

"Rex, stay down!"

A stream of bullets from above gnawed the next two necro-mutants into oozing heaps of twitching flesh. A golden light started from behind me, then something sizzled through the air and the heavy stench of ozone cut through the charnel-house stink in the tunnel. The plasma bolt hit one necro-mutant in the chest. Golden lightning played over its body, and the corpse began to dissolve from the inside out. Its swarthy flesh grew translucent, then blackened before the body burst into flame.

The burning body formed enough of a bulwark for me to regain my feet and retreat up the corridor. The first step on my left foot shot pain from my ankle to my hip, but I forced myself to continue backing up. I gave Jan the right side of the hallway for her to shoot down, and I unloaded the last two grenades in my launcher back down that tunnel. Between them and a couple more plasma bolts, we slowed pursuit, but could not stop it.

I finally reached the first of the circles. Jan yanked me aside as Ash stepped into the opening and fired down the tunnel. I landed heavily as Ash's spent cartridges peppered me in a hot hail. Jan slapped a new clip into her plasma carbine, then knelt beside me. "You okay? You were limping."

I glanced at a flashing light the computer had displayed in my field of vision, and a schematic of my body came up. The image focused on my left ankle, then zoomed in. It gave me a full readout of the damage, including recommended treatments and a probable date for full recovery.

I snarled. "My ankle's broken."

"Can you go on?"

"You think I'm going to stay here?" I glanced up at Ash. "You're our Roland at the pass."

The Attila's head swiveled toward me. "Information download to complete the cognitive association is unavailable at this facility."

"No, of course it isn't. Next time download everything

you'll need for a mission *before* we head out." I shook my head. "Roland means nothing gets past you."

"Roland. Acknowledged."

Jan helped me to my feet. "Follow when you can."

"Acknowledged."

I sent Jan on ahead of me, and I limped after as fast as possible. The computer deadened most of the pain from my ankle, but could not get rid of all of it without numbing it entirely. If it did that, I'd lose my ability to know where my foot was, and I'd stumble and fall a lot more than I would without the minimal amount of pain the computer let through.

Two more landings farther on and I found an open door leading out into one of the balconies overlooking the nave. The rest of our crew had run out and around to another corridor leading deeper into the Chapel. I followed as quickly as I could. Scattered gunfire skipped off pillars and walls around me, but none of it hit me. Occasionally I stopped and shot at necro-mutants trying to climb up pillars to reach my level. More often than not I sent their limp bodies sailing down to the floor to be pulped beneath the hooves of raging Ezoghouls.

Up ahead I heard shooting, and it sounded more heavy and concentrated than our group was capable of generating. As I came around the corner of the corridor, I saw our crew hunkered down behind cover on one side and a handful of the Brotherhood's Sacred Warriors on the other side. Backing down the hallway and through a huge double doorway, a cohort of undead Legionnaires and necro-mutants fired their weapons at us. They formed an undead wall between us and two large and incredibly strong, green-gray-skinned humanoids, each of which bore a human under one arm.

Though I never saw her face, I knew the female captive had to be Sandra. Her size and shape were difficult to judge at that distance, but the monster's jealous care for her and harsh glower back at us told me she was somehow sacred to it. The other monster, looking more sullen yet just as protective of its prize, bore a man wearing the red robe of an archbishop.

"Mitch," Alverez's voice crackled over the radio, "You

have four choppers and two fighters coming in from the Citadel to the north. All black technology."

"Don't engage, Julia, bug out if you can."

"I have no choice but to engage. This SkyRay may be a slow pig, but it's a well-armed pig. I'll be back when I can."

"Good luck."

We could hear the rhythmic whooping of a helicopter's rotor through the doorway, and Titus pointed toward it. "There is a helipad out there. They are getting away with the hostages."

The urgency in his voice rippled through me like an adrenaline booster shot. I suppose, somehow, in the back of my mind I knew that Ash would fall when he ran out of ammo for his cannon, and necro-mutants would surge up through the Cardinal's path to trap us. The Ezoghouls might be too large to use it or even the more conventional corridors spiraling up through the Chapel, but those wider passages would easily accommodate Razides. We were trapped and that would mean we would die.

Dying without having rescued Sandra was something I could not contemplate.

Dropping to my left knee, I jammed a new clip of four grenades into the AR3000's launcher and pumped all four straight into the middle of their formation. Bodies flew high into the air, cartwheeling into collisions with the walls. Sliding back down to the floor, they made smears amid the gore-spatter the explosions had created. The hole the blasts had torn in the necro-mutant formation was slow to fill.

The taller creatures snapped orders at the Legionnaires. A half dozen of the undead sought to close the doors to the chamber while the rest started howling and screaming. Guns blazing, they charged out at us. Even though the corridor offered them no cover for their assault, the distance between us was quite short, and they fell upon us before we could do more than cut their number in half.

In close quarters combat my assault rifle proved useless except as a club. Because my most recent training had been in unarmed combat, I didn't need a club. The metal armor sheathing my body both protected me and made my attacks even more lethal than they would normally have been. I threw the empty rifle at one necro-mutant, knocking it down, then braced myself to fight more of them.

I ducked beneath the initial attempt of a zombi to bat my head back down the corridor with his clubbed rifle, then stabbed the stiffened fingers of my right hand up into his armpit. The blow pierced his side and severed both muscle and ligaments. His enthused follow-through of the attack meant he tore his own arm off. Black blood spattered all of us as he pirouetted on past me.

A stamp-kick hyperextended another necro-mutant's right leg to the point of its knee popping, then I punched his nose back into his brain stem. Throwing myself forward, I flew beneath a Legionnaire's snap-kick. My head-butt to his groin upset him, then I scrambled forward and landed with both knees on his face. His skull crunched between my leg armor and the stone floor.

Springing up, I found myself all the way through to the other side of the Dark Legion formation. Ahead of me one of the tall necro-mutants forced his Brotherhood captive back through the narrowing gap between the doors, then drew a wickedly barbed sword and stalked toward me. As the blade cut through the air the weapon seemed to torture a shriek out of it. Not laughing, but cunning and confident, what my computer scanned, cross-referenced, and confirmed as a Centurion closed with me.

It angled in at my left side, which meant it had noticed I was not fully mobile. Drawing my left leg back, I lowered myself into a crouch. Raising my hands in a guard, I waved it on in. "Do your worst."

The first attack came high from my left to my right and I slid away from it. As the Centurion recovered himself, I saw his grip shift on the sword. The return cut came in faster, letting me know the monster was left-handed. As I'd moved *toward* his strong side with my first retreat, this information came late, but still had its uses.

Darting forward, I got inside the tall creature's attack circle. I grabbed his wrists in both of my hands, then turned my body around so, for a second, my back slapped up against his belly. Continuing my move, I slid back beneath his left arm, then dropped to my knees and yanked

down with all my strength. The Centurion flipped in the
air and hit the ground hard on his back while his sword
struck sparks from the floor.

He was ready to bounce up, but I shifted my left hand
down to lock his left wrist and twist his arm around. If he
leaped to his feet, his own weight would snap his arm or
dislocate his shoulder. His only escape was to flop on his
belly and then yank his hand from my grip. In a straight
contest of strength, his left arm against my left hand, he
would have no trouble winning. He knew that and probably already had begun planning his attacks once he got
the sword back in his hands.

The reason I only used one hand to delay him was because my right hand was busy drawing and aiming my
Punisher. The Centurion's eyes grew quite wide as I
pressed the gun to his forehead and pulled the trigger.
The first bullet only seemed to anger him, but the second
and third snuffed the light of evil in his eyes. With the
fourth and fifth I felt the strength leave his limbs, so I
used the seventh and eighth to further scramble his
brains, then I stood.

Hunter smashed the butt of his assault rifle into the
face of a necro-mutant, and Yojimbo bisected one with a
huge samurai sword. I waved the Mishaman forward,
then pointed to the door. "Mitch, blow it."

Hunter dropped two grenades dead on target and blew
one of the big, bronze doors off its hinges. It spun into
the room beyond like a top, whirling on a corner.
Yojimbo and I leaped in through the gap and saw the door
whip through two necro-mutants, then totter and fall on a
third. I capped a fourth with two shots from the Punisher.
Yojimbo parried a bayonet attack by one and then split
him skull to breastbone with an overhead strike.

Out beyond the glass wall we saw a strange flying
craft. It appeared to be a helicopter, and clearly had metal
and plastics as part of it, but I could not recognize it. My
computer could find no match because the craft had been
warped and changed by the Dark Legion. Odd bumps and
bulges, like tumors, twisted the metal of its flesh. It appeared as if whatever the original craft had been, biolog-
ical elements had been grafted to it to make it into
something else entirely.

The other Centurion tossed Sandra and the Brotherhood hostage through the side door, then climbed in itself. It kicked a last necro-mutant in the face to drive it back toward us, then the helicopter leaped up into the air and raced off toward the south. Out of frustration, I fired at the necro-mutant on the helipad and struck him at least once. I didn't kill him, but drove him off the edge of the landing area and had the grim satisfaction of hearing him scream for a couple of seconds before he hit the ground below.

The others poured into the room with Jan and one of Hunter's men, Redfield, taking up positions at the door. Aside from Ash being gone, I noticed two bodies in Capitol armor and two more Sacred Warriors being laid out in a corner. Lane seemed to be favoring his right arm, and Wendy Levin, the medic from Mitch's squad, was tending a nasty gash on Titus's forehead.

Mitch shook his head. "We lost three of ours, have three wounded, but pick up four Brotherhood Sacred Warriors. Not a good trade."

"Who did you lose?"

The special forces captain glanced at the corner. "Venneti and Halston."

I looked around the room. "This appears to be as good a place as any to make a stand. We can hold it until Alverez can bring the SkyRay in and pick us up."

Mitch shook his head. "Never work. SkyRay is too heavy for a pad made for helicopters. If we can't get to the ground, she can't pick us up."

"Captain, I have incoming. Nonhostile."

Two more Sacred Warriors came through the doorway. Behind them two dozen very frightened men, women, and children ran into the room. They started screaming when they saw the necro-mutant bodies. They probably would have continued to do so, but Scythia marched to the center of the room, her black cloak flowing around her armor like a piece of shadow itself, holding aloft a black, leather-bound copy of the Book of the Law. The Brotherhood's crossed-arrow insignia glinted gold from the cover and combined with her sheer presence to cow the civilians into mewing calm.

She consulted briefly with one of the half dozen Sacred

Warriors who had shepherded the pilgrims into the room, then approached Mitch. "I have been told this is all that remains of the pilgrims here at Eternal Vigilance. An earlier convoy did head out to the south, but their fate is unknown and probably doubtful. It appears that the unit that assaulted Eternal Vigilance was originally meant to hold the flank in the Dark Legion counterattack against the Imperial assault at Cereberus. It diverted here to destroy Eternal Vigilance and, apparently, to take your Lorraine Kovan."

"I'll be sure to file that in the report we leave behind with our bodies here." Mitch loaded a new clip into his M50 assault rifle. "Holding the high ground is good strategy, but not when there is no way down."

"But there is, Captain Hunter." Scythia gestured at the helipad.

"SkyRay can't land there."

"No, there is the requisite emergency evacuation equipment as required on all helipads." Scythia's voice made it all sound very matter-of-fact. "While this is a place of worship, it was not constructed without consideration for the safety of our personnel and guests."

That comment seemed incongruous with the slaughter around us, but I didn't point that out. "If we're going to try to get to the ground from here, we'll need to draw them up here so they have a hard time getting back down to pursue us."

"Agreed." Mitch looked up at Scythia. "Organize these people into evacuation parties and brief them on what they'll be doing. We'll send your Sacred Warriors down first to hold the ground for them. I'll get my people to shift this door around and rig it with explosives, so we'll turn it into one giant Claymore mine. I'll need some rabbits to tease the enemy while we do this."

I raised my hand. "Rabbit reporting for duty." Jan, Pam, and Yojimbo joined me. Having lost my AR3000 in the melee, I appropriated Halston's Gehenna Puker, and we went out to make the Dark Legion very, very angry at us.

TWENTY-EIGHT

Making the Dark Legion mad at us was not one of those things that was easier said than done. Yojimbo made very good use of Venneti's Mephisto Sniper Rifle to do cranial volume surveys on Razides, Centurions, and necro-mutants. The vast majority of undead Legionnaires seemed deathly afraid of the Gehenna Puker's fire. I guessed that was because cremation somehow put them beyond the possibility of being reanimated yet again. While being an undead warrior might not be much of a life, as the saying goes, it beats the alternative, even if only by a slender margin.

Picking off the intelligent among the horde and terrifying the rest seemed to work pretty well for buying time up until the point when the pressure of those below forced the ones above forward. At the base of the Chapel tower, Ezoghouls exhorted their minions to assault us. Even though the Ezoghouls were too big to traverse the corridors to punish the necro-mutants and Legionnaires, the lesser creatures took their threats to heart and gradually forced us back.

When we reached the melee corridor, the four of us broke and ran. We vaulted over the bronze door that had been wedged crossways in the corridor. On the other side of it various explosive charges had been arranged to convert the whole thing into a sleet-storm of shrapnel. Nodding once as I visualized what that would do to the monsters following us, I cut around the corner and limped as quickly as I could to the helipad.

Two huge yellow evacuation tubes—one at each external corner of the helipad—ran all the way down to the ground. The civilians would have used them to slide to safety. The rest of us, because our armor and weapons would have shredded the tubes' soft fabric, had to use the slide cables to go down. Harris linked himself on to one, and Pam, Jan, and Yojimbo took the other three. Mitch Hunter and I would have to wait until they had cleared the lines before we could use them, but we both had last-minute work to do.

Hunter looked up from the small LCD screen on the detonation control box. "They're at twenty meters. Rex, use the Puker." He pointed at the center of the helipad where our four fallen comrades had been laid out. "We won't get them away now, so burn them. Don't want the Legion using them against us. Ten meters."

I immolated the bodies, then started flooding the room in the temple with fire.

"Down!"

I hit the deck with Mitch's shout. A tremendous explosion shook the Chapel, and the back blast blew fire into a roiling ball that ascended toward the heavens. Glass fragments from the windows pelted us, but broke like waves on stone against our armor.

The two of us scrambled up and ran to the escape lines. "Lines one and two are clear," Pam told us over the radio.

I used the Gehenna Puker to ignite the evacuation slides and lines three and four. Taking a snap-link from the escape provisions basket near line two, I clipped my armor onto the line and slid to safety. Wind whistled past the angles in my armor as I accelerated, then I hit hard and white-hot agony punched up through my left leg.

Hunter picked up the Puker from where it had fallen and torched the other two lines while Jan and Wendy dragged me back from the edge of the Chapel tower. Fiery loops of rope twisted and snapped through the air as they fell to the ground. The evacuation slides sent a thick gray smoke into the sky, and the stench of burning plastics spiced the death miasma with a waxy scent.

Hunter turned toward the front of the Chapel and shot a gout of flame off toward the entrance. Around the corner galloped three Ezoghouls, each bearing a huge sword in one hand and a pistol-gripped assault rifle in the other. Mitch's attack forced them to shy off, but they cut in closer to the Chapel and threaded their way through burning rope snakes to face us.

One of them gestured at us as I attempted to shake Jan and Wendy off. "Go!" I shouted, but my word trailed off into a terrified shriek. Something pulsed out from the Ezoghoul at the head of their wedge. I felt it in my soul the way I could feel heat from a fire on my flesh, and this burned me with utter terror. I fell down as Wendy and Jan ran away screaming.

I wanted to run with them, but the throbbing pain in my ankle told me that was not possible. I had no weapon left with which I could kill the Ezoghouls, so fighting them was not an option. I had to fight, but I could not. I had to run, but I could not. The alternatives ricocheted around inside my skull, colliding with each other and getting boosts in vitality from the fear gripping me. Though a small part of me knew the numbing horror I felt was artificial and projected by the lead Ezoghoul, that logic could not command me to move or act.

As terrified and as helpless as I had been when my spine had been shattered, now I was yet more so frightened and hopeless. Even Parabellum Rex, the part of me that had fought so hard to stay alive, could not have defied or denied or defeated what I felt. I was going to die and not a living thing could prevent it.

The first sight I caught of my rescuer came when the sun sparked gold from his glittering armor. Having leaped from the helipad, Ash landed with both feet square on the spine of the lead Ezoghoul, right in the middle of its back. I heard its spine snap as cleanly as mine had. Ash's weight bore the beast to the ground, shattering ribs and pulverizing internal organs. The creature's inhuman shriek of agony thundered through me and started my ears ringing.

Ash bounced off the first Ezoghoul and rolled up in front of the one on the right. I noticed then that Ash had lost his left arm. His left leg had been stripped of armor, and a number of frayed adductor cables hung down from his hip joint. His SSW4200P had no ammo belt feeding into it, and the barrels had long since warped because of the heat generated by the gun's use. In fact, the barrels twisted down and had been wrapped around the hilt of a Centurion's barbed sword.

Ash thrust the makeshift bayonet into the second Ezoghoul's abdomen. Steaming green blood started to bubble around the wound, but the Ezoghoul did not cry out in pain. It glared defiantly down at Ash. Its expression seemed to ask if that was the best he could do, then it raised its own sword and shouted contemptuous epithets at the Attila.

Ash hit the switch on his gun, and the barrels began to spin. Lunging forward, Ash let the weapon drill into the Ezoghoul's belly. Viscera and blood the color and consistency of creamed spinach poured out over Ash, but he ignored it and the Ezoghoul's flailing hooves. Pushing forward and down, Ash levered the sword up higher into the Ezoghoul's body cavity, then drove it up further until I saw the spinning blade shred the Ezoghoul's throat from the inside.

The Ezoghoul Ash's jump had crippled went and flopped on its side in front of me. It dug its hands into the red earth and pulled itself closer to me. My sense of terror increased, but the sides of the equation that had made me incapable of action before became unbalanced. Unable to flee, I was forced to fight, and the monster's being forced down to my level meant I could strike at it. While I might not have the weapons I needed to kill it outright, I remembered that Hunter had doomed one by destroying the pulsating breathing apparatus on its face.

As it crawled nearer and I gathered my arms beneath me, the third Ezoghoul leaped over its crippled leader and attacked Ash with its sword. The Attila tried to pull its weapon free of the Ezoghoul corpse, but the whirling blade hung up on the breastbone. Unable to parry, yet unable to retreat since its software commanded it to somehow defend me, Ash gave the Gatling cannon one final tug. The sword carved its way out of the corpse, but too late to help. The Ezoghoul's sweeping struck Ash's head off and sent it sailing out toward my retreating compatriots.

Pushing off with my good leg, I leaped above the first Ezoghoul's clumsy attempt at grabbing me. Throwing myself forward, I landed on my right knee and hand inside the circle of the Ezoghoul's arms. I stabbed my right hand forward and punched it into the gelatinous parasite clinging over the Ezoghoul's snout. I felt the protoplasm quiver and saw mucous gush at the edges of the seal, then I felt the Ezoghoul's teeth close on my forearm.

Posting up on its arms and scrabbling to get its front hooves under it, the Ezoghoul reared its torso back and pulled me from the ground. The breathing device poured down my arm and hung from my shoulder. The monster started to swing its head back and forth, to shake me and snap my limbs. The unforgiving power in the creature's broken body convinced me that it could easily accomplish what it desired.

As I started to swing back to my left, I kicked off the Ezoghoul's bony chest with my right foot. This accelerated my swing. Reaching up with my left hand, I grabbed one of the horny protuberances on its brow and swung myself around to where my body's weight wrenched my forearm sideways in the monster's beak and let me get my legs around its neck.

The Ezoghoul shifted its weight to its left arm and tried to grab me with its right hand. As it did that, I hammered my left fist down on its snout and left eye. I heard something crack and part of the beast's face caved in. Another punch completed the fracturing of its maxilla. I pulled my right arm free of its broken maw just as its right hand grabbed my right thigh and hammered me into the ground.

My armor absorbed most of the tooth-rattling impact. Kicking wildly, I dug my heel into its forearm and the hand released me. As I spun away from the Ezoghoul's hands, the terror that had seized me vanished, leaving me unarmed, on one knee, before a dying Ezoghoul, facing yet another that was uninjured.

And the computer took that moment to inform me that, though I could not feel it yet, my collision with the ground had dislocated my right shoulder.

The last Ezoghoul reared up and flicked a hoof at me. I managed to partially avoid the blow, which meant that when it hit me in the chest and knocked the wind out of me, it only tossed me half a dozen feet farther through the Martian air. I landed hard again on my right shoulder and heard a pop. I waited for the pain, but the computer reported my arm was back in its socket and suggested that arching my back would help me regain my breath.

Almost prancing, the Ezoghoul charged at me, then stopped as if it had hit a stone wall. I saw sparks glint off some of the metallic bits of the Ezoghoul's body, and flesh peel back in ribbons as bullets fragmented upon impact. Its head snapped back, and the Ezoghoul stumbled backward as gunfire caught it high, but the creature regained its balance just on the far side of its leader's corpse, and I knew it was far from dead. Using the gun in its left hand, it sprayed fire out at Mitch and the others shooting at it, then it lowered its sword like a lance and pointed it directly at my chest.

Fortunately for me, its retreat returned it to the spot where it had beheaded Ash, though it faced me instead of him. The headless Attila unit's proximity sensors registered its target and the limbs, having stored the final command the head had given them, plunged its weapon's whirling blade into the Ezoghoul's body. The sword augured its way into and through the monster's chest, then the Attila wrenched the blade upward and pulled it free in a verdant spray of blood and vertebrae.

The monster's dying scream sounded more out of frustration than any agony. Its forehooves shattered red rock and peppered me with fragments as if sought to somehow stomp life out of me. I scrambled back away from it despite the agony in my left leg. Sparks struck as the creature's front end succumbed to the damage Ash's body had done to its back half. It crashed down in a ocher cloud and finally lay very still.

Jan and Diane Parker—another of Mitch's snipers—ran up to me, hooked their arms through mine, and pulled me back away toward where the others had gathered.

"We're going to try to clear a place for Julia to land the SkyRay." Mitch dropped to one knee beside me and scanned the skies for our plane. "Ammo is low, but we might be able to hold it. If she gets back soon."

"No," I gasped weakly. "Let's move. Let's get up to the top of the plateau."

"High ground is good, but we won't have escape chutes for the other side."

"Mitch, trust me. Let's work up the side of the mesa here."

The man stopped for a second, then looked down at me. "Do you know something I don't?"

"I think so, and we both better hope I really do."

Titus and Scythia led the trek up the side of the mesa. The rough path there was usually five feet wide, but erosion in the rainy season had worn it down to a foot or less in some places. The Sacred Warriors helped the pilgrims along, with Lane and me in the middle and the rest of our unit playing rear guard. We made progress slowly, and as the heat rose off the desert plains below, we stopped more frequently to rest the pilgrims.

To the north and west hundreds of distant black-smoke plumes dotted the landscape. Black dots hovered in the air, then darted around. Other specks wove in an out among them, and occasionally something exploded. Always, though, the black dots pushed farther north, relentlessly and remorselessly.

Hunter sat down beside me. He dropped his helmet between my helmet and Ash's head. "Kind of ghoulish, your carrying that thing around."

"I know, but Ash is still in there, and he's working on our situation right now." I pointed out at the distant air battle. "Would I be guessing wrong if I said it looked like Imperial's drive is heading in reverse."

"Nope. Serves the bastards right, too."

"What do you mean?"

"Pam, Lane, and I were with the banshees when the Dark Legion first started to build over here. Capitol launched a huge air attack against the beginnings of their Citadel. Alverez can tell you about it—she told me about it on the flight here to Mars. Imperial's Automatic Air Defense came online and knocked down about eighty percent of what we were sending in to attack the Dark Legion. They got a bunch of kills out of the attack and extended their control over a lot of territory, but now the Dark Legion is encroaching on them. Had they not ambushed us, the Dark Legion never would have gotten its beachhead on Mars."

Diane Parker cradled her sniper rifle to her chest as she squatted down next to us. "Captain, I think we have trouble. The Legion guys from the Chapel have stopped following us."

I glanced down at the base of the plateau and saw she was correct. The Razides appeared to be assembling their troops away from the head of the trail we were on. In fact, they were moving them back from the base of the mesa. Had any of us had grenades left for our weapons, we might have been able to kill quite a few in those tightly packed formations.

Parker pointed off at the far battle. "I've been watching some of the choppers out there, and I think we have some headed our way."

"Great! We'll be sitting ducks up here." Mitch stood up and started pointing both up and down along the trail. "We have incoming aircraft. Disperse and find what cover you can. Parker, see what you can pick off. Yojimbo, do the same." He shook his head. "This will be ugly, so if what you know that I don't is a way to conjure up miracles, enlighten me."

Ash's head beeped. I picked it up and stared him in the eyes. I got a command-code sequence that I immediately fed to the software controlling my cellular phone link. As the program loaded and ran, I smiled at Mitch. "Ask and you might receive."

All of a sudden a white curtain parted before my eyes, and I saw Carl dressed in casual slacks and shirt standing on the ledge beside Mitch. "This is highly irregular, Rex."

"Desperate times call for desperate measures. I remembered your saying this was your hideaway."

"I shut it down long ago, Rex." Carl shook his head. "In fact, I contacted you only because the repeated attempts to make contact through Ash alerted me to tampering. Had I not identified him, your effort would have gone unanswered."

"Forgive me for ignoring protocols, but this is a highly dangerous situation we're in, and we're desperate."

Carl nodded as he looked out at the growing black spots in the sky. "So you are. The thing is, this is a hyper-secret installation. We shut it down after the Dark Legion arrived. The board would revolt if I used it to succor your band of survivors—the majority of whom are of the Brotherhood. Even worse, Lorraine Kovan is not among them."

"Carl, if you don't help us . . ." I started to protest that he had to help us, but letting us die would keep his secret. At some point in the future whatever he had inside the mesa might be valuable and help stop the Dark Legion at a crucial point. To waste it on us might do more harm than good, and someone in Carl's position had to consider such things when making a decision.

I frowned. "I'm asking for a favor, Carl. Saving us may not be cost-effective or even expedient, but it *is* the human thing to do. It is good, and injecting some more good into the world will hurt the Dark Legion in more ways than you know."

"Eloquently put, Rex." Carl nodded slowly. "An excellent mix of abstract thought blended with emotion under the guise of logic."

"Then you'll help?"

"I will." He shrugged. "Besides, I've wanted to play with the toys in here for a long time."

Carl's image grew to titanic proportions as he stepped off the ledge and fell toward the ground. He strode away from us and sprang up to the height of a kilometer. As he did so, I felt a rumbling in the mountainside and heard someone say, "Damn, those look like missile launching bays!"

Carl bracketed the first Dark Legion helicopter with his hands, and a missile streaked skyward at it. Carl's hands continued to enfold the chopper as if it were a butterfly intent on fleeing, and the missile spiraled through the sky at it. When the missile hit, the helicopter exploded, but Carl walked through the fireball unharmed.

In similar fashion he directed other missiles at the four remaining choppers, then lobbed one in on the Dark Legion's ground forces. Their remnants scattered screaming in complete panic. Our people started cheering, and Mitch banged a fist against my shoulder pads; but looking farther to the north, I saw something that drained all relief and pleasure out of me.

The far Citadel grew brighter for a moment as a miniature sun ignited beneath a rocket ship. It rose from the horizon slowly at first, then more quickly and finally hurtled through the sky like one of Carl's missiles. I watched it, and my computer continually updated its estimated range and velocity in ever increasing numbers.

I shivered. "'That's it, Mitch. That's a ship carrying Lorraine away. Taking her from Imperial on the Moon broke their plan, but sending her back here fixed it up again."

"Where do you think it's going?"

I shook my head as I slowly stood up beside him. "I don't know, and without that information, there's no way we'll ever get her back."

TWENTY-NINE

Alverez managed to land the SkyRay on the plateau and took the lot of us back to San Dorado. It was a bit cramped, but we were all too exhausted to notice the conditions. The rescued pilgrims were very happy with us, and a number of them made us promise that we would visit them when next we were on Venus or the Moon or had free time on Mars. Wendy Levin, while she was working on my ankle, said that sort of euphoria was normal, but the offers were likely genuine.

Back in San Dorado the team broke apart and retreated to our neutral corners, myself being the sole exception to that rule. I co-opted part of the suite my brother had taken in the Coprates Arms. A doctor set my ankle and put it in a fiberplast cast. He also gave me a sling for my right arm even though he could not find any permanent damage done to my shoulder socket.

My brother, on the other hand, had all sorts of permanent damage to contend with. "Win Raleigh is furious with me for commandeering that SkyRay. He'd have my head on a stick except that Anna would never speak to him again. I also managed to get Lieutenant Alverez a medal for her part in your assault, and the Brotherhood has been very happy with the results of the rescue."

I smiled at him. "Did we get a letter from the Cardinal?"

"No, because that would require explaining how Eternal Vigilance had fallen to the Dark Legion, and no one wants to saddle the unsuspecting public with that sort of information." Nick chewed a burr from his thumbnail. "The Brotherhood has assured me that if our operation requires anything at all, they will move heaven and earth to provide it."

"Great, they can get us a spaceship so we can follow Sandra."

Nick grimaced. "Anything save a spaceship. Just because of shipping schedules, everything in port right now is controlled by Win. Either the ships belong to Capitol, or they're using our storage and loading facilities at the spaceport. Of the three ships in port that Capitol doesn't own, two belong to Imperial and one to Bauhaus."

"The two corps not invited to our party."

"Exactly. We aren't moving from Mars until Win says we can move."

I limped over to a chair in the suite and dropped down into its padded embrace. "Doesn't matter, at this point, because we don't know where Sandra is headed." The logistics of finding, catching, and boarding another spaceship are so prohibitively expensive and so prone to disaster that even I wouldn't endorse that sort of thing. Our only chance to get Sandra back would be to assault the location where her ship went down.

"The ship is still heading out away from the sun. We're looking at three weeks until they hit the asteroid belt and another three before they reach Jupiter."

"Six weeks is a lot of slack time to make up for a split-second rescue." For the first time I began to feel Sandra was truly lost to us. That annoyed me, and I refused to surrender to defeatism. "At least that would give me time to heal from the ankle break."

"And might be enough time for Win to cool down."

I heard a gentle knock on the door to our suite. Nick got up to answer it, and I awkwardly levered myself to my feet using my left arm and my right leg. I steadied myself against the chair as Nick opened the door and admitted Titus Gallicus. "Favor of the Cardinal upon you, Inquisitor. Has Scythia abandoned you?"

"May the Book of Laws bring you comfort, Mr. Dent, and you, Mr. Kell." The tall, slender Brotherhood Inquisitor looked rested after our ordeal. If not for the bandage on his forehead, it would have been impossible to tell he had been involved in any sort of expedition. "No, Scythia is not with me, but it is on her behalf that I have come."

Nick waved him to a chair. "Please, be seated."

The Inquisitor shook his head. "Another time, perhaps. I would like the both of you to accompany me, if you would. I have a car waiting down on the street."

My brother draped a jacket around my shoulders and got me the aluminum cane the doctors had provided for me. Titus remained silent in the elevator down to the ground, then ushered us into a black, stretch limousine. Once inside he told the driver to head out, then smiled and rested his hands on his black-robed knees.

"I hope you will not think this overly dramatic, but I cannot tell you where we are going. Because you are with Cybertronic, Mr. Dent, it is necessary that this vehicle's passenger compartment be totally shielded, so external communication will not work. I hope you can appreciate the need for secrecy and will make no attempt to solve the mystery of our destination. I assure you that no harm will befall you."

I nodded. "After Eternal Vigilance, I'm willing to trust you. What is all this about?"

"Our organization, as you know, is vast and has people involved in it on various levels. Most come to us as I did—answering a divine calling to my vocation. I saw that my life could be no better spent than devoting it to bringing the Book of Laws and its message to my fellow man. It is an arduous task, and often a thankless one, but this is the burden laid upon my heart, and one I struggle daily to uphold."

Outside the limo's darkened windows, buildings slid by as shadowy monoliths. "I was impressed by your Sacred Warriors at Eternal Vigilance, Inquisitor. Their actions in defense of their faith were impressive."

"Thank you, Mr. Dent. The Sacred Warriors who served there were a credit to the Second Directorate. They remained loyal to the precepts that we all hold as sacred. The Abbot of Eternal Vigilance might not have been as high-minded as they. There is some indication, now, that he sought to build a coalition within the Brotherhood that would facilitate his elevation to the position of Cardinal when His Holiness completes his mission. He apparently agreed to help Lorraine Kovan recover from her trauma as a favor to a friend who would be seen as valuable in the future to the Brotherhood."

Nick and I exchanged glances. Titus had all but confirmed Win Raleigh was a Brotherhood sleeper, and apparently did so because Win's patron, the Abbott of Eternal Vigilance, had been exposed.

Titus smiled carefully. "Because we put Mrs. Kovan in danger through the actions of one of our members, we felt responsible for her. Since the original Dark Legion plan called for her to be sent to Mars and then moved from here to another place, we surmised that the Dark Legion must have had a cell on Mars, similar to the one that took Mrs. Kovan from Capitol on Luna. We surmised that it probably had Imperial connections. Knowing Saladin's Citadel was the logical destination for Mrs. Kovan, and bearing in mind the penurious nature of most Imperial citizens, we began searching for reservations to travel to the Chapel and then the sudden cancellation of the same before and after her rescue from the Imperial facility on Luna."

I blinked. "That's one hell of a search. You should have let me know, and we could have had some computers at Cybertronic do it."

"We have found that a sufficient number of devoted monks employed in the proper manner can be almost as efficient as a computer. Indeed, they produced a number of likely targets that we investigated, and we finally settled on an individual we believe is the ringleader of the Dark Legion group here on Mars. Scythia took him into custody, and we wanted you to be present to witness his interrogation."

My brother and I again exchanged glances, and made no attempt to hide our surprise. Nick watched Titus warily. "You are going to allow us to witness one of your Inquisitors questioning a suspect?"

"The decision to do so is not without precedent. The process we use to break down resistance and extract a confession is not that much different than the one you employ when making inquiries of suspects. In fact, the Brotherhood views this portion of the Reconciliation process to be secular. We believe it is important, especially with heretics such as this, to produce a confession without relying on theology or philosophy. Only once the heretic's errors can be shown to him in a secular environment will he be open to an exploration and recantation of his false beliefs."

I frowned. "Break him down as a man, then rebuild him as a person within the Brotherhood?"

"Metaphysically speaking there is much more to the Reconciliation of an individual, and reconstruction as a human being is part of the process, but you have the core of it in a nutshell there." Titus shrugged, then smoothed wrinkles from his black cassock. "We are concerned with having the individual make a break with his past so we can save him in his future. As the Brotherhood is generally not part of his past, using it to break him would be difficult."

"But eventually he is remade in the image of the Brotherhood."

"Much as you were remade in the image of Cybertronic."

The vehicle's sharp descent down a ramp and gradual slowing to a stop prevented further discussion of the Brotherhood's techniques for dealing with heretics. I gathered from Titus's early remarks that the Reconciliation was sacrosanct. Because of that I'd learned nothing more from him about the sacrament, so the end of our conversation was not as premature as it might have seemed.

We quit the car in an underground garage and were immediately led down a stairwell to a level sunk deep into the red planet's stony flesh. I brushed my fingers over the ferrocrete blocks making up the walls and felt none of the heat common on this world. I knew Nick was similarly collecting data and that if I invoked my computer, I could get an infrared reading that would be able to approximate the depth of this level.

I did not, in keeping with my agreement with Titus. I knew I always would have the chance to take such measurements on the way out, but that alone did not stop me. Something told me he was pushing the actions allowed an Inquisitor by bringing us to the interrogation. While the Brotherhood might have permitted outsiders to be present before, I had no doubt they were from accredited law enforcement agencies, not civilians like Nick and me.

Titus led us through a fire door, then down a short corridor and into a dimly lit room. Across from the door a window slanted back and away to let us look down on a room beside and below the one in which we stood. I leaned on the cold metal railing and stared down into the brightly lit room. Looking up at eye level, I saw a mirror opposite my position in the other wall, confirming my suspicion that I was looking through a one-way mirror. In the room, two black-robed Inquisitors stood before a dark-haired heretic and plied him with questions.

The heretic sat in a curious device. It looked like a wooden chair, but he sat in it so his chest rested against the back. His legs had been fastened with leather straps to boards that ran straight out from the seat of the chair, and his arms were fastened straight out on other planks that stood out from the back of the chair. It looked as if he were seated on the floor doing toe-touches, then frozen and fitted to this chair.

It did not look comfortable, and he looked rather ill-at-ease. Sweat soaked the back of his T-shirt and darkened the waistband of the surgical scrub pants. I wasn't certain if he was a doctor who they had dragged out of an operating theater, or if they had supplied him that garb. His arms were bare, likewise his feet, and his head lolled from time to time with extreme lassitude.

I looked over at Titus. "He looks as if he's been down there a long time. You worked fast if you found him and brought him in during the twenty-four hours since we escaped Eternal Vigilance."

The Inquisitor stared down at the man. "The search for a Dark Legion Cell on Mars began around the time you left Luna. Our agents arrested Dr. Woods when we set off for Eternal Vigilance. He has been questioned three times and is two hours into the new session. He is near breaking, and Scythia will see that he tells us what we want to know."

As he spoke, a door opened in the wall below us, admitting Scythia. Woods glanced at her and stiffened his spine. Though I only saw his face in profile, I recognized the hint of a lecherous smile, and I had difficulty reconciling the idea of lust or attraction with Scythia until she moved away from the door and started to pace around the room. Her fluid grace and the fire in her eyes *did* make her more seductive, but I could still feel the cold press of her palm against mine when we first met.

The other two Inquisitors quit the room and the lights dimmed until only a single spotlight in the ceiling pinned Woods in place. Around him, existing like a ghost in the light reflected from the floor, Scythia circled him. Passing behind him, she let a long fingernail lightly scratch along the flesh exposed where his shirt ended and his pants began. Woods started, and Scythia smiled cruelly, then made her expression more benign as she moved into his visual arc again.

Her black cassock had been slit to the hip, and flashes of white thigh peeked through above knee-length black boots. The sleeves had been shorn from her robe, and fingerless black gloves covered her hands. Eye shadow and mascara sunk her eyes into dark hollows while blush and rouge heightened her cheekbones and gave her a vulpine appearance. Moving sinuously, she appeared a winter vixen out to attract a mate, but when Woods could no longer see her, she became a vengeful revenant who glared hatefully at his back.

"Dr. Robert Woods," she began with a seductive whisper, "you have allowed yourself to become involved with forces that are evil beyond your comprehension. When you became a doctor, you took an oath. You pledged yourself to do no harm. Yet in your alliance with the Dark Legion, you do more harm to your fellow man than you could possibly know."

She stopped before him and drew her hands up in an attitude of prayer while her forearms pressed her breasts back against her chest. She stood between his arms, yet was so slender that he could reach her with neither hand. For a moment she looked innocent and virginal—a reward silently promised him for his compliance with her wishes. Woods craned his head back to look up at her.

"You have done something horrible, Doctor. You are part of a conspiracy that has doomed a woman—a woman who could easily have been one of your patients, someone who would have trusted you completely with her life.

You have betrayed her, and she is most assuredly lost for all time because of what you have done."

Scythia slowly squatted down. Her cassock pooled on the floor as her knees poked free of the slits and her elbows came to rest on them. Woods' head followed her descent, keeping his eyes locked on hers, and studied her as she extended her hands and placed one each on the inside of his knees. "There is a chance, of course, that you could help us get her back. You can atone for your transgression against your fellow man, and you will even be rewarded for your actions in this matter."

She stood, slowly, shifting her right hand to the inside of his right leg, and letting it drift in along his right thigh as she began to circle him again. The smoothness and certainty of her actions made her almost hypnotic. As I watched her fingertips pluck at each wrinkle of fabric on his pant leg, I could feel a sympathetic tickle on the inside of my own thigh. I found myself becoming aroused, and I wondered at how Woods—half-delirious from fatigue—must have been reacting.

Scythia drifted around behind Woods and ran her fingers around the collar of his T-shirt. Grabbing the cloth in each hand, she tugged gently, then split her hands apart. The collar snapped in half with a pop, then the cloth slowly tore in two as she pulled at it. She made her action teasing and playful, yet the violence of it sent a chill running down my spine.

With the shirt torn open at the back, Scythia peeled it off the man's sweat-slicked flesh. She let her index finger delicately work its way down his spine, leaving a red line in the valley between his back muscles. The man's shoulder blades moved beneath his flesh as she hit a ticklish spot. She let her finger linger there, then moved it on down farther, centimeter by centimeter, until a droplet of his sweat hung from her fingernail like venom oozing from a fang.

"Yes, Doctor, you could be rewarded if you help us." Her left hand ran up into his long, dark hair. Her fingers separated it into distinct hanks. "Your rewards would be most delicious. More than the Dark Legion ever could give you."

Then her fingers tightened, and she jerked his head

back. His Adam's apple jutted out far enough to land SkyRay on it, and all color drained from his face. Whereas he had been dreamily listening to her voice with half-closed lids, now terror widened his eyes until I saw more white than color. His mouth gaped open, and she held his head back so far that he could not close his jaw.

She stabbed her right index finger into the flesh over his spine and a droplet of blood trickled out. "Your punishment, should you choose to resist me, Doctor, will be most horrible. You can feel my finger, for now, and you know where it is pointed. If I exert pressure here, you know what will happen. Your legs will tingle, then go numb. You will see them, but you will not feel them, nor will you be able to move them. They will be lost to you as the woman is lost to us without your help.

"And if I keep pressing, you know that your loins will shrivel. You will lose control of your bladder and your bowels. If I press hard enough—and I assure you that I can do that—your spine will be shattered and your spinal cord cut. You will never walk again. You will spend your life sitting in your own filth, dreaming of days when you functioned fully as a man."

My stomach tightened as she spoke. I heard her words, but before she actually verbalized them, I knew what she would say. Part of me wanted to believe that I read her lips before the audio pickups in the room could feed us the sound through the speakers mounted behind me, but I knew that was not the explanation. I had heard her before, and I had been where Woods now sat. That which she had used to threaten him had been done to me.

As strange as it had been to watch the video of my funeral, I now found myself staring at a reenactment of my death.

She released his head for a second, but had grabbed a handful of the hair on top of it as she whirled around in front of him. Holding his head aloft, she dropped her snarling face right in front of his frightened visage. "And you might think that you could last me out, deceive me, and I would let you go and your masters would heal you, but that will not happen. If you do not tell me what I wish to know, if you lie to me, I will crush your skull and leave you in a gutter so rats can feed on your corpse."

Tremors wracked me, and I turned away before I could begin burbling as did Woods. I tasted fear in my mouth and wanted to scream for Woods and for myself, but I did not. I knew that had I been in his situation, tired, disoriented and terrorized, I would have told her everything. I could not have resisted her even if I had been fortified by some belief in the powers of Dark Legion Apostles.

Watching her work, I discovered the reason why I had murdered the two Brotherhood Inquisitors who had followed me back on Luna. Though I did not remember what she had done to me on a conscious level, somewhere down in my animal brain I had recognized the threat Brotherhood security personnel posed to me. What I had done had puzzled me and made me wonder about myself.

No more. Lethal response in defense of self is no character flaw.

It's a survival trait.

Down below, Woods told her everything she wanted to know about Lorraine and the place the spaceship was taking her. After his third confession matched the first two, Scythia left him unmolested and the original two Inquisitors came to take the man away. She came up and joined us in the observation room.

My brother complimented her on her technique. "That's the fastest breaking I've seen. Fascinating protocol you use."

She shrugged casually. "The others prepare the subject, and I just concentrate pressure on him. Hinting at sex as a reward, especially with men, makes them vulnerable, then I threaten them with taking the lower half of their body away and they cave in. It always works."

Licking sweat from my upper lip, I looked sidelong at her. "Always?"

"There may have been one exception," she smiled coldly, "but then, it's the exceptions that make the rule, don't you know?"

THIRTY

Somehow her casual dismissal of me as the exception to her rule allowed me to push past the shock that had knotted my stomach and focus on the situation at hand. We had come together to get Sandra away from the Dark Legion. Had I chosen to dwell on the fact that Scythia—or someone enough like her to be her twin—had crippled me and had killed me, our chance to save Sandra would have passed completely. I filed my knowledge about Scythia away, knowing I would somehow avenge myself when all this was over, and concentrated on rescuing Sandra.

Titus took us back to the hotel, and from there my brother made contact with the Martian Cartel staff. While he set up a meeting with the local representatives from the various corporations, I set Ash—now housed in a new Attila body with black hair and brown eyes—to downloading all the data we'd need to get us out to the minor planet known as Themis and back. Titus headed off to brief his superiors about Lorraine's location, and I went to the nearest Cybertronic facility to go subreal and consult Carl.

Once through the wall, I found him atop his Martian plateau. Once again the horizon was pristine, and I could not see Eternal Vigilance or Saladin's Citadel in the distance. "We've found Lorraine Kovan. The Dark Legion is taking her to a little planetoid called Themis. It's just over 240 million kilometers from here."

"I am aware of its location. It is within 100,000 kilometers of our facility in Caliban."

Carl sounded more cold and distant than I had ever heard him before. "Again I am sorry I compromised the security on your hideaway."

The computer construct shook his head. "I am not concerned with that. The base would have been discovered relatively soon anyway. Right now I am selling it to Imperial so they can lose it to the Dark Legion and save me the shame. The fools are even willing to pay me for that privilege."

My head came up. "But you are concerned about something."

He nodded slowly. "You've come here to garner my support for a mission to Themis to rescue Cassandra Raleigh, correct?"

"Yes."

"Winchester Raleigh is claiming you have suborned a Capitol executive and were influencing him to interfere with internal Capitol affairs of which you have no part."

"My brother did help here, but our action had Cartel sanction."

"Your mission covered finding Lorraine Kovan and bringing her back to Luna, not extorting a ship from Capitol."

"Carl, you know the real story here. You know why we had to work around Win Raleigh." I opened my hands. "He's posturing because he's gone nuts. He wants her dead, and she's the victim here. She still needs rescuing."

"Capitol has issued a demand that the woman be left to them to deal with. The matter has been placed in Win Raleigh's hands."

"No!" My own vehemence surprised me. "If it is left up to him, she will die."

Carl nodded. "I understand that, but Capitol is pressing a very successful argument before the Cartel's High Council that suggests we have a victory in what has already happened here. Capitol won't make trouble if the matter is turned over to them. Your mission here is over."

"That can't be. My brother is speaking with his people right now about the need to rescue Sandra."

"Yes, but I doubt his people are listening. Your brother has been reprimanded and is facing disciplinary action when he returns to Luna City."

My hands balled into fists. "I can't believe this. How can the well-being of a person be ignored?"

"Corporations do not think like people, Rex." Carl started tracing with a finger in the air, and white letters hung in the wake of his motion as if his finger were made of chalk. "The fact that we know the Dark Legion has a base on Themis is important. We have a number of ways to destroy it. The Brotherhood believes that watching it may teach us a great deal about the Dark Legion. For this reason they are reluctant to disturb the base."

"But if we don't disturb it, Sandra will be their prisoner forever." I frowned. "That's hardly a victory to my mind."

"But your mind is not a corporate mind. A rescue operation has negative value to a corporation. The little jaunt your team took to Eternal Vigilance cost dearly in personnel and equipment. The fact that the Brotherhood now feels a debt to the corporations involved is a plus, but it is hard to put a value on that debt that we can enter into a balance sheet. Going to Themis is even worse because even if you succeed in your rescue attempt, the corporations involved cannot even get propaganda value from the effort. How can we applaud such a daring mission if, to do so, we have to reveal the true nature and extent of the Dark Legion's threat to humanity?"

"But in not going after Sandra, are we not conceding defeat to the Dark Legion? If we let her go, might we ignore the loss of Pluto or Neptune? When and where will we draw a line if it is not now and on Themis?"

Carl gave me a superior smile. "Philosophical arguments seldom prevail over the cold, hard facts and figures of an audited company report."

"So you are saying all is lost?"

He shook his head. "Nothing is lost. Your mission on Mars, as it has been subsequently redefined in the annals of the Cartel, was a complete success. You relieved a raid on Eternal Vigilance and saved a dozen civilians. This mission is considered top secret, to save the Brotherhood embarrassment, but each participant will be roundly rewarded. Each of you, in fact, have been given two months of rest and recreation there on Mars. Take it. Forget Sandra Raleigh Ellsworth."

"Won't work."

"No?"

"No. Telling me not to think of her is like telling me not to think of pink elephants." I clenched my fists. "I can't stop thinking about her. I put her on Venus."

"Quentin Kell put her on Venus."

"Dammit, I *am* Quentin Kell!" I plucked at my clothes, and the computer fed the sensation of cloth running across my flesh to my brain. I commanded the fabric to be changed to barbed-wire, and I stiffened at the sting. "I'm not the same as I was when my brother and I sent her away, but I am enough myself to want to help a friend."

I released the sharp metallic threads of my shirt and pointed a bloodied finger at Carl. "You said you chose me for who I was and what I was. You wanted someone with imagination and discretion and all the other things that the vacs don't have. Well, loyalty is one of those traits. No, I didn't tell you about Sandra's real identity because it was not important for you to know that. I won't betray my brother or my father because I am still loyal to them. And I am loyal to Sandra, which means I can't accept her being left to die on some cold rock out in Jupiter's shadow."

Carl shrugged slowly. "It seems to me you are being given little choice but to do exactly that."

I watched him carefully. "Are you *ordering* me to do nothing to help her?"

He slowly smiled. "You are of Cybertronic. You are a Diamond. My only orders to you are to continue to cause difficulties for the Dark Legion and our competitors. Your methods, provided they do not cause Cybertronic undue shame or cost, are open, but discretion is urged."

I narrowed my eyes. "You're not going to help me do this, are you?"

"Do what? You are on leave. Ash will be with you to serve as your bodyguard, and Jan will continue her training with you." Carl shrugged. "I trust you will find something to amuse you during your vacation."

"Now I'm confused. You say individual concerns don't matter to corporations, yet you refrain from restraining me. Why?"

Carl folded his hands together, interlacing his fingers. "When you become what we have—part man and part machine—you learn to value those properties that machines do not possess. Take Ash, for example. He is loyal and follows orders, but cannot see beyond those orders or improvise new orders. He cannot grow and, with the universe being in a state of progress at all times, that which cannot grow stagnates and dies.

"Corporations are prone to that same stagnation. Decisions are not made to maximize gain, but to minimize exposure and loss. The easiest answer to any request is 'No' because it requires no gamble. Cybertronic was able to attain megacorporate size and power during an earlier period of corporate stagnation. In fact, had our executive raids not forced a shake-up and a renaissance among our competitors, each would have collapsed inward because of paralysis caused by caution."

He opened his hands again. "Stagnation in the face of the Dark Legion is, as you noted before, surrendering to them. The personnel of Luna's corporations need to be reminded that before they were comptrollers and actuaries and managers and directors, they were human. If it requires people who are partially or wholly mechanical to do that, so be it."

I smiled and wiped my bloody hands on my pants. "I won't fail."

"No, you won't." Carl's grim visage hardened into a steel mask. "Just for going on this mission, the other corps will pressure me to have you killed. If you do not succeed, I will do what I must to appease them."

THIRTY-ONE

I stared at my brother as if he'd suddenly become a snake. "What do you mean you won't help?"

He held his hands up. "Win has everyone so stirred up that I'm pulling duty assigning priorities to Sundiver shipments. The only way I could be busted lower is by being assigned to move the damned stuff on board the ship, then pilot it out to shoot the trash into the sun."

"I would have thought Sandra would have been worth that risk."

"She would have, Quentin, but I was shown a few things while trying to drum up support for a rescue mission." Nick looked miserable, but his natural combativeness helped hide how hurt he was. "Wendy Levin reported, based on her examination of Sandra on Venus, that Sandra has undergone severe trauma. While she had brain function, a lot of her higher brain processes had been disrupted or altered. Her neurochemical makeup is different. While Levin seems to think Sandra could be brought back to being who she was, the whole operation would take a long time and require dedicated care."

Fury blazed in my eyes. "Don't tell me you're going to start talking cost-effectiveness."

"I wouldn't, but I have some serious decisions to make here. I have a wife and kids to think about."

"And Sandra didn't?"

"No, it's not that, damn you, and you know it. For all we know, Sandra is already dead."

"And if she isn't?"

"Levin's report says the person we knew as Sandra *is* dead."

I thumped a fist against my chest. "*I* was dead, but I'm not now. I can't live with the idea that somewhere, locked up in her brain, Sandra is screaming for help—help that only we can give her."

Nick shook his head as he crossed to the suite's bar and poured himself three fingers of Martian whiskey. "How are you going to do it? Win Raleigh has every ship in the planet sewed up."

"With your help I could get a ship."

"If I help you, Win will have me loaded into a Sundiver canister and shot into the sun."

"He wouldn't do that. You're Anna's husband."

"And Sandra was his own daughter."

I hammered a fist into my open palm. "I can't believe you're being like this."

"Look, Quentin, I wish you all the luck in the world, but I overstepped myself when I commandeered the SkyRay." He opened his hands helplessly. "This is one play I can't make."

At Hunter's insistence I met him at a greasy café two levels below Mars' red surface. "Sorry about the place, but this is probably the only speakeasy left in San Dorado."

I frowned. "What are you talking about?"

Hunter hunched forward over lukewarm beer. "Capitol uses a lot of listening devices in its construction here. Sawyer, the proprietor, likes his privacy, so all the bugs have been exterminated. Now what's on your mind?"

"What are you and your people doing for your vacation?"

The Capitol warrior shrugged. "This 'n' that. You have something special in mind?"

"I want to finish what we started at Eternal Vigilance. Lorraine's heading toward a little planetoid called Themis. It once was used by Bauhaus as a mining station, but they abandoned it about fifteen years ago when the valuable metals played out. I want to crack it open and get Lorraine back."

Hunter leaned back in his seat and began to drum his fingers on the table. "It's going to take more than a SkyRay to get us there. Driving a spaceship into the vicinity of an enemy base is not going to be easy."

"Themis is big as far as planetoids are concerned. It's 249 kilometers in diameter. It was undetected as a Legion base until given up by a heretic."

"Okay, that's big, but it's hard not to notice a ship landing on your rock."

"The ship isn't going to land." I lowered my voice. "We have the ship heading to Jupiter, and we pop four life-skiffs. We run them into Themis, raid it, and get off. We'll have the range to get to Caliban from Themis if we don't get picked up by our ship first."

"Skiffs are fine for short-term runs, but what if we have pursuit."

"Mitch, if we don't leave anything alive on Themis, nothing will come after us."

The warrior nodded his head. "I like your thinking. Do you have us a ship?"

"I'm working on that."

"How about supplies?"

I shook my head. "Might you be able to do something in that direction?"

"I have a few favors left over from my days with the Banshees. That might get us a bullet or two." Mitch leaned forward. "I don't know how many of my people I can get to go with me, but I'm in. If I'd killed Ragathol on Venus, this would have been over a long time ago. I don't like leaving things undone."

"I didn't think so." I placed two Cardinal's crowns on the table to pay for our untouched drinks. "I'll meet you back here in twenty-four hours."

"It's okay if I bring Pam and Lane in on this?"

"Yojimbo, too, if you want. They have as much of a stake as we do." I thought of Scythia and shuddered. "I'll check with Titus and see if he has anything to offer. You realize this is off the books."

"Yeah, just for bragging rights." Mitch shrugged easily. "I don't know about rest, but this is just the sort of recreation I want."

* * *

I hooked up with Ash and asked for a download of the data he'd gathered concerning ships. He told me he had 4.55392 terabytes of data, so I settled for the list of ships in port. Ash had been thorough and showed everything from Mishima *Tobi* class luxury starjammers to Capitol's *Regina* class of liners like the *Red Corsair* that had brought us to Mars from Luna. In each and every case the ships had been assigned extra security or were undergoing maintenance that meant they couldn't fly at all. That presented more of a problem than the extra security, though I didn't want us to have to shoot our way on to a ship just so we could go off on a wild rescue mission. Committing suicide was one thing, but murdering others for that privilege seemed decidedly extreme.

"Ash, these are all the ships on Mars capable of making the trip to Jupiter?"

The Attila stared at me. "That is a list of all the ships inspected, licensed, and approved for interplanetary travel."

I raised an eyebrow. "There are other ships *capable* of such travel, but not approved for it?"

"Many craft used for local orbit missions are decommissioned but still capable of intra-orbit travel."

I smiled. "Would you have a file on *those* ships?"

He shot it over to me. I opened it and laughed as I saw a name come by. "Nick, you son of a bitch."

"The reference suggests the presence of a dog, but sensors detect none."

"That's okay, Ash." I slapped him on the shoulder then shook my left hand until the sting went out of it. "I want a full schematic on the Sundiver *Suzy Coulson*. And get me a file on Emil Cusder, her new captain. I'm going to go get Titus Gallicus, and we'll see if Cusder still has some religion in him."

Titus joined me, and we discovered that Emil Cusder was both very religious and cooperative. Though the computers on board the *Suzy Coulson*—newly commissioned as such when Cusder took over at the helm— actually flew the ship, Cusder took being in command very seriously. He was more than happy to help us out on our jaunt, though I suspect that was because his bodyguard, a bubbly blonde who looked quite fetching in her short-skirted, nautical attire, simply could not be left behind on Mars while he went jaunting about.

Mitch Hunter's unit, save Alverez and Taylor, agreed to come along on the rescue mission. I would have liked to have had the aviators with us, but Win Raleigh exerted influence through the Capitol Air Force and attached them to a Martian air wing until they could return to Venus. In addition to Hunter, that meant we had Corporal David Redfield, Corporal Diane Parker, Sergeant Wendy Levin, and Corporal Mark Harris.

Yojimbo, Pam, and Lane also agreed to go on the mission. Like me, Lane would use the trip out to Themis to heal up from the Eternal Vigilance raid. He'd fractured his humerus, but it had not dislocated, so the bone would be mostly knitted by the time we reached our destination. Likewise my ankle would be operational by then. Having more time to heal would have been nice—and healing up in a normal gravity situation would have been better—but beggars couldn't be choosers.

Counting Ash, Jan, and me, our squad strength came in at eleven. Titus Gallicus, Scythia, and a dozen Sacred Warriors brought it up to a full twenty-five, which was far fewer a number than a full assault would prudently suggest, but we were planning a raid. While we were going in against an unknown number of enemies, the lack of activity reported in and around Themis made us hopeful that Ragathol's sanctuary was lightly staffed. As I'd never seen anyone other than him during my fugue states, and given that Themis had evidence of his betrayal of Algeroth, I let myself believe resistance would be minimal.

That didn't mean it wouldn't be tough. As the *Suzy Coulson* lifted off from Mars and headed up to its ejection station, all of us began memorizing the labyrinth of mine shafts and galleries Bauhaus had chewed in Themis. Given the seemingly random nature of the maze, Themis might as well have been an apple that a dozen worms ate their way through. Though the confused tangle presented a problem, the fact that numerous tunnels actually provided external entry points to the interior meant we had several points of attack for our assault.

Sundivers like the *Coulson* attract little attention. They normally fly up and away from the plane of the elliptic, then launch huge garbage canisters down the gravity well toward the sun. The object is to miss inhabited planets, but many Sundiver captains like to make tricky shots, using planets and asteroids to slingshot their canisters around. Doing this is a dubious accomplishment, but when your life is spent dumping trash into the big bonfire at the center of the solar system, almost anything will suffice as excitement.

Once the *Coulson* had been cleared by planetary control, it wouldn't be contacted again until it requested a return vector. Normally such a request would come within a week of liftoff, but off-the-scope is out-of-mind for traffic controllers. The only person who could raise an alarm about the *Coulson*'s being overdue on its return was the load manager. However, my brother, being new in his position, happened to overlook the *Coulson*'s tardiness.

My brother's inexperience as a load manager also evidenced itself in the nature of things found in one of the trash canisters. An incredible amount of munitions and explosives had been shipped on the *Coulson* for destruction. It turned out that two digits had been transposed on the disposal date, meaning it was all still very good. The transposition problem also supplied us with medical supplies, better than normal rations, and some very expensive environmental suits in case we had to function in vacuum.

That latter situation did not arise. Small though it was, Themis had a weak atmosphere—roughly equivalent to that at the top of some of Mars' taller mountains. Mitch located a large pit mine on the surface that had actually gone deep enough to connect up with a tunnel from the interior. Our surveys said the nexus had been sealed with a steel bulkhead, but we had enough in the way of thermite charges to burn through it very easily.

While traveling through the vast distances of space is not very conducive to rescues in the nick of time, the *Coulson* had engines of sufficient power to let the ship take a considerable amount of trash off Mars. Once away from the planet, we ditched the two canisters of true garbage and started burning for Themis. We were able to travel faster than the ship carrying Sandra, reducing a four-day head start to a mere ten hours by the time our life-skiffs dropped away from the *Coulson* and shot across the third Kirkwood gap toward Themis.

We were at our most vulnerable in the skiffs. Packed tightly, everyone in full armor and bristling with weapons, we braced for defensive fire from Themis. I thought we'd been hit when I felt the first bump of atmosphere, but we continued on unmolested. At the bottom of the pit mine, Harris burned a hole through the bulkhead, and we were in.

Huddled in the darkness of a mine shaft, I tapped Hunter on the shoulder. " 'Welcome to my lair,' said the spider to the fly."

" 'Lock and load,' said the fly captain to his warriors." Mitch waved us forward. "This time the spiders have bitten off more than they can chew."

THIRTY-TWO

We pushed on deep through the mining tunnel. Its surface bore the spiraled scars of the huge boring machine that had gnawed its way through the rocky surface. Dust rose with our footfalls and, because of the lighter gravity on Themis, hung in the thin air longer than it should have. While the dust cloud hanging at our rear could have led to our detection, I thought of it as an easy way for us to figure out which tunnel to take to get back to our skiffs and escape.

Inside ten minutes we hit our first interior bulkhead. It was the first of two that made up a crude air lock. We could have fitted the whole squad inside, but Mitch had us come through in small groups to avoid getting us all bottled up. The Dark Legion had not set up a trap, so we passed through what we had seen as the first choke point without incident and within a half hour of our landing, we approached the first of the habitat galleries.

The galleries had been constructed as needed during the mining operations on the planetoid. The earliest ones—numbers One, Two, and Three—formed a rough triangle toward the lower part of Themis and all connected one to another. The second set—numbers Four, Five, and Six—formed an offset triangle higher up and all connected one to another. Habitat Two linked up to Four, and Three connected to Five. The last habitat—the one created for executives and their families—had been located at the top of the asteroid and connected to habitats

Two and Six, though it also possessed its own dock for the CEO's private starship.

Because Bauhaus had abandoned Themis before the general paranoia about high technology set in, when we hit our next objective, I went into action. Doffing my helmet, I used the computer jack cable in my tooth to link into the old Bauhaus 80030VRX system. Moving swiftly through the network, I hit the environmental control database and raided it for a current snapshot of conditions within the complex.

I pulled out immediately, but in less time than it took me to replace my tooth, the computer in my brain finished the three rounds of comparisons I demanded of it. It matched the current conditions against old Bauhaus benchmarks for the base. First it flagged any place where conditions met Bauhaus standards, and the only hit in that category came in the infirmary complex in habitat gallery Two. We'd agreed that normal conditions probably marked where they were keeping Sandra and any other human captives, and both Pam and Wendy had suggested the infirmary as being a logical prison, given Sandra's special medical needs.

I flashed Mitch the hand signal for the infirmary, and we moved out. As I refastened my helmet, I studied the computer's second-round results. The second set of search parameters looked for carbon dioxide and methane levels. We didn't know if the necro-mutants, being dead, respired or not. If they did, we figured they'd give off carbon dioxide. Also, being corpses, we figured they were still decaying, even if only a little bit, so a search for methane concentrations could pinpoint them.

The computer found suspiciously high levels of CO_2 and methane in habitats Two, Three, and Five. This worked to our advantage because by blowing the connections between habitat Two and Three and Two and Four, we could force the troops in Three and Five to take long detours before they could get to us. The only other connection out of Two was to the Executive gallery, and since we could get out to the surface through it, we needed it for an alternate escape route in case gallery One became nasty.

The last operation results sent a shiver down my spine.

I'd asked for atmospheric volumes, figuring I could use that information to determine the extent of alterations of the galleries or mines. All sectors reported back as normal except the core sector in the Executive gallery. It actually demanded less atmosphere, which meant it had been filled in with something.

The only *something* that sprang immediately to mind was the statue to Muawijhe. If it had been constructed in the Executive gallery, that meant Ragathol would be located closely to it. The idea of being forced to retreat through a nepharite's stronghold did not fill me with joy, but when I related the information to Hunter, he accepted it with a grim grunt and no further comment.

We passed through gallery One without opposition, which made me feel a bit better about the intelligence I'd gathered. Harris rigged the mouth of the tunnel leading to gallery Three with explosives, then similarly booby-trapped the tunnel to Two behind us. When all hell broke loose, he could detonate either tunnel with a radio command.

Waiting in the dark for him to finish his work, the utter desperation and futility of our gesture slammed into me. Like the chill leeching heat from my body, it sucked my confidence away. While I had no doubt that what we were doing was right, I knew it was not expedient nor wise. At best we would get one woman back—a broken woman who might never even realize she had been rescued—and perhaps kill a number of Dark Legion troops. We were a defiant gesture, a curse shouted into the teeth of a storm. That many of us would die in making that gesture just rendered the whole operation ludicrous.

Yet we were here, voluntarily, in defiance of our superiors and their desires. Each one of us, save perhaps Ash, knew our chances of survival were minimal, and our chances of success even more slim than that. Even so, we had chosen to accept the risks and jam our heads deep into the throat of the Dark Legion's lion. Why?

As Carl had noted, philosophical questions have little to do with corporate policies. Likewise philosophies are often cited as sufficient reasons for martyrdom, but it took more than a statement of principle to motivate us to put our lives on the line to save Sandra. As much as I could make a case for her captivity lessening the freedom of all humanity, even I could not deceive myself into thinking that spilling my blood here would somehow liberate mankind.

I could not answer why the others had come, but in response to my own internal inquiry I felt a curious peace. I felt as if I were marching toward a point that would define my life and make me complete. I did not know if this was just the end of one chapter of my life, or the end of the whole thing, but I just knew it was the thing I had to do. My life, my death and rebirth had all, somehow, been shaped by chance or design to place me here, on Themis, at this point in time.

What would happen in the future I did not know. I only knew that whatever it was, it had been ordained since before my birth. I was but a piece in a puzzle that is reality, and I was about to be snapped into place.

Hunter pointed down the tunnel, sending Ash, Jan, and me forward. Our enhanced vision allowed us to see more clearly than any of the night vision devices carried by the other troops. We worked our way forward cautiously, with Jan advancing on one wing and me on the other. She'd get ahead of me by a dozen yards, then stop, and I would go beyond her position by another dozen. Ash lurked behind Jan and moved up when I did.

We reached the opening into gallery Two, and I gave myself a full minute to conduct a full survey of the area. The foyer was a right triangle with a convex hypotenuse. Our tunnel entered midway along the one hundred meter wide base and the tunnel to gallery Three headed off to our right about a third of the way up the longer arm. Bisecting the long arm, just a bit beyond the tunnel to Three, I saw the dark opening of the tunnel that sloped up to the Executive gallery. The tunnel up to gallery Four joined the triangle near the nexus of the arc and long arm, roughly two hundred meters from where I crouched.

The infirmary complex lay at the middle of the arc, making it most convenient to the tunnel leading down from the Executive gallery. The walkway along the front of gallery Two's second level overhung the infirmary entrance, and somewhere in back of that upper precinct I knew we would find the barracks that housed the necro-mutants and undead Legionnaires my survey had detected. Infrared and ultraviolet scans of the area revealed nothing out of the order, though I did detect a faint heat source through the infirmary wall.

I waved Hunter forward, and he set Harris to rigging our tunnel. Ash, Jan, and I sprinted across the open court-yard and reached the infirmary door unmolested. Ash pushed it open, Jan went in low, and I came in high, but no one shot at us. In fact, we found only two people in the ward, and neither of them was capable of doing anyone any harm.

As the rest of the team, save the demolitions man Harris, filed into the infirmary, I crossed to where Sandra lay on a bed. She looked even more gaunt than when I had seen her on Mars. Her hair hung in greasy strings around her shoulders and grime formed black lines beneath her fingernails. Her arms and legs had been strapped to the bed rails while angry red scratches near the site of the IV needle stuck in her arm suggested why she had been restrained.

I smiled. "That's the Sandra I knew. Still fighting."

Wendy Levin came up on the other side of the bed, pried open Sandra's eyes, and flicked a light across each one. "Pupils equal and reactive, but slow. She's doped to the gills." Without comment she eased the needle out of Sandra's arm and slapped a bandage over the bleeding hole.

The Sacred Warriors had their own medic going over the ward's other occupant. Because they formed an armored Phalanx around the bed, I could not see what was going on, but the machinery at the head of his bed was decidedly more complex and strangely warped than what the Dark Legion had been using on Sandra.

Pam pointed at the bloated black instrument from which wires led to a skullcap. "Looks like what they had Lorraine in the first time we found her on Luna."

"Do you think they were trying to do to him what they did to Lorraine?" I reached out to caress her cheek, but held back because she needed human contact and my armored gloves would deny it to her.

Wendy shook her head. "I don't know. Lorraine's hospital workup on Venus said she had abnormal brain chemistry. I don't know what that means to the Dark Legion, but in Lorraine's case it means the total suppression or erasure of her life. Think of it as a stroke or amnesia—she doesn't know who she was. She might not even know *what* she was."

I looked down at Sandra, then back up at Wendy. "Could the amnesia be a result of trauma instead of the neurochemical changes?"

"Are you talking hysterical amnesia?" Wendy frowned for a moment. "It's possible her mind shut down to cut itself off from what she saw. Catatonia, which she has exhibited, is possible in such cases. Hell, the trauma could have been sufficient that her personality fragmented, and what we have here is personality that remains catatonic when threatened."

I shuddered as her remark hit close to home. "If that were the case, she could be reintegrated?"

Levin eyed me closely. "You a shrink, Dent? If so, you're more qualified to deal with her than I am."

"Informed amateur, Sergeant."

"I see." She nodded toward Sandra. "Integration is possible, but it won't be easy. And it won't happen here."

Titus came over and stood at the foot of Sandra's bed. "We have confirmed the identity of Brother Claudius Turba—his captors have not treated him kindly."

Behind him Scythia removed her gloves and screwed a silencer onto her Punisher. "What's she doing?"

"Administering the sacrament of Extreme Termination. He is now a creature of Darkness, so we will give him peace."

I heard a muffled *chuff,* then Scythia came walking over to Sandra's bed. Smoke drifted up from the barrel of her gun, but she did not blink when wisps of it grazed her pale eyes. "If you wish, I will take care of this poor unfortunate as well."

"She doesn't need a bullet, Inquisitor." I reached down and pulled my knife from the sheath inside my right greave. I presented the hilt to her. "If you want to care for her, cut her loose so we can get her out of here."

Scythia accepted my knife, but before she could provide me with a bit of wisdom from the Book of Laws, the phone on the wall beside Sandra's bed rang. Without thinking I started to reach for it, then stopped. I saw Mitch turn and look toward me, but his battle mask hid any reaction. I started to lower my hand, then every phone in the ward starting to ring.

Mitch nodded, and I pulled off my helmet, then answered the phone. "Yes?"

I recognized Ragathol's voice and felt my stomach flutter. "You are beyond succor. You were allowed to reach the infirmary because that is where you will spend the rest of your life."

My nostrils flared. "You don't expect us to throw down our arms and surrender, do you?"

"No. You are expected to die screaming in agony, then you will be resurrected to serve my master in the Dark Legion."

"Your master? Would that be Algeroth or *Muawijhe?*"

"What?"

"Prostrate yourself before his idol again, Ragathol, and pray hard." I smiled at my companions. "We're beyond succor because we didn't want anyone else to have the pleasure of your dying moments."

"You are but two dozen." I heard a burst of gunfire and a scream from outside. "You cannot prevail."

Though it was rude, I slammed the phone down on the receiver. "Ragathol," I shouted to Hunter. "He wanted to know if we deliver."

Mitch slapped his assault rifle affectionately. "Piping hot, hits the spot. C'mon campers, service with a smile."

THIRTY-THREE

I took my knife back from Scythia and resheathed it.
With her help, Wendy and Pam managed to tuck Sandra
into a kevlar cocoon. They capped the hybrid sleeping
bag/body bag with a combat helmet, then eased Sandra to
the floor. Wendy attached lanyards from her armor to the
shoulders of the bag and dragged Sandra along like a sled
behind a string of malamutes.

Securing my helmet, I closed my eyes and had the
computer paint IR signatures in great detail in the inside
of my eyeballs. Looking toward the door, I saw the outline of a man with a fair pool of heat around him. "Harris
is down. Lots of blood. And he's being moved. Ash,
cover me."

Snapping the safety off on my AR3000, I dashed back
out through the door and sprinted toward where Harris
lay. The two Legionnaires dragging him toward the executive tunnel saw me coming and looked up with surprise
on their faces. At least I think it was surprise because a
whining lead sleet storm exploded both their heads. They
fell back against the wall in a smear of blood and brains,
and Harris slumped to the ground again.

I popped two rifle grenades down the tunnel to Three
and saw Legionnaires backlit by the explosions. Corpse
debris—fingers, teeth, and patches of flesh mostly—
sprayed back out into the courtyard in sufficient quantity
to make the footing treacherous. My right foot rolled over
a fat thumb, and I started to fall. I fought to regain my

balance, but knowing I could not, I tucked myself into a ball and rolled.

That move saved my life.

From the overhang on the second level, a zombi squad opened up on me with a heavy machine gun. Tracer rounds struck sparks all around me, but I remained untouched. Given the lighter gravity and the blocky nature of my armor, my roll became a bump-and-bounce display that they could not track accurately and that I could not control.

I hit the wall and would have rebounded back into the courtyard except that one of the re-dead Legionnaires absorbed the impact with a sickening crunch. I crushed her rib cage when I steadied myself with my left hand. Holding the AR3000 like a pistol in my right fist, I burned a clip walking fire along the overhang, but the ferrocrete safety wall provided cover for most of the Legionnaires up there.

Mitch darted out of the infirmary and arced a satchel charge up and over the safety wall. The bomb detonated with a thunderclap and shook the whole gallery. Directly below ground zero, the walkway crumbled and collapsed. The safety wall channeled most of the explosive force out toward either end of the walkway, blasting apart the Legionnaires who had been seeking cover behind it. A few were blown out into the courtyard, but they bounced bonelessly off the ground, then lay very still.

I looked down at Harris and saw a huge hole where his left shoulder should have been. From the twisted metal around the wound, I could tell a machine-gun burst had hit him from the flank and pushed fragments of his armor deep into his body cavity. I had no doubt he was dead.

I looked for the detonator to activate the satchel charges he had left behind, but all I could see on his equipment harness was a bullet-riddled pouch from which sprouted brightly colored wires and chips of plastic. I knew satchel charges had a digital timer that could be used to manually set them for a ten-second countdown, but the only charge I could reach would be the one set in the mouth of the tunnel to Three. Sealing the tunnel was certainly important, and likely suicidal, but no more so than any other part of this exercise.

"Ash, scour the tunnel to Three!"

The Attila unit dutifully turned his SSW4200P on the tunnel as I crawled across the floor toward it. Ash's gun looked very much like a blowtorch as muzzle flares lit the front of the infirmary with brilliant fire. Silvery tracer afterimages circled the tunnel and stabbed deep into it. The Gatling cannon's whine filled the gallery with ghostly shrieking.

Behind him, illuminated by the violent strobing of Ash's gun, the Sacred Warriors poured out of the infirmary. Two of them joined hands beneath the hole in the catwalk, then boosted a third and fourth of their number up through the hole. Those two warriors sprayed the catwalk with gunfire, then took up covering positions to be able to shoot Legionnaires coming in from deeper in the gallery itself. More of their compatriots joined them, then the rest of our party began to spread out and prepare a retreat back to the skiffs.

The Attila stopped shooting when I reached the satchel charge stuck to the mouth of the tunnel. Thick-fingered in gloves, I fumbled with the strap holding the canvas bag closed. Cursing to myself, I shook my gloves off and started to work on the straps. I almost drew my knife to cut through them, but the first one came loose and the second started to give, so I kept at it.

Even as I peeled the canvas back to expose the timing mechanism and its little touch pad, a howling pack of necro-mutants burst forth from the Executive tunnel. Most bore strangely altered guns whose barrels swelled then convulsed down as if each bullet were being expelled like darts from a blowpipe. Others—the ones streaking mindlessly in at my compatriots—carried wickedly barbed blades slathered with a dark liquid that absorbed all the available light.

They would have been fodder for my companions' guns except for the figure striding from the tunnel behind the Dark Legion formation. His flesh as red as the Martian soil and muscles bulging so much that they threatened to burst his skin, Ragathol paced into the courtyard as if an ancient, earthly noble on the trail of quarry with a pack of dogs. He brandished a saw-toothed halberd in his left hand, raising it above his spiked head, then gestured in a circular motion toward the infirmary and my companions.

As one they started shrieking and firing their weapons wildly. Mitch Hunter rolled on the ground, tearing at his armor as if it had become red hot. Yojimbo sank calmly to his knees and drew the shorter of his two swords, then started to rake it across the belly of his armor. Pam and Lane collapsed near the infirmary doorway, clutching each other tightly. Even Titus and Scythia staggered and sank back against the walls, jerking and making signs against evil.

Ash turned his fire on the necro-mutants and cut the swordsmen in half with a concentrated stream of bullets. When the muzzle flashes died, he did not pause to reload the SSW4200P with another drum of ammo, but waded out into the necro-mutants, crushing them with blows from his gun or free left hand. Their bullets washed over him, but his armor held, and he advanced. His assault reduced the unit guarding Ragathol to a carpet of puling, bleeding organisms as effectively as a bear dispatching a pack of starveling curs nipping at it.

Ragathol whipped his halberd around and sliced a full foot from the muzzles of Ash's gun. The Attila tried to lunge forward and stab Ragathol in the belly with the ragged metal barrels, but the nepharite brought the butt end of his halberd up and caught Ash in the chest. The Attila flew up and back, bouncing off the catwalk's restraining wall, then dropped to the ground again. Ash lost his gun, but climbed to his feet and prepared to receive Ragathol's continued attack.

I punched four seconds onto the detonator, then hit the activation switch. Grabbing the shoulder strap on the canvas satchel, I rose to my feet and whirled the explosive package around. "Ash, shield Lorraine!" I screamed and let the bomb fly.

At the sound of my voice, Ragathol turned and brought his halberd around in a guard position. That saved his life, because the weapon's massive head deflected the satchel charge and started it off toward the tunnel to gallery Four. That meant it was about six feet from Ragathol's left shoulder when it exploded.

The blast sent the nepharite spinning into the infirmary

wall with enough force to drive one of his head spikes into the ferrocrete, then snap it off. I lost sight of him for a second in the fireball's incandescent glow, then his form shredded the curtain of smoke in the center of the courtyard. Blackened flesh hung in crispy ribbons from the left side of his neck and torso. His left arm swung wildly amid a tangle of tissue threads. His left eye bounced off his charred cheekbone as he ran before me and on up the tunnel to the Executive gallery.

Leaving my gloves where they lay, I picked up my AR3000 again and ran to the mouth of the Executive tunnel. I triggered two bursts that ricocheted around a corner in the tunnel, but I could not tell if they hit anything or not. I did see a copious amount of a thick liquid smeared on the tunnel wall. It shimmered with an oily film, and I might have taken it as some sort of industrial fluid had it not trailed from the point of the explosion into the tunnel. Ragathol had been hurt badly.

Mitch shook himself as he staggered up. "Damn that bastard. He made me think I was bleeding beneath my armor so I couldn't staunch my wounds."

Yojimbo solemnly resheathed his sword. "And he filled me with the dread of having failed my master."

"He's bleeding a lot." I jerked a thumb at the tunnel. "Shall we take the wolf by the ears?"

Hunter nodded. "Inquisitor, have some of your explosives people seal the tunnels. We'll be using the Executive gallery to get out. Rex, Yojimbo, we go first. The rest of you follow, but carefully."

I think Mitch admonished them to use caution because the three of us were anything *but* cautious. Like tigers that had tasted blood, we stalked up the tunnel. It leveled out for twenty meters, then went up and in for another thirty. As we mounted that slope, Mitch slammed a new clip home in his M50. "Remember, we can hit him from range, which is advisable because he still might be able to use some strange power to incapacitate us."

Yojimbo nodded, then we crested the passage and all stopped. Even if Mitch had not cautioned us to avoid a close engagement, I don't think any of us would have taken a single step forward. What we saw below was too strange and pitiful to invite our interference. All I could do was lower my gun and stare.

Fifteen meters down, at the base of a blood-spattered causeway, Ragathol knelt before a huge statue. I recognized the seated figure at once, from my encounter with the mirror at Larkspur. Chipped out of pure obsidian, the representation of Muawijhe sat back and stared down mercilessly at the torn and bleeding nepharite. Aside from spectral green lights reflecting on the statue from above, the only color in it came from the ivory set in its eyes.

My blood ran cold as I realized that ivory came from *my* bones. I had looked out of those eyes because they were part of me until Muawijhe had severed the link between us. I had been in this chamber before, in spirit, and I had seen Ragathol beg from the vantage point so high above him.

"Master," he wailed, anointing the statue's feet with his blood, "I have been defiled and abandoned. I am yours. Do not let me fall to ruin. Do not waste all that I am. Let me serve you without subterfuge and smite thine enemies for thee."

I took off my helmet and bowled it down the causeway. It hit Ragathol in the ass, and he jerked as if he'd been hit with an antiaircraft missile. "He thinks you are a wretched failure, Ragathol. You'll get no help from him."

The nepharite looked back at us, then slavishly draped himself over the idol's feet, licking them clean of the blood he had splashed over them. "Go away. This place is sacred."

Hunter nodded, then raised his assault rifle to his shoulder. "You better hope this place really is sacred, because this is where we bury you."

I raised my gun, and Yojimbo did likewise, but before we could shoot, something happened.

Ragathol began to glow.

THIRTY-FOUR

The pale green reflections from the statue leaped off it and enfolded Ragathol in a milky, translucent shroud. It draped itself over him, then enfolded him and lifted him into the air. The shroud rippled as if it were a liquid sphere and rose up into a crest as waves slid around the globe and collided with each other. It contracted slightly and appeared to have solidified, like an egg being boiled, yet it did not become opaque. Instead it cleared to an emerald hue within which we could see Ragathol and two sinuous, serpentine threads of the pale green plasma.

The glowing ribbons bound Ragathol's wrists and ankles together, then drew his arms against his chest and his legs up until the nepharite huddled in a fetal position at the heart of the emerald globe. Slowly, as if teased by unseen winds or carried by invisible fairies, the ribbons wound themselves around Ragathol. They grew more swift as they covered more and more of him. Within a minute or two they had mummified him in an intricate plasma braid, then all the seams smoothed and again his form lay encased in a puss-green skin.

Things began to change at that point. The remaining spikes on his head atrophied, and I thought I saw black holes open in his skull where they retreated. If they were there, they remained present only for a second or two, then were replaced by pulsing, phallic things that stretched the green membrane. The cylindrical shapes shot in and out, first up at the top of his skull, then down and out at a temple or his forehead. They moved cautiously at first, then grew bolder, pushing and pushing against the elastic green film surrounding him.

Suddenly his arms pushed out from his chest and cracks appeared in the emerald. His legs extended slowly, and his back hunched as he tried to straighten within his prison. More cracks appeared, popping and snapping like glass being ground beneath steel boots. When he brought his head up, the emerald crumbled over his chest, then his hands reached out and pushed the halves of the gemstone egg apart.

The green tissue covering him split down the middle, and Ragathol emerged glistening and dripping a crystalline liquid. His flesh had been drained of its livid, sanguine hue and replaced with a greenish corpse-like pallor. Where there had once been spikes, now huge, fat worms stuck their heads forth and waved their mouths through the air. Leaner than he had been before, he bore no scars or signs of the abuse he had endured at our hands.

He gave us a lipless grin. "It was insanity for you to come here. Now you shall have what you so richly desire. This is the word of Glathoar, nepharite of Muawijhe!"

He gestured at us, and the world went black for me, yet I knew I had not lost consciousness. I found myself in a black void looking at a small wooden simulacrum of myself. I looked like a marionette and above me, wearing robes cut from a nightmare cloth, Glathoar manipulated me. At his whim I jerked and twitched. I capered around and around, casting my assault rifle from me, spinning and leaping, pirouetting and hopping down the causeway on my tiptoes.

I tried to stop myself, but I could not. Looking up again at Glathoar, I saw him raise a thin pipe to his mouth and somehow blow a tune out through it. His fingers writhed like the worms in his head, coaxing a twisted, blasphemous song from the simple flute. I could not hear the song, but every fiber of my being responded it to. As commanded by this song of madness, my limbs flopped back and forth, utterly beyond my control. The sheer torque of some maneuvers threatened to tear my body apart from the inside, but the insane melody always prevented that from happening, and yet promised that it would soon, sooner, soonest.

From somewhere inside me, I heard a growl. The sound could not cut through the song driving my body, but it somehow wrapped itself around the notes and began to insulate me from their influence. "The tune has been called," it said.

INIT EVALUATION.TGT

"Now it is time for the piper to be paid."

THREAT_ASSESS LEVEL TGT.1 = 32

From the darkness of my mind an ebon and silver warrior congealed. Insane fire flared from his eyes like muzzle flashes. With a hand shaped of razored daggers like the one sheathed on my calf, he threw me a brief salute, then he turned and leaped at the image of Glathoar.

PRIME_TGT = 1

Suddenly I recognized the warrior leaping to my defense. Parabellum Rex, stripped of anger and aggression by our partial reintegration, still possessed my total capacity for hatred. Had I thought about it, I might have noticed that I did not hate Scythia for killing me, or Win Raleigh for his repeated attempts to kill his daughter. I did not hate Ezoghouls or Razides or the other denizens of the Dark Legion. And it was not because they were not worthy of hatred or I was incapable of seeing how much they deserved to be hated.

I could not hate them because Parabellum Rex *was* my hatred.

INIT EVALUATION.WPN

Parabellum Rex's claws slashed into Glathoar, and the tune faltered.

INIT PUNISHER.ONE

Ribbons of Glathoar floated out into the void like tatters of a wind-shred flag in a gale. Parabellum Rex clawed and dug, bit and scratched, gnawed and gouged. With each strike a note sounded sour and ended prematurely, creating gaps in the song. In those infinitesimal silences I felt my body again, and I tried to make myself stop dancing madly.

INIT MOVE_COMPENSATION.AIM

The dancing marionette had drawn his Punisher and sought vainly to aim it at Glathoar, but he could not. Even though the puppet jerked with the starts and stops of the music, each hole in the song failed to come when the gun pointed at him. The long tendrils of Glathoar began to blow beyond Parabellum Rex's glittering fingers and weave themselves back together behind him. As they did so, the tune became coherent again.

CONT MOVE_COMPENSATION.AIM

Parabellum Rex leaped up to snip at bits of Glathoar, but the nepharite had risen above his reach. The silver and black figure fell back to the unseen earth, then dropped to one knee. I saw his chest heaving and the fires in his eyes receding until they only licked at his eyebrows.

CONT MOVE_COMPENSATION.AIM

Rex looked over at me. "Help me. Help us. *I* cannot win, but *we* will prevail."

CONT MOVE_COMPENSATION.AIM

I reached out to Parabellum Rex and flowed into him as if I were fluid being poured into a mold. As I geysered up into his hollow head, he granted me the last of the memories I did not possess. They exploded in my brain like a satchel charge, yet they did not bring destruction with them. Instead they gave me healing and completeness. With them, with the total integration of who I was and what I had become, I knew I was not insane.

Parabellum Rex's memories did not begin with my death and resurrection as I had supposed before. He had been born when Scythia's fist slammed into my spine, crushing vertebrae. I had resisted her, refusing to tell her where Cassandra Raleigh and her husband had gone. As she had done with the heretic, she titillated me, cajoled me, and threatened me. She told me that I would talk once I could not walk, but I refused to speak, so she crippled me.

With that single blow she brought Parabellum Rex to life. His job, as he saw it, was to preserve us and resist her. He gained my hatred and aggression and combativeness, but he did not take my memories. He could not have told Scythia where Cassandra had gone because he did not know. He laughed in her face, knowing he would frustrate her forever. And when she killed us and then Cybertronic brought us back to life, he remained in control and resisted learning anything that might give him the information she so dearly desired.

Then, when the image of Muawijhe touched me at Larkspur, Parabellum Rex attacked the seed of insanity that the Apostle had planted in my brain. Rex stripped off things like aggression and pugnacity, leaving himself nothing but pure hatred. He swarmed over the seed, crushed it, and devoured it. Like a macrophage he learned to recognize Muawijhe's spoor and lay in wait for it to come again, so he could destroy it.

I cranked my head back and saw Glathoar standing above me, breathing lunacy through his pipe. I stabbed my right hand upward, willing my arm to grow long. My bladed fingers sliced up into him. They minced and diced him, pushing up beyond his intestines, through his liver and heart and lungs. They coursed along his spine and up through his soft palate. Firmly lodged in his brain, I began to twiddle my fingers, blending gray matter and worms into a lifeless puree.

INIT PUNISHER.ONE

My index finger tightened, spasmodically.

INIT PUNISHER.ONE

And again.

CONT EVALUATION.TGT
THREAT_ASSESS LEVEL TGT.1 = 16

I spun to the ground and slammed into the statue of Muawijhe. I saw Glathoar staggering backward with two bullet wounds in his face. As he caught himself and started to step toward me, the crisp staccato of Hunter's M50 filled the chamber. From his knees Hunter kept the assault rifle on target and bullet holes stippled Glathoar's chest. Brackish, black fluid began to ooze from the holes, but somehow the nepharite remained on his feet and staggered forward when Hunter paused to reload.

Yojimbo's sword slash caught Glathoar below the jaw and swept through his neck as if the nepharite had been no more substantial than a wraith. Glathoar's mouth hung open in surprise, then slowly began to spin as a writhing worm overweighted it. The body buckled at the knees, hit them hard on the stone floor, then flopped onto its back.

CONT EVALUATION.TGT
THREAT-ASSESS LEVEL TGT.1 = 0

I holstered the Punisher and looked over at my two companions. Blood dripped from Yojimbo's sword and steamed on the ground. Smoke slowly settled around Mitch as the last of the brass cartridges spun to a stop off to his right. "We got him."

Mitch stood and pointed his gun at the body. "What happened to him?"

Yojimbo shook his head. "I don't know. He started glowing and then . . . wait, he's glowing again!"

I turned back toward the body and saw Yojimbo was right. The green glow had begun again, but before it could cover the body, a reddish fungus covered the corpse and dissolved it. "What in hell?"

The red fungus collapsed into a black pool that then rose up in a dark mist. That mist swirled around, then solidified itself into a huge humanoid figure. Even more heavily muscled than Ragathol had been, this being had cables and tubes running across his red flesh. A red-gold battle mask covered his face, or so I thought until I saw the metal begin to move and tighten like flesh. I saw parts of his skin shimmer like liquid crystal displays and arcane data flashed across their surfaces as if he were some living union of organic creature and machine—a huge, primal and terrible godling who had fashioned a Cybertronic chasseur like me in his image.

The metal mask contorted itself into a pitiless grin. "Blessed are thee, bellicose and lethal, for you stand before Algeroth, the Apostle of War, and you have pleased him."

THIRTY-FIVE

"Forgive us our trespassing here." Algeroth opened his hands slowly, but as they moved apart, I saw various weapons fill them and again disappear. It seemed, as his body moved, the computers integrated into him calculated threats and made available the things necessary to counter those threats. "We would normally never have interfered with our brother Muawijhe and his operations, but we had tired of this game."

Hunter pulled his helmet off and frowned at the biotech giant standing before us. "What game are you talking about? I've lost people, which means this is no game to me."

Algeroth nodded slowly, a myriad of phantom helmets ancient and futuristic haunting his head as he did so. "Our brother Muawijhe is yet youthful and prone to foolishness. Among us, the Apostles, there is a certain contention for position and primacy. We sharpen ourselves by testing each other. My brother sought, by corrupting and co-opting Ragathol, to bring discomfort or disgrace to our threshold."

I shook my head. "He picked a singularly poor vessel for his ambition."

Yojimbo smiled. "Ragathol was driven from Luna by a force barely half of what we brought here."

"And his defeat on Venus cost you a citadel." Mitch grinned wolfishly. "And this expedition was mounted without serious corporate support, yet he could not prevail."

"We are aware of all this. Muawijhe saw an opportunity and took it." Algeroth gestured graciously toward the obsidian statue. "We have been at odds with him and his goals when we chose to reject his desire to join with us and inject insanity into warfare."

"There's already enough madness in war."

"This case has been advanced before, cyborg." The Apostle's metal mask smoothed into a serene and thoughtful expression. "Muawijhe wished to make insanity dominate war, not remain at the fringes of it where it belongs. He wished to make us his disciples, but we resisted subordination. So our brother began to look for ways to bring our efforts into disrepute. He fastened upon Ragathol and seduced him. Our brother promised our minion consideration and dominion. He spent time and resources on enabling Ragathol to follow his own plans."

I shook my head. "All good money thrown after bad."

"Correct. He squandered power in his quest to discredit us by using one of our own against us. He saw in Ragathol an excellent tool." The Apostle began to smile. "When we created Ragathol, we saw him as something else entirely."

I smiled. "Bait."

Yojimbo looked at me. "Bait?"

Algeroth knit his fingers together, and a phantasmal sword flickered in and out of his grasp. "A stalking horse. We intended him to be corruptible. We knew not which of our kin would pervert him, but we suspected it would be Muawijhe. We considered Ragathol a project to keep him occupied. Without such a diversion it was possible that Muawijhe could have done something that would have caused trouble for us."

Mitch casually tracked the muzzle of his gun across Algeroth's body, and I saw a line of ruby shield blink into existence to protect the Apostle. "Why'd you end your brother's fun now? If he kept bringing Ragathol or Glathoar back, we'd have eventually run out of bullets and he would have destroyed us."

"First and foremost, our brother foolishly compromised himself when he answered Ragathol's plea for aid. As the cyborg knows, Muawijhe had a mystical system for keeping his communication with Ragathol outside our notice."

I narrowed my eyes. "You mean to say that until Ragathol prayed to your brother and he responded, you had no way of knowing which of your kin had taken your bait."

"Your thoughts on this matter are not wholly without reason. Muawijhe's system frustrated our inquiries, which is why we had the vessel, the woman you came to save, filled with scenes from an utterly insane slaughter on Venus. We surmised that once Ragathol had tasted of the pain and madness in her brain, he would conduct her to Muawijhe, and our brother would receive a very nasty surprise. That trap was not sprung, but your efforts forced our brother to reveal himself, and for that I ruined his fun."

Again the Apostle gestured toward the statue, but the array of weapons flickering through his grasp belied the benign arc of his hand. "More importantly, though, our brother sought to deny you victory. We had luxuriated in Ragathol's defeat on Luna and again on Venus. We admired your work here on Mars and found your action here entertaining. We decided to eliminate the immediate threat to your existence. As Glathoar was consumed, so were all my necro-mutants and the Legionnaires remaining here on Themis. You no longer face a threat from the Dark Legion."

Yojimbo's eyes sharpened. "You honor us with this gesture, but I would not think honor is in your nature."

"Let us speak as one warrior to another, Yojimbo. We have an appreciation—nay, an adoration—for you and your skill. You—all of you—are known to the Apostles and even feared by some of us. We chose to come here and show you our deep respect for your spirit and abilities." The Apostle bowed and samurai armor faded in around him, then evaporated as he straightened up again. "We have also come to make you an offer. Join us and we will give you power beyond your wildest dreams."

I shook my head. "Power beyond my wildest dream would mean nightmares for you and your kin."

Yojimbo bowed his head. "I have no wish but to serve my present master for as long as I am able and he desires my service."

Mitch thrust his chin out defiantly. "I'll fight against you, never for you."

Algeroth clapped his hands and laughed in a voice that came as a thousand million trumpets sounding charges and retreats. "You who fight against us *do* fight for us. We are the Apostle of War. We embodied all that war is."

"Including defeat," Mitch growled.

"Including defeat." Algeroth's mask took on an almost bemused expression. "Very well, you have earned your freedom. As our abilities are whetted in contention with our peers, so shall we pit our troops against you so they may be honed to perfection."

"Beware sharpening a blade too often, Algeroth, for it may be worn away to nothing." Yojimbo rested his hands on the hilts of his blades. "What you send against me, I will destroy."

The Apostle appeared locked in thought for a moment, then smiled. "What glorious Legionnaires you will make."

Hunter frowned. "Reneging on our promised freedom already?"

"Though we keep our word, we also plan ahead." Algeroth smiled as he began to turn back into mist. "You will be ours soon enough. Your Sundiver's captain just received a message from Luna demanding him to bring the ship around, lock the throttle on full speed, and ram Themis. He has complied and is on his way to Jupiter in a life-skiff, so nothing can turn that ship. Impact is in five of your minutes."

"Wait," I reached out toward him, "can't you stop it?"

"We have given you a temporary truce with the Dark Legion. It is up to you to defeat threats from your own allies."

As he vanished, the rest of our group came running down the causeway. "What's been going on?" Pam pointed back up toward the tunnel. "We walked for miles without seeing anything but tunnel, then suddenly we found ourselves here."

"We have five minutes to get back to the skiffs!" Even as I said it, I knew that path was hopeless. If they had followed Mitch's instructions, all the tunnels were blown and even if they had not, we could not get back there fast enough to be able to escape. "We're sunk."

"Wait a minute. Ragathol had an escape vessel on Venus." Mitch pointed off at the small passageway located in the wall behind the statue of Muawijhe. "He might have one here."

Lane snapped his fingers. "He *has* got one here—the ship they brought Lorraine on, that *Tobi* class thing."

"Go, then, go!" I pointed everyone toward the passage Mitch had indicated earlier. "The Bauhaus manager had his own private docking silo. The ship has to be there."

I let everyone else trail out of the room and I waited a second, alone, in the dark. I saw no light glowing from the statue of Muawijhe, no trace of life in it. It seemed, as Algeroth had said, the game was over, done, dead, and gone.

I decided to take no chances.

I shot out Muawijhe's eyes and then raced after my friends.

My computer had started a countdown when Algeroth mentioned five minutes, and I reached the ship at 4:15 still on the clock. The *Tobi* class of runabout is normally known for its clean lines and aerodynamic styling. They're generally bought by executives who like jaunting between planets on vacations or used by black-marketeers who want to move contraband between planets. Treasured for their looks as much as their speed, they are the ship of choice for heroes of all sorts of video adventures.

Looking at this *Tobi,* I hoped like hell it still had its speed, because the Dark Legion's modifications to it had destroyed its esthetic value. The bridge, mounted halfway between the needle-nose and the stubby rear wings, looked as if the metal and ceramics had been boiled into bubbles and then left to cool that way. The rear looked as if some extra engine pods had been grafted on, and I wasn't certain what in hell the grassy fringe around the edges of the hull was or what purpose it might have served.

I hopped aboard, and Lane shut the hatch behind me. Ash was helping Wendy strap Sandra into a daybed in the aft lounge. I patted him on the shoulder as I squeezed past. "Glad I didn't have to carry you home in my pocket on this one."

The Attila said nothing, and I worked my way forward to the middle cabin. Six rows of seats running six across supplied ample room for the rest of our contingent. I noticed Scythia sitting alone while the rest of the Sacred Warriors mingled with our people. I returned some smiles and nods as I passed down the central aisle, then I stopped in the cockpit doorway.

"We're not going anywhere, are we?"

Mitch and Yojimbo, sitting in the pilot and copilot seats respectively, turned back toward me and sighed in unison. The cockpit instrumentation had suffered the same sort of boil-up as the exterior of the cockpit. The lenses distorted the various gauges and displays and a furry, gelatinous *thing* covered the central console between them.

Mitch reached out toward the fur-covered throttle, but tiny tendrils came up like cobras and waved back and forth as they tracked his hand. "Normally you can call up an auto-launch sequence, but I can't find the switches to do that. I've got basic power up, but I'm stuck after that. I can't fly it manually."

"Nor can I." Yojimbo shrugged. "I thought, because Mishima made this, I might be of help reading things, but this is well beyond my abilities."

I reached back and plucked an intercom mike from its clip. "Thanks for flying Desperation Spaceways. Does anyone know how to get this monster out of here?" I saw no volunteers in the mid-cabin, so I hung the mike up and squatted down for a look at the console. As I brought my right hand near the gray gelatin, little pseudopods started adroitly tracking my hand.

"Gray like brain tissue." I pointed up along the console. "That's where the computer navigational and launch core normally goes. Do you think this thing thinks for the ship?"

"I don't know." Mitch shook his head. "What do we have to do, beg it? Please, ship, take off?"

I smiled to cover my panic. "Ships are usually personified as women. Sweet-talk it."

Yojimbo bowed toward it. "I would be honored for the pleasure of your company in orbit around Mars."

Mitch laughed aloud. "Mars? At least promise her a good time on Luna."

I joined his nervous laughter, but cut it off abruptly when I felt Ash's fingers sink into my armpits and move me into the navigator's seat behind Yojimbo. "Ash, what are you doing? Put me down. This is serious."

"Compliance with your request." His right hand reached up and popped open his skullcase. Following the last command given it by Ash's brain, the hand scooped his memory core out and jammed it down through the gray jelly. The stuff liquified and flowed out over the cockpit floor, but left us staring at Ash's memory core nestled in the launch and navigation slot.

The ship shuddered as the engines ignited behind us. Mitch looked back at me with wild eyes. "Your robot can fly this thing?"

"I told him to download everything we'd need to make this trip. Since a *Tobi*-class ship was one of our possible rides out here, I guess he took me seriously and down-loaded *everything*!"

Yojimbo smiled. "Never again do I complain about a literalist."

"Me, neither!" I patted the console affectionately. "It's your turn to carry me home, Ash. To Mars, as fast as we can."

THIRTY-SIX

The return flight from Themis to Mars would have taken us nineteen days, if we had traveled at the approved speeds dictated by transportation contracts, safety standards for spacecraft and the common conception of prudence. Throughout the history of mankind, our machines have always been able to perform at higher standards than the human body could stand or human society thought correct. Allowable speeds within the solar system had been determined not by the capability of the spacecraft, but by some bureaucrat's idea that interplanetary travel should have some logical analogue to terrestrial time-scales.

This meant interplanetary travel could be *slow*.

As the *Coulson* showed by its impact with Themis, flying a spaceship at excessive speeds in a crowded area of space can be extremely dangerous. The *Coulson* hit Themis dead-on, shattering the planetoid like an ice cube hit with a sledgehammer. Ash had pulled us up and away from Themis on a vector that closely paralleled the *Coulson*'s incoming course. As a result, while we got to watch a brilliant explosion on the aft-monitor view screens, we escaped being peppered by debris.

Because of the collision, we declared a medical emergency, and the Cartel gave us immediate clearance to return to Luna instead of Mars. They also advised us to "proceed with all dispatch." I let Ash push the ship as fast as it could go, considering that a good definition of "all dispatch." He matched the accepted speed used on the run from the asteroid belt to Jupiter, turning what should have been a month-long trip to Earth into something that took just less than a day to accomplish.

We landed at the Furnerius spaceport on Luna, and the Brotherhood immediately impounded the ship. I recovered Ash's brain and returned it to his body. My brother, who had returned to Luna to face disciplinary actions for letting us use the *Coulson* to get to Themis, met us at the spaceport with a vehicle and some basic medical supplies. Titus Gallicus ran interference for my brother and me while we got Sandra out and safely ensconced in my apartment. We decided that was the safest place for her in the short term because Winchester Raleigh did not know who I really was. When he learned Sandra and the rest of us had survived the *Coulson*'s collision with Themis, we expected a reaction, but figuring out where we had stashed Sandra would be all but impossible for him.

Wendy Levin, Jan, and Ash remained there to watch over her. Nick, Titus, and I met covertly in Luna City to discuss the implications of all we had learned since we left Luna and came up with a rudimentary plan for eliminating the threats to Sandra's safety once and for all. I immediately headed off to Cybertronic Headquarters and enlisted both Miss Wickersham and Dr. Carter in the plot. They did their parts, but I waited until I had confirmation from both Titus and Nick that things had gone well before I went subreal to face the music for my actions.

The bemused expression on Carl's face surprised me because I had expected him to be angry. Instead of meeting me at the simulation of his Martian retreat, he wove around himself a replica of my apartment. With feeds he was getting from Jan and Ash, he let me keep an eye on Sandra's treatment, and I appreciated that.

"Am I to gather that you approve of my actions?"

Carl shrugged and dropped himself into my favorite chair. "Since your discovery of who you were, and even before that, I would have said you were clever, but since your total reintegration, I find you positively insidious."

"That doesn't really answer the question."

"I know. I can't answer the question until I satisfy myself as to how much of what you have done was done for Sandra Raleigh or Cybertronic or for yourself."

"Or some combination thereof."

Carl shook his head. "Others might consider your actions as having eliminated two bugs with one line of code, but you and I know each other too well to know that is true. Instead of having your brother forge and plant a transfer order ceding the *Coulson* to Raleigh's Transportation Division of Capitol—a move that will surely end Raleigh's career—you could have simply created another new identity for Sandra and had her hidden away again. He never could have touched her."

I frowned. "We tried that once, and Raleigh learned she was alive. That's the reason Raleigh met me outside my brother's apartment and transported me to a place where Brotherhood Inquisitors—including Scythia Scipio—questioned me about her location. If Win had learned how to break the identity we set up for her once, he could do it again."

"Ah, but he hadn't learned that trick at all." Carl gestured and a copy of the *Chronicles* appeared in his hand. "Munnsinger Ellsworth used personal ads to remain in contact with you after he and Sandra had gone to Venus, correct?"

"Yes, but he used the *Citizen,* not the *Chronicles.*"

"To send messages to *you,* yes, but he used the *Chronicles* to send messages to Winchester Raleigh."

"What?"

"I reviewed Ellsworth's files from Capitol. Your assessment that he was a very nice guy is confirmed by every evaluation he ever had on the job. His supervisors noted he was a conciliator and peacemaker." Carl smiled weakly. "He was too nice for his own good."

"Of course." I slapped my forehead with my hand. "Munnsinger would have hated the fact that Sandra and her father were estranged. He used the *Chronicles* to send a message to Win, and that alerted Win to the fact that his daughter still lived. But with Raleigh's ties to the Brotherhood, he should have been able to learn where Munnsinger and Sandra had gone."

"Should have, but apparently did not." Carl tossed the paper over his shoulder and it dissolved into static before sinking into the dark screen of my television. "The *Chronicles* are managed by one of the more conservative factions within the Brotherhood. Win's connections came with a spur group, and cooperation between the two groups was not good enough to get the data he wanted. I suspect the *Chronicles* group withheld that information to use at a later date to co-opt Winchester for their own purposes."

"So Winchester used the resources of his friends to try to break me." I nodded slowly. "From me he got nothing, and Scythia must have been convinced that I was the one who had made all the arrangements concerning the move. That or he didn't want to make a move against Nick for Anna's sake."

"That's possible, though it is more likely his friends in the Brotherhood urged caution upon him and were working for a year and a half on getting at the *Chronicles* information about Munnsinger. There *were* more messages to you and him during the period after your death. Winchester obeyed his handlers because Sandra had been promised him as a reward for his continued status as a sleeper agent within Capitol."

"Well, then, taking him down is an advantage for Cybertronic. It cuts the Brotherhood's power in another corporation, and that should relieve some of the pressure against us." I smiled. "See, I did it for Cybertronic."

"That *is* possible, but you're smart enough to see that having Winchester on a string could have been useful for us as well. Taking him out of play means no one benefits from his position. Still, I am willing to allow that you did think that was the only way to protect Sandra."

I nodded. "Sandra's protection and recovery is important to me. My brother has gotten Wendy Levin detached from the Capitol military and reassigned to his division so she can help treat Sandra."

"Where will you send her?"

I shook my head. "I don't know. My brother is making the initial arrangements, and he's also teaching Wendy enough that she'll be able to drop the both of them out of sight whenever she thinks its necessary. I don't know and will never know, which is the only way I can guarantee her safety. And if you don't think that's in Cybertronic's best interest, I don't care. It had to be done."

Carl held his hands up. "I understand and appreciate

your situation concerning Sandra. My only regret there is that if we could have been of some aid in her rehabilitation, her going underground will prevent us from being able to help."

"The key, Carl, is that *she* knows how to reach us, not the other way around. Wendy's got a good head on her shoulders. If she needs help, she'll ask."

"Very good." Carl inspected a fingernail, then smiled slyly at me. "Now, about what you have done to Scythia . . ."

"Another threat to Cybertronic gone."

"Ah, I see." He clearly did not believe me. "I very much like your method for handling her. You've got her fingerprints on the knife with which you killed Jan's partner in Capitol Security, and you've had the body thawed out. There should even be blood residue still on the knife. I take it Titus Gallicus is investigating the murder?"

I nodded. "It's part of the overall inquiry into the Eternal Vigilance's faction within the Brotherhood."

"Did you decide on a motive?"

"The guy was a go-between who carried messages to Scythia from Win Raleigh. She killed him to sever that connection. Spur of the moment thing—she's known for having a temper."

"But would she be stupid enough to have left a weapon with her fingerprints on it lying around where it could be discovered?"

"I think you'll find that Titus, visiting his friend after our return from Themis, walked in on her as she was trying to dispose of the body. He was forced to kill her when she attacked him to cover her tracks."

"And dead women dispute no frames?"

"Something like that. The Brotherhood is anxious to purge that Eternal Vigilance faction, so they'll accept anything right now. Case closed."

Carl frowned. "Titus Gallicus is willing to participate in this conspiracy?"

"He is. I told him how the man died—self-defense— and that I knew Scythia had murdered someone else at Win Raleigh's orders. I also told him I had no evidence to back up my charge against her. He'd seen Scythia execute the Abbot of Eternal Vigilance, and heard her offer to kill Sandra on Themis, so he had no doubts as to her homicidal tendencies. The conspiracy brings Scythia to justice and cuts off inquiry into many more potentially damaging things."

"Besides," I shrugged, "If not for me and Cybertronic, all of us would have died at Eternal Vigilance and again on Themis. Titus Gallicus pays his debts."

"And *you* collect yours."

"Do I?"

Carl nodded slowly. "While you've done some excellent work in safeguarding Cybertronic, I notice that the man who ordered your interrogation and death is now in disgrace and will never be able to recover. Your executioner is dead, framed for a killing you did."

"And your point is?"

Carl stood and extended his hand to me. "I think, Mr. Quentin Kell, you will have a great future here at Cybertronic."

EPILOGUE

Rex,

Two years is a long time to take to say thanks, but I've had a lot to learn. Thanks. Remember Anna's birthday is a week away.

Love,
Lorraine.

MUTANT CHRONICLES

From the darkness of the void emerged nightmares beyond our wildest fears. As man penetrated deeper into space in the far future, a hurricane of evil destroyed and corrupted all that lay in its way. It was a time to conquer all fears and stand up against the tidal wave of the Dark Symmetry.

In Volume I of The Apostle of Insanity Trilogy, *IN LUNACY* by William F. Wu, the five MegaCorporations unite against the common enemy despite their ongoing skirmishes among themselves. It's up to a handful of freelance mercenaries to save the world from total destruction in a time where the struggle for survival continues.

In Volume II of the Apostle of Insanity Trilogy, *FRENZY* by John-Allen Price, the battles for supremacy among the five MegaCorporations continue on Luna, Venus, and Mars. Now they are all vying for possession of one comatose woman, the lone survivor of an attack that had destroyed her entire settlement. Yet the five Megacorps were not the only ones interested in the woman known as Lorraine Kovan. For the Dark Legion had made her their Receptacle of Vision, and they couldn't afford to let the humans rcover any of the knowledge locked away in her mind.

And so the hit-and-run war between the humans, Nepharites, Necromutants, and the traitors known as Heretics began. Only time would tell whether the human forces could withstand the mind-control magic and the seemingly endless invincible foe. . . .

If you and/or a friend would like to receive the *ROC Advance*, a bimonthly newsletter featuring all the newest and hottest ROC books and authors, on a complimentary basis, please fill out this form and return it to:

ROC Books/Penguin USA
375 Hudson Street
New York, NY 10014

Your Address
Name _____
Street _____ Apt. # _____
City _____ State _____ Zip _____

Friend's Address
Name _____
Street _____ Apt. # _____
City _____ State _____ Zip _____